Standing on the Promises

A Trilogy of Historical Novels about Black Mormon Pioneers

BOOK ONE

One More River to Cross

MARGARET BLAIR YOUNG
AND DARIUS AIDAN GRAY

BOOKCRAFT
SALT LAKE CITY, UTAH

Visit us at www.deseretbook.com

Library of Congress Cataloging-in-Publication Data

Young, Margaret Blair
  One more river to cross / Margaret Blair Young and Darius Aidan Gray.
    p.   cm. (Standing on the promises ; v. 1)
  ISBN 1-57345-629-2
  1. African-American Latter-day Saints—Fiction. 2. Latter-day Saints—Fiction.
I. Gray, Darius Aidan II. Title.
  PS3575.0825 O54   2000
  813'.54—dc21

                                       00-039280

Printed in the United States of America   72082-6631
10 9 8 7 6 5 4 3 2 1

We lovingly dedicate this novel to our parents:
Robert and Julia Blair, and Elsie and Darius Gray

Though our upbringings were worlds apart, we both
received from our parents not only love and
guidance but the inspiration to seek the best in life
and the constant assurance that the Lord loves us
and would direct our steps

Standing on the promises of Christ my King,
Through eternal ages let His praises ring!
Glory in the highest I will shout and sing—
Standing on the promises of God,
Standing on the promises of God!

—R. KELSO CARTER, "STANDING ON THE PROMISES"

FOREWORD

It would be hard to dispute that the events of June 1978 opened a new era for members of The Church of Jesus Christ of Latter-day Saints. But these events hardly marked the beginning of the story for black members of the Church. Elijah Abel, Jane Manning James, and other free blacks joined the Church in its formative years. Some early white Church members owned slaves, and three of these "colored servants," as they were often called, were in the first pioneer company to enter the Salt Lake Valley.

During the following decades, other black members pioneered as they joined the Church despite the challenges that membership brought. One of these later pioneers was Darius Aidan Gray, who joined the Church in 1964.

When I first met Darius, he was a TV news reporter. He soon became my friend.

I was public relations director of Brigham Young University for President Ernest L. Wilkinson during the late 1960s and early 1970s. In discussing the blacks-and-BYU controversy with a group of black students at the University of Wyoming, I mentioned that black members of the Church accepted the policy that prevented blacks from holding the priesthood and were still glad to be members.

"You've got blacks in your church?" I was asked.

"Yes, we do."

"I'd sure like to meet one," said one black student.

"Let me see what I can do," I told him.

I went to my motel room and called Darius. "Could you hop a plane over to Laramie?"

"How soon?"

"There's one leaving in thirty minutes."

He was in Laramie almost before I could arrange transportation and meet him at the airport.

I had tried to get him a motel room, but every room was taken by cowboys and cowgirls from all over the state who had descended upon Laramie in force for this basketball game. Because I had two double beds in my room, I invited Darius to stay with me.

The next morning, early, I woke up to the sound of Darius laughing loudly. "Go back to sleep," I said. "Can't you see it's the middle of the night?"

"Look over there on the desk," he said. "Two telephones: one black, and the other one white."

Through bleary eyes I could see he had made an accurate observation. "If you need to use the telephone," I quipped, "just be sure you use the right color." I rolled over and went back to sleep.

Darius met with several groups of blacks during the next two days. Just his presence in a meeting did more than all the preaching I could do. A determined black in one meeting kept pressuring him about being a disgrace to his race by having joined the Mormon Church. Finally Darius responded, "I'm not getting through to you. Don't you understand? I was born black. I am black now. I will die black. I am proud of my black heritage. And I will fight for just black causes with every power I have." He paused for a moment and then continued: "I am also a Mormon. And I am proud to be a Mormon. The Mormon Church has answers for me I have found nowhere else. There is no conflict between the color of my skin and my religion!"

Darius, just being Darius, did more to open understanding between nonmember blacks and Mormons at that meeting than everything all the rest of us had done during the previous two years.

Darius and I made many such trips together. Always, his honesty and straightforwardness were of tremendous value in increasing understanding between the two groups.

The day the revelation giving blacks the priesthood was announced by President Spencer W. Kimball, June 9, 1978, I went home at noon to share the news with my wife. On returning to the office, I opened the door and saw Darius Gray looking fondly out the window at the Salt Lake Temple. He rushed to me, and we threw our arms around each other and wept for gratitude and joy. When we regained a little composure, I whispered, "I never thought . . ."

"I always knew," said Darius. "I just didn't know if it would happen on this side of the veil."

" . . . in our lifetime!"

Darius looked at me, then out the window at the temple, and then at me again. He closed his eyes, opened them slowly, and said softly, "God is good."

I know of no one who can express a more objective, more compassionate, more honest portrayal of blacks and the Mormon Church than Darius Gray.

He is joined in writing this novel by Margaret Blair Young, a lifelong white member of the Church with pioneer heritage. She has felt deeply over the past few years the inspiration of her pioneer forebears, many of whom knew the Saints of color portrayed in this novel. An accomplished writer, Margaret has published two novels and many short stories and has won prizes for her work. But for her, this trilogy of novels about black Mormons is something different. She feels a deep kinship with Elijah Abel, Jane James, and other early black Church members.

Both Margaret and Darius have been inspired by the faith of those early black Saints, have felt sorrow at the suffering of these remarkable people with their unusual burdens who joined a "white" church during a time when racism was condoned, and have marveled at the patience of these black Saints through the long years when the full blessings of the priesthood were not available to them.

We are living at a special time in our history. Members of the LDS Church and people of other faiths—white people, black people, and people of other races—are ready to hear and treasure the stories of the great African-Americans who have been members of the Church since its early days. Not only are we ready but we *need* to know these stories. We can no longer afford to live with the folklore and the speculations of the past. We need to know the real heritage created by black Latter-day Saint pioneers of both the nineteenth and the twentieth centuries.

Though much of the dialogue presented in these novels is of necessity imagined, the stories you will read are based on extensive historical research and present the personalities and experiences of these pioneers as faithfully as possible. The novels of the trilogy *Standing on the Promises* invite all readers, regardless of race or church membership, to open their hearts and imaginatively experience the heartache, trials, joys, triumphs, and faith of some of the Church's greatest pioneers.

HEBER G. WOLSEY

Former Managing Director,
Public Communications,
The Church of Jesus Christ
of Latter-day Saints

PREFACE

Demographically we have come a long way since 1964, when I became a member of The Church of Jesus Christ of Latter-day Saints. Then it was estimated that worldwide there might have been 300 to 400 Church members of African descent. Today's statistics reveal a dramatic change: more than 100,000 black Church members on the African continent, at least 20,000 in the Caribbean, and countless thousands in South and Central America. Although dramatic, the changing hue of the Church is only part of the story. Equally important are the hearts that have swelled to accept these new converts.

Growth in the numbers of black Church members outside the United States has burgeoned, but within the United States there has been no similar surge in conversions. Today, many black converts in the United States merge with a seamless ease, but for some the experience has been less pleasant. Notwithstanding the distance traveled, the journey towards total acceptance is not yet complete.

Within the Church, an enormous legacy of misinformation concerning blacks remains to be corrected; and outside the Church, large elements of the black population cling to misconceptions about Mormons. As might be expected in any culture of eleven million people, some members are more tolerant of diversity than others. In addition, folklore surrounding blacks and the Church is damaging and begs to be corrected if we are to move forward as true brothers and sisters.

Standing on the Promises is a series of novels about the lives and testimonies of some remarkable men and women. These black Saints teach us volumes through the ways they faced the degrading battlegrounds and endured the dank trenches of this country's racial conflict. These Negro pioneers pierce our eyes and hearts with their examples and make real the conflict experienced by early Latter-day Saints, both black and white.

This volume, *One More River to Cross*, introduces readers to several of those black Saints from the shadows of history, pioneers who gave much to the early LDS Church and who offer still more today. Elijah Abel, Jane Manning James, the two Isaacs (Manning and James), and Samuel Chambers are names faintly familiar to some Latter-day Saints but unknown to most. Their experiences deserve to be better recognized, for they provide precious examples of faith sufficient to meet and transcend tribulation. Although thousands of pioneer stories have been told and retold, these accounts infuse a fresh perspective—not better, not bitter, but certainly distinctive. By looking at these lives of color, we hope that a healing will occur, that wounds will be attended, and a new perspective will be gained.

In the LDS faith, we regularly speak about turning the hearts of the fathers to the children and the hearts of the children to the fathers. Jesus Christ also taught that we need to turn our hearts to one another. The Great Physician calls us to heal one another from the degenerative disease of prejudice. Let me share a personal experience.

One summer day, a number of years ago, a twelve-year-old neighbor boy set up a lemonade stand. My son, who was a few years younger than this entrepreneur, visited the stand and headed home to get money to make a purchase. As soon as my son was out of earshot, the older boy stated (as several other children reported): "We don't serve niggers."

I was reminded of those bitter words every day as I passed the home of that young man. But the most painful moments came on

Sundays when this same individual, a deacon, offered me the sacrament.

The parents of the children who reported the incident had asked my wife and me to let them approach the young man's family. Our immediate instinct was to act quickly and directly, but we agreed to the request. The approach to the family was not well received, however, and nothing came of the effort.

Some time later I approached our bishop and asked that he speak not to the boy or his parents but to the ward as a whole about tolerance. I envisioned that such a talk would bring about heartfelt change. Months went by, and no message was given. Again I met with the bishop and repeated my request. Several years passed, and the hoped-for words never came.

The good man who was our bishop was released, having served faithfully and well. He had my love and had earned my eternal respect for the much good he had cultivated in the ward and for his demonstrated charity. Pivotal to my view of him is the remarkably honest answer he gave when years later I asked him why he had never addressed the issue. With admirable candor he expressed his lack of ease or facility concerning matters of race. It wasn't that he hadn't cared; he simply hadn't known what to do. To me it had seemed an easy matter; to him, the subject of race was entangled with past Church policies and pronouncements. He had feared speaking on a subject full of taboos and contradictions. Fear and uncertainty had prevented an opportunity to teach truth and provide healing.

It can be hard to step away from past positions, but boldly stating any truth, though it may be awkward, is potentially redemptive. Elder Boyd K. Packer remarked about this tendency in his book *The Holy Temple*. Speaking of the benefits of the interview necessary to obtain a temple recommend, Elder Packer observed:

"Sometimes it is difficult to talk about mistakes. But it is a great blessing in the Church for us to have the privilege of cleansing ourselves. One of the steps of repentance is to make proper confession, confession to the Lord in the normal course. . . .

"Repentance is something like soap. It can cleanse us from our transgressions. Yet some people stay unclean when it is not necessary to do so" (*Holy Temple*, 54).

In trying to overcome past misconceptions and prejudices, we often struggle to understand that a person's color is relatively insignificant, that there are other realities of far greater importance. As Elder Packer noted:

"The reason the teaching of the gospel ofttimes is so difficult is that ideals in the gospel are such intangible things as faith, repentance, love, humility, reverence, obedience, modesty, and so forth. The dimensions of size and shape and color and texture just do not serve us there" (*Holy Temple*, 40).

One More River to Cross is about moving forward by looking back. Such an exercise may require an examination of ourselves and of our adherence to the old truths of "size and shape and color." As we gain an appreciation for correct values, false attitudes must make way for greater light and knowledge.

Some reading this series may be troubled by the depiction of actions and philosophies which, while historically accurate, contradict the way we might wish to see our history. As presenters of these humble lives, we have chosen honesty over comfort and truth over convention.

Latter-day Saints have a profusion of material written by historians, lay persons, and past general authorities, each sharing insights about various aspects of the restored gospel. Countless lives have been enriched by this repository of views, but the blessing of having living prophets supersedes the wealth of even this library. On the topic of certain past writings, Elder Bruce R. McConkie honored us by speaking plainly:

"I would like to say something about the new revelation relative to our taking the priesthood to those of all nations and races. . . .

" . . . There are statements in our literature by the early brethren which we have interpreted to mean that the Negroes would not receive the priesthood in mortality. I have said the same things, and people write me letters and say, 'You said such and such, and how is it now that we do such and such?' And all I can say to that is that it is time disbelieving people repented and got in line and believed in a living, modern prophet. Forget everything that I have said, or what President Brigham Young or President George Q. Cannon or whomsoever has said in days past that is contrary to the present revelation. We spoke with a limited understanding and without the light and knowledge that now has come into the world.

"We get our truth and our light line upon line and precept upon precept. We have now had added a new flood of intelligence and light on this particular subject, and it erases all the darkness and all the views and all the thoughts of the past. They don't matter any more.

"It doesn't make a particle of difference what anybody ever said about the Negro matter before the first day of June of this year (1978). It is a new day and a new arrangement, and the Lord has now given the revelation that sheds light out into the world on this subject. As to any slivers of light or any particles of darkness of the past, we forget about them" ("All Are Alike unto God," 1–2).

Our journey through the words and experiences of numerous black pioneers will testify of God's goodness, His unchanging fairness, and His embracing love. Eternal truths will link Elijah the prophet with Sister Jane Elizabeth Manning James; Elder Elijah Abel with Joseph of old and with Joseph Smith Jr.

Why have we not heard more about these black pioneers? And why was my former bishop so ill at ease with matters of race? We have been afraid to speak about race openly, honestly, and most important, lovingly. Race is a reality. We need to come to grips with it. Our necessary growth will not emerge from an embarrassed avoidance of past statements.

Let me end with a final citation from Elder Packer's book *The*

Holy Temple. Written two decades ago, its perspective is still valid. Elder Packer witnesses that we and our prophets are ordinary men and women with a work to do:

"Men called to apostolic positions are given a people to redeem. Theirs is the responsibility to lead those people in such a way that they win the battles of life and conquer the ordinary temptations and passions and challenges. And then, speaking figuratively, it is as though these prophets are tapped on the shoulder and reminded: 'While you carry such responsibility to help others with their battles, you are not excused from your own challenges of life. You too will be subject to passions, temptations, challenges. Win those battles as best you can.'

"Some people are somehow dissatisfied to find in the leading servants of the Lord such ordinary mortals. They are disappointed that there is not some obvious mystery about those men; it is almost as if they are looking for the strange and the occult. To me, however, it is a great testimony that the prophets anciently and the prophets today are called out from the ranks of the ordinary men. It should not lessen our faith" (*Holy Temple*, 102).

It is my hope and prayer that we win our own battles as best we can—that we overcome our fears and uneasiness about the sensitive subject of race. Doing so will require personal appraisal and the sacrifice of preconceived judgments. Our goal is nothing short of first inspecting and then healing the innermost recesses of our hearts. May we come to truly embrace and share the love that emanates from the Father and the Son.

DARIUS AIDAN GRAY

AUTHORS' NOTE

We have been true to all the facts we could find but have freely fictionalized the spaces between the facts. We do not know, for example, much at all of Elijah Abel's life before his conversion to the Church in 1832, except that he was born in Maryland and very possibly used the Underground Railroad to escape slavery by traveling to Canada. From the point of his baptism, we can track his steps by Church documents, which reveal his work on the Kirtland, Nauvoo, and Salt Lake Temples, his mission to the northern states and Canada, his service as the Nauvoo undertaker and a member of the Nauvoo Household of Carpenters, his departure to Cincinnati and subsequent marriage, and lastly his trek to the Salt Lake Valley and his final mission—again to the northern states. Everything we have said of Elijah's life before 1832 is purely conjecture, though we do know his parents' names: Delilah and Andrew Abel. Several historians, Newell Bringhurst and Lester Bush perhaps being foremost, have provided essential data for us to fill in the blanks with some direction besides our imagination.

We know that Samuel Chambers, born May 21, 1831, in Pickens County, Alabama, was baptized at age thirteen in Mississippi, after hearing the preaching of Preston Thomas, who was himself a new convert. We know that Samuel Chambers was a slave at the time and therefore not free to join the Saints in Nauvoo, though, as he put it, "God kept the seeds of life alive within me" ("Saint without Priesthood," 18). We know that after the Civil War he worked as a sharecropper and a shoemaker to pay for his trip west. We know, too, that he and his wife, Amanda, were loyal members of the Salt Lake Eighth Ward for the rest of their lives; in fact, thanks to the work of William Hartley, we have a number of his testimonies, as recorded by his stake clerk.

Our depictions of the first black pioneers to enter the Salt Lake Valley—Hark Lay, Oscar Crosby, and Green Flake—use some data from Kate Carter's *Negro Pioneer*—with care, though, for much of Carter's information is flawed. Her book is nonetheless a vital contribution to our subject. Other sources—including the autobiography of James Madison Flake; *Southern Grace*, by Charmaine Lay Kohler; fine research compiled by one of James Flake's descendants, Joel Flake; and the research of Lester Bush, Newell Bringhurst, and Ron Coleman—are more reliable, and we have used them copiously.

Jane Manning James's life is considerably better documented than those of the aforementioned pioneers, as we have not only Church records of her but her own recorded life story and a number of corroborating documents. We have drawn heavily on all the fine work compiled by Henry Wolfinger. Though one source lists her husband's name as Sherman, all other sources (including Jane's own history, as dictated to Elizabeth J. D. Roundy) call him Isaac, as does his gravestone. Because Jane's brother was also named Isaac, we have referred to him by his middle name, Lewis, to avoid confusion. In actuality, however, Jane's brother was almost certainly called Isaac, and in their final years in Salt Lake City, the two were known as Aunt Jane and Uncle Isaac.

We hint at the use of black vernacular English (which some linguists designate as BVE) by the characters in this text, though we do not attempt to duplicate their language phonetically. Some readers will think the dialect Southern and wonder whether blacks from Connecticut or Maryland would have spoken as we depict. The truth is, pronunciation did vary according to location. But all blacks, with common African ancestry somewhere in their genealogy, would have learned a language that had progressed from African grammar behind English words, to a creole, and finally to a particular black vernacular. We have relied on some linguistic work by Marvin Loflin in our dialect creation, on many studies of slave language in such books as *Lay My Burden Down* and the more recent *Remembering Slavery*, but we have relied mostly on the childhood language of Darius Gray, who was raised in Colorado by parents and extended family with deep Southern roots. In a world that had oppressed blacks, Darius was once ashamed of the "flat-talk" dialect used by many Southern blacks. He is now proud of it, seeing it as the language of survivors. Our process consisted of Brother Gray's reading the text aloud and intuitively changing syntax or grammar while Sister Young, trained in the process by her linguist father, typed in the corrections. We hope we have produced something that approximates the ways our characters really would have spoken.

Besides the fine researchers whose work we have used, we gratefully acknowledge the personal assistance of Margery Taylor and Bill Hartley and the painstaking detail work of Bruce Young. We are also thankful for a grant from the Utah Arts Council (sponsored by the National Endowment for the Humanities) which supported the beginnings of this work.

PROLOGUE

Mormon folk know all about the white pioneers. You ask any one of them and just listen. They'll tell you stories of the Martin Handcart Company plowing through the snows, freezing and dying. They'll tell you all about Brigham Young weeping out loud when he learned there were Saints mired out in the frozen prairie. The Mormon folk will tell you all about Winter Quarters and Jim Bridger warning the first pioneer companies that the ground out West was useless—not one ear of corn would grow there. Listening to the stories, most don't imagine there were any pioneers of color among those Latter-day Saints. But we were there—slaves, some of us; former slaves, some of us; free blacks, some of us. We were there. We were like flies in buttermilk, a few dark specks in a sea of cream.

Our presence started with the conversion of Elijah Abel way back in 1832. Now there was a good man. You sit back and read, and you'll learn all about him. And Jane Manning James, too, and Samuel Chambers, Green Flake, Hark Lay, Oscar Crosby—there are many names and histories, sad and sweet, to the black faces that came across the plains.

Elijah Abel
1831

1

HIDING IN THEE

*For thou hast been a shelter for me, and a
strong tower from the enemy.*
PSALM 61:3

"It's time!" Delilah Abel whispered into her sleeping son's ear.

Elijah opened one eye. "Mama?" There was no dawn light he could see. Seemed he had only just gone to slumber. Elijah's toes, peeking out of the flannel, let him know this was one cold November night. He sat up.

"Wake up y' brothers, 'Lijah."

"Wha—"

"Hush!"

"Ain't mornin'." He looked at her. It was dark, but he could make out Mama's face wearing the most serious expression he had ever found—on her, anyways. His mama was a happy sort when she was home, loved dancing. In the years when they had gone to church, Mama did the clap-sing better than anyone. But this moment, she was either set to do murder or run away, and it wasn't hard to guess which. Elijah knew the information he had given her yesterday had set her mind. He knew what "It's time" meant, and yes indeed, the time had arrived. He just wished it had come calling on a warmer night.

Elijah watched Jeremiah and Daniel on the bed next to his. Daniel was on his stomach snoring peaceably. Jeremiah's eyes were fluttering like he was dreaming something fast. When he shook their shoulders, Daniel waved his hand as if swatting a fly. Jeremiah just lay there, didn't move a finger.

"Up," Elijah ordered.

Daniel moaned, "You d' new rooster? Lemme 'lone." The mattress ticking was corn husks. They used corn husk ticking a lot back then, and truthfully, these boys were lucky to have a mattress at all. The husks rustled when Daniel rolled over.

"Mama say so," Elijah stated. Those words, you know, had about the power of God. When Mama say something—you listen. That's the way it was then and the way it ought to be now.

Daniel moved his mouth like he was saving up spit for an answer. He was older than Elijah by a year, give or take (they were both near twenty), but shorter by a hand span and heavier by twenty pounds. He sat up and punched Jeremiah, which was pretty typical. Jeremiah cried out loud enough to make Mama flap her arms and hiss, "Hushhh!"

Jeremiah was the oldest of the boys. He was high yellow of complexion and looked right then like he'd been sucking lemons in his sleep. "Massa callin' us 'gain?" His voice was tired-raspy.

"Not Massa this mornin'," whispered Mama.

Then Jeremiah's whole face woke up. Lightning had struck.

It was no secret Massa's tobacca crop was a failure. Only the Abel boys and Delilah were left as slaves, where once there'd been thirty. One by one the others had got sold down the river. Including Elijah's woman, who a fortnight before her sale had birthed his daughter. That baby had gone with her without a name, though Elijah had named her in his mind: Delilah, after his mama.

They knew Mama had been scheming her own plan for over a year to keep her boys put. And they all knew Massa was getting old and falling down drunk more nights than not. Massa didn't take pleasure in Delilah Abel as he once had. His own wife had passed to her glory some time ago, and then grief had settled onto the farm like permanent fog. These last months, Massa had been talking—at least to Elijah—about abandoning tobacca altogether, selling off his remaining fields, limiting himself to carpentry, maybe moving north.

And Elijah, who had helped Massa with woodwork these past long years, had some special information, which on this cold not-quite-morning made perfect sense.

Yesterday, Massa had given him a paper, making him promise on his soul not to tell. They had a table in need of sanding between them, and Massa started in on the work, no more explanation.

"What is it?" Like many of us in those days, Elijah couldn't read much. Just what he had figured out making furniture and wagons. He knew numbers fine and maybe ten or twelve letters.

"It's a table."

Elijah shifted his weight. "Sir, the paper?"

Massa sanded two hard strokes before answering. His answer was more mumble than word: "Freedom."

"Sir?"

Massa looked up. He had old blue eyes, one cloudy and half blind, both of 'em narrowed by fallen lids and looking sore and sad. "Setting you free, boy. That's your free papers."

"Free?"

"Your ears are working fine." Again he sanded, fixing those sad eyes on the table.

"All us free?"

Massa kept his eyes down.

"Massa? All us free?" Elijah repeated more loudly but not full-voiced. He never did use full voice with Massa.

"You become an echo, did you?"

"My brothers? My mama?"

Massa let out a long breath. "'Lijah, you promised on your soul to keep this secret. You break that promise, the devil like to climb in your bed and haul you straightway to flames—flames that burn out your eyeballs and consume all your flesh."

"Why?"

Massa sighed. "Because, though I hate to say it, the devil loves black flesh. Black flesh don't house no soul."

Any other day, Elijah would've laughed and said, "How can I promise on my soul if I don't got a soul?" But this was a serious day. Elijah waited. His voice was almost the one he used with Mama during their "talks": solemn and deep. "Why you set me free?"

Massa still didn't look up. "Been my plan." He shrugged. "All 'long. Every time you fashioned a chair to sell, I saved up some profit, 'til there was enough to satisfy me as your price." He shrugged again, lopsided, like he had a pain in his back. "You bought your own self free."

Elijah went to his knees.

Now Massa met Elijah's eyes and spoke softly. "Don't you kneel, boy. Not to me." Massa mumbled to himself, "I ain't worth even no niggah kneeling to me." Then loudly, straight into Elijah's ears: "If you got a mind to, you could slip away this second. Dash out that door, and I won't follow. My word on that. New York. Ohio. There's talk of setting up a college down Ohio. College for Negroes and whites and all manner of damned abolitionists. There's folk fixed on educating niggahs like—" Massa looked away "—almost like they was white." Massa sniffed. His sinuses had been bothering him of late, what with autumn shuffling between frost and sun. "You could go to Ohio. Work your way there. You got the wood skills. You know how to walk the chalk. You could leave this second." He returned to hard sanding, staring at his hands to hint that Elijah should run now and Massa wouldn't even peek.

Elijah stood. "But you ain't said nothing about my brothers and my mama. Just about me."

"Maybe best you should leave right now."

"And my family?"

Massa sanded. "Ain't earned theirs yet."

So Elijah knew. Now, he may have promised Massa, but Elijah would never keep such a secret from his mama, even if the devil was holding a pitchfork directly overhead. The Abel family, even without a father, had managed to form a knot in the slippery ties of slavery. Delilah was the threadworker. Like so many of our women back then—the ones who managed to hold on to their children—she had looped her sons together, needling them into the kind of loyalty that undercut or overhung any order Massa might give. No sir, neither Elijah nor his brothers kept secrets from Mama. (Well, except maybe one. And Mama had figured out about Elijah and Nancy anyhow. Mama had the woman's way of knowing.)

He told Delilah about the free papers directly after leaving Massa's side. She gave him a long look, moving her eyes across his face like her whole life was written there and she might read it.

Everyone knew a masted ship was waiting down Baltimore harbor. Surely the famous trader Austin Woolfolk had come to town to buy slaves for the Carolinas, where the overseers whupped their blacks easy as taking in air. And here were Daniel and Jeremiah Abel: two big slave boys, full grown, tall, muscled, fit for a fine price. And here was Delilah—too old for pleasuring a white man anymore but not too old to keep up a kitchen. And the good Lord knew Massa needed money.

"What we takin'?" Jeremiah asked.

"Ourselves," Mama whispered. "Wear all the clothes you can get into. We can't tote a thing."

"Mama—" Jeremiah began.

She held her finger over her lips, wouldn't let him finish.

They wore as much clothing as they could, and their hand-me-down wool coats, too full of holes to do much good. Elijah's was the best one: a thick felt cloak, a gift from Massa two years ago, and it still fit fine.

He didn't quibble, never even mentioned he didn't have to do this flight. He put his free papers down his shirt. His brothers and mama needed him, and he would do his best to get them north. This was the Abel family. No one got left.

It was a half-rain night, more like sweat in the air than actual drops. No light to make shadows, no stars, just nervous clouds playing against each other, taking turns at blinding the moon. Mama wore a black head wrap, not the white one she usually used, which would've been visible as a rabbit's tail to a hunter. She hiked her dress around her hips and tied it. She was wearing Massa's pants underneath, and Massa's boots. If they should get caught, Elijah realized, his mama might dangle on a rope for being a thief—that is, after she was whupped for being a runaway.

If Massa dared do it. Massa was not a strong man, and he wasn't a bad one, either. He could be a bully, but it was mostly bluff. He had lost the brunt of his authority. There was only this one slave family left to respect him, and they didn't much, except to his face. Which was why the tobacca crop was a failure: Nobody worked it, though they pretended to, and acted perfectly stupid if they got caught loafing.

Daniel was the best at it. He could make the monkey face, talk the slave talk, and only his family knew how sly and smart he truly was. Jeremiah hated following the plow and would give himself a rest with the slightest excuse.

Elijah, for his part, never had worked the fields. From his earliest years, Elijah had been the favorite of the Massa and the Mizzus. He hadn't made much sound even as a baby, and by and by no one expected more than a "yes sir" or "no sir" from him—which silence his owners approved. The pale, powdery Mizzus took him early as a kitchen boy. After Mama had hearth-cooked the white folks' dinner, Elijah would tote it from the smell of dried herbs hanging on the stove brick to the smell of the main house. He'd whistle in the catwalk that divided the black world from the white, so the Mizzus would know he wasn't stealing any food on his way. (The slave food was different from what the whites got. The whites ate ham and sweet potatoes, while the blacks gave thanks for mustard greens, pork rinds, and corncakes.)

A few years later, when Elijah was too tall to negotiate the catwalk without stooping, Massa took him on and trained him in working wood. And all the time, Elijah said hardly a thing, but he did apply himself—which Massa approved. Elijah even tried his hand at whittling and created a sort of flute. He could eke out "Yankee Doodle" through its holes, even approximate some hymns.

And he took to woodworking. Elijah made picture frames and simple supports, and it wasn't long at all before he could see there was more to carpentry than nailing balsam. There was beauty in fashioning a tree trunk into a desk, inventing it a whole new purpose. Massa soon saw, Elijah had him a gift.

Maybe that was when Elijah Abel started to hope. For if he could make something so good from a lowly stick or a dead tree, then improvement was possible everywhere. Even in a slave. He started carving his own designs into table legs, maple leaves into chair backs. He was a carpenter, a joiner, a woodsmith, and Massa knew it. And he, Elijah, was himself like wood, just waiting for someone to take an interest in his improvement, make him into something good, maybe redesign him.

Did Delilah sense that kind of promise for her son? He was the youngest of her three remaining boys, and she favored him in subtle ways—such as waking him up first on the night of their escape.

None of them spoke as they headed north, the cold air licking their nostrils and ears, making ghosts of their breath. They had climbed two frost-slicked fences and three big hills before the clouds lifted and revealed a sprinkle of sunrise stars. Before the sky started blushing and a distant cock crowed, they had made it over another good-sized hill, flattening its yellow grass into their own trail. Though the clouds had calmed and mostly parted, there was yet a mizzling rain, and Mama was coughing every now and again. Still, she moved with long strides and purpose, seeming to know exactly where she was headed. Sometimes she looked at the fading North Star, but she never stopped walking. They crossed through a mostly dead peach orchard and a grove of hickories, lichen sprawled over the crotches of trunks and limbs. A weak stream, dark and thick as molasses, stinking of swill, stopped them for a moment. They leapt over it, Elijah and his brothers first so they could help Mama across. The dawn mists kindly parted to reveal yet another good-sized, grassy hill. They hiked it and descended in silence save Mama's repeated cough and repeated prayer, "Lord have mercy."

Then up ahead, in the midst of more fog, appeared a lantern. That was an answer of some kind, and Mama sighed. When they were almost to the light, she slowed and turned to Daniel. "Bark," she ordered.

"What?"

She swayed to a stop. The boys stopped too. "I say for you to bark. Like a dog."

He gave her a look, shrugged, and then barked. Coonhound bark.

"Again," Mama commanded. "Louder."

He barked again. You didn't say no to Mama, and you didn't question her reasons.

A woman in a black cape stepped from the mists. She lifted the lantern, showing her face and nodding.

The dawn clouds had gone gold. The sun was announcing itself with a fan of light that seemed to Elijah a promise.

"You the best dog I ever birthed," Mama said to Daniel, smiling for the first time since they woke up. She untucked her skirt, let the dress fall like it was supposed to, and they all approached the lantern.

"Thee must be hungry." That was how the Quakers talked then. The woman with the lantern was old and white, wearing a black bonnet with thick lace ruffles all around her face. Her skin was like paper, face half glowing where she held the light. Though her voice was soft, until now the Abels had been using only whispers, so it sounded near a shout.

"Yes, ma'am, sore hungry, thank you," Delilah Abel said.

"I have plenty." She gestured to the simple brick house behind her. Elijah hadn't noticed it until that moment.

On the porch, Delilah looked over her shoulder. The rising sun was just a dazzling sliver between the hills. She collapsed, weeping, and then coughed so hard she could barely find her breath. Even inside the Quaker house, as they fed her chamomile tea and set her in a rocking chair, Mama coughed and cried.

She had had the cough for some time but not this bad.

Elijah stayed with her next to the fire, one hand on the rocker. Daniel and Jeremiah stood against the wall, watching.

The Quaker woman went for paregoric. That put Mama to sleep, but she kept waking herself up with the cough. Elijah, though his joints and bones ached for slumber, hardly closed his eyes.

"We can't stay here," he said to no one.

The Quaker woman answered. "True, thee cannot. Thee art too near danger."

"Yes'm." He nodded. "That put you near danger, too, ma'am?"

The woman stirred the fireplace ashes with a stick, blew on the flame bud till it took to nursing a log. "I never have felt myself in danger. God's eye won't shut itself while I'm about his business. I'm certain of that." Her voice had a sweet, fluty tremble but sounded full assured.

"You help slaves often?" he asked.

"No." She blew the flame again. "I have never in my life helped a slave."

His mouth dropped. "We the first?"

"I am a Friend, a Quaker. We do not believe any human being is a slave. Not in God's mind. I have opened my door to human beings of somewhat darker skin than my own, but I have never helped a slave." She stirred the fire like it was soup.

"I heard there was people doing that. Making up a secret path for slaves to get north."

"No. Not for slaves."

He laughed low. "For colored men and women, then."

The woman smiled. "Can thee sleep? Thee should sleep," she said.

He tried to, but Mama's coughing wouldn't let him relax. Daniel and Jeremiah had no such difficulty. Both were deep dreaming, huddled against each other on the floor.

Then it was dusk. Elijah must have found a bit of slumber, for he did have to pull himself from some dark comfort when his mama said once more, "Time!"

They ate sop-bread as Mama listened to the instructions on how to reach the next stop. Their whole journey seemed to have been planned by Quakers. The woman put a brown shawl around Delilah's shoulders and opened the door.

At the next place, a Quaker man—the old woman's son—waited with an empty wagon. The Abels climbed into it, and the Quaker man covered them with hay, never uttering a sound. That's how they traveled, bumping over the road and itching. Sometimes they could hear horses' hooves, other voices, and their driver talking innocently about his big load.

Come night, they were walking once more, hay sprigs in their hair.

As long as they were moving, Mama's cough stayed calm. And they were moving fast—through a grove, down a long, overgrown path, and across a marshy field of wild grass. They saw the next lantern before morning gave a hint.

Once again, soon as they stopped, Mama's cough hit hard. The hay had aggravated it, she said.

They were housed this time by a whole family of blond, blue-eyed Quakers, including seven children who looked like copies of each other. The Abels ate the porridge offered them, Delilah coughing between every spoonful. Again, she was given tea and paregoric. Again, they all tried to rest by the fire. This time, Elijah fell fast asleep, too, until he heard his mama call his name.

He opened one eye.

"'Lijah, wake your brothers."

Was it a dream? Was he reliving their escape? Had they escaped? Or had this been one long night of dreamtales?

"There's danger, 'Lijah!"

He didn't have to wake the boys. The heavy knock at the front door did that job.

The Quaker man, looking steady rather than scared, directed them to a closet and lifted a piece of the floor. A ladder led to the root cellar.

Elijah was the last to go down. He heard the outside voices. Not Massa's voice, but white voices nonetheless, describing a family of fugitive slaves. There was a law, the white voices said, passed in 1793—didn't the Quakers know of it?—that let a man claim his property even if that property had legs and used them. And anyone hiding that man's property was bound for jail, be he Quaker or Baptist or heathen.

"We have no slaves here," said the Quaker woman.

"We would not house slaves here," said her husband, his voice just as steady as his steps had been.

Elijah grinned.

Then footsteps. Hard ones. Right above their heads.

Mama's face puckered. She had to cough, but she couldn't let herself. Not in this circumstance. She folded her arms over her mouth, squeezing her face.

More footsteps, muffled, now outside.

Delilah squeezed her face harder and then let out a cough she couldn't contain. With a look of horror, she fainted. Elijah caught her before she hit dirt, but they had made a noise, and not a small one.

They waited. Someone was banging on the cellar door, a white voice demanding, "Come out!" Then another white voice, a woman's: "Thee can come out! Danger is past!"

The cellar door opened, and they knew light again.

"Mama done faint," said Daniel.

He and his brothers hoisted their mama's limp body into the arms of the Quaker man, who observed, "She's taken fever."

Mama woke up to the smelling salts—coughing hard and deep and then spitting up what looked to be blood and hay. Her bandana was part way off. She pulled it all the way off, holding it to her mouth. Her hair was a turmoil, matted to her head like moss, some gray sprigs of it sticking straight up.

"That blood?" She looked at her kerchief. Whatever she had coughed up didn't show any color on the black bandana, but a string of spit fell over her wrist. Red spit.

They moved her to a bed in a room barely big enough to hold it. The Abel boys and the Quakers stood in the doorway.

"We safe now, Mama," Elijah said.

"How long has thee had the cough?" asked the Quaker man.

"Off and on, I say—." She took in a shallow breath. "Long time." She showed the bandana and her wrist to the man. "Maybe the hay disturb my throat," she said.

"Is it night yet?" asked Elijah. There were no windows in this house.

"Near dusk," said the Quaker woman.

"'Cause cough or no, we headed for the Lion's Paw," said Mama. Canada.

"Thee is quite ill," said the man.

Mama sat up straight as she could. "If I die, then I die in freedom, sir. I feels better now I coughed up that bit of blood." Her face lines deepened. She was struggling against another cough. "You been most kind. You risk y'own freedom for us. We won't tarry." She forced a smile that looked more pained than happy. Elijah hadn't realized until that moment how wrinkled Mama's face had gotten. She was trying hard to look glad, but every hurt her slave years had etched into her face showed like the lines Elijah might slice into oak.

Another cough took her, sent her to the floor.

"Thee cannot leave in such a state," said the woman after Mama had coughed up more blood.

Mama breathed two long sighs. The cough spell was over, but it had roughed her voice, stole a good part of it. Her speech was more wind than sound now: "If I die, I will die free—and my boys free too." Delilah Abel stood.

There were more hills and rivers before them, and a string of Quaker helpers, often with wagons and always with food. Two weeks later, a Quaker woman pointed to a large sycamore in the distance. "On the other side," she said, "thee crosses the waters into Canada. A Friend will be waiting with a flatboat to carry thee over."

That's just how it was too. The only thing Mama said as they crossed into freedom was, "This be holy water. You boys remember this day. You remember this water."

"Yes, ma'am," Elijah answered.

Notes

The chapter title, "Hiding in Thee," is from the title of hymn number 70 in *Hymns for the Family of God*.

According to the records of baptisms for the dead, Elijah's mother, for whom he was baptized, was named Delilah, as was his daughter, of whom we have no record other than this ordinance. Bringhurst ("Elijah Abel," 142, n. 20) cites the Nauvoo Temple record Book A100 as follows: "Delila Abel bapt in the instance of Elisha Abel. Rel son. Bapt 1840, Book A page 1" and "Delila Abel Bapt. in the instance of Elijah Abel 1841, Rel. Dau. Book A page 5." In Elijah's ordination to the priesthood office of seventy, his mother is listed as "Elila" rather than "Delilah."

According to Bush, "Abel was born in Maryland, [but] his family was later from Canada, raising the question of his having made use of the underground railroad" ("Commentary," 33). We know that his mother had once been a slave in South Carolina, which lends credence to the possibility of their having escaped slavery. "Free papers" would have been hard to come by (Bush, "Commentary," 42, n. 8).

Although most of the stories we hear about the Underground Railroad come after the passage of the Fugitive Slave Law in 1850, when Harriet Tubman was at her heroic best, in fact there were already fugitive slave laws on the books, dating from 1787 and 1793. "It was accepted by all as a just law, permitting the owners of slaves to reclaim their property" (Cockrum, *History of the Underground Railroad*, 9).

Austin Woolfolk (actually Woldfolk) was a famous slave trader whom Abel likely would have heard of in Maryland. Frederick Douglass, also from Maryland and Abel's contemporary, mentions him (Preston, *Young Frederick Douglass*, 61). Douglass was born a slave and for a time worked at buying his freedom but soon became a fugitive slave and ultimately a great Abolitionist orator, often giving speeches in the same forums as William Lloyd Garrison and Elizabeth Cady Stanton.

2

THE BOND OF LOVE

By this shall all men know
that ye are my disciples.
JOHN 13:35

Delilah Abel lived a few more months, until some hints of spring appeared, though the ground was still hard. Daniel and Jeremiah had left her—not because they wanted to, mind you, but because she insisted. Parting time had come, and the Abels had divided themselves freely here in the Lion's Paw. Elijah, with his manumission papers—he was safe. And Mama declared she'd be perfectly safe herself before long, curled in the bosom of Jesus. But she wanted Daniel and Jeremiah farther north. Rumor had it there was gold up there. A fine life might be waiting for them, so she told them to set forth and discover it. They had resisted some but not for long. Elijah gave them his cloak as a good-bye gift, telling them they'd surely meet again—the Abels were meant to be together— and he'd more than likely want it back, so they'd best care for it well. The boys nodded, hugged Mama close, and set out.

In the poor shelter—part dugout, part cabin—that the brothers had framed from half-burned wood and rusty, bent nails from an abandoned camp, Elijah held his mama's hand in her last hour. She said simply, "Better."

"You feelin' better, Mama?" he asked.

"No. You be better, son."

"I'm fine, Mama."

She gazed at him. "Listen. You be better, 'Lijah."

"Now Mama," he laughed, "I ain't the one sick."

"Make yo'self better." She coughed. He wiped her chin with her good head wrap—the white one—stiff with blood, though he snow-washed it daily. All her coughs had blood in them now.

"Massa told me," he said, "there's to be a college. Down Ohio. They take black and white."

Her eyes went wide. "Back in United States? You plan on—."

"Ohio."

"Slave country?"

"Well—Ohio."

"'Lijah." She coughed. "Don' you know? Even with them papers you got, down in the United States, some mean soul might take you for a runaway and sell you south."

He took her hands. "Not if I outruns 'em."

"You outrun a musket ball, do you, son?"

"Oh, I be fast!"

"What you need to be is careful."

He smiled. "Mama, you believe in the devil?" he asked.

She closed her eyes, didn't answer for quite a while. Then, "Man make enough wickedness without no devil helpin'," she said. "That's what I thinks. Though I guess there's a devil somewheres, laughin' away." She watched Elijah, her eyes glassy, waiting—either for his response or for the real cough spell they both knew was building.

"You believe in God?" Elijah asked.

Her face wrinkled itself up. "Now why you ask that? You know I prays." This was the weak version of her scold-voice. Years ago, she could've used it like thunder and stopped a body in its tracks. Now it was the echo of what it once had been. "You sees me pray."

He shrugged again. "I ain't askin' does you pray. Askin' does you believe. For sure."

She looked at him long, her face so full of pity and love it would haunt him for the rest of his life.

"I know you prays, Mama," he breathed, not moving his eyes from hers. "What I don't know is if God ever hear your prayers. It just seem you ain't been treated fair. That's all. *If* there's a God."

She coughed. Another prelude, not a long spell. "'Lijah," she said, "you listen." He had to move close to her lips to hear. "They is a God. They *is* a God."

He answered quietly, "Massa say to me once, the devil love black flesh."

"Massa?" Sounded like she was damning Massa by hissing his title with one of her last breaths.

"He was part jokin'."

"Not much joke," Mama whispered.

"What if—" Elijah started. Then he turned his head away. "What if God don't love black flesh?"

"God." She sighed out long, like this would be her final word. "God know colored folks even better than he know white. That be the biggest secret this side of heaven."

"Know us better?"

She took in a shallow breath, trying to gather enough air to make a fine departing speech. "God's got him one good heart, 'Lijah. The best heart of any." Another cough. "That heart ache for the one what suffers most. Ache for us, 'Lijah."

"Preacher say that?" He couldn't recall any preachment about God's heart, couldn't even recall any particular preacher talk, only the hand-raising energy and the mention of what kind of soap God used—soap so strong it could bleach blood. Not lye soap, but something like whole soap or full soap. "Who preach that?" he asked, for he truly wished to remember.

"No preacher. Just my own self. What I feels."

"You got the call, Mama?" he chuckled.

She gave him a wry look. "Oh, the call comin'," she said. Then once more, "God."

"Who is God?" he asked as though she could really tell him. "What you feel when God be talkin' to you?"

"Well, ain't you feeled it yo'self?"

"Not for sure."

"Some nights when the stars is fallin', ain't you feeled it?" Now her voice was gone dreamy.

"Not too much."

"Like them stars is set to rip the night open and show us the very face of God with tears streamin' down his cheeks just for us? Oh, I feel that some nights! Ain't you?"

He wanted to say yes but couldn't. "Not any I recall just now." He wondered if God's face looked like a bright version of Massa's, or if a colored man's God wore a colored man's face. How were God's eyes? Did he smile?

Mama grasped his hand. Hers was cold and dry. "Jesus," she said.

Pictures of Jesus most generally showed reddish hair, blue eyes. Was that Jesus? He wondered if his mama might be seeing the Lord this very moment. "What 'bout Jesus?" he asked.

"'Lijah, Jesus feel the whip ever' time it hit black skin. Jesus knows, honey. And if they do be a devil, you know what I thinks?"

"No, ma'am."

She tried for a smile, which didn't amount to much. "I thinks every time he watch that ol' cowskin lash up slave flesh, it make him laugh same way it done when they hit Jesus. That ol' devil, he know Jesus love us. Every time Mr. Devil watch us suffer, why, that's like watching Jesus gettin' one more hit. That's what I thinks. Must make the old devil howl." Her mouth puckered like she was set to kiss her son good-bye. Instead, she expelled a little cough, still nothing serious. "And then the white folks go to church, don't they, and fold they hands under the man on the cross. They never even imagine they doin' Jesus' torture all over again, every time they rope up slave hands and pull out that whip. Good joke, ain't it."

"Not much," Elijah said. He had seen only one slave whipped—his own daddy, Andrew Abel. That was the first memory of his life: the long-gone overseer taking a curling whip to Andrew Abel's back and cutting to blood with every lick. The whipping was because Andrew had run off. But he had not run far enough. Dogs smelled him out in two days. Delilah Abel had wrapped her husband's back in a grease cloth after that punishment. Andrew stank of lard until the day he got sold off, which wasn't long after. Now that was another picture Elijah kept in his head, though he never did actually see it: his daddy standing like a statue on a block. He could not remember his daddy's face but figured it must've looked like his own face did now. Yes, Andrew Abel would've been somewhere near Elijah's age when he tried running off.

With effort so strong it showed her neck tendons like bones, Delilah lifted her head and propped herself on one elbow. "Jesus know you, son. Jesus got big plans for you. Settin' you free!" The words were rasps. Her face lines were looking more like silver than charcoal, and he knew she was going fast, all her blood coming to a halt, settling down for a long rest.

"Then why—" Elijah began.

"Why he let us get hurt?" She took in wind that sounded more like dry grain. "It make us brave. Son, that be the refiner's fire. That be the fuller soap."

There it was—the name of God's soap! Fuller. God's was fuller soap than any human could concoct. One whiff would clean out a set of lungs. Elijah repeated the name so he wouldn't forget it. "Fuller soap."

"Jesus," she said again, "he want us glitterin' like a diamond, same as him." Her skin was wearing the death sheen now.

"I believe in God," he said.

He had considered God seriously years ago. He had said those very words to himself one afternoon and not said them again until this day.

Before the rest of the slaves had got sold off, they had a happy church with good singing and sometimes a circuit preacher to quote them Bible verses. Later, there hadn't seemed much point to church. Besides, the nearest colored congregation was half-day's ride from Massa's place. So they had pretty much quit religion—though indeed, Mama still prayed every day of her life and many times during the day. And there had been that particular afternoon—oh, so many years back he had mostly forgotten it—when Elijah himself had declared there was a God. He didn't know how to picture this God or even if a body could picture God or even if a body should. But he had said those words, said them alone, in private, talking to a half-finished table. He hadn't repeated them until now nor made any steady progress towards whatever or whoever God was. Only at this moment, next to his dying mother, did he recall having declared himself a believer.

Delilah traced his nose and jawbone with her finger. "I done this when you was born," she whispered. "You know that?"

"Don't remember so far back, Mama."

"Well, I done it. I touch yo' face. My first baby got took away 'fore I ever see him. They say he be dead, but I never know for sure."

"You ain't ever told me."

"Then Jeremiah come, then Daniel. I make sure every time, my baby full-made and lively. And then you." Her coughs were not growing deeper, just weaker, and her words were coming so soft and slow. "I try to picture how you might look this very day, in your manhood. My, my, you even better than I thought! 'Lijah, you everything to me."

"Mama, I do anything in this world for you," he whispered.

She smiled dimly and then asked him to pray God let her die quick, not drawn out over days. She didn't want to go hacking and breathless the way she had seen some do, when it was consumption strangling them so tight their souls could hardly find a pathway out of their bodies.

He didn't want to pray this woman dead, but he did it—in the first out-loud prayer of his life: "God? Whoever or whatever you be, if you wants her that bad, would you please take her quick and don't make her to suffer any worse than she already done."

"Say 'Jesus,'" she whispered.

"You see him, Mama?"

"My Lord!" Delilah inhaled deep, lungs rattling.

"Jesus!" he said, and repeated the name as a breeze came around him. "Oh, Jesus! Take my mama!"

And with those words, on the wings of that breeze, Delilah Abel passed.

Elijah wondered what kind of power might be waiting inside him if God would hear his request and answer it so quick.

He didn't weep. Elijah Abel had never been a weeper. He built his mama's coffin—the very first he ever made. He used wood from the poor shelter he and his brothers had built, and a rusty old saw a stranger had left as though for this very purpose. Then he heated tin after tin of water and poured it on the ground until the dirt was soft enough to dig. The stranger had provided him a half-broken shovel too, which worked fine enough for this end.

The moment his mama passed, an other-world peace filled him. But the deeper he dug, the thinner that peace stretched, the more his sorrow turned the edge towards anger, until he had sweated away every drop of comfort and was out loud cursing the dirt, then cursing Massa, then cursing whatever slave ship it was kidnapped his kin from Africa, and finally even cursing the very God he had said he believed in. By the time he buried his mama, he was fit to find someone to kill. He had never suspected there was such fury inside him and such an ability to shout when nobody was around to hear. Every inch he dug into the earth, he was digging into his own soul—the soul Massa said he didn't have—and finding not any residue of peace, only anger and ice.

NOTES

The chapter title, "The Bond of Love," is from the title of hymn number 544 in *Hymns for the Family of God*.

According to Margery Taylor's research, Elijah Abel reported his mother as "[D]Elila Williams [Abel]" (she is listed as "Delilah Abel" in baptism for the dead records, as noted in chapter 1) and his father as "Andrew Abel" in the missionary registry (microfilm 025664—Missionary record books, A–C, 1860–1906). The fact that he named his father seems to contradict the once popular idea that Elijah Abel was an unusually fair-skinned mulatto, the son of a white man—possibly his master. (Elijah's father, for whatever reason, did not remain with his family, for Elijah's patriarchal blessing mentions that his father "[had] not done his duty" towards him.)

Though we do not know the exact racial mixture of Elijah Abel's lineage (slavery brought a legacy of very common—though hidden—interracial relations), it is vital to dispel the folklore about Elijah, which has sometimes cast him as so white that his race was not discernible and that (as Zebedee Coltrin falsely claimed) when Joseph Smith learned of Abel's black lineage "[Abel] was dropped from the quorum and another was put in his place" (Bringhurst, "Elijah Abel," 139). Brother Coltrin's claim was contradicted by apostle (later President) Joseph F. Smith, who discovered two certificates "attesting to [Abel's] status as a Seventy; the first 'given to him in 1841' and a 'later one' issued in Salt Lake City" (Bringhurst, "Elijah Abel," 139). There is even more persuasive evidence that Elijah Abel was indisputably black and recognized as black during his lifetime: Census takers, who were to identify a person's race by appearance only, identified Abel as black. (The choices the census taker was given were W [White], B [Black], and M [Mulatto].) Margery Taylor's research shows that the 1850 census in Cincinnati, Hamilton County, Ohio tenth ward, page 89, lists Elijah as B (Black). Though a Salt Lake City census lists him as "M," the census taker could not have so identified him without noting African characteristics. Finally, the one drawing that depicts him (reproduced in Van Wagoner and Walker, *Book of Mormons*, 1) shows a man with distinctively African features.

3

MUST JESUS BEAR
THE CROSS ALONE?

If any man will come after me,
let him . . . take up his cross.
MATTHEW 16:24

The loneliness surprised him, after he had screamed himself
hoarse while earthing his mama. Elijah had never been alone in all
his life. He started imagining ghosts sneaking up on him or slave-
catchers setting up to rope him throat first.

After his mama's death, he mostly walked, eating roots and an
occasional cluster of shrunk-up, leathery berries that had somehow
defied the snow. Around his neck, he wore the shawl the Quaker
woman had gifted his mama—the Freedom Shawl, he called it.
What with his cloak gone, it was all he had against the cold.

By and by, he invented his own companions, usually characters
from the Bible. He had heard a few Bible stories in his church-going
days, and sometimes his mama had told him the tales. Joseph of the
Rainbow Coat was his most favorite. He'd hold conversations with
the old prophet as he made his way towards—he supposed Ohio,

though it was really Maryland beckoning. Maryland, his slave place, was still home, the only one he'd ever had. He wanted to see Massa. Not to thank him. To kill him maybe. And to demand of him exactly whereto he had sold off Elijah's woman and baby.

He didn't bother with the underground network, didn't feel the need of it, what with that paper in his pants. Still, his mama had surely been right that there was danger all around, for he looked like a runaway: skinny and unwashed, his cheekbones like sharp rocks, hair outgrown and half-matted. His top trousers were tattered, the right pantleg torn clean off at the knee, the left one near that bad, a big rip that got bigger by the day. Under the top trousers, he wore two more pair, but they weren't in much better condition. His shirt was in fair shape, and the Freedom Shawl was a good one, even though it was a woman's and he knew he appeared silly wearing it.

He didn't talk out loud, even when he was making up conversations with Old Testament Joseph, though he listened to everything around him and to everybody—when there was a body to listen to. He listened especially one bright Sunday, hardly a cold day at all, when he found a group of free blacks in a little makeshift church. They were amening a fancy dressed preacher man who looked to be about half the size of the church itself. They were shouting hallelujah whenever that preacher quit talking to take in breath.

Elijah stood outside the open door, listening. Though it had been a while, he could still hold on to a good sermon like his brain was painted with horse-glue. He knew how to wrap his memory around good words, always had. As the preacher quoted scripture, Elijah let his mind gnaw on the verses until he was sure he could repeat them. The preacher was talking about the Lord being tried without justice. And then, said the preacher, his voice a low whisper like what he was about to say shouldn't be repeated outside the church walls, those Romans prepared a cross for Jesus to die on. And those Romans laid hold on a certain man to carry that cross through those streets and up that hill. That certain man, said the preacher, was called Simon, and Simon was black. Yes, Simon was a Cyrenian, an African! and he was black "as you and me." The big preacher read, "On him they laid the cross, that he might bear it after Jesus."

Elijah had never heard anything like this before, that a colored man had carried the cross for the Lord!

"And we still carryin' that cross," the preacher said more loudly. "We still carryin' it for Jesus—who ain't nothin' like any massa we ever knowed in this sorry land. He is the redeemer of our souls, not the oppressor of our bodies. And don' you go thinkin' Simon left the Lord's side when Jesus got lifted up on that cross—oh, no. Simon knew that cross, and Simon stayed right there watching. Weeping, I say. Now Simon, bein' colored, he may've knowed—like we know—how it felt to be whupped and spat on like Jesus was."

The crowd shouted, "Yes, Lord. Preach on, preacher!"

"But then, three days later, that same Jesus arose from the dead, and other dead folks made they way past the tomb right behind him. Make me wonder if Jesus might have repaid Simon for his kindness. Make me wonder if the Lord mighta come to him before too long, walking hand in hand with a child or mother of Simon's who had died long ago."

Elijah could picture the scenes the preacher described. He had seen enough of human life up close that he knew how a man looked dying and how a woman's face changed as she watched her son get hanged. He knew the defeated arms, the slack jaw of a caged man, and the lit-up grin of someone finding the way north of Mason-Dixon. It wasn't just the scripture words he held in his mind but real eyes and hands and toes, parched mouths, swollen joints, weary people waking up to the spread of dawn. They were colored folks he pictured, for he couldn't quite imagine a white face understanding the true meaning of "north." Elijah saw not just this Simon but even Jesus himself, with dark skin and hair like a black lamb's.

"He is not here, for he is risen, as he said." Yes, Elijah had that scripture down, and he could imagine Jesus saying to Simon, "Thank you for helpin', brother."

"Death is swallowed up in vict'ry," said the preacher. And that verse swallowed Elijah's own anger—for a minute, anyways. Those words felt warm and good easing their way into his thoughts and settling. He could imagine Jesus with Delilah, Jesus saying, "Welcome, sister."

When the preacher finished his sermon, Elijah echoed the congregation's amen and joined as best he could in singing a hymn. Shortly afterward, an old man approached him. "Happy Easter, stranger. You look like you could eat somethin'."

Elijah nodded. There was surely nothing to fear in this old, dark face. "It be Easter?" Elijah asked.

"Yessir."

"Well, happy Easter, then."

The man took him home, where most of the congregation followed, home being a simple frame cabin. The sun was full up, and so bright. It was the prettiest day Elijah had seen since escaping, quite a bit greener than where he had left his mama. There were patches of green with yellow flowers like women in bonnets peeking up to spy on any remaining snow. And there was an outdoor table spread with potatoes and greens and the sweetest blueberry jelly Elijah had ever tasted. The congregation—all free blacks, not a slave amongst them—greeted him like he was an important guest.

They called their town Little Egypt. They were farmers, mostly, who traded food more than money with each other and kept within their own borders, not associating much with whites except to purchase medicines or necessities they couldn't manufacture themselves. Little Egypt was a good place, they told him, a happy place, and he should stay. One old woman motioned towards a sweet-looking girl near Elijah's age, a slight miss, thin at the ankle and collar bone, her skin dark as a ripe berry. Her face was pretty, but it was not the face Elijah loved. The face he loved was Nancy's. That's what sealed his determination to move on.

"That girl need her a husband," the old woman said in a high, scratchy voice.

"I wish her well," Elijah answered, moving his eyes away from the girl's. "Maybe someday I be returnin'."

"You could start up anything—includin' a new family—right here, you know. 'Less'n you got yourself a family already," the old woman said.

"I ain't sure if I do got a family. That's what I need to find out."

Twice more he was invited to stay, and twice more he declined. Elijah was set to find his old Massa and learn who had bought Nancy and the baby. He wasn't ready to lay down roots, though these good people did make the prospect pleasant. The old man gave him fresh clothes and directions to Maryland, which was quite close, he said. Only three days by foot.

More like six. Finally, though, Elijah found a familiar road, and in one more day, the place he had lived his whole slave life.

There had been changes. All the slave quarters were torn down. Old Massa's house was sitting lonely in the midst of foxtails and stinging nettle. And there was Massa himself on the porch, rocking in his chair—a chair Elijah had made—and lifting a bottle to his lips. He was wearing pants almost as raggedy as Elijah's old ones and a shirt that once had been white but was yellow and brown-specked now, like he had spattered himself with coffee.

When Elijah approached, Massa squinted like the sun was too bright, though it was down. The clouds were still reflecting the sunset. Maybe they held too much light for those drunk old eyes.

"'Lijah?" His voice sounded rusty, like he hadn't used his mouth in some time for anything but guzzling liquor. "You one brash boy, coming back here after what you done."

Elijah stepped forward. Not defiant-like. He had nothing to

defy, just personal business. "I 'spect you be right, sir." What surprised him was that he was using his regular voice, not his slave one.

"I gave you freedom. Then you ran off with my property."

"You referrin' to my brothers and Mama, I suppose."

"Each one worth five hundred dollars. Or more." Massa aimed a shaky finger at him. "You owe me fifteen hundred dollars, boy. Ought to sell your black hide to recover my money."

Elijah thought his former Massa would at least stand to threaten him, but Massa just sat there and took another long draw on the bottle.

Elijah stayed silent a moment. "I come back here to know something."

"You know too much, that's your problem. I was too good to you."

"Where you sell off my woman and baby to?"

Massa wiped his mouth with his dirty sleeve. "Your woman?"

"Nancy." He hadn't spoken her name out loud in years. He sighed it, as if "Nancy" had been stopping up his breath since the last time he had said it.

"Who's she?"

"Nancy." Her name came soft, couldn't come any other way. Standing here, next to the porch, he could picture her wearing a pink cotton dress, white apron, white head wrap, balancing a laundry basket on her head and gliding up the walk, singing. Her songs were always about Jesus. The one Elijah remembered now said, "When we all meet in heaven, there is no parting there."

"You own her since she been four years old, sir. She have a baby when you sell her off. That baby was *my* baby."

Massa belched.

"Where you sell my woman and baby off to?"

"You got fifteen hundred dollars to pay for that information? You owe me, boy." He spat into the nettle.

Elijah took another step towards the old man. Oh, he did look old, feeble, near pathetic, that pink scalp gleaming between greasy strings of white hair. Elijah's voice stayed calm and soft from the influence of Nancy's name. He thought, *I got me strong hands could wring your neck*, but he didn't say it.

Massa's eyes filled. "I treated you like a son. Then you up and steal my property. I shoulda listened. My brother told me to never trust no niggah. Give a niggah an inch, he'll take a ell."

"Where you sell my woman and baby off to, Massa?" His voice stayed low, but anger was filling up the words like they were pig bladders.

"You was always my favorite. I never done you wrong in my life. I treated you like a white man. I freed you. Coulda sold you for more'n your brothers, you know that? But I didn't. Then you up an'—"

"I didn't mean you no harm. Now, where you sell them off to?"

Massa's face was crumpling up for a good cry. "I loved you, 'Lijah."

"You owned me, Massa." Still soft but puffing up steady with the breath of his newfound, life-held anger.

"Virginia. Sold the lot of them—all my slaves but Delilah. And them brothers of yours. Virginia. I expect they're all dead now." His face straightened. He emptied the bottle, holding it an inch from his lips, waiting for the last drop, then licking his mouth with a slow, thick, white-coated tongue. "There was a ruckus down Virginia. A slave uprose against his master." He coughed out a drunk laugh. "Imagine that! Probably not hard for you to imagine it."

"No sir. Not all that hard." Still quiet.

"Then a bunch of slaves joined the ruckus. Ended up sixty whites or more died and, oh, a couple hundred, maybe five hundred niggahs. Maybe a thousand. Likely them I sold. Maybe including the girl."

"Nancy."

"Nancy," Massa mimicked. "Give up any hope there, boy. Ain't no use for it." He held the bottle above his mouth.

"That all there is, Massa. That whiskey gone like Nancy gone. Like my baby gone."

He lowered the bottle. "You wanting to kill me, boy?"

"Whereto in Virginia you sell them?"

"If you try it, you'd best give it your all."

"I ain't goin' kill you, Massa. Just tell me who you sell them to."

Massa waved like he was slow-swatting a lazy gnat. "I don't remember. I sold the lot of them to some slaver. Forgot the name. Never knew the name. He made the deal, not me. I don't know where any of them went, except to hell. Far as I'm concerned, you can go there too." He gazed at Elijah, his face still weepy. "Be quick."

"I ain't goin' kill you. I already say that."

"You heading for Virginia?"

"That's my business."

Massa threw his bottle down. It exploded into sparkly shards. Seemed he wanted that sound to be his anger, for his voice was too weak to come out anywhere near as mad as he surely wished. "'Lijah!" Massa tried to stand up, wobbled and swayed, then fell right back down into his chair.

Elijah waited.

"I am not a bad man, 'Lijah." He paused for a response, but none came. So Massa himself described what he wanted to hear: "Come Judgment Day, you remember all I done for you. I could send the law after you right now. I could have you in ball-and-chain by night-fall. Lynched at dawn. But I won't. If I was a bad man, I would. But I am a good man."

Elijah fixed his eyes on the old drunk, thinking, *Just because you ain't bad, that don't mean you good!* and taking note all over again how yellow and sick his once-proud owner looked. Massa would stand before God's bar soon enough. With a half-smile, Elijah said, just as he would've in the old days, "How you think I'm goin' take your part if I don't got a soul? Besides which, you just told me to go to hell. Now, if I'm in hell, how am I goin' stand up for you when you before God?"

Massa let his own mouth make the almost-smile too. "Maybe I can call your name, and you can take the stairs."

"Maybe I can take the stairs all right. But I might have to take the *down* stairs to visit you."

Massa whispered, "I don't care what else you remember, but if I was a bad man, you'd be picking cotton this moment. Or worse."

"Keep sayin' it, and you might convince a angel. A white one, anyways. I wish you the best of luck when God be counting up your marks."

Those were the last words Elijah spoke to him. Then he walked on towards his destiny.

He asked at the Baltimore shipyard if there was any record of twenty slaves being sold south towards Virginia. He was met with laughter. He had no date of sale, no name but old Massa's. When he mentioned he might head towards Virginia in search of his woman and baby, the black sailors, who had sea papers—which were even better than free papers—told him any Negro in Virginia was asking for a lynching, so he should go there only if he was no longer particularly attached to his heartbeat.

They were interesting boys, these colored sailors: rough, proud, feisty. There were some slaves in the shipyard, too, working to buy themselves free. Fred Bailey—a strong, tall, sullen man with a head like a black lion—he was one of these. He worked as a caulker, sealing ship seams with pine pitch and oakum. Most of what he earned, he got to keep. He would have his freedom full bought before long.

Did they need a carpenter, Elijah asked.

Laughter again. Now, a slave might follow any craft to help his master, but no free Negro was allowed to compete with white labor, no sir! White men claimed the privilege of keeping blacks from the best trades. Why, some white carpenters would up and quit work if a free black should hire on. So the answer was one mocking no—they had no need of a carpenter.

It was common labor, then, that Elijah sought. And found. Wasn't hard. He worked a year in a shipyard down Chesapeake Bay—until he got beat up, robbed, and half-drowned by a couple of mulatto sailors.

At some point, Elijah decided to seek out another destination than Virginia. His time in the real world of sailors and new styles of oppression had persuaded him he dreamed too easy. Besides, if God was going to return Nancy and his baby to him, it wouldn't neces-sarily be in Virginia. No guarantee they hadn't got sold off from there too. He started thinking about the college Massa had men-tioned. Maybe he should head towards Ohio and find that college. Instead of poking his head into every slave house down Virginia, maybe he should just choose a promising path and pray. If the Lord and Mama were watching out for him, he'd get his family back somehow.

Heading west, he worked his way across the hill country, hitch-ing free rides on farm carts, if it was a colored man at the reins, and using his two good feet. In Cincinnati there were jobs for the tak-ing, he was told. Carpenter jobs too. In Cincinnati, he decided, he'd get his money for the Ohio college and find some good Quaker man to teach him letters. Surely if God could answer a prayer and take a woman out of this world on a single breeze, God could return a woman to her man and their baby too. So Elijah took to praying, exactly as he had seen his mama do, that God would lead him wher-ever he should go.

NOTES

The chapter title, "Must Jesus Bear the Cross Alone?" is from the title of hymn number 504 in *Hymns for the Family of God.*

We have extracted information on Little Egypt from Cleary, "Little Egypt." In fact, there were several African-American villages in New England, often with such names as Little Canaan or Little Egypt.

Simon the Cyrenian (Luke 23:26; Matthew 27:32), who was "compel[led]" (Mark 15:21) to bear the Savior's cross, may have been black, inasmuch as Cyrene was a town of Libya (Acts 2:10).

The reference of Elijah's "Massa" to a slave uprising is an allusion to the historical uprising in Virginia in 1831, headed by Nat Turner, a slave who felt called upon by God to deliver his people, even by violence. The "Nat Turner Affair" is also referred to in Chapters 6 and 9. Information on Nat Turner may be found in various sources, including Johnson, Smith, et al., *Africans in America*, 308–12.

Frederick Bailey, as Frederick Douglass was then known, was a caulker in the Baltimore harbor, where, indeed, whites might refuse to work if a black man was hired on the job (Huggins, *Slave and Citizen*, 15).

Oberlin College, which was open to both black and white students, was founded in Ohio in 1833.

4

HIGHER GROUND

Ye do well that ye take heed, as unto a light in a
dark place, until the day dawn.

2 PETER 1:19

It was late spring. Elijah was sleeping on a clover field in a place
he didn't know, though he was sure it was Ohio and he was pointed
towards Cincinnati. When he awoke, a large white man was leaning
over him. This man was dressed as a farmer: brown pants and sus-
penders, an old shirt, and a wide-brim hat, which he was holding in
his left hand. The sun was behind this man's hair like it belonged
there and was content to follow this particular head wherever it
went.

"And who might you be?" From the man's harmless voice, Elijah
knew he had nothing to fear and stood. He was the man's same
height.

"I'm Joseph Smith," the man said, offering his hand. Elijah
shook it. This Joseph Smith had a strong grip.

"Elijah Abel, sir. Free man. I got my papers."

Joseph waved away that information. "You don't need those here."

"No? What city this be?"

"You are in Kirtland, Ohio. And welcome."

Elijah scratched his head. "I figured I was in Ohio. Kirtland. That near the college that takes colored men alongside whites, sir?"

"And what college might that be?"

"Don't know the name. Don't know if it even got built. I heard it was goin' to get built."

"Is it Oberlin College you're speaking of?"

"Like I say, I don't know the name."

"Must be Oberlin. It's underway. Not finished, though. Not yet."

"Am I near Oberlin?"

"No, not too near." Joseph Smith gave an easy smile.

"Am I near Cincinnati then?"

"Not too near there, either."

"Well, what am I near to?"

Joseph's smile grew bigger and brighter. His front teeth were chipped like someone had hit them with a hammer. "Near God, Mr. Abel." He spoke with a little whistle.

Elijah stepped back. "I ain't dead, is I?"

Another good smile. "You don't look dead. A little on the skinny side, though."

"I been walking a while. Destined for Cincinnati. Hoping to find carpenter work there."

"You're a carpenter, then?"

"I am."

"Are you any good?"

Elijah looked down. "If I say so, I be right good."

"Well then, I guess you've been sent to us by God."

"Is there need of a good carpenter here?"

"There is indeed, Mr. Abel." Joseph Smith clapped him on the back. "God has always found excellent use for carpenters." He smiled again. It seemed his most natural expression. Elijah thought maybe Joseph Smith slept smiling.

"The people I'd be working for—they don't mind I be colored?"

"I don't imagine they'll question the color of what God's sent. If you have the will and the skill, they'll be pleased to have you. Are you hungry, then?"

"Yes, sir."

"And thirsty?"

"Oh, yes."

"You'll be filled, Brother Elijah. Better than you've ever been filled before. Allow me to invite you to a meal and conversation."

Joseph Smith's cream-colored stallion was standing nearby, munching clover.

"Your horse," Elijah observed. "It stand all right without being roped up tight?"

"Oh, yes," said Joseph. "But I suggest you never trust property to the mercy or judgment of a horse."

"He's having him a fine meal, looks to me, sir."

"He does enjoy clover—in moderation. And we enjoy being on a first-name basis in Kirtland, Brother Elijah. My horse's name is Charlie. And I am Brother Joseph."

Elijah mulled the names over. "Brother Elijah." He had never been called that. "Should I call your horse 'Brother Charlie' then?"

Joseph Smith released a full, free laugh. "You'll join us for dinner, won't you?"

"Thank you, sir. Yes, sir," Elijah said, feeling almost giddy with gratitude.

So that was the day Elijah Abel met the Mormon prophet, who took him home and gave him not only corn pone and prairie chicken but a set of fine clothes. Sister Emma, the prophet's wife—a sweet-faced, willowy woman with brown hair and browner eyes—gave him a nice big slice of apple pie like a welcome home. He knew right then his life would never be the same.

And he learned that nothing happened in Kirtland without the Mormon gospel getting preached at the same time. Every bite of pie came with cinnamon, sugar, and gospel.

Elijah didn't talk much as he shared his first meal with the founder of the Latter-day Saint religion, just ate. But when Sister Emma offered him a second helping—and that was surely inspiration, for he had been silently praying for one more slice—he said, "I used to go to church."

"You stopped?" Emma set the pie before him. "Why?"

"Oh, ma'am," he said, "I ain't never had nothin' this tasty in my life."

She smiled. "Why did you quit religion, Brother Elijah?"

That was the third time he had heard himself referred to as "Brother Elijah." It gave him gooseflesh. "I didn't quit. Things got difficult, that's all. My church-goin' time was before I come free. Massa sold off all his slaves but me, my mama, and my two brothers."

"Sold them off?" Emma repeated.

"Including my baby, yes, ma'am."

Joseph shook his head. "Makes my blood boil," he said and pounded the table with his fist. "When will these things cease to be?"

"I'd say that's a pretty good question, sir."

"I fear for my country sometimes. Mob violence, injustice, cruelty—these seem to be the darling attributes of some."

"Yessir."

Emma asked Elijah again why he had quit religion.

He hedged and then admitted, "Jus' wasn't nobody to go to church with once they all got sold off. I don't even remember the hymns, except one or two."

Brother Joseph spoke now. "Well, Jesus can tell you whatever you need. Hymns. Knowledge. You just ask Jesus; he'll know all about it."

Elijah forked a circle in the sugary glaze on his plate and took another bite of pie. The apples squirted sweet juice in his mouth. "I heard many things in my time. Once, a man even told me blacks ain't got no souls."

Joseph leaned back in his chair. "And do you believe that, Elijah?"

"Same man said only the devil loves black flesh."

"And do you believe that?"

"Well," he said, not sure he should give the answer he really believed, "I feel like a baby—just a child—answering such a question as that."

"Brother Elijah, if the Lord comes to a little child, He'll adapt himself to the language and capacity of the child. You ask the Lord."

Elijah ate the last bit of crust and stared at his fork. "What do you think, sir? Do the black man have a soul?"

Brother Joseph paused a long time, like he was waiting for someone else to speak—maybe God himself. "Why, Brother Elijah," he said, "you already know the answer to that."

"My mama say," he began but stopped himself. He wasn't ready to talk to these folks about his mama.

"Jesus aches for everyone who suffers," Joseph said. It was practically straight from Delilah Abel's dying speech.

"And God maybe knows the colored man even better than he knows the white one?" Elijah said, hearing his mama's voice right behind him, more a prompt than a memory. Then he wondered if he should take the words back. Surely they would offend white folks.

Joseph Smith pursed his lips and raised his brows, examining the idea, maybe, to see if it was plumb and level. Finally he said, "Could well be. Oh, yes, Brother Elijah, could well be. He knows the ones who seek him. And we seek him most when we suffer."

Elijah felt himself sweating but didn't want to use Sister Emma's clean napkin to wipe his face. He palmed his wet temples and wiped his hands on his pants. "Mr. Smith—"

"Please call me Brother Joseph."

Now Elijah sensed something deep in his own soul, like warm light growing under his skin.

"What your heart tells you is true," said Joseph. "Of course the colored man has a soul, and God has full acquaintance with all souls. Why, you know that! The Negroes are certainly subjects of God's salvation. You, Elijah, are a subject of God's salvation. And God knows you."

Again, the words were almost Delilah's.

"God knows you personally," Joseph Smith declared. "Your name. Your history. He knows your heart. Knows your mission in life. It was God who brought you here."

"To America?"

"To Kirtland. Why, Elijah, I've seen black men—even slave boys—far more refined than a good number of whites. Many a black boy will take the shine off those they brush and wait on. You know that every bit as well as I do." The Prophet leaned across the table. "And I sense you'll outshine many, in days to come. God's been keeping his watchful eye on you. He wants that shine to get radiant—glittering."

Elijah nodded. The Mormon prophet had just used the very word Delilah Abel had spoken in her dying moments: *Glittering.* Elijah's voice came quiet. "My mama said somethin' similar to me. One of our last conversations."

"And God wants to hold conversation with you same as your mama did. But he can't much do it if your ears are stopped up, can he?"

Elijah shook his head.

"So," said Joseph. "You ready to join God's purpose and open your ears?"

"Sir?"

"You need to be baptized."

Elijah squirmed. "Now listen, sir—Brother Joseph. You should know. I ain't what you might call a—a full righteous man. I—I swears sometimes."

Joseph's face went stern. "No! You swear? I had no idea." He wagged his head like disappointment itself. Then his face broke into another full grin. "I love the man who swears a stream as long as my arm—provided he's good-hearted. I love that man much better than the smooth-faced hypocrite."

Elijah said, "I tries at a good heart, Brother Joseph."

"And I don't want you to think I'm an entirely righteous man either. I'm not. You see, God judges men according to the use they make of the light he gives them."

Elijah nodded. "That makes good sense."

"I suspect you're rather like me: A rough stone. Oh, the sound of the hammer and chisel was never heard on me until the Lord took me in hand. It'll be so for you as well."

Elijah breathed deep. "Then I guess," he said, "I maybe should get myself baptized."

Brother Joseph agreed that was a sound idea. Sister Emma asked if he'd like yet another slice of pie, to which Elijah answered, "You sure now I ain't died and gone to heaven? Thank you, but I'm so full I couldn't take in even one more bite."

The year was 1832, the year Elijah Abel was baptized and knelt to receive the gift of the Holy Ghost, becoming a Latter-day Saint, a fellow citizen in the household of God.

In December, Brother Joseph told the Mormon people the Lord wanted them to "establish a house, even a house of prayer, a house of fasting, a house of faith, a house of learning, a house of glory, a house of order, a house of God." Construction on the Kirtland Temple was started up the following June.

Brother Elijah helped dig a trench for the foundation, hauled quarried rock to the site (Brother Joseph himself serving as quarry foreman), sawed wood for the frame, and, under Brother Truman Angell's direction, carved out stair rails. Alongside the other Saints,

Elijah Abel built up a temple to God, the outside like a regular church, but its inside something special: two big halls, the upper one for education in all things, both of this world and the unseen one; the lower room for worship. It was the most magnificent building he had ever seen, and he was a part of it. The women had dedicated their best china to the cause; it had been crushed into a sparkly finish. Elijah gave his whole self—muscles, sweat, time, devotion. Everything he had to give. And he felt God was watching, nodding approval.

Elijah did much of his work next to Father Smith, Brother Joseph's daddy. The relationship these Smith men had was something to envy. Elijah did not think of his own father much. He had been so young when Andrew Abel ran off and then got caught and sold that he wondered what he was truly recalling and what he was making up. Once, though, when Elijah caught a glimpse of himself in a glass, he saw an image he knew was memory: his daddy. But his daddy was wearing some sort of harness with bells on it. It was something like what fancy horses wore when they carried newlyweds. But this harness wasn't fancy. This harness was worn around the neck, and there were spikes sticking out between the bells. A runaway slave wearing such a contraption wouldn't get far—which was surely why the overseer had put it on Andrew Abel. That was the last sight Elijah had had of his daddy.

He could not go into detail about this memory. It hit him so fast and went away so fast, he could hardly catch it. He thought he remembered his mama's whisper, "Andy—why'd you run? Why'd you run?" but he wasn't sure. Anyway, even if Mama had turned bitter over her husband's failed escape, she got inspired by his example eventually, didn't she! But by the time Delilah and her boys lit off, the overseer was gone, the slave-catching dogs were gone, and the Quakers were holding up lanterns to show the way north.

What he said to Father Smith was simply, "You and Brother Joseph get along grand, don't you, sir?"

Father Smith answered, "From his first day on this earth, we've been good friends."

"Ain't that somethin'!" Elijah said, and then, "My daddy ran off." That was as much as he could tell Father Smith—or anyone—about that long-past event. It was a part of the life he had left behind, and no white man, not even a man as good as Father Smith, would understand all that might make a slave run. Elijah had always imagined Andrew Abel planned on buying his family's freedom once he got beyond slave country, though he never had a chance to find out.

On Sunday, March 27, 1836, the temple was dedicated, the Prophet offering a long prayer that "no unclean thing be permitted" to enter this sacred building, which was God's house; that those who went forth from this holy place would do so in Jesus' name, with glory "round about them" and angels tending their path. The Saints waved white kerchiefs after the prayer and shouted "Hosanna! Hosanna! To God and the Lamb!" Elijah also shouted the words and thought he heard angels, sounding like rushing wind—strong enough to wake the dead, yet soft enough to leave lilies unalarmed. Then, somewhere beyond him, Elijah saw a light—not a full vision like some others claimed to get, but for sure a light—and heard a voice he thought was his mama's: "It's time, Elijah!"

He straightened his back, straightened his legs, whispered: "Mama?"

"Wake up, son."

"I remember that night so good. I never forget it," he thought at his mama, who was again by his side. He was remembering her from younger days, from before her hair got its silver threads. He was recalling her tall dignity, her high, round cheeks, her strong, calm eyes, her rich voice.

"Wake up yo' brothers, 'Lijah."

"They gone, Mama."

"Say to them, time come to be free," the voice whispered to him from across the years, or across the hall maybe.

Again he cried, "Hosanna!" with the other Saints.

"God make you be free."

"Hosanna!" he said once more and then "amen!"

"There's more to you, Elijah," said his mother's voice, "than you ever before supposed."

"Amen!" he shouted with the others.

"Wake up yo' brothers, now. Son, you help them to the sacred waters."

"Amen!" he said.

"Be better," her long-gone voice whispered to him. "Let God breathe into your nostrils the breath of life."

He felt a breeze, something like he had felt when he said "Jesus!" just before Delilah died, though this breeze was warmer than the one that had swept off her spirit. This, he thought, was that breath of life God was blowing into the temple. Elijah inhaled deep to catch a whiff of God's sweet air and let it fill him.

He heard another voice then, a child's, inquiring, "That him, Grandma?" He could see no one.

"That's him," he heard his mama say. "Yo' daddy."

He knew the voice must be his baby's. Yes indeed, the two Delilahs—and God—had been watching over him all this time.

Notes

The chapter title, "Higher Ground," is from the title of hymn number 469 in *Hymns for the Family of God*.

The statement by Joseph Smith referring to slavery, "It makes my blood boil within me," is from *History of the Church*, 4:544.

The statement by Joseph Smith "They have souls, and are subjects of salvation" is from a conversation Joseph Smith had with Orson Hyde, as reported in *Teachings of the Prophet Joseph Smith*, 269.

The statement by Joseph Smith "We may come to Jesus and ask Him" is from *History of the Church*, 3:392.

The statement by Joseph Smith "I love that man better who swears a stream . . . than the long, smooth-faced hypocrite" is from *History of the Church*, 5:401.

The statement by Joseph Smith "I am a rough stone" is from *History of the Church*, 5:423.

The statement by Joseph Smith "Never trust property to the mercy or judgment of a horse" is from *History of the Church*, 5:390.

Elijah Abel was baptized by Ezekiel Roberts in September 1832 (Bringhurst, "Elijah Abel," 131). We do not know the location.

The use of a "cow bell . . . or a tall instrument with several prongs covered with little bells attached to his head" was frequently a punishment for recaptured slaves who had run away. This is documented in various sources, including Blassingame, *Slave Community*, 109–10.

Quotations from the dedicatory prayer of the Kirtland Temple are from Doctrine and Covenants 109. The scripture referring to building "a house of order, a house of God" is in Doctrine and Covenants 88:119.

Jane Elizabeth Manning

5

Nobody Knows, 'Cept Jesus

The things which are not seen are eternal.
2 CORINTHIANS 4:18

Now, all the time Elijah Abel was making his way towards the Latter-day Saints, a particular black child was growing up in Wilton, Connecticut. Her name was Jane, and she would have much to do with the Mormons before too long.

Some few years after Elijah Abel had heard those holy words in the Kirtland Temple, Jane Elizabeth Manning was running smack into hard times, though her times would get harder yet. This was just a prelude to all the trials awaiting her. It was good she didn't suspect what lay ahead. Good thing most of us can't predict our afflictions. We just take a step at a time and hope we ain't on the edge of a cliff.

The trial before her now was that, barely into her teen years, Jane had got made pregnant.

She wasn't a slave, by the way. Slavery had been done away in

Connecticut. But she still had had to go into service at age six when her father died. Widow Fitch, Jane's mizzus, sent her back to her mama to give birth.

Now, the widow Fitch had always been somewhat hard on Jane, but she was not a mean woman. In fact, she considered herself very righteous and blessed by God. She was rich and grand. Her pull-back hair was a pretty, shimmery gray and her arms fat as a good duck. Her round face was lined with sixty years of easy tears and laughs, though she hadn't laughed much of late—not since Jane's stomach had swelled up and her state become clear. The widow said to her then, "I know the ways of you people, but I had hoped you'd show yourself an improvement."

You can be sure Jane knew better than to tell her who the father was: the widow's own white minister, Presbyterian pastor Enoch Sylvester. So she mentioned nothing about the night when Pastor had taken her into his church office, showed her a Bible picture of Jesus on the cross, another of Mary at the tomb, and one of a half-naked angel, and then said, "You are one comely nigger, Jane. Brown velvet, that's you. Eyes so dark, so soft. Your hair smells like cornsilk. Forgive me, Lord, but she moves me so strong! I do wish I was a better man!" He had stroked her cheeks, her neck, and then forced her to the floor.

Jane had resisted, but she was only fifteen years old and no match in size or weight for the pastor.

So she was back home, set to deliver a child who wouldn't have claim on a father. Jane's mother, Phyllis (more like a sister to her, since Jane had been with the Fitches for near a decade), did ask who the father was, and Jane told her. No more questions passed between them over that. It was understood territory.

And it was time. Jane lay on the birth bed, Phyllis coaching her to bear down.

Jane moaned. There was pressure like a boulder sitting on her womb.

"Push, baby," said Phyllis, her own body tensed to show the way.

"Oh, Mama, this so bad!" she cried.

"I know the bad part," Phyllis said.

A punishment, that's what it was, thought Jane. It didn't seem fair she should get the full hit of God's wrath while Pastor Sylvester went on preaching like he kept a halo under his hat.

"You know what? That man should die," Jane groaned.

"He will," Phyllis answered. "They all does."

Jane wasn't certain who "they" meant. Her father had died, but that hadn't seemed exactly the will of God, just an accident of drowning. To keep her mind off the labor pains, which had stopped for a moment, Jane remembered her daddy from before she went to the Fitches, how he'd toss her into the air and catch her, nuzzle her cheeks and neck, sing her songs like "When dat ol' chariot come, I'm goin' leave you; I'm boun' for de promised land . . ." She missed him, and she didn't care at all for the old fellow her mother had married last year: Cato Treadwell, a relic of the Revolutionary War who had scarecrow bones and hair like cotton.

Or did "they" refer to white men her mother had never mentioned?

Phyllis Manning Treadwell had been a slave until her twenty-fifth year, owned by the rich Abbotts, given to the oldest Abbott daughter as a wedding gift and later sold to a Stamford man before freedom was given, bit by bit, to all Connecticut blacks. Had there been white men who'd taken Phyllis? Everyone knew about the sort of bedwarmers some white owners used: not a coal-filled, long-handled kettle, but a coal-black, two-handed female. Jane wouldn't ask about that—not now, not at this moment, not with that big boulder sitting on her again, pressing her inside parts, turning her muscles to hot stone.

Her mother helped her sit up, told her the job was nearly done, wiped Jane's brow with her fingers, and asked, "You feel to push, baby?"

"I do," Jane shouted.

"Then push!" Phyllis said.

After some time, Jane's whole body moved to birth the child. Jane was crying and screaming, shivering as though it was winter in this room, damning Reverend Sylvester to hell by name. And then, like fire coming through her, her son was born.

A plump, grayish form, wet and a little bloody, with sweet-smelling, white cream in all his skin creases—around the eyes, in his joints, between his toes—the baby cried, showing a tongue pink as the peonies in Widow Fitch's garden. His skin started looking better presently—brown, not gray. Jane held him to her breast, and after a moment, he figured out what it was for.

Phyllis told her to push one more time, and she did, easing out the afterbirth with no pain at all.

"Good girl," said Phyllis.

Jane's brother Isaac Lewis (she called him "Lew") had been a baby not much older than the one she was holding when she had gone to the Fitches. And there was Lew at the door, eleven or twelve years old now; long, lean and raggedy looking, woolly hair cropped close to the scalp. "Heard the cry," he said.

"Well, come see, why don't you?" Jane said as Phyllis covered her with a blanket.

Lew came in. "Now look at this!" he said.

"You can hold him," Jane offered.

"Naw. 'Fraid I'd drop him."

"You ain't goin' drop him. Hold out y'arms."

"He so little!"

"Hold out y'arms!"

Looking scared and embarrassed, Lew presented stiff arms and then curled them around the baby. "He got a name?"

Jane was smiling now, relieved and full of wonder at what she had done: given birth to a fat, healthy boy! It was good to see Lew holding him so tender. "What do you think—babies come with names printed on they tummies?" she asked.

"I know better'n that," Lew said.

"His name's Sylvester," Jane announced. "It's writ across his little 'hind end, not his tummy."

"I know better'n that." Lew used his saucy voice, but it was half-reverent too.

Of course Baby's name would be Sylvester. Sylvester Manning.

After six weeks of nursing him, watching his brown cheeks get plump as a chipmunk's, Jane would leave the baby with her mother and then return to the Fitches as though nothing had happened.

It was even harder to leave this time than the first. There was Lew holding baby Syl and waving her good-bye. Her youngest brother, Peter, was hiding behind the cabin. (He had been born shortly after Jane started work at the Fitches and still treated her like a stranger.) Everything she loved was staying at her mother's place, and Jane was leaving.

What was harder yet was attending Pastor Sylvester's sermon the next Sunday. But Widow Fitch, dressed in dark silk and a white cap, her hair brought back in a twist so tight it made Jane's jaws ache just seeing it, forced her to go. Melissa, the widow's aging, maiden daughter, wouldn't have forced her if it had been up to her. But it hadn't been up to her.

Melissa herself was bored by church, though she attended faithfully, because that wasn't up to her either. Every now and again, she glanced up at Jane, who was sitting in the colored section. Sometimes Melissa rolled her eyes at the sermon.

Melissa—Missy—had pretty much raised Jane. And it appeared Jane would be the only child Missy would get to raise, what with her buck teeth, big mouth, big nose, and never-gone sunburn. Her face was more like a pink horse's than a white woman's, and men didn't generally favor it with a second glance. Which was a sad thing, because Melissa had a good heart. But her face didn't say one thing about her heart.

Pastor, in this sermon, was talking about the Ten Commandments, in particular the one about adultery and not doing it. Jane watched Pastor's wife, who was sitting statue still and beaming like she worshipped this man. Her hair was the shade of buttermilk, and she had the swollen stomach too.

Pastor was a young man, half bald, his belly too big under the preacher robes. He wore glasses when he preached. He hadn't worn them when he took Jane to the floor. His voice was deep and resonant from the pulpit, could make you feel to weep regret at your sins or weep pity over another's. Mrs. Fitch dabbed her eyes throughout the sermon.

Jane didn't weep. She knew Pastor's lies. His sermon was full of put-on power he hadn't had when he took her.

"And will God ever tempt us beyond what we are able?" Pastor was shouting. "I say to you, nay!" His gaze fell briefly on Jane and darted to his worshipping wife. As his cheeks flushed, Jane spoke to him through her eyes: "I know you. You pretend power, but you are one puny bug in God's fingers. He will squish you like grapes, which I hope he do soon." Jane could feel the milk leaking onto her black dress as she thought curses at him. "Like grapes!"

After church, Jane went to her room, wrapped her breasts in cold rags, and took a few minutes to cry over her lonesome arms.

The next week, Pastor's sermon was on lust; the week after, on the sanctity of marriage. Jane sat still through each one.

Jane would meet the Mormon missionaries before long. But at this time, Elijah Abel was one—a missionary! Elder Elijah Abel, a colored man, was preaching God's news in St. Lawrence County, New York State, not all that far from where Jane was living. An Ohio-licensed minister of the Mormon gospel—yes, he was. He had been ordained an elder by Joseph Smith and then a seventy by

Brother Zebedee Coltrin. He had helped build that temple in Kirtland and been washed and anointed in it against "the powers of the opposition." And now he was spreading the word to all his brothers and sisters in the wide world, railing against the devil's slavery, praising God's deliverance. Elder Abel was a servant of the Most High, a regular missionary of Zion, and, from what one ancient black man told him, "a mighty powerful preacher." He was dressed like a preacher, too: long black coat, stiff white collar, gray vest. His hat didn't look church-fit, being a wide-brim of straw, but it kept the October sun from his eyes just fine.

The missionary who would teach Jane, Elder Charles Wandell, would be dressed somewhat finer, but the message would be the same: The Church of Jesus Christ had been restored to the earth in all its power and authority.

NOTES

The chapter title is from "Nobody Knows the Trouble I've Seen," a traditional Negro spiritual.

Jane's birth date is rather elusive. It is reported as 1818 in her patriarchal blessing but as 1814 by her brother Isaac. Wolfinger estimates it in the late 1810s or early 1820s ("Test of Faith," in *Social Accommodation*, 126). Jane's gravestone lists her birth date as May 22, 1822. Aligning her life events with the provided dates is a little complicated. Jane's life history claims she was fourteen when she joined the Presbyterian church and that she joined the Mormon church about eighteen months later, leaving for Nauvoo a year after that. She had her son, Sylvester, by then; he was reported by at least one man as being "five or six years old" when the family arrived in Nauvoo, though the record (from Elizabeth J. D. Roundy) states Jane was "about eighteen" when he was born (Wolfinger, "Test of Faith," in *Social Accommodation*, 156). The dates become problematic when we see that Jane did not arrive in Nauvoo until at least 1843.

To try to make sense of all the conflicting data, we have accepted the fact that records were not commonly kept for black births (Frederick Douglass, for example, could only estimate his age), and so a reasonable estimate is the best we can do. We also believe Sylvester could well have been three or four rather than five or six when the Manning family arrived in Nauvoo, though he was certainly at least six when they left for the west.

Our best estimates, taking all the conflicting data into consideration, are the following:

1822	Jane is born.
1838	She joins the Presbyterians and around this time gives birth to Sylvester (she is fifteen or sixteen).
October 1841	She joins the Mormon church.
October 1843	She goes to Nauvoo.

We can better trace her steps from Nauvoo onwards, for we have others' journals, which either mention her or detail the journey of her pioneer company. Numerous legal records and newspaper articles give us accurate dates for her activities once she reached Utah.

We have similar problems with the name of Jane's mother, reported in some records as Phyllis and in others, including Jane's own history, as Eliza. Wolfinger is the best source on this. It appears that Jane's biological mother was Phyllis Manning, whose first husband, Isaac, had apparently died, for she had married a Cato Treadwell. A Phyllis Manning is listed in the 1830 Wilton, Connecticut, census as the head of a free black household. We have no information on Phyllis Manning's death, but we know that Cato Treadwell remarried, his new wife being named Eliza (hence the confusion). Treadwell died in 1849 in Connecticut. At least one source claims that Cato made the trek to Nauvoo with his stepchildren (Wolfinger, "Jane Manning James," in *Worth Their Salt*, 261, n. 13).

Wolfinger further records: "According to later family gossip, [Sylvester's] father was a White preacher. After Sylvester's birth Jane returned to the Fitch family while her mother kept the child. . . . The circumstances of Sylvester's birth were a matter that Mrs. James refused to discuss with even her closest friends, and she omitted all mention of the incident in accounts of her life" (Wolfinger, "Jane Manning James ," in *Worth Their Salt*, 261, n. 13). We have invented the minister's name.

Jane almost certainly did not call her brother Isaac Lewis Manning by the name Lew. We have substituted his middle name for his first to avoid confusion with Isaac James, Jane's eventual husband.

Elder Elijah Abel
1838

6

I'll Tell the World

For I am not ashamed of the gospel of Christ.
ROMANS 1:16

At the moment, Elijah Abel was on his own. He had offended his missionary companion, Elder Christopher Merkley, by stating what he knew for true: that even as an elder and a black man, Elijah had as much authority as any high priest in the kingdom of God and that someday there would be stakes of Zion throughout the world.

Merkley had humbled and humiliated him with the same scripture whites of all persuasions seemed so fond of, that Negroes, being the descendants of Cain and Canaan, "were set to be 'servants of servants' all their days." That, said Merkley, was from the Bible and true as corn, so Elijah had best adjust to it and not get above himself.

Elijah knew the scripture story well. He had heard it not only from white men but from a black one too, who was explaining slavery to him: "God gave religion to Noah and Noah had three sons, and when Noah got drunk on wine, one of his sons laughed at him, and the other two took a sheet and walked backwards and threw it over Noah, and then Noah told the one who laughed, 'Your children will hew wood and draw water for the other two children, and they will be knowed by they hair and by they skin being dark.' So that is the way God meant us to be."

No, that story didn't hit him right—out of a white mouth or a black one. Elijah couldn't understand why he should be punished for sins done in ancient times. And this marked the first time a fellow missionary had used the Bible against him. It made Elijah mad, made him burn behind his ears and down his neck. Before he knew it, he had told Christopher Merkley that he'd maybe knock him down right that moment, knock him smack into Lake Ontario, just to see who had more priesthood strength. Half a head taller and lean but not so scrawny as Merkley was, Elijah had stepped forward. He hadn't even raised his voice, but his words had been strong enough. Truth told, he hadn't intended them to come out quite that strong or quite that bold.

Merkley braced himself to get hit and then said in the same self-righteous monotone he always used: "Violence will be an offense to God and maybe bring you a good-sized wallop of lightning."

Elijah stepped back and laughed gently. He had learned how to undo a threat through years of practice, especially during his Chesapeake Bay time. A colored man in America had to know how to cool his blood, disconnect himself from his heat, at least momentarily, at least when it was a white man on the other side. There was nothing a white man liked better than bruising a colored man's anger.

"Aw, the elders in Kirtland don't make nothing of knocking down one another," Elijah sighed. He smiled like he was stupid.

Merkley, who looked about eighteen, though he was thirty and married, said maybe he'd just report Elijah Abel to the Church. Or maybe he'd call after some lawmen. If this talk continued.

That was the moment Elijah decided it might be best if he set off by himself for a while. So when they hit New York land, Elijah forked down a different trail from Elder Merkley, saying, "Give me some calm time; I'll get back to you. That all right, brother?"

Calm time for Elijah meant lonely silence, a space to let his anger settle.

Of course, anger served him when it was channeled. Anger made energy. Some of his preacher power came from that raw place inside him that he had dug up when he dug his mama's grave. With his anger focused, Elijah Abel could tell folks how God always meant a man to be free and burn his words into the air.

The first time he delivered a public sermon, back in the Kirtland days, his fellow Mormons stared, amazed, like angels were dancing on his shoulders. They had hardly heard him say two words since his baptism and surely didn't know what conversations and images had been building in him since babyhood. What they did understand was that suddenly "Black 'Lijah" was a great sermonizer, so probably God and the Holy Son had filled him with their revelations. Maybe, said one Mormon man, when Elijah opened his mouth, it was Moses himself doing the talking.

What none of them realized was how crowded his silence had always been, especially after he earthed his mama's remains and took to wandering, keeping company with poplars and bracken and occasional long-tailed critters. That silence, wherein most of what he heard was his own footsteps, was crowded with scriptures he suddenly remembered from his childhood days and also with anger, with images of his past (him as a skinny boy whistling his way from the slave world to the white one, toting the tray of white-folk food he wasn't allowed to touch or even breathe on) and of his future, his robes glittering in the heavenly courts, which Brother Joseph's father had prophesied would happen. Elijah's silence had always been crowded with fear and hope and story upon story.

When the time was right, preaching came to him as a gift, the very thing he had been saving up for—or the very thing God had saved him up for. He opened his mouth, stuttered around for a moment or two, and then the words flowed: Bible verses and life-tales and every human thing he had seen in all his years came pour-ing like Niagara. Now he was capable of sounding just like any one of the whites, but it always made them suspicious when he tried it. Such talk from black lips was seen as more than uppity; it was threatening. But when he moved into his preacher life—natural as the last skim of ice melting off a spring-ready pond—he used more white tones, more Bible-sounding words than ever he had in white company. Nobody seemed to object.

"Moses say to Mr. Pharaoh, 'God command you let my people go.' And Mr. Pharaoh say to Moses, 'Now you tell me, who is this God, that I should worship him?' So Moses show him. Oh, yes. Moses put down a stick, and it become a snake to swallow up the magician's staff—swallow it up like it be nothin' more'n squirrel meat. Now brothers and sisters," Elijah had said in his first preach-ment, "do you know what it is to be a slave? To be somebody else's property, do his biddin', make his whole world for him, never mind your own world, or even your own babies? You know about that? Well, I do know about it. What you call sometimes 'The Peculiar Institution,' now, that was my life."

He knew, he told them, what it was to have your back whipped, because he'd seen the marks of the cowskin. And he remembered, though he didn't say, his own daddy collapsing after the overseer's lashes. There were hordes of freed slaves and bond slaves in the Maryland shipyards whose bare backs were crossed with purple welts like long worms or gold ones like stripes of butter. They could make you hear the whip with their breaths, make you feel it when you looked into their secret eyes. Thirty-nine lashes was the common punishment for anything from a nasty look to thieving. And thirty-nine lashes from a white master was better anyhow than Judge Lynch's price. Elijah had seen some lynchings too, even shook a condemned fellow's hand right before one, and didn't care to see another.

"Tell us, 'Lijah," a Mormon elder had called out.

Elijah told it like he had been telling it forever, like it belonged to him to tell, every inch of him feeling the power, his fingers and hands moving just right, his voice stirring up drama like he was setting a tornado to fly. He never planned a thing, it all just came: "There was a time of my life," he said, "when I could not partake of the best fruits God put on this earth. I was not allowed. The best fruits, they was hidden from me. And then God brought me here to Kirtland, and God, through his Prophet, God says, 'Lijah, why don't you come on in and eat freely—anything you fancy! You jus' delight yourself in fatness, why don't you! For this here is Zion, the promised land, and your bondage is over. So get yo'self immersed in this River of Jordan and then you enter this land, why don't you!" He smiled on these white folk, who seemed in that instant to love him. Then he shrugged and said, "So you know what? That's exactly what I done."

The Saints applauded.

After that meeting, Brother Joseph called him on a mission, and Elijah knew he had as much priesthood, as many blessings as any white man. He knew it from head to toe and in every sinew. That, he guessed, was what troubled Elder Merkley: that Black Elijah understood his own worth.

He tried not to be boastful, hadn't meant to brag on his strength. Didn't usually. Most often, he was quiet as a caterpillar when he wasn't before a crowd. But he had the power in him, and he knew it. Upon taking a pulpit or just standing on a box, Elijah could speak with inspiration. His everyday voice was deep; his preacher voice was deeper—a rumble of thunder that could rise in fury and shock the trees. His fingers would splay themselves like lightning was in them as he testified that the fullness of times was come. Sometimes after a missionary sermon, he'd be shaking. His hair would buzz. He liked that. It said his preaching had been strong. And he liked making folks' eyes pop by telling them the bold truth of the gospel—in all its colors—and telling it through scripture words and his own hot rage.

Elder Merkley was a one-voice fellow, practical to a fault. Elder Merkley could get him going, which was why Elijah needed this calm time.

"Give me calm time. I'll get back to you."

Skinny Merkley had not answered Elijah for a moment, just stood there, straightened his collar, straightened his hat (shiny black, much nicer than Elijah's). Skinny's face was a stone. Finally, Merkley had said "calm time" would probably be a good idea, and then strode away, calling back without turning, "You know where to find me, 'Lijah."

Which, yes, Elijah did know. But he preferred being called Elder Abel or Brother Elijah, not just 'Lijah, which was hardly better than "boy." Elder Merkley referred to his white companions, Arza Adams and William Snow, as brother—then why not him?

Elijah knew, only wished he didn't.

So at the moment, Elijah's missionary companion was his favorite dream: Joseph with the Rainbow Coat. Elijah made him up simply to have company, as he didn't particularly enjoy the lonely, even when the lonely was needful. He chose Joseph because that coat was the prettiest thing he could think on—stripes of every color of the wild flowers. Walking through brambles, Elijah conversed with him ("You feeling tired yet?"), and Joe answered in the sweetest voice, like a gentle bear: "I don't think I die just at the moment. Could use me some good apple cider, though."

"If that don't sound good!" Then Elijah dreamed they had some. He could taste it. Made his mouth pucker and well up.

They talked religion too, and politics, and Joe was never argumentative, never sent Elijah beyond the simmer point.

"Why is it, Joe, that the Almighty God let slaves get whupped and sold off, do you s'pose?" he said in his mind. He had asked the question many times. He was picturing Nancy when he asked it. She was wearing a white head wrap, sitting in the flatcart, the way she had been the last time he saw her, feet dangling over the edge. Nancy hadn't met his eyes or waved then. She was holding their baby in one arm and clutching the cart side with her other hand, so waving might've been hard to do. She probably didn't even know he was watching her from Massa's window. Her faded blue dress was too tight on her, for she had birthed Baby Delilah (whom Elijah named the moment he saw them carted away) so recently she still pooched out at the stomach, and her breasts were too round for the bodice. She was squeezed into the cotton like meat into sausage. Her buttons would no doubt burst any minute. Her skin—oh, that soft, gold skin—puffed out between each button like it was trying to breathe. For sure, Massa had not thought to send another dress with her, and Nancy had but two anyway, plus a frayed apron, which the baby was wrapped in. Something like the "swatting clothes," Elijah thought, which one circuit preacher had said Mary used for Jesus after she birthed him.

"Swatting clothes" seemed precisely what white folk thought a slave baby should have: cloth to get swatted in. Sweet Lord, he hoped Nancy and his baby were not going to where they would get swatted. Nancy's eyes looked empty, blind. Not that she couldn't see, but that she didn't care what sights her eyes took in. She was holding the baby loose, maybe afraid of getting too attached.

"Well," said Ancient Joe in a respectful tone, "I don't guess the Almighty like seeing it."

"No, I don't guess so." Elijah didn't move his lips, because he didn't want any folks who might be spying to think he was crazy.

Joseph said, "I guess he watched them ol' Romans whuppin' his very Son, though, just like your mama say."

"I guess that's true." Elijah broke off a willow, thrashing it around, since gnats and flies were gathering. Then Elijah saw what they were gathering for: a dead rabbit lay just before him, already bit into by some wild critter, its gray head half off, entrails glistening like pomegranate seeds. He stepped over the death, whipping flies away, and thought he'd best head for a town. Oh, was he hungry! What he wanted was rabbit stew. Lashing the air, Elijah moved himself towards a smokestack just beyond a sugar maple grove. A horsefly danced around him for a bit, troubling his neck and ears. He felt to command that fly to drop down dead but didn't want to go wasting God's power on a bug, so just let it be.

Ancient Joseph was saying, "And I guess God figured everything'd come out all right before too long, it being The Plan and all. Them that done the whuppin' would get their own taste of it sometime, be naked in the pit, and them that was whupped would be wearin' their glory."

"Like that rainbow coat you got you." Elijah sliced the air.

"And better."

"Robes a-glittering."

"Yessir—like that."

"Them's the very words in my blessing. I tell you that before?"

"I reckon you did, sir."

"You know what a patriarchal blessing is, then?"

"Does I? I've gived and I've received."

"The patriarch, whoever he be, he sets both his hands on your head, and he speak for God himself, tells you things you need to know about your life, even about your future."

"Like I say, I've gived and I've—"

"I got my patriarchal from Father Joseph Smith himself. You know that?"

"Oh, yessir, I know that. I got mine from—oh, that—whazzisname."

Elijah stopped, rummaging his mind for the name his dream companion needed. Now what was that old fellow's name—the father of the twelve tribes? The one who once fought angels and climbed up a ladder and got him a new name? What was that? Then, in a fine case of revelation, he knew.

"You forget your own papa's name?" Elijah teased Joseph of the Rainbow Coat.

"My memory do slip on occasion," Joseph admitted.

"Well, let me help you out, then. The name's Jacob. Well, it been Jacob at first, and then it get changed to Israel."

"I know," Joseph laughed. "Jus' testin' you, 'Lijah."

"I reckon I pass pretty good then."

"Yessir. Father Israel set his hands on my head, and he tell me God will make me get fruitful."

"Father Smith say to me," Elijah said, "I be made equal to my brethren, my soul be white in eternity, and my robes glitterin'."

Joseph asked the question that had troubled Elijah's mind more than once: "You think God need your soul white before you enter them gold gates?"

"Ain't that so?" Elijah led his companion through a wheat field, stopping twice to taste the grain. Dry as dust.

"Me, I reckon a soul's a soul," said Joe.

"You white, aincha?" Elijah asked, though in his imagination Joseph was deeply tanned.

"Married me a Egyptian, 'member?"

"Ho-oly! You did that, dincha!"

"My twins—the ones my papa adopted as his own heirs? They come from her."

"Ephraim and Manass, right?"

"Yessir. I wondered if you remembered they names."

"Ephraim and Manass. No, I don't forget 'bout them boys." Of course, he hadn't forgotten, as he had this conversation every now and again with his imagination, but he liked the words, so he pretended. He wasn't sure just who had brought that to his attention— Joseph of the Rainbow Coat being married to an Egyptian and then later Moses taking an Ethiopian to wife—but it might've been the Prophet himself. "How them boys of yours doin'?"

"Brown as leather, both of 'em."

"And you love 'em fierce."

"Like you can't count it, that's how."

"That's the best way, Joe," Elijah mind-talked him. "I got me a father's blessing from Father Smith himself. Because I'm like a orphan."

"That a fact?"

"I ain't really no orphan, but good as."

"Good as?"

"Molasses. Good as black strap molasses." He let out a hearty laugh and stung his thigh with the willow. "My patriarchal says to me, 'I seal upon you a father's blessing since you mostly an orphan.' Those are the words exact. I think." He stopped as he recited them in his head and drew the willow across the air, underscoring the unwritable—too sacred to get written. Besides which, he couldn't write, though his reading was coming better, what with Skinny Merkley helping him set down his letters.

"Nice words." Joseph tightened his belt. It was a purple belt, the shade of a fresh bruise, thick and wide and shiny as a brand new razor strop. Joseph's arms were like a fieldworker's: dark and muscled, veins bulgy. He was wearing a white rag on his head, wrapped tight above his brows, hanging to his shoulders. His painted eyes were black as a crow's. "I lost my papa too—for most my life, anyhows. Whilst I was busy gettin' powerful in Egypt. Didn't see him for like to twenty years."

"That happens with slaves." And Nancy's face was with him again. She was smiling this time, looking up at him before he kissed her the night they made Baby Delilah.

"It do."

"Once a slave gets big enough to protect his woman, they sells him off. Or sells her off. And maybe even a baby they had between them."

"It do happen. All the time."

"For a fact."

They stepped out of the field and onto a dirt road. A mile down, the dirt became cobblestone. Elijah could see a blacksmith shop and a buggy. He broke into a run when he saw a stone wall curving around two dressmaker stores. That wall would be his preachment stand.

The moment he leapt up it, he could smell—for sure!—rabbit stew coming from somewhere near, like an instant reward for his courage. If things went as usual, he would have that stew in his belly within the hour, provided his sermon was strong enough. He stood quiet a moment, let the smoky scent fill his nostrils.

There had been some argument back in Kirtland about whether Elijah should preach to whites as well as coloreds. Some of the elders had said no, America wasn't ready for that. But most didn't care, and nothing bad had happened as yet—though up till now, Elijah had had a white companion beside him.

Removing his straw hat, he called to two chatting farmers: "You hear the news?"

The farmers stared. A young, aproned man with a sooty face and sooty arms emerged from the blacksmith shop. Inside the shop, Elijah could see another smith pedaling at a wheel, honing a scythe blade. But the smith's eyes were focused on him, not on the scythe. A bald store tender poked his head out of his door. A woman in a blue dress wearing a fancy hat all decorated in knots of cloth that resembled true-life violets stood on the dressmaker porch. Two well-suited men appeared from somewhere Elijah didn't notice. Clearly, this was something unusual, even up north: an unaccompanied colored man preaching to whites!

He began. He had the speech memorized: how the true gospel had got restored to this earth. Which Elijah knew for true and testified of it. He had felt himself getting turned towards Kirtland, he said, back when he was twenty years old or thereabouts, not knowing why he should be moving that direction, thinking he was headed toward a college whose name he didn't even know, or towards Cincinnati, but going with the wind anyways because it was calling him. And there he found himself looking dead up into the kind, hazel eyes of a real prophet. And that prophet—Brother Joseph—welcomed him into the Restoration. Elijah had felt his limbs afire with the Spirit, he said, every bone and heartbeat telling him, "Here's your leader!" And he swore to God he'd be loyal forever no matter what. He'd preach the word, which was exactly what he was doing now. And the "peculiar institution" had been his life for many a year but now he had been delivered from bondage, and wouldn't they like to learn more about that?

There were six listeners now, five men and the woman in blue, three on either side of him. And suddenly, there was one more man, directly in front.

This was the moment Elijah saw The Man. There was something familiar about him, something he had seen before. He wondered if The Man had maybe been following him since Kirtland. The phrase that came to his mind was "white trash."

He would know him later—years later—as Tom Brown, a bitter fellow who had lost eight distant cousins in the Nat Turner rebellion. Tom Brown hardly knew his cousins, but the hate, like a stink, had reached him all the way from Virginia.

Tom Brown's eyes were murky as mudwater. When Elijah saw those eyes swallow him up, he knew this was a man in need of God's mercy.

"Guess you got papers." That was Tom Brown's answer to Elijah's testimony. Tom Brown's voice was stiff as frost. Everything about him was sharp, brittle: his pointy beard all silvery like an icicle, edgy cheekbones, black hair pomaded into an arrow under his slouch hat. What Tom Brown referred to was freedom papers, not required or even asked for in New York state. No one had ever asked for Elijah's papers in New York. No one!

Of course, Elijah had them, along with a paper presenting him as a bonafide preacher, licensed and certified. He displayed both with a low, friendly chuckle, asking, "You hear the message just now?"

"Mormonite." This was one of the farmers—a smiley man with a pig face, eyes hardly visible in his flesh folds, squinty because he wore no hat.

"Latter-day Saint," Elijah corrected as The Man approached and took his papers.

"You Abel?" the Man said.

"Able to do what?" Elijah smiled.

"You sure you're Abel, not Cain?"

"My name's Elijah Abel. I'm a free man. Missionary of the Restoration. Ordained in the holy priesthood of God." He had this memorized too and used his lowest, most reverent tones.

The man glanced at the farmer, whispering like Elijah wasn't meant to hear it, "The devil was a preacher."

"The devil was?" Pig's voice was like a woman's.

"Black Turner," said The Man.

"Oh, *that* devil," said Pig.

Holding onto his smile, Elijah stepped off the wall, just as invisible Joe next to him said, "Maybe we'd best git."

"We—me and my companion," said Elijah, "we be doin' some preachment over the next day or two. I invite you all to give a listen." He was using the soft voice he employed around proud whites, not his preacher voice, not his preacher words.

"You got you a companion?" It was The Man asking. No one else was speaking nor appeared ready to.

"Elder Christopher Merkley, yessir."

"A black one?"

"No, sir. White as you."

"You wouldn't know a Mrs. Nash, would you, boy?" The muddy eyes were measuring Elijah's suit.

"No, sir, I wouldn't." He felt The Man setting up to grab him, the hate was that strong.

"You wouldn't know her children?"

"No, sir, I wouldn't." He smiled bigger, even as Joe was saying into his ear, "They goin' throw you inna pit now, 'Lijah. I know these looks. I seen 'em."

The six other listeners were backing away, like Elijah had just then gone dangerous. He thought at least one of them might mention to The Man that free papers were not required in New York state, didn't he know that? No one said a thing, though. They just backed up.

"Where'd you get that suit?" The man thrust his hands into his overall pockets. Elijah full expected him to pull a knife and waited a long moment before answering, in case he was called on to run. His smile quit. He licked his lips.

"From a prophet of God." His voice was the deep rumble now. "It was Brother Joseph Smith's. He give it to me."

"Prophet?"

He brought out the smile again. He was standing directly before The Man and was considerably taller. "God's prophet of the latter days. I'd like to invite you—all—to hear me and Elder Merkley preach tomorrow. We plan on explaining all about the Prophet and the principles of the everlasting gospel." Elijah began backing away too. "Meanwhile, you enjoy this good autumn sun."

He didn't run, just walked away using very big steps, not looking back until he had gone a good distance. He snaked through a yellow cornfield, down a canyon, up two hills, into a grove. Then he looked. Praise God, he was alone.

"See, 'Lijah," said Joe—the first words Elijah had heard from him because his heart had been pumping up his neck and drumming in his ears—"God always makes a way to deliver us. You remember that."

Elijah looked up the trees—poplar, yellow birch, and all manner of oak with leaves like shiny fiddles. Their boughs looked as tired as he felt. The sun was coming through in weak-pleated shafts, and the wind was toying with the leaves. There were many autumn shades to answer his eyes: yellow-green and grey-green, sparkly green and green like the sea, brick-red and daisy yellow, orange like fire and orange like sunset.

That was another habit he had adopted from his Maryland days: the study of hues. The blacker the skin, he had seen, the more likely the whip. There were purple-black skins just one generation out of Africa, despite the laws against new slaving. There were coffee-colored skins with gray heels and palms. And there were skins like his: deep brown with gold in all the creases. White skin came in gold tones too and in ruddy ones. The whitest skins belonged to names like Larson or Bjarnson, who sometimes had rust-hair. The whitest people could hardly pronounce an English sentence.

"Now," said Elijah in his mind, "the question is, where we be?"

"On God's good earth."

Elijah looked around. The ground was all tree roots, dirt, moss, acorns, new fallen leaves in all those shades of yellow and red, and old lacy gray ones from seasons past. "Damn," he said out loud. "We lost, Joe."

"Never lost, 'Lijah. Not unless we choose to be. That's the promise."

"We lost temporary, then. Damn."

"You'd best not use that word, being as you a missionary, 'Lijah."

"A hungry one."

"You'd best not."

Elijah groaned. "Aw, no. No!" He slapped his forehead. "The man got my papers." The realization shivered through him. "Aw, how'd that happen? The man with the hate-eyes, Joe—he got my free papers!" His stomach was churning panic like hot cider. His hat was bunched in his fist.

"So?"

"Somebody catch me, sell me to Austin Woolfolk, Woolfolk take me down Carolina and chain me up a slave—I know it!"

The sun was sinking. There were only branches around him.

"So? What you doin'? Ain't you goin' run, 'Lijah?" Joe asked this because Elijah was kneeling on the cold, bumpy earth.

"My papers is gone." He hugged his coat to him, praying out loud for help. Then he lay down, and eventually slept, though it wasn't a sound sleep, because moonlit ghosts were dangled over his dreams, all chanting "Austin Woolfolk." He cast them out again and again, but these spirits were stubborn cusses—sent from the opposition, no doubt—and they didn't respect his authority. Not until dawn did he arise and head where his instincts told him was civilization. But when morning was full up, something told him "Stop." So he did, waiting again for the harvest moon, sitting up against a maple, inventing more conversations with imaginary prophets, letting his thoughts fold up and relax.

Somewhere in the distance, he heard a man's voice calling what sounded like his own name: "Elijah Abel." He heard footsteps but couldn't tell how close they came. He heard sighing, which he thought must be the wind.

It was cold. A pair of white-tail does walked before him, pausing and staring like he was a curiosity, then moving on without alarm, their hooves cracking sticks. He decided they were surely a God-sent sign of comfort, though he wished he had a gun, a good carving knife, and a cooking fire.

He slept against the maple—still fasting—then walked again, praying God to guide him to his companion and not to The Man or—please God!—not to Austin Woolfolk. There was a train, he knew, somewhere in New York state. If he could grab hold of a train car, his escape would be made. He had no idea where a train might be, though, and walked miles (it felt like ten or more) to where he thought tracks could be set. He listened hard for that long whistle. It was acres of barely-tampered-with land he found and orchards of apple trees with wrinkled, yellow fruit. No trains, not that he could see. Not even a stagecoach or a good road to hold one. Not even a cart trail.

Elder Merkley would think he had died or abandoned the cause. Elder Merkley, who believed in the curse of Cain and Canaan, would probably testify against him and get him excommunicated.

No, Elijah could not permit that. The Church was his identity now and held the best times he had had since long before his mama died. The best times since Nancy. And what would Brother Joseph answer if he heard Elijah had skipped off? Above everything, he didn't want to disappoint Brother Joseph.

Why was he so scared anyway? Nothing had happened. Surely he had seen hate-eyes before. What made The Man's hate-eyes any different from others? It was all in his imagination—had to be, he told himself. He had a bad habit of inventing danger and then running from it—running for weeks sometimes, churning up fear with every step. It had to stop. Elijah Abel, freed slave and holder of the Mormon priesthood, needed to get back to his mission work and quit acting like a scared pigeon. He had been running and walking and swimming away from his own fears since Maryland days. No more.

"Lord," he prayed, "you take me to my companion, please, Lord."

Well, the good Lord did exactly that, though it took four days, with one of them rainy. It was just before he found the meeting place that Elijah saw a thing which was not his imagination and which put ice in his bowels. It was a handbill, showing the badly drawn face of a black man, words framing it. He read slowly, sounding out each letter and then shaking his head and sounding the letters again. The words couldn't say what he thought they said. After three reads, though, he knew they did:

"WANTED FOR MURDER."

It was his name—ELIJAH ABEL—beneath the drawing.

"WANTED: FOR THE MURDER OF MRS. MARGARET NASH AND HER FIVE CHILDREN."

"Ho-oly," breathed Elijah.

Not even Old Joseph answered. Old Joseph had disappeared.

NOTES

The chapter title, "I'll Tell the World," is from the title of hymn number 648 in *Hymns for the Family of God*.

Information on Elijah Abel, one of very few blacks to receive the priesthood in the early Church and reportedly ordained by the Prophet himself—Walker Lewis being another, under the hands of Joseph's brother William (Lythgoe, "Negro Slavery and Mormon Doctrine," 136)—is available in a variety of sources. Most notable are Carter, *Negro Pioneer*, which is certainly the earliest, though not the most reliable, account of black pioneers, and Hill, *Joseph Smith*. Hill documents the fact that Elijah was ordained a seventy on December 20, 1836, by Zebedee Coltrin (*Joseph Smith*, 381–82). The sentences quoted from Abel's patriarchal blessing are authentic (Bringhurst, "Elijah Abel," 131; Bush, "Mormonism's Negro Doctrine," 102, n. 30).

The passage about a black man explaining "the curse of Canaan" is taken directly from Botkin, *Lay My Burden Down* (15), a compilation of slave narratives. We include it here to show that the "curse of Canaan" idea as a justification for discrimination was widely held throughout Christian America, as was the "curse of Cain" tradition, referred to, for example, in a poem by a black woman, Phillis Wheatly, in the 1700s:

> Some view our race with scornful eye:
> "Their color is a diabolic dye!"
> Remember Christians, Negroes black as Cain
> May be refined, and join the Angelic Train.
> (In Wangeman, *Black Man*, iii)

That Joseph of the Old Testament married an Egyptian woman (around 1715 B.C., according to Young, *Analytical Concordance to the Bible*) is found in Genesis 41:45, 50–52: "And Pharaoh called Joseph's name Zaphnath-paaneah; and he gave him to wife Asenath the daughter of Potipherah priest of On. . . .

And unto Joseph were born two sons before the years of famine came, which Asenath the daughter of Potipherah priest of On bare unto him. And Joseph called the name of the firstborn Manasseh: For God, said he, hath made me forget all my toil, and all my father's house. And the name of the second called he Ephraim: For God hath caused me to be fruitful in the land of my affliction."

We cannot identify the race of Asenath, because the Egyptian ruling classes were so varied, including the Hyksos and the Ptolemies. We know from the book of Abraham that a particular pharaoh was a "righteous man . . . but cursed . . . as pertaining to the Priesthood" because he was "of that lineage by which he could not have the right of Priesthood" (Abraham 1:26–27). But so much changed in Egypt's ruling classes that it is not really possible to say what the race of Joseph's wife was. Because the references to Ephraim and Manasseh in this chapter take place in Elijah Abel's mind, however, it is not really necessary to document the possibility of Joseph's sons having "black blood." That Moses' Ethiopian wife was black is not in question (Numbers 12:2).

The accusation of murder leveled against Elijah Abel is historical. Indeed, according to one source, the non-Mormon residents of St. Lawrence County, New York "accused Abel of murdering a woman and five children. 'Handbills were pasted up in every direction . . . and a great reward was offered for him.' He was apparently successful in refuting these charges and left the community 'unmolested.'" And he did, in fact, run into problems with the Saints, for "threatening to knock down a fellow elder" and claiming that "an elder was a High Priest and he had as much authority as any H.P." (Bringhurst, *Saints, Slaves, and Blacks*, 38).

Though Christopher Merkley does not mention Elijah Abel in his autobiography, Jedediah M. Grant "communicated to the council a short history of the conduct of Elder Elijah Abel . . . that in addition to threatening to knock down Elder Christopher Merkley on their passage up Lake Ontario, he publicly declared that the Elders in Kirtland made nothing of knocking down one another" (Van Wagoner and Walker, *Book of Mormons*, 2–3). It was also reported, as a scandal, that Elijah Abel had said that someday stakes of Zion would dot the world (Bringhurst, "Elijah Abel," 131).

The "cowskin" (a whip) was a "heavy, three-foot long sticklike object, made of strips of dried oxhide bound together, tapering to a point, painted ghastly blue. It was springy as a hickory stock" (Preston, *Young Frederick Douglass*, 61).

7

GOD MOVES IN A MYSTERIOUS WAY

Heaven is my throne,
and the earth is my footstool.
ISAIAH 66:1

Elijah knew where Elder Merkley was staying: at the Day home in Great Bend. Skinny Merkley had been inspired to stop there once, and it turned out the Day folks were already Mormon. Old Sister Day had seen him in a vision the night before and was waiting for him with victuals and drink.

Might she have had some vision of Elijah's troubles too? Surely God could visit her again and tell her to keep the soup warm!

He was set to knock when the worst thought slapped him. What if it wasn't The Man who had set that murder charge against him? What if it was Elder Christopher Merkley? Elijah had been betrayed once by a curly haired white boy, back in Maryland when he was just beginning to aim his steps towards Ohio. The boy had told him he could sleep in the barn, but come morning a big farmer was standing before him, the boy laughing at the farmer's side. Elijah was fined for vagrancy and had to surrender his best possession in the world: his leather hat. What if Skinny Merkley had turned traitor too?

Elijah didn't want to welcome anger, but it was oozing into him, braided up with fear. It had joined his blood and was flowing, steady and cold, into every muscle and joint. His stomach was so tense it ached.

"And God," he thought towards the stars, "I am truly puzzling over why you did not warn me of The Man. Now God, you did not go put him in my path as chastisement—did you?" He knew God could feel his anger. No use trying to hide it, so he didn't. "And what surprises have you got behind that door for me?" he asked the sky. Then he lowered his eyes to the knocker. He could either trust Elder Merkley or he could leave now and never come back.

His hand was already fisted. He knocked.

Sister Day, a slip of a grandma-woman in brown silk and a white cap, opened the door to him. Elder Merkley stood just behind her, a full head taller than she was.

"Brother Elijah," sighed Merkley, breathing out like it was the whole world's relief.

Elijah searched out his companion's eyes for meanness. He didn't find any.

"Praise God," said Elder Merkley.

Elijah kept his own silence.

"Have you had a thing to eat since you walked away, brother?" Merkley seemed to be going out of his way to act polite.

Elijah gave a small shrug. "Four apples."

"You're hungry."

He nodded and breathed, "Trouble."

"I know." Merkley's long face was all pity. Elijah hated pity.

"There's trouble." His voice was stronger now, almost the preacher-voice, not even quivering.

Elder Merkley turned to the little woman in brown. "Brother

Abel is hungry," he said, his voice so full of goodwill and pity it made Elijah tense all the more from suspicion. "Can you feed him?"

The woman was headed towards the kitchen before Merkley completed his question.

Elijah eyed him: tall, skinny, honey-eyed, honey-haired Christopher Merkley with the clean, squared-off chin. There was no apparent vengeance in him, though he was going a little overboard on the niceness.

"Look at your coat, Brother 'Lijah. There's burrs all over it. And dried mud. Take it off, why don't you?"

He handed it over.

"How'd it happen?" Merkley asked. Elijah wasn't sure if "it" meant the dirt on his coat or the murder charge. Or did "it" mean the murder itself?

Elijah commenced pacing.

"How?" Merkley repeated.

"I did not do it," Elijah said.

His companion was picking burrs from the coat and slapping the fabric, raising dust.

"You see the handbills, sir?" Until now, he had called his companion Elder Merkley or Brother Christopher.

Merkley hummed. "I thought you was in jail, more than likely."

This, considered Elijah, was a fairly casual response to an accusation that could send him to the gallows.

"I've been visiting jails two days now, looking for you," Merkley continued. "Preached the gospel to some ready prisoners too. Therefore, this must be the will of God. Therefore, this must be God's very way of getting through to places we might not have visited otherwise."

Elijah stopped pacing to raise his brows in amazement. He was thinking, *Well now, lucky me to get called on to help out Almighty God like that! Having my name stuck on every tree and post and saying I killed a whole family! How lucky can a body get to take on such a privilege as that!*

"There are some good men in jail who need to know God's still in his heaven," Merkley went on.

Elijah didn't answer, just folded his arms hard. Couldn't God have suggested in a dream or a revelation that they pay a kindly visit to some prisoners? And how might Elder Merkley have felt if it was *his* face plastered everywhere as God's way of getting them behind some bars?

"Indeed yes, there are good men, ready men, even in the jails," Merkley finished.

Elijah stood still for a long moment. He could hear Mrs. Day's feet on the dining room floor, hear her setting plates on the table. The wind outside was rustling leaves, and a goat was bawling just behind the back door.

Elder Merkley waited, wearing an oily sort of smile, stroking the coat, raising himself to his toes, and then falling back to his heels. "Indeed," Merkley repeated.

Then Elijah Abel testified: "By God, I am innocent. As a lamb."

Pulling two more burrs from the coat, Elder Merkley said, "You didn't murder a soul. You're here saving souls, not killing them. Besides, you couldn't have. That murder happened one week before we set foot in St. Laurence County."

"You was with me, sir!" Elijah breathed low.

"I was. And I'll sign an affidavit to that effect." Elder Merkley shook the coat like it was possessed, sending up a cloud. "There are witnesses."

The last of Elijah's suspicions dissolved. It was clear Merkley hadn't set him up. It was also clear Merkley was dumb as a white donkey and didn't have an inkling what happened when a black was charged with murder, even in civilized New York. Elijah started pacing again.

"Out of curiosity, sir," Elijah asked, "you ever see a man get lynched?" The man Elijah had shaken hands with moments before that man was hanged had said: "I swear by the blood of Jesus, I didn't commit no crime." But he hanged anyway for violating a white woman—or because someone thought he had. Blacks were lynched every day over suspicions; they all knew that. Accused, convicted, no time for a trial, and even if there was time, who'd believe a nigger? The white man thought nothing of noosing a black, just in case an accusation might be true.

Elder Merkley pursed his lips, wrinkled his chin. "Can't say as I've had that—"

"Privilege?" Elijah stopped, his shoulders squared into fighting posture before he could calm them.

"—horror. Can't say as I've had that horror. I do not enjoy witnessing anyone suffer."

Elijah commenced pacing again.

"Slow down, brother. You'll wear a hole in the floor." Merkley's voice, still the monotone, was easy. "Besides, that neck of yours is too stiff and orn'ry to stretch." He folded the coat over his arm and offered a quick laugh. "You ever heard the story about Elisha and the hosts of heaven?"

Merkley had been telling him Bible stories since the first day of their mission. A lot of these tales Elijah had never heard. The Bible made for fall-back conversation. When other words failed, there were scripture stories to recite.

"It don't come to mind," Elijah said.

So Elder Merkley rehearsed the story about some warriors surrounded by enemies, seeing hosts of angels beyond and knowing God's power was greater than any man's.

"No, sir," Elijah said, "I ain't never heard it."

"You understand its meaning?"

Elijah gave him a "What do you think?" look.

"God always makes a way to deliver his children," Elder Merkley said. "So, quit pacing the floor and don't forget what you already know."

Elijah stopped, swaying a bit. His temples were sweaty. When he wiped them with his sleeve, he noticed how dirty his shirt was. It didn't seem right to wear such clothes in a clean, white-folk house. Merkley had told him not to get above himself. At that moment, Elijah felt like a sullied nothing, like he ought to be whistling so Sister Day would know his black lips weren't touching any of her good food or kissing her walls.

She appeared just then, directing them to her table, smiling without a hint of judgment. A steaming bowl of barley soup and hot bread were waiting, set on porcelain. Sister Day was serving him!

He sat in the maple chair—his favorite wood. Many times, he had worked it into tables and hutches and stair rails. It was a good chair, the seat carved for comfort, fan-shaped seashells whittled on the back. He blessed the food and ate slowly because it was so fresh and warm and because it felt so fine to get fed. He wanted the moment to last.

Elder Merkley gave the coat to Sister Day, who said in an angel's voice, far younger than her face, she'd be glad to wash it, have it ready tomorrow afternoon, provided the sun come up.

Elijah nodded, and Sister Day went for more beeswax candles, the ones on the table being near used up.

In her absence, something amazing happened. Elder Merkley told Elijah Abel a piece of his own life. This marked the first time he had gotten personal since they left Ohio. Usually, it was just scriptures and scripture stories he shared, teaching (sometimes as though Elijah were a child) and practicing his missionary tones but keeping himself a mystery. Now he mentioned an actual time God had delivered him.

Christopher Merkley had been passing through some woods, when two gunslinging men appeared and ordered him forward. Then they sounded a bugle that twelve other men answered on horseback. "So they hold a few minutes' talk together," Elder Merkley said, "and then they ask where I'm from. I tell them from Canada. Then they want to know where I'm going. I tell them I don't know; I'm looking for a place."

Elijah nodded. This didn't feel like a sermon. It felt like real conversation.

"And they ask me if I had any arms. My answer was 'No.' 'Any letters?' 'No.'"

"Was you scared?"

"Scared? With the Spirit of God upon me?"

Elijah smiled. No, surely Elder Merkley would not let himself seem vulnerable. "'Course you wasn't scared."

Merkley looked down. "Trembling in my boots. My faith wasn't strong then as it is now."

Elijah stopped eating, he was that shocked at the admission. "I guess faith grow up like a baby," he said at last.

"So, the men searched me, found no arms nor letter but a Bible in my breast pocket. Which they said was a good weapon to carry."

"They say that?" He spooned soup to his mouth, regretting that every spoonful making it down his throat left less in the bowl.

"Those very words—with a few others I'd best omit. They wanted me to pull off my boots, since the British generally carried letters in their boots, but I said I wouldn't do that."

"They thought you was a spy for the Brits, then, Brother Christopher?"

"They did."

"And you square refused to take off your boots?"

"I did."

"Elder Merkley, you either brave or you stupid." Elijah shook his head and wiped his chin on the napkin, leaving gray streaks in the fabric. One thing was plain: he needed a washing.

"Some of both, I dare say. Well, they cussed me and said I should, and I told them I should not, and then one of them said if

I'd tell the truth I'd be unharmed, and he asks me, 'How many are you in number in Dewitt?'"

The soup was gone. Elijah scraped the bowl with a bread crust.

"I said, 'I don't know.' 'Are you five hundred?' I said, 'I don't know.' 'Are you three hundred?' 'I don't know.' So he says, 'How is it you are such a fool?' And I says, 'I don't know.'"

Elijah laughed at that one and then sat back, warmed through, full, calmed, grateful.

"One of them wanted to ride me to their camp, but the other one says, 'No, he's too big a fool to have at camp.' So they let me go."

Elijah laughed big. "Pays to be a fool sometimes," he said.

Elder Merkley didn't answer, only waited like he was listening for God.

"Fear not," Merkley said at last, "'for they that be with *us* are more than they that be with them.'"

Elijah dropped his voice to an apology. "You know I didn't mean what I said about knocking you down. I guess God's punished me pretty good."

Elder Merkley's eyes, which had seemed like a dumb cow's during Elijah's anger, now looked sincere and bright. "There's nothing easy about preaching," he said. "Sometimes our lesser selves come out despite who we are. We say things. We get above ourselves."

Elijah winced and cut his eyes away. He noticed Sister Day's china hutch. It was pine wood—not the best choice. He would have made it from oak, had he been her carpenter.

"We're going to forget and forgive everything we need to, Elder Abel. You and I. Isn't that right?"

Elijah shrugged.

"It is possible I got above myself too, in saying what I did." Elder Merkley did not meet Elijah's eyes but looked down and scanned the room. "Brother Joseph did ordain you, isn't that a fact?"

"He did, sir." He addressed the hutch. He didn't want to look at his companion when his companion was not looking at him.

"He called you on this mission."

"He did."

"And he is a prophet."

Now Elijah turned his eyes to the white man, who met them. "He is a prophet," Elijah whispered. And Joseph was his brother too, and Father Smith his father. They were his restored family. They saw him in visions even Elijah hadn't imagined—where pigment made no difference and all were equal in love and wealth and power, with robes glittering. But this last part was his alone, not to be shared with Christopher Merkley.

"Is God with you, Elder Abel?" The question seemed sincere, like Merkley really wanted to know.

"Yessir. He is."

The room got brighter. It wasn't angels paying a visit, just Mrs. Day come with fresh candles.

"Then don't worry," Elder Merkley said.

Elijah moved his eyes to his soup bowl, scooted his finger across it to get one last lick of flavor. After a moment, he said with the best humor he could summon, "So you think God made all this to happen so's you'd go visit some folks in jails?"

"God moves in mysterious ways."

"God ain't printing handbills these days, thank you, sir."

"Mysterious ways," Merkley repeated, not even smiling.

For himself, Elijah was not sure he wanted to be the black part of God's mysteries.

I suppose Jane Manning felt the same way.

NOTES

The chapter title, "God Moves in a Mysterious Way," is from the title of hymn number 603 in *Hymns for the Family of God*.

According to Christopher Merkley's autobiography, Sister Day "had seen me in a vision the night before, and said I was going to help Brother Day and another brother out of trouble, which I did" (12). The passage about Merkley's confrontation with the horsemen in the woods is also taken from his autobiography (5–6).

The scriptural references to Elisha are found in 2 Kings 6; the passage "Fear not: for they that be with us are more than they that be with them" is verse 16.

The reader should note that any apparently harsh judgment of Christopher Merkley is manufactured in Elijah's mind at a stressful time. All historical evidence indicates that Christopher Merkley was a devoted Latter-day Saint.

8

IN CHRIST THERE IS
NO EAST OR WEST

*In every nation, he that . . .
worketh righteousness, is accepted with him.*
ACTS 10:35

When preachers started traveling through Connecticut with
their new religions or new slants on old ones, Jane Manning went
to hear what they had to say. She usually liked what she heard.
Melissa Fitch sometimes accompanied her, though Widow Fitch was
content with Pastor Sylvester.

As I said, the first minister of Mormonism Jane Manning heard,
nearly three years after Sylvester's birth, was Elder Charles Wesley
Wandell.

That was a cold day in October 1841. Jane leaned against a bare
elm to listen to this young man—well-born, he appeared from his
clothes. Charles Wandell declared that the heavens were open, and
God had called him up a prophet named Joseph.

Jane wasn't sure what all was meant by *prophet*, but she liked the
idea of God holding conversation with a mortal man rather than

just carving his dos and don'ts into stone and then ambling away. She especially liked the idea of joining a church that was not Pastor Sylvester's. A number of colored folk were in that little group listening to Charles Wandell. Perhaps that was why he sang them a hymn that mentioned Africa:

> Go pass throughout Europe
> And Asia's dark regions,
> To China's far shores,
> And to Afric's black legions,
> And proclaim to all people,
> As you're passing by,
> The fig trees are leaving—
> The summer is nigh.

His voice wasn't great, but the hymn was lively. He seemed a little embarrassed by his singing but not by his message. "Pray about what I've told you," he said. "Pray God to know the truth of it."

She did, and she dreamed that night of a white face rather like Charles Wandell's but broader of cheek, thinner of lip, the eyes as blue-green. The face smiled and nodded as though saying, "It's all true," and she felt it surely was.

Dinner was on when she returned to the Fitches after a second night of preaching. Pastor Sylvester and his wife were guests, their baby toddling around the dining room. Melissa was at the table too. By all their expressions, Jane might have guessed she was dessert. She backed away, set to retreat outside.

No use. Seated beside the pastor, Widow Fitch stopped Jane's exit with a shrill call. "Girl!"

"Ma'am?"

"You must hear what the pastor is saying about those terrible new preachers!"

Pastor Sylvester looked up from his ham steak. He wasn't

wearing his glasses. She didn't enjoy seeing the same face she had seen when he had sinned against her.

"Why Jane!" When he smiled, she saw his dog teeth were missing and his other teeth were coffee-stained. Also, his face had gotten chalky. She hadn't looked at him quite this close since that night.

"Where are you coming in from, Jane?" Mrs. Fitch's voice was still high and desperate. Melissa was sending apologies through her eyes, and Jane understood what for. Melissa wouldn't be able to help her here.

"Outside, ma'am."

"Now, Jane," said Pastor as though she were a babychild, "you haven't been listening to Mormonites, have you?"

The white folks, all except Missy, laughed.

"Me, sir?"

He leveled a fork at her, his face a happy lie. "Because they are the worst of the lot, you know."

Mrs. Fitch stood. She offered Jane a plate with a potato and invited her to get comfortable at the table.

This was not Jane's normal setting. She had servant's quarters. It was a rare time indeed when Jane ate with the Fitch family.

"Sit here, ma'am?"

"Certainly. Enjoy a meal with our guests, Jane. As though you were one of us."

Jane sat as far away from Pastor as she could. She was opposite Melissa, who was seated beside Mrs. Sylvester. Pastor was seated in Mr. Fitch's place at the head of the table. His wife, next to him, was in reach, so he periodically stroked her hand.

Widow Fitch stood. "Well, Jane? Answer the reverend. Have you been there?"

"Yes, ma'am."

Patting his mouth with the napkin, the pastor said, "Now now now, Mrs. Fitch. Our dear colored girl simply may not know better."

"She has been trained," Mrs. Fitch declared, like her own salvation was at stake. Her eyes were tearing. Jane could've predicted that.

"Consider, madam, that children follow the condition of their parents, not necessarily that of their overseers."

"I know," Widow Fitch mewed.

"You, for example, Mrs. Fitch, are a native of New England, are you not?"

The widow served Jane a half-sized ham steak. "My father fought in the great War for Independence, you know." Her voice was close to cracking.

"Yes, yes. I believe you've mentioned that," said Pastor.

Jane thought, *Every time we've talked, you've mentioned that,* but didn't voice it.

"Oh my, yes! The Fitches have been proud New Englanders for generations," said Mrs. Fitch. "Jane, have some gravy." She was forcing a smile, but her voice was tear-roughed.

"Well," said Pastor, "you prove my point exactly. The natives of New England are not savages, like the aboriginal Indians, but an enlightened, civilized, and Christian people, are they not? Quite after the fashion of their Puritan forefathers." He leaned back in his chair. Jane thought he was either showing off his watch chain or giving his belly a rest.

Widow Fitch stood still, nodding and pretending this was a profound bit of information. "Quite so." She surveyed her tea service—all sterling silver, which Jane polished weekly.

The pastor patted his wife's hand and explained like it was the truest and easiest fact in the world: "You see, the posterity of Abraham inherited by divine providence, we may say, the privileges which their father's faith earned for them, as well as for himself." Pastor cleared his throat, making space for his full voice. "And the descendants of Ham have likewise been born to the curse anciently pronounced upon their progenitor. So you shouldn't wonder that

your Jane may not be so understanding of these grave issues as yourself." Once more he smiled and patted his wife's hand.

Mrs. Fitch moaned, "I had hoped——."

"Perhaps I might persuade her, though," Pastor said.

"Alone?" Jane's eyes flew open.

Pastor laughed, though Jane saw his cheeks go pink. "I do not
believe my wife would precisely approve of my preaching alone to a
negress."

"Nonsense, Mr. Sylvester," said his wife. These were the first
words Jane had ever heard from the buttermilk-haired woman. Mrs.
Sylvester's voice was breathy and sweet, but it was a girl's voice, not
a woman's. It suited her pink gown and the pink rosebuds braided
into her side curls. "I trust you."

Pastor said, "I mean, I might persuade our young colored friend
against these Mormonites right here, right now, this moment."

"Sir?" Jane said. She caught Melissa's helpless expression and
tried to communicate to her that she'd survive this. She wondered
sometimes if Missy suspected who Sylvester's father was. They had
never talked about it.

"My girl, do you know who these Mormonites are?" Pastor
leaned across the table.

"Preachers, sir? Like you?" She held a piece of ham on her fork,
couldn't quite get it to her mouth.

He laughed louder than he needed to, and Mrs. Fitch joined in.
Then Mrs. Sylvester laughed too—timidly, behind a lace fan. Even
the Sylvester baby—not much younger than the other Sylvester
baby, the darker one—laughed with the grown-ups. All the white
folk were laughing at her. Except Melissa.

"Preachers, yes," Pastor said when the hilarious moment ended,
"not quite like me." Again, everyone but Jane and Melissa laughed.
When Pastor hit his spoon against the table, though, all laughter
ceased. "They're the devil's messengers, Jane. Wolves in sheep's

clothing. False prophets. The Bible warns us against them specifically."

"Wolf in sheep clothes?" Jane touched the meat to her lips, couldn't get her teeth to part. "Sir?"

"Yes?"

"Oh, I wasn't addressin' you," she said. "Just makin' certain I understand." She saw Melissa bite down on a laugh, purse her big lips against it.

Again, Pastor flushed, though his voice came full force when he answered. "The Mormonites say God has spoken to a man. The Bible labels such a claim as blasphemy. Do you know what blasphemy is, girl?"

"No, sir. I only know a few of the sins by name. That one is new to me."

"Blasphemy means treating a sacred thing as naught!" He waved his fist.

She put her fork back on her plate. The meat was still tined.

"The Bible says no one can look on God and live. And here come these fine men, and what do they claim?" He was making wide gestures exactly as he did at the pulpit. She thought he might slap his wife by accident or maybe just knock a rosebud out of her hair.

"Sir?"

He lowered his voice and made his face sickly sweet, like he was dying of sugar. "They claim their prophet beheld the very God of the universe—held a conversation with him!" After a stunned moment, wherein Widow Fitch gasped loudly, Pastor laughed again.

"But I seen him," Jane said.

"What?"

"In a dream. His name's Joseph."

Pastor leaned across the table again. He was squinting as though he'd dissolve her right there. "You've seen God? And his name's Joseph?"

"No, sir." She stared at her plate. "That be the Prophet's name. I seen him in a dream."

Gasping again, Mrs. Fitch apologized to the pastor. "A lot of the niggers dream," she said. Her voice wasn't so high as before, seemed just weary now.

"Indeed." He sniffed.

"Part of the curse, perhaps." Widow Fitch blinked back fresh tears.

Jane's eyes stayed locked on her plate. "This meat sure smell good, ma'am."

"Well, eat it, girl! You haven't touched a thing!"

Jane brought the ham to her mouth, bit it, chewed. It was rubber, and her throat too dry to swallow. She chewed. They all were watching her. She chewed again, feeling her teeth grinding circles into the meat, but not getting through. Finally, she forced it down her throat, where it stuck like wood. There was ale on the table, which she wanted but didn't dare ask for. So she swallowed her own spit to push the meat down, though her mouth wasn't producing much spit at all. She swallowed again and then stood and asked to be excused.

"Look at that!" Mrs. Fitch said like the devil had come to dinner and put his leftovers on Jane's plate. "Hardly touched the meal!"

"Mama, let her go," Melissa said. Jane turned grateful eyes on her. Missy's were defiant. "Let her do what she wants."

"Well, she always has, hasn't she," murmured Widow Fitch. "Yes, go, girl." She sighed and then finished like a queen, "You may take your leave of us, Jane."

Imitating the same dignity, Jane left the room.

The next Sunday, she went to where Elder Wandell was preaching. After he had read a good passage from his new-revealed scriptures, the Book of Mormon, she approached him. She said simply that she would be baptized, please. So he led her to a little pool between two streams and immersed her in the name of the Father,

the Son, and the Holy Spirit. Then, with Jane kneeling, he con-
ferred on her the gift of the Holy Ghost.

"How do you feel, Sister Jane?" he asked afterwards.

"Wet," she said. "Wet and happy."

"Then share the joy." He gave her the very book he had been
showing to the congregation. She couldn't read, but the book felt
good in her hands.

"Preach unto all the world," Charles Wandell told her.

"I will do that," said Jane. "I sure will."

Notes

The chapter title, "In Christ There Is No East or West," is from the title
of hymn number 685 in *Hymns for the Family of God*.

The material on Jane's conversion to Mormonism is extracted from
Wolfinger's two "Test of Faith" articles, one in *Worth Their Salt*, edited by
Whitley, and a more complete version in *Social Accommodation in Utah*, edited
by Knowlton. Jane's own history, taken from the Wilford Woodruff Papers and
printed as notes in *Social Accommodation*, 151–56, states the following (punc-
tuation, spelling, and grammar as in the original, which was dictated to
Elizabeth J. D. Roundy):

"When a child only six years old I left my home and went to live with a
family of white people their names were Mr. and Mrs. Joseph Fitch, they were
aged people and quite wealthy, I was raised by their daughter, when about
fourteen years old I joined the Presbyterian Church. Yet I did not feel satisfied it seemed to me there was something more that I was looking for. I had
belonged to the Church about eighteen months when an Elder of the church
of Jesus Christ of Latter-day Saints was travelling through our country
preached there. The pastor of the Presbyterian Church forbid me going to hear
them as he had heard I had expressed a desire to hear them, but nevertheless
I went on a Sunday and was fully convinced that it was the true gospel he presented and I must embrace it.

"The following Sunday I was baptized and confirmed a member of the
Church of Jesus Christ of latter-day Saints. About three weeks after while
kneeling at prayer the Gift of Tongues came upon me, and frightened the
whole family who were in the next room."

"There's a Feast of Fat Things," the song Elder Wandell sings in this chapter, was a hymn in Emma Smith's first hymnbook (Bush, "Mormonism's Negro Doctrine," 103, n. 39).

For the conversation we have created between Pastor Sylvester and Jane in which he talks about natural law, we have drawn language and ideology from a prominent New England minister, Reverend Samuel Seabury, who wrote about natural law as a justification for slavery. We have quoted some of his words verbatim (Seabury, *American Slavery*, 127). The Reverend Seabury wrote his book in an effort to prevent the Civil War—obviously to no avail. It is important to note the prominence of such ideas, for they were as commonly believed by the Latter-day Saints as by most Americans during this time, through the Civil War, and beyond it. Many things Brigham Young said during his tenure as president of the Church seem to have their foundation in the same philosophy of natural law Seabury promulgated.

9

THROUGH IT ALL

As a sheep before her shearers is dumb,
so he openeth not his mouth.
ISAIAH 53:7

Jane wouldn't meet Elijah Abel for many years, though she would hear about him. No doubt all the Mormons of color, which included a number of slaves, would hear about Elder Elijah Abel. There was some fame attached to him, especially for black folks dreaming of some sort of equality with whites—or at least of a place where no white man could whip a black without God making lightning and thunder.

As you might understand, the turn of events in his mission territory in 1838 helped Elijah decide it was just about the right time to head back to the Saints, who had mostly moved from Kirtland to Missouri now, Caldwell County, their settlements called Adam-ondi-Ahman and Far West. Elijah got homesick for a home he'd never known. Besides which, he wasn't particularly enjoying missionary work at the moment. Not when folks were inking handbills with his name and making accusations that could wind him up in a twist-rope.

By the time Elder Merkley signed the affidavit testifying to Elijah's alibi, another man had confessed to the Nash murders and then shot himself. A suicide note spelled out his blame. He was Mrs. Nash's husband. One day before his suicide, the murderer had sworn that his family had been killed by a black man. The sheriff returned Elijah's papers at Elder Merkley's request.

Elder Merkley did not join his companion on his trip back to the Saints. Instead, he gave Elijah a blessing and a letter to convey to Mrs. Merkley in 'Diahman, paid for the stagecoach, and waved once it set off.

It looked more like a butcher's wagon than a coach, the side curtains having no fastenings, flapping up and down all through the journey, letting gusts of cool air into the compartment. The two horses attached were sorry-looking, spotted gray critters with all their bones and veins showing.

For the first day, Elijah's riding companions were two white brothers who never said a thing to him nor much to each other, either. Mostly, they just slept. The second and third days, Elijah was by himself. At the Missouri border, an elderly white man with a beard like a snow drift entered—a lawyer, who asked him point blank if he thought to settle in Missouri.

Elijah said to that, "I don't know, sir."

"You belong to somebody?" the lawyer asked. He was reading a thick book. He looked up to make his question and then went straight back to his pages.

That was not an uncommon inquiry, of course, especially in the South. Elijah had heard it many times. But he hadn't heard it in a long while, and it made him tired to hear it now. His heartbeat got faster, but all he felt was tired. He wanted to reply, "I belong to Jesus," but didn't, only shook his head.

"Law says no free blacks or mulattos can enter the state without

receiving ten whip strokes. And then another ten until they leave."
The man was reading all the time he spoke.

"The law?"

"Missouri Compromise."

Yes, he had heard about the Missouri Compromise, though he
didn't understand exactly what it meant. Still, he had been in
Missouri before, and no one had harmed him. If it was a law, it
couldn't be a serious one, though he did know there had been
Church problems in this place, and slavery behind them. Elder
William Phelps, a personal acquaintance of his, had published an
article called "Free People of Color" in *The Evening and the Morning
Star*—which the Missourians thought was telling slaves to leave
their masters and gather to Mormon Zion. And even though
Brother William ran a retraction the next day, the Gentiles were
bone-sure Mormons would agitate their blacks, abolitionism would
rear itself up, and the Nat Turner affair would look like nothing. So
the Missourians, mostly restless Southerners originally from
Kentucky and the Carolinas, they held a secret meeting, formed a
"secret constitution," and then tarred and feathered Bishop Edward
Partridge and Brother Charles Allen instead of using any argument
of words.

This all happened before Elijah made his way to Kirtland, but
he had heard the stories and wrapped his memory around them
same way he did with scriptures. "Missouri Compromise" was a
phrase in the story. As the lawyer explained things, "Missouri
Compromise" seemed to involve mostly whipping.

"Stay close by me, and no one will ask questions," the lawyer
offered.

Elijah wasn't sure he should. "I do belong to someone," he said
at last. "To the Latter-day Saint people."

Setting his book down, the lawyer fixed him with hard eyes.
"Mormon! You're not one of them!"

"Yessir." Elijah looked straight at him.

"Say again? My ears don't work like they once did."

He repeated himself. "Yes, sir. I belong to the Latter-day Saint people."

The old man moaned. "Well, that's no good luck, boy. Not now. You'd best leave that band. My sympathies are with you, but I must say, the Mormons are getting it bad. Last I heard, the Mormon leader and some of his cohorts was set to be shot. He's in jail, you know. And not without cause." He went into some detail. There had been a fray, Mormons resisting arrest and making battle. It had started when a Mormon tried to vote, for many a man in Missouri felt a Mormon had "no more right to suffrage than had a Negro."

Elijah tensed at this but kept quiet. The old man was speaking in a matter-of-fact voice, like he was telling nothing more important than a day's business. These were mere facts; he didn't mean to offend, even when he reported in that same tone that Missouri's Governor Boggs had ordered Mormons "exterminated" or "driven from the state for the public good." Mobs had attacked a Mormon settlement, killing a good number of Saints (seventeen, Elijah later learned, with another thirteen wounded, the settlement being Haun's Mill). The leaders had "their fate sealed," for they had simply assumed too much power in this frontier territory. Besides which, it was a bad idea for any church to worship a man, said this riding companion of Elijah Abel's.

Elijah swallowed hard. "Brother Joseph?"

"Speak up."

"Brother Joseph Smith?"

"Yes, that's the name. Set to be shot. They were taking him to Independence, last I heard. I disembark there. You stay with me, and we'll find your man." He returned to his book.

"We don't worship Brother Joseph," Elijah stated.

"Say again?" The lawyer didn't look up.

"We worship Jesus, the Son of God."

"Well, good for you, then." He turned a page and adjusted his monocle.

Elijah was shivering, his back throbbing when he followed the lawyer off the stagecoach into the center of Independence City. But he forgot that pain a moment later. For the first sight he saw was a cage for humans, its contents on display. There, in the midst of the prisoners, was Brother Joseph himself, chained up like a slave, a cut on his forehead, dried blood down his cheek, his shirtsleeves torn.

When Elijah approached, Joseph shook his head like there was danger. Elijah knew better than to brave it.

He followed the lawyer home and discovered the man owned fifty slaves himself. Elijah didn't think he'd want to join this particular household, or even preach the gospel to it. So he left without notice before supper.

NOTES

The chapter title, "Through It All," is from the title of hymn number 43 in *Hymns for the Family of God*.

The Missouri Compromise and its consequences are explained by Roberts in his introduction to volume 3 of *History of the Church*.

William Phelps published "Free People of Color" in *The Evening and the Morning Star* 2 (July 1833): 109, as documented in Bush, "Mormonism's Negro Doctrine," 98, n. 7.

Joseph Smith and several others, including his brother Hyrum, were put on public display in Independence during early November 1838. According to *History of the Church*, 4:29: "This last persecution began at an election, which was held . . . August, 1838. A 'Mormon' went to the polls to vote. One of the mob standing by, opposed his voting, contending that a 'Mormon' had no more right to vote than a negro; one angry word brought on another, and blows followed. . . . The 'Mormon' was not the aggressor, but was on the defensive."

The reference to the Mormons having "made battle" refers to the Battle of Crooked River, in which the Mormons—still on the defensive—fought their enemies. Elder David Patten, a member of the Quorum of the Twelve, was killed in that battle.

Louis Gray

10

Didn't My Lord Deliver Daniel?

And all thy children
shall be taught of the Lord.
ISAIAH 54:13

Christopher Merkley's house in 'Diahman was empty. It took two hours of searching and asking questions before Elijah learned what had happened to his fellow Saints. A slave boy named Louis Gray in Marshall, Missouri, told him: "The general say Mormons can stay the winter, but they can't plant crops. He wants all ya'll gone come spring." Louis was pitchforking the last of the fall hay, leaning on the fork while he talked.

"What general is that?"

"Some fancy-name fellow—Lucky or somethin'. I don't recall."

"Well, that general ain't goin' be so lucky or so fancy once the angels tell God about his sayin's. General Lucky done everything 'cept eat us." Elijah used his black voice. His breath made a plume in the air.

"And likely do that to ya'll, if ya' ain't outa here come spring."

107

Louis, dressed in a homespun old coat, already had the slave sidle: hips forward, feet apart, arms limp so as not to appear threatening. He was about fifteen but sluggish in the bone. He pinched his mouth between sentences like his teeth hurt—or like he was practicing being old.

"I reckon I do what I wants, and he can eat me whole if it suit him," Elijah said.

Louis raised his brows. "So you must be one."

"A Mormon?"

"No. A stupid. Setting yo'self up to get whupped and lynched! Lawd, Lawd, Lawd! You sumpin' else!"

Elijah looked at him square. He didn't like disrespect, especially from someone younger than he was. "I ain't stupid, and I is Mormon, ordained in the holy priesthood, and just now come back from bein' a missionary up in New York State and the Lion's Paw."

"You ain't no slave, then?"

Elijah rolled his shoulders so his coat would fall on him better. He had used it as a pillow in the stage and it looked it, though Missouri's damp air would soon ease out the wrinkles.

"I resemble a slave to you, boy?"

"You black, ain'tcha?"

"Me and freedom rides together, and so does me and the Mormons." He wished his teeth wouldn't chatter whilst he was saying important words.

"Mormons lettin' the black man be full part of them—that's why they catch so much hate, I reckon." Louis Gray puckered his mouth and nodded.

There was truth there. Elijah didn't inform the slave boy of all the details but did decide this was a good time to recite a Book of Mormon scripture: "All are alike unto God, black and white, bond and free, male and female." He used his preacher voice, bearing testimony of Joseph Smith and testifying that Brother Joseph would get delivered by God and neither general nor governor would stop the Holy Hand from that. He asked finally, wouldn't Louis like to get baptized now?

"In that col' ol' Miss'ippi? I don't think I be doin' that right at the moment, thank you kindly." Louis's grin showed two missing teeth. *Too much sugar,* thought Elijah. *Either that or a good beating with someone's boot in his mouth.*

He didn't say that out loud. What he said was, "You just remember what Elder Elijah Abel taught you. When you see the Prophet Joseph getting delivered by God, you find you a Mormon man with the priesthood to take you down to that river and get you born into the Restoration."

"Massa wouldn' 'preciate that, I don' expect."

"Then do it secret. And remember I told you. Your faith can get mighty as mine." Elijah stretched himself tall. He felt tall and strong.

Louis Gray laughed and then went serious. "Don't disbelieve a Missouri threat, Mister," he said. "These folks have pushed a people out of they places before."

"What people they push?"

"That be our people."

"Negroes?"

"That's right."

"Well, you still here! How you pass for white? You must be one fine actor!"

"The free Negroes is who they sent off or killed. Many a year ago, but they done it, and they hearts ain't change, from what I see. So don't disbelieve any threat in Missouri." Louis turned back to his fields like he was scared not to, started running towards the bales.

Yes, fear was branded into a slave, along with the sense of rules and rulers: You go to this point, not beyond. Beyond here is every trouble, bad as you can imagine.

Louis was certainly right about the Missourians driving free colored folk from the state, but that wasn't what Elijah dwelt on. He was observing this slave boy. "There's more to you yet, Louis Gray," Elijah whispered into the air, willing his sound to the slave. "Lift up your head, boy. Don't go fearin' everything. God will make you free." Then Elijah Abel blessed Louis Gray's posterity as though he could see them lined up in the heavens, blessed them by the power of the priesthood, which he hoped they themselves might experi-ence once they took on mortal bodies. "Let God make them all be free," Elijah whispered.

Louis Gray was loping towards a hay bale, arms flapping.

Old Joseph with the rainbow coat was beside Elijah then, and they watched Louis. "Joe?" said Elijah. "You move like that when you was a slave?"

"No. But I wasn't born a slave like him. I knowed I was set to better things. That boy don't know who he is or who he can be."

"Nope. He don't," Elijah said.

"I knowed, though. I trusted in the Lord, kept his commands, jus' waitin' for the time he deliver me and make me strong. Waited years 'til I was head of ol' Master Potiphar's house. Then years in jail until somebody 'membered me."

"And somebody did remember you at last, and you got yo'self delivered. Then you switched things up good, and you delivered them!" Elijah chuckled.

"I did that, yessir. And you, 'Lijah, you be something like me. Why, you was holed out there in them woods with your name gracin' all them handbills, and then God delivered you and now you be preaching to the people—to that boy there, for one example."

"And blessin' his seed too. Seemed the polite thing to do."

"More than polite. It was the godly thing, once you was moved to do it."

"Well, I have to agree with you there."

"And God's goin' deliver you again. But then maybe you got to wait again, and then he deliver you again, and on it goes. Darkness to light, darkness to light, 'til the sun be up permanent and all the shadows get gone."

When Joseph walked away, Elijah watched how strong and straight his back was, how high he held his head. Elijah wanted to walk that way too.

"And God will deliver his prophet," Elijah told the thin clouds above him. "You watch."

He wanted to work at freeing Brother Joseph, which seemed a fine work to do. But Brother Joseph was quickly sent up to Richmond and then to a half-underground dungeon called Liberty Jail, with walls like mountains. Elijah could do nothing save pray, and he could pray as well in Illinois as in Missouri—better, maybe, for he imagined Missouri skies were stopped up with Missouri sins.

And the Saints were sure suffering under those stuck-in-the-sky, stinky-rotten sins. Maybe General Lucky had said the Mormons could stay till spring, but they had been driven from their homes in the dead of winter. The little town of Far West, which was about the right size to hold four hundred families, was keeping thousands of homeless Mormons. They were living in tents, wagon boxes, and quick-made huts—nothing to compete with the cold. Father and Mother Smith turned their whole yard into a campground—an acre covered with beds. Elijah could hardly bear seeing it and hearing all the hungry, crying babies, for he didn't have a thing to give them. He made slight greetings to Father and Mother Smith, but this was no time for extended conversation. This was the time for Mormon folks to move on.

To Quincy, Illinois, they went in February, Elijah and hundreds of other Mormons, most of them driving ox or horse teams, but many on foot. It would be a twelve-day trek, two hundred miles.

Elijah had been told their stories by now. Among the refugees was Amanda Smith and her five children. Sister Smith had lost her husband and ten-year-old son, Sardius—the child shot point blank even as he was begging for his life—in the Haun's Mill massacre.

She was driving her own team to Quincy, saying nothing to anyone, just staring straight ahead. Watching her, Elijah muttered, "They was slavers, them mobcrats. Full accustomed to see human faces as things, not people. Full accustomed. Ten-year-old boy!" Elijah had seen whip marks on a slave boy's back once, the boy being no older than nine or ten. He couldn't imagine how heartless the whipper had been but hoped angels had been taking notes with strong ink. He hoped Sardius's guardians had had their paper pads ready too. Or gold plates, which would be better yet.

Asahel Lathrop was driving a team of horses and a wagon. Lathrop had been warned of the mob and, when his wife insisted, he left his home. Some fifteen rascals pushed through his door the day after, took full possession of his place, and robbed him. They ordered Lathrop's wife to cook for them whilst they stole everything of value she owned in this world. Asahel Lathrop's son died of some disease—probably a mix of cold air and fear—and the mobbers buried him without even letting the mother say good-bye.

Brother Asahel and his wife appeared more worn out than angry now.

Timothy Clark was leading a sorry-looking mule. His ox team— two yoke—had been stolen by mobbers under the banner of the United States government. These soldiers had taken Brother Clark and his three sons prisoner, destroyed all their crops, and commandeered whatever looked useful, including the oxen, three horses, two wagons. "For the army," they said, like it should be an honor for Mormons to take on poverty so a United States brigade could be supplied and then "exterminate" the Saints. The Clarks hadn't been broken, though; they seemed powerful now, running ahead of the Mormon line and yelling, "Ya'll look like tired old turtles! Put some grease in your shoulder bones there!" They were met with weary laughter or just groans.

Yes, the Mormons were a sad-looking bunch. Every one of them had felt the sting of that Boggs order. Some had been whipped.

Many had lost family. All had lost their homes, either to mob fire or the threat of it. They were leaving Missouri in defeat.

Elijah made no comment, though he understood what it was to lose everything, to be driven hither and yon at some powerful body's whim. He was used to that kind of thing. Why, all blacks in America were used to such during those years! It wasn't hard to believe Louis Gray's tales of how Missouri had rid itself of free color. But he hadn't seen whites treated this way, not once in his entire life. He had seen whites wielding whips but never their own backs ripped. Those were cruel folk, those Missouri frontiersmen. They were low-down, nasty-minded, mean-thinking, evil folk, he thought, and they'd get theirs. God would serve it up good.

He had heard Brother Joseph say there would be a great war between the states before long, probably over the question of slavery. He figured Missouri would pay dear for its present victory. "Go on, you men," he thought back to them over the half-frozen prairie. "You go on and whup us away. God be watchin' you, though. Every move."

He liked thinking *us* with the Mormon people. He knew their gospel. He had preached it; he had learned it. He knew the Mormon life and what all it meant—even the hard, leg-stretching parts like this journey. And now the Mormons were coming to understand how it was to be declared less a man because of something you couldn't just drop like a corncob. This something was in your blood and in your heart. This was who you were, your forever identity. Mormons and Negroes—they were coming to understand each other. He only wished Elder Merkley could participate in this long parade.

Of course there was a certain irony in Elijah's place among the Saints. All those years of his youth, he had been searching out a better life, and once he found it, the very people he chose got mowed down to poverty. It was almost funny once he thought on it.

But he wouldn't go back to his young self, his young dreams. No matter what, he wouldn't go back. He was a Latter-day Saint, sure as he was colored. They were one licked people for now.

At one point, there were hundreds of families stuck on the west of the Mississippi. The weather had been favorable at the journey's beginning, but now so much sludge and rushing ice cut through the river that they couldn't cross. They made tents out of their bed-clothes. A few women delivered babies in such conditions. Oh, this was sad! This was a sight to make the Lord himself weep!

Maybe that's what the rain was—God's tears. But Elijah wondered if Jesus couldn't have cried warm instead of cold. Maybe passing through the Missouri skies, the tears turned to sleet. The more it rained, the colder it got. Snow and hail before long, and every step so swampy that a foot would sink in mud up to the ankle. Elijah's eyebrows and lashes were frosted, and he couldn't even open his mouth to speak.

Maybe they had abandoned Missouri, but they hadn't abandoned God, and God still remembered them. The state of Illinois "deplored" what Missouri had done and said to any Mormon leaving that lawless place, "Welcome hither." As though it were God himself speaking through the people of Illinois, calling across the plains with the wind, "Here's the promised land!"

In Quincy, Elijah found Mrs. Merkley and gave her Brother Christopher's letter. Samuel Smith—whose life was in danger in Missouri, because he had fought in the Crooked River Battle—he had already escaped to Illinois and built Father and Mother Smith a split rail cabin there. The Smiths fed Elijah in that cabin, and listened at last to his mission report, now that there was time and comfort to tell it. And he loved telling it: the story of the handbills and how God had watched out for him and even arranged for Elder Merkley to teach some prisoners in the bargain. Mother Smith—stooped, bony, white-haired—sat by the fire. Elijah sat next to her, and wondered if any of them would ever really thaw out. She was wearing a white cap with fussy pleats and tatted lace across the brim, and a black dress like a woman in mourning, which seemed just right. As he unfolded his stories—puffing them up with all the drama they deserved, and maybe a little extra just for luck— she smiled and shook her head. Father Smith, still a tower of a man despite his years and these most recent trials, said little, just nodded.

He could've lived with the Smiths had he chosen to, but their Quincy place was so tiny. Four other families shared it, including Hyrum's wife and children, for Hyrum was in jail with Joseph. The Smiths were feeding anyone who dropped by, though they had little themselves. He was certain he'd be an inconvenience. Besides, Mother and Father Smith were still in agony over the Saints' expulsion and their sons' imprisonment; they didn't need the pressure of another mouth to feed.

"All this been so hard on you," Elijah observed to Mother Smith once when her husband went out for wood. He didn't mention how much older she appeared even since their brief interaction in Far West nor how shaky her hands had gotten.

"Been hard on everyone, 'Lijah," she said.

Of course, he already knew the details of Far West and that hellish journey to Quincy, but he hadn't heard the details of Joseph's capture. Now Lucy told it: She and Father Smith had stood in the doorway. They could hear yelling like it was fiends at a party. They thought sure the mob was murdering Joseph. "Father cried out, 'They've killed him!' and, oh, he clutched his heart," Lucy said. "For two days running, my husband wept. He said that if Joseph was dead, he'd die too." She described how later, when they learned Joseph, and their son Hyrum too, were still alive but caged up like condemned men, she had gone to them, reached her hand into the mobile jail as it was being carted away towards Independence. She told how Joseph clasped her fingers and said—she could hear the tears in his voice: "God bless you, Mother." She dabbed her old eyes as she remembered. "They was set to shoot him, 'Lijah. Hyrum too." Her voice trembled. "But that didn't happen, did it. God is with us."

"God is sure with us," Elijah answered.

"I haven't lost them yet."

"You won't," he said.

She gazed at him long. "Not yet."

Within a week, Elijah found employment and a good bed in a carpenter's shop—another sign of God's mercy that Mother Lucy and Father Joseph nodded their heads about. Elijah visited them every few days, and Mother Smith talked about her sons, reciting the account of Joseph's captivity three times more, so Elijah could almost mouth it with her. "I'm repeating myself," she'd say, and Elijah would tell her, "I never get tired of it." Then she'd work letters with him, until one day he could read the entire story of Joseph and the Rainbow Coat without even pausing to think what sound each letter made.

Come March, he heard that Sister Emma had crossed the unstable ice of the Mississippi on foot, holding two children, with Julia clinging to her skirt on one side and little Joseph on the other. Elijah would hear later that under Emma's skirts, tied in heavy bags, had been all the Prophet's papers.

Come April, he had the best sight of his life: At the ferry, a tall, unshaved man emerged, dressed in old boots, torn pants, blue cloak, and a wide-brim black hat, rim down.

It was Brother Joseph, delivered as promised, and the spirit of Zion come with him.

Now was the hour for all Latter-day Saints to make a permanent home, Joseph said. But not in Quincy. They'd buy up land, settle into it. Commerce, they called it at first. Then, after further consideration, they renamed it.

Nauvoo.

Notes

The chapter title, "Didn't My Lord Deliver Daniel?" is from Burleigh, *Spirituals*, 184.

Louis Gray is an ancestor of Darius A. Gray. Though we have freely fictionalized his personality, dates and locations are according to genealogical record. We are portraying him in this novel as a young man fully accustomed to slavery, though perhaps more fearful than he was in his actual life. He will be more completely treated in the second volume of *Standing on the Promises*, which covers the Civil War years and the Emancipation Proclamation.

That Missouri had once driven out free blacks is indicated by a letter to the editor in the *Missouri Argus* (quoted in Hartley, "Exodus," 14). The letter, dated 20 December 1838, objects to the treatment of Mormons and says, "Public opinion has recoiled from a summary and forcible removal of our negro population—much more likely will it be to revolt at the violent expulsion of two or three thousand [Mormons]. . . ."

The general Louis Gray refers to is General Samuel D. Lucas, who "ordered that Mormons surrender their firearms, that those who had taken up arms surrender property to pay debts and indemnify for damages, that leaders be given up to be tried and punished and that everyone else leave the state when so ordered" (Hartley, "Exodus," 9).

The description of the Smith household and yard is from Lucy Mack Smith's *History of Joseph Smith*, 292.

The views of Lucy and Joseph Smith Sr. about their sons' imprisonment and mistreatment are recorded in *History of the Church*, 3:194.

Joseph Smith's revelation on the Civil War was received on December 25, 1832, "at a time when the brethren were reflecting and reasoning upon African slavery on the American continent and the slavery of the children of men throughout the world" (D&C 87, headnote).

Samuel Smith's fleeing to Quincy with other participants in the Battle of Crooked River is documented in Sarah De Armon Pea Rich's journal, quoted in Godfrey, Godfrey, and Derr, *Women's Voices*: "My husband was allso with David Patton when he was killed . . . and my husband and some others were compelled to flee for there lives as the mob swore they would kill him. I do not remember the names of all the brethren that left with Mr Rich but Hose[a] Stout, Samuel Smith a brother of the prophet and Seamor [Seymour] Brunson and Phineous Young were among that number that had to flee. . . . the[y] expearenced maney hardships. . . . they ware five days lost. . . . One of those days the company of six only had one black bird among them to eat.

They finely come upon a camp of indians who received them friendly and fed them . . ." (100–1).

Samuel Smith's building his parents a cabin upon his arrival in Quincy is documented in Lucy Mack Smith, *History of Joseph Smith*, 294–97.

The description of the February exodus is paraphrased from John Greene, "Facts Relative to the Expulsion of the Mormons or Latter-day Saints from the State of Missouri, Under the Extermination Order" (quoted in Hartley, "Exodus,"11).

The fact of Sardius Smith's murder is documented in *History of the Church*, 3:324. The account of Asahel Lathrop's troubles is from his affidavit, recorded in *History of the Church*, 4:66. Timothy Clark's account is from his affidavit, also recorded in *History of the Church*, 4:58.

The description of Emma Smith's crossing the frozen Mississippi is from Newell and Avery, *Mormon Enigma*, 79.

The description of Joseph Smith's arriving in Illinois is taken from a number of sources, including Flanders, *Nauvoo*: "In April 1839, Joseph Smith escaped prison. He assumed that his detention had been unlawful as well as unjust, and that once he was beyond the borders of Missouri his trouble with that state would be ended. He fled eastward unmolested and arrived in Quincy on April 22, where he was greeted with joy" (34).

Commerce was the name of the abandoned settlement before the Saints renamed it Nauvoo.

Elijah's Calling
1840–41

11

THERE IS A BALM
IN GILEAD

Go up into Gilead, and take balm.
JEREMIAH 46:11

Brother Joseph's voice was never angry and never hopeless.
Nothing could get Brother Joseph to lose faith in God or in the
Mormon people. And in that certain, peaceful voice, in one easy
sentence, he asked Elijah wouldn't he like to live with him and
Emma? And would he mind serving as Nauvoo's undertaker?

Yes to the first, but lemme think on the second.

Undertaker! But he was trained in woods!

"That's why. The Saints should have the best coffins in North
America." They were standing in a weed-spiked field that would
one day house a whole block of stores, according to the Prophet. It
was late spring now. The weeds were mostly young thistle and jim-
son, but the land was so boggy there were some random cattails too
and clumps of swampgrass.

"Bury my gifts, you mean?" Elijah said. "Do my best work I can and then put it under the ground?"

"It's always been considered a great calamity, Elijah, not to obtain an honorable burial."

"I know that, Brother Joseph."

"One of the greatest curses the ancient prophets could put on any man was that he should go without a burial."

"Is that so? Me—a undertaker!"

Death had spooked Elijah since he was six years old and stuck in Massa's parlor keeping watch over a life-gone girl, her skin pale as birch bark, her mouth hung open. And oh, how he remembered his first experience as an undertaker: building his first coffin and burying his mama somewhere in the Lion's Paw. It wasn't an activity he had thought of taking on as a career. Besides, he knew what dead bodies he'd deal with in Nauvoo: those folks who had been battling exposure from the Missouri days and couldn't fight it any longer, and those who would face the summer ague in their weakened condition—that ague which brought chills and fever and nosebleeds and then twisted air out of the lungs until there was no air left—that ague which was contagious as pollen off the goldenrod.

"Will you?" This was Brother Joseph, those brilliant green-blue eyes already certain of the answer.

But Elijah didn't want to give his answer just yet. So he looked at his boots, which were in need of blacking. He kicked a pebble gently. "Aw, why you want that?" he asked.

"You think I'm the one who wants it, brother?"

There was going to be no way around this. Elijah rolled his eyes, still watching his boots. "It's God?" he said, already resigned.

Joseph didn't reply, just smiled when Elijah finally looked up at him.

Elijah sighed. "Awright. If you bless me so I don't get sick,

Brother Joseph, I'll do what you and God wants." He looked at his boots again. "All right, even if you don't bless me, I'll do it."

Later on, Joseph laid his hands on Elijah's head—not in the marshy field, because that was no place for kneeling, but in the simple frame house Joseph had put up as his temporary place. Elijah's soul got peaceful. There was some reason he was being called as undertaker, and before long, he'd know it.

So here he was: Elder Elijah Abel, black man, carpenter for a temple of the Lord, former minister of the Mormon gospel, now called by the Prophet to carve out coffins from pitch pine because God said.

It was babies first—those that didn't make it out of the womb breathing and those that caught the whoop before their cheeks got fat. Then it was the old women and old men—yes indeed, the very ones who had been stripped of their strength in the icy, muddy journey from Governor Boggs's order and General Lucky's threats. Come July, with the steady hum of mosquitoes down the swampland and the jeers of cicadas, it was everybody dying.

Elijah didn't have to do the laying out. The midwives did that most often—almost always when it was a woman dead. Sister Sessions was the best. She'd get the body cleaned up even under the fingernails, dress it in good clothes, get coins on the eyelids to keep them shut, tie a cloth around the face to keep the mouth closed. Everything would be set by the time Elijah arrived with his wagon, hauling a coffin so new there'd still be sawdust in the corners. He'd pick the body up, lay it in its box, then—alongside the family men—carry it first to the sitting room (if the family had one) where mourners could weep over the corpse and snip off mementos of hair before the lid was nailed shut, then to the Grove for the funeral, and finally to the grave.

He didn't know most of the people he coffined, so their deaths didn't melt or wreck him. He simply stood back and watched grief settle into the mourners' face lines. Death was the ultimate slavery, that was it. A living, breathing soul became a thing to get boxed up, not even human anymore. And he, Elijah, was supervising the process: measuring the remains, cutting the wood, putting the box together with strong nails to withstand the weight of centuries. He was the carpenter measuring out the division point—brothers divided from sisters, husbands from wives, children from parents. He took the money for his pains and theirs and watched the white folk become one mass of weeping humanity, hardly any distinctions between them: all dressed in black, all teary.

Elijah had always loved open space and hated boxes, and now he was building them. It got so he was sometimes shocked by color, as when he left his shop before dusk and saw calico dresses, green polka dot slippers, magenta silk, and all the hues of apples and applesauce swirling around the Mormon women, especially around the English converts. There was a whole world of greens and blues and purples outside his door, and for days at a time, he hardly saw it.

Within a little while, he got too used to death. He became gentle but unemotional as he took still babies from their mothers' arms, lifeless husbands from sobbing wives, lifeless wives from sobbing husbands. And he never did get sick, even when Brother Joseph and Sister Emma got sick during the bad summer and lived in a tent on their homestead. Elijah's health showed more of God's mercy: keeping him whole so he could care for the ones Jesus was claiming. He saw heaven's mercy in Brother Joseph too, for Joseph looked ready to go under one moment and was healed the next, blessing the ones still sick, sending his red handkerchief when he couldn't get to a bedside himself.

Elijah got fast accustomed to funeral sermons too—and learned a thing or two in the process, including more scripture stories and new revelations.

After Brother Seymour Brunson's death, Brother Joseph told the Saints they could do baptisms for their loved ones who had died without it, which they commenced to perform in the Mississippi. Elijah, unconnected to about everyone, couldn't think of any dead folk he'd want to stand in and go under for, excepting the two Delilahs who surely had kept watch over him: his mama and his baby. So he walked into the river holding their names in his heart and let another elder immerse his live body for their dead ones.

When Zina Huntington passed, he heard Brother Joseph tell Zina Diantha, the dead woman's daughter, "You'll see your mother again—and you'll see your eternal mother, the wife of your Father in Heaven." Elijah had never thought of God being married, though it made good sense.

In time, he learned the undertaker's words and tones of comfort, though mostly he kept quiet. He certainly didn't use his powered talk when he was prying a woman's fingers off her gone baby (mothers would often grab the body when it came time to box it) but spoke softly of God's love—if he spoke at all. In Nauvoo, God was as real as a neighbor you saw only occasionally but whose presence you felt by the lantern light in his window, which was always burning. Elijah took to addressing God just as he would that neighbor—usually in an out-loud voice, because he didn't want to trouble the Almighty into mind-reading. "Now God," he would say, "what need did you have of this child that you'd take it away from its mama?" He didn't picture a face for God, just the brilliance of the sun that warmed a body through and burned away anything impure. That brilliance was God, though he understood and accepted the doctrine that somewhere at the nub of all that radiance was a flesh-and-bones body. He did not picture that body with any particular pigment, just beams of light for eyes and sun-struck clouds for hair. And Elijah knew God wanted him serving as the undertaker, because that warm peace filled him whenever he questioned his job. "Now Lord," he might say, "there must be occupations a lot more fun than this one here. But I ain't turnin' my back on anyone in need of my services." Peace would come as the answer.

Maybe God had wanted him to build coffins so Elijah could see the Saints in their tenderest, most vulnerable moments, so he could expand his store of human pictures to include white faces alongside the colored ones. He pitied them, these poor white slaves of Massa Death. He knew their faces, and he did pity them.

Sweet Eliza Partridge, just a slip of a woman barely turned twenty, looked set to faint from grief while Elijah measured her father, Bishop Edward Partridge, for his coffin. The bishop had suffered too much in the Missouri persecutions. After the loss of his oldest daughter, Harriet (who Elijah had also attended in death), the bishop's body could endure no more. He passed on May 27, 1840, and Eliza appeared ready to join him. Her face was blue-white except for her flushed cheeks. Indeed, she got too sick to attend her own daddy's funeral, and Elijah wondered how long it would be before he was making one more wood cage for a Partridge.

He had never imagined he'd see so many teary faces in such a short time. And he certainly never thought the teary faces would include the Smiths' or that he'd tend the corpse of Father Joseph.

The old man hadn't been well since he and Mother Lucy arrived in Nauvoo. By September, he was vomiting blood. Consumption, maybe, brought on by all the pain and pressure of the Missouri time and the sludge and to-the-bone cold of the trek to Illinois. It was bad. Elijah had experience now; he knew death had come stalking. He sat at the bedside, September 12, 1840, not so much waiting for last moments as just keeping the patriarch company.

The day was muggy hot, air so stale you could taste it. It hung on the skin, compelled water from every pore, and invited mosquitoes, which hummed everywhere. You could flap them away or slap them dead, but there were always others troubling your ankles or tempting you to hit your ears. Elijah's clothes were wet, his face dripping. Father Smith, lying there, seemed too dry and cold to perspire much, though a film of sweat gleamed on his forehead.

Elijah would wipe it, but a moment later it'd be back, though never drippy.

Most of the Smiths hardly noticed him sitting in the room like a shadow and never asked him to leave, so he heard every last word between them, heard Father tell Mother Lucy in a strangled breath: "The world does not love us. Hates us because we are not of the world." Which sure was the truth, and something Elijah understood. The old man tried to lift himself up in bed, and Elijah, calling him "Father," said, "You best not try." Father Smith moved his eyes towards him. They were glazed blue, lit up with last lights; his eye-whites had taken on bile. The old man moved his gaze to Lucy, who was weeping without a sound, and he said, "Such trouble and affliction on this earth. I dread to leave you surrounded by enemies." No one offered reassurance that he wouldn't be leaving anytime soon. They all knew what was ahead. It was no use pretending otherwise.

Brother Joseph came in towards dusk, hardly recognizable for being so sad. His head was down, shoulders stooped like he had been preparing to kneel the whole day, which he did now at the bedside, collapsing to his knees. Tears and sweat rolled down Brother Joseph's face. Elijah whispered to him yes, it looked bad, and then watched Father Smith raise his hands high as he could—which wasn't high—and pronounce a last blessing on his son: "You are called to do the work of the Lord. Hold out faithful and you shall be blessed, and your children after you. You shall even live to finish your work." The blessing spoken, Father's hands dropped like the life had gone out of them, though Elijah saw he was still breathing.

That was the first time he saw Brother Joseph weep like a baby, bowing his head to the blankets, crying out, "Oh, Father, shall I?"

In a thin breath, Father Smith promised: "You shall live to lay out the plan of all the work God has given you."

Elijah stood, wiped the sweat film from Father's brow again, and told him to rest, no use straining himself. The patriarch looked straight at him and said, surprised, "I can see and hear as well as ever I could."

"Now that's a blessing'," said Elijah. "You best lay you back down, though, sir."

The old man didn't pass until two more days had come and gone. Elijah, with all the Smiths, was with him when the final summons arrived. Father said he'd live seven or eight more minutes. Then his breaths got deep, then further spaced, then they stopped. As the women wailed, Brother Hyrum told Elijah to do his best job for this particular dead man.

Which Elijah did, measuring the body like it was sacred—as it was. This was his own father by adoption, the man who had laid hands on his head and blessed him beyond what any black in this slave-loving nation had ever received, he supposed. This was the man who had joked with him, fed him, prayed with him, hauled temple rocks with him. This was the man who had looked at the woodwork Elijah had given the Kirtland Temple and called it "consecrated." Tears dripped down Elijah's cheeks as he gave his own blessing to the old man's body and noted its dimensions for the coffin. This was the first time he had ever wept so hard doing his duty.

"You gets this back in the resurrection," Elijah said, though this version of the body didn't seem much worth reclaiming. Gray skin hung on the bones; all the blood had stopped, the veins gone flat. The fight Father had put up against the sickness seemed carved into his face—around the half-open mouth especially, like a frown— though he had been such an easy-smiling man, just like Brother Joseph. Serious about the work of restoration but easy-smiling. In his prime, Father had weighed near two hundred pounds like his sons. The last ague, Elijah guessed, had stolen fifty or more. "Only you gots to wait some before resurrection happens. It will be worth it, though. This old body goin' get young again, every hair put back in its place." In the resurrection, the two Josephs, father and son, would most likely look like twins. "And health in the navel and marrow to the bones," Elijah said.

Though he didn't need to, he sat with the body after the mourners had left, being scared only once during the night, when a blast of wind came at him through the window and lifted Father's white hair like the life had come back to it.

At the graveyard, part of his own self got buried with Father Smith—not just the coffin, which was the best one he could make, but a portion of his heart. By the time he ate the funeral meal, he realized he had hardly touched a morsel since Father started dying. He was hungrier than a hog, and Isaac James, another black Mormon living in Nauvoo, brought him catfish, fried corn, and ginger cake, and then talked to him about everything that had gotten buried in that grave with Father Smith's body.

Notes

The chapter title, "There Is a Balm in Gilead," is from the title of hymn number 48 in *Hymns for the Family of God*.

That Elijah Abel was given "the calling of an undertaker" by Joseph Smith is substantiated by Van Wagoner and Walker, *Book of Mormons*, 3, and by Bringhurst, "Elijah Abel," 133.

We have used Flanders, *Nauvoo* (40), in describing the initial appearance of Commerce (Nauvoo) and its peninsula and bluffs.

The deaths of Harriet and Edward Partridge are described in Eliza Partridge Lyman's journal (transcribed in Carter, *Treasures*, 2:219).

Hill's biography of the Prophet, *Joseph Smith*, gives information we have used in recreating the death scene of Joseph Smith Sr. Hill relied partly upon Lucy Mack Smith's biography of Joseph for her text. Elijah Abel recalled being present at Father Smith's deathbed "during his last sickness" in 1840 (Bringhurst, "Elijah Abel," 133).

In the early baptisms for the dead, performed in the Mississippi River before the Nauvoo Temple was completed, men often did the work for women, and vice versa. As documented in the notes to Chapter 1, the Nauvoo Temple ordinance records show Elijah's having been proxy in baptisms for two "Delilah's"—one his mother and the other his daughter. He also was baptized in behalf of at least one friend.

Joseph Smith's description of a mother in heaven as given to Zina Diantha Huntington (Smith Young) is taken from Susa Young Gates, as quoted in Holzapfel and Holzapfel, *Women of Nauvoo*, 200. Since Zina and Eliza R. Snow were great friends, one often speaking in tongues and the other translating, it seems likely that Zina shared Joseph's teachings with Eliza. Or possibly, because Eliza was a plural wife of Joseph Smith, as was Zina, she could have heard the doctrine directly from him. In any case, there is clearly some foundation for Eliza's poetic description of a heavenly mother in the hymn "O My Father."

The account of the introduction at Seymour Brunson's funeral of the doctrine of baptism for the dead is from Holzapfel and Holzapfel, *Women of Nauvoo*, 90.

Accounts of the many deaths in Nauvoo from malaria (called ague by the Saints) can be found in any history of the Church, which describe the undrained swampland around Nauvoo, the ubiquitous anopheles mosquito, and the consequent contagion.

Our descriptions of funeral customs and an undertaker's duties are drawn from Jones, *Design for Death*, and Habenstein and Lamers, *History of American Funeral Directing*. Indeed, it was common for carpenters such as Elijah Abel to take on undertaking duties as well as upholstery. Sometimes the undertakers did "lay out" the bodies (embalming did not begin until the Civil War years), but it was far more common for family members or midwives to attend to those duties. Patty Sessions, a preeminent Mormon midwife, mentions laying out the dead numerous times in her journal (Smart, *Mormon Midwife*).

Isaac James
1841

12

ALL CREATURES OF OUR GOD AND KING

*Sing unto the Lord a new song, and
his praise in the congregation.*
PSALM 149:1

Isaac James had come alone to the City Beautiful, having joined the Church in Monmouth County, New Jersey. He was a farmer, as long as farming seemed profitable, and planned on sowing grapes in Nauvoo. The white Saints seemed to assume that two free colored men would become best friends—which they didn't, though they didn't dislike each other, either. There just wasn't much to talk about.

Except women.

There were only a few colored women in Nauvoo, and these women were Mormon-owned slaves. It was risky to marry someone's property. Certainly white women were not an option, unless you enjoyed wearing a noose for a necktie.

Food was another favorite subject between them. Pork rinds and cornbread; catfish, mustard greens, purple grapes, and rutabagas;

prairie chicken and pumpkin pie. The two of them could make up a four-course supper in their minds and share it like it was real, which they did when hunger came calling. And hunger stopped by a lot. Hunger wore out its welcome. Nauvoo was just getting itself started, and food was scarce too often. Someday soon, though, there would be food aplenty and everywhere. They knew that. Nauvoo was growing like a fine crop of zucchini squash, spreading out and swelling up.

When Elijah had come to Joseph's city, right at its beginning, Nauvoo was a tangle of trees, vines, and bushes, the ground all wet. The Saints started out living in huts and tents and some abandoned stone buildings from former settlers who lacked a vision of what this swampy place could be and gave up trying. The Saints, though, were not quitters, and they did have a vision. Brother Joseph provided it. So it wasn't long at all before frame homes went up by the tens and then by the hundreds, and brick ones soon followed. Now the Prophet was set to build a mansion house to replace his log homestead.

Nauvoo was a river city, occupying two levels: the flatlands—or peninsula—near the river, and the much higher bluffs. The air smelled of frying fish, river rock, new leather, and hot metal being forged in the blacksmiths' shops. Boats of all sizes floated up and down the Mississippi, clanging their bells and announcing their great clouds of steam with shrill whistles. Industry was peeking around the corner too, with the beginnings of an iron foundry, a steam grist, saw and water mills, limestone quarries, match and powder factories, pottery shops, wagon shops, brick makers, blacksmiths, tailors, milliners, cobblers, storekeepers, tanners, coopers, and, of course, undertakers.

Most important, a new temple was set to go forward. Brother Joseph ordered it, placing the cornerstones himself on April 6, 1841. Elijah worked his skills and muscles on the site whenever death took a break. This temple would be even better than Kirtland's—

richer, bigger. And Brother Joseph had hinted at new revelations for this one. Not just washings and anointings but bigger things. New things.

Isaac James hadn't been washed or anointed and didn't hold priesthood like Elijah did, and Isaac didn't seem to care much about anything except getting wifed and fed. He was in Nauvoo because a black man was treated right in this place, he said.

Elijah hoped that would stay true.

For himself, Elijah was doing fine. He had proved to be a good undertaker and was a founding member of the Nauvoo carpenter's guild—officially, the House of Carpenters of the Town of Nauvoo—and a generally respected Latter-day Saint. There was no argument at all in renewing his certificate as a seventy, signed again by Zebedee Coltrin. The white Mormons seemed to full accept and even admire him, perhaps because he had seen them in their pained, vulnerable moments, perhaps because they needed him.

Granted, there were still plenty of Saints who either owned blacks the same way they owned ox teams or thought slavery was God's will—even showed him the Prophet's own words in the *Messenger and Advocate*: "The Negro is to be 'a servant of servants unto his brethren.'" But what else did they expect Brother Joseph to say back then? Why, that was years ago when they were in slave country, threatened by slavers with boiling tar and feathers!

Anyhow, Elijah had seen in his own life how a person can change, how a person can grow. You understand things according to your light, and that light was always getting brighter in this Restoration, new things coming all the time—new promises, new fulfillments, just like Nauvoo itself. Brother Joseph had said to a group of priesthood holders in Kirtland, "You know no more concerning the destinies of this church and kingdom than a babe upon its mother's lap." That's what they all were—babes in the faith. So who were they to name-call and label and box up one another? The Prophet had said the Church would fill the world, which meant

Africa too, and all the races of man. "People from every land and from every nation," Brother Joseph had said, "the polished European, the degraded Hottentot, and the shivering Laplander— persons of every tongue and of every color shall with us worship the Lord of Hosts in his Holy temple." Elijah remembered all those words, even the complicated ones. Elijah remembered that no one got left out. And he had his own personal assurance in Father Smith's blessing: "You shall be made equal to your brethren."

So when exactly would equality happen? Next year? Tomorrow? Next life? And where? Heaven? Nauvoo? Or just in the human heart as it changed itself for better? People could pick and choose what the Prophet said to support their own schemes, but Elijah knew how Brother Joseph responded when asked what he'd advise a new Mormon with a hundred slaves: "Set them free—educate them and give them equal rights." Freedom was God's way and the Prophet's way, and that wasn't likely to change anytime soon.

Isaac didn't fret over such questions. A Mormon, yes he was, but he still lived moment to moment without a solid feel for the future. Nauvoo was a good place for him now, mostly because there were parties. Not being an undertaker, there was nothing solemn amongst the Mormons that Isaac paid mind to. What he heard was music— two bands' worth. What he saw were corn-husking parties, quilting parties with supper after, cotillion parties, Christmas parties, New Year's parties, riverboat tours, and dancing under a full moon. It was a merry life in good company. Granted, he was usually serving the food before he was eating it, but it was still a better life than the one he had left behind. If the parties stopped, and things suddenly got nasty for blacks in Nauvoo, no one could predict where Isaac might head off to, but he was content for now. More than content. He liked being Mormon.

Elijah imagined he himself would stay in Nauvoo forever, though he couldn't fathom making coffins the rest of his life.

Changes were coming, though, for trouble had followed Brother

Joseph across the Mississippi. Just when it looked like the Saints had found home and peace, ugliness set in. Maybe it just took the devil that long to find them again.

It started in June 1841 when Brother Joseph visited Governor Carlin at his home in Quincy. News came back to Nauvoo that right after the visit the Prophet had been arrested by a posse. No one knew why this time. Debt matters saved up from the Kirtland years, most likely. Or charges of adultery, plurality of wives. Or maybe agitating slaves. The accusation itself was not clear, but the need was. So Elijah and six white men, Mormons all, set themselves towards Quincy to make a rescue.

At least one of the men, Bill Hickman, had a reputation for violence. He would be good at a righteous rescue of the Prophet, even if it involved bloodshed. Like Hickman's good friend, Porter Rockwell—that long-haired, till-death-do-us-part-I'll-shoot-anyone-between-us—guard of Joseph Smith, Brother Bill was rumored to have been a Danite back in Missouri, one of the mysterious band of vengeful angels who took it upon themselves to protect the Saints' rights with muskets and gun powder.

There were those who said the Danites didn't exist. Elijah Abel thought they probably did exist and probably should. In fact, he wanted to ask Brother Bill if a colored man could join up. But he didn't ask. A good Mormon didn't talk about Danites, especially to a fellow who might be one. Hickman seemed capable of anything, though, and Elijah was glad to have him on board.

The river winds were fierce.

Elijah was not quite as tall or as heavy as the dark-haired, thick-browed, jaw-whiskered schoolteacher Hosea Stout, who was also part of the rescue troop, but he was considerably stronger anyway. So he took the skiff oars, fighting not just the rapids but powerful gusts that spat into his eyes and worked against his arms. The devil was riding these waters, that was clear—kicking the currents into froth. The devil had cursed the river, given it a mad case of rabies.

Fast, foamy water was trying to bite anyone who'd brave it. And Elijah and the others were loyal enough to take it on.

They made Quincy by dusk, only to learn that Brother Joseph had already been returned to Nauvoo in the company of two officers. Still, he'd do it again if he was called to, Elijah said as he rowed the skiff back Nauvoo-wards. The Prophet would get persecuted over and over, and God would deliver him over and over, and Elijah would ford any rivers between Joseph Smith and safety. He'd fight any man fist and skull to protect Brother Joseph.

He hadn't been present in Hiram years ago, when the Prophet was tarred and feathered and clenched his teeth against a vial of acid held at his lips—which was how his front tooth got chipped and why Brother Joseph spoke with a little whistle. But if he had been there, he would've answered the mob. Anyhow, he liked to imagine he would've. At the very least, he'd do his undertaking duties the best way he could, even if he hated death and even if it was the Prophet's own family (which meant Elijah's too) dying.

Which it was again, come August.

The deaths started with Brother Joseph's youngest brother, Don Carlos Smith, twenty-six years old.

Elijah had known him, having worked on the Kirtland Temple at his side, and having served in the same mission territory up north. Just two weeks previous to death's call, Don Carlos had been administering to the sick, commanding The Destroyer to depart in Jesus' name, the sick to arise and walk. And now Don Carlos was claimed by swamp fever, his six-foot-four frame gone bony, skin turned from pink with green shadows to yellow with purple ones. He had become a limp, heavy sack of flesh and blood, bound for the tomb. Bound.

Don Carlos was the first corpse to haunt the undertaker.

Elijah dreamed of him right after the death night, while the body was laid out and the casket not quite finished. This was his first ghost-visit since he got to Nauvoo. It would not be his last.

Though Elijah was in his own bed, the dream sent him to Don Carlos's side. The dead man's skin glowed, as if all his goodness was radiating from his remains. He had been laid out well, eyes closed, mouth almost smiling.

No, his mouth *was* smiling, his eyes fluttering, and Elijah knew they were burying this man premature. He ran for a mirror and held it before Don Carlos's mouth. Sure enough, the mirror misted.

"Aw, no," moaned Elijah. "Aw, no! How we done this?"

Don Carlos's pale lips worked themselves into limberness, and then he spoke in his soft, familiar, friendly voice. "How's the coffin coming, Brother 'Lijah?"

"Oh. Good coffin," Elijah answered. "One of my best." This was not entirely true, as most of Elijah's nails had gotten rusted by the damp air—a nail's way of taking in malaria. He had ordered new ones from Jeremiah Bingham, the nearest blacksmith, but what with all the construction, there was a line of people needing nails. He wouldn't get his for some time. "Only—" Elijah started.

"Only what?"

"Only—look—you premature dead! You ain't dead!"

"Dead enough," said Don Carlos. "The nails? How are the nails?"

He was panicking. "Fine."

"I hope so. If I should break out of the box underground, I should certainly have to haunt you."

"Aw, you wouldn't do that, would you? You be my brother!"

"Wouldn't want to. But would. As punishment."

"You'd do that?"

"Oh, yes. So build it strong."

"Strongest ever," Elijah dreamed himself saying.

He was sweaty waking up, which he did long before dawn. He went back to the coffin to place more rusty nails. Come morning, he went to Don Carlos and held a mirror to the mouth. There was no mist. Two hours later, he carted the finished coffin to its purpose.

There were full military honors at Don Carlos's gravesite. The Prophet looked as strong as ever Elijah had seen him, not bowed by grief as when Father Smith had died. Moved by it, but not bowed. This was strength Elijah envied and pretended at, but he knew he didn't have it like Joseph did. Not when his dreams could spook him into losing sleep and hammering rusty nails like his life depended on every one.

Isaac James thought the military honors made the best fun since cold butter. Rifle shots and all the Nauvoo Legion in uniform, including Lieutenant General Joseph Smith, who even wore a feather in his hat and toted a sword.

"I wants that at my funeral," Isaac told Elijah.

"Don't talk on dying." Elijah was suited up in black, looking exactly like his job. Even his cravat was black.

"I wants it."

"Naw, you doesn't. Ain't no use dying if you can help it. Even if you gets everyone dressed in their fanciest. You ain't seen what I seen." He was thinking not just on the haunting but on the last moments of Don Carlos's life, which he had witnessed: painful, raspy breathing with lungs that wouldn't open for air. He had stood by the body after measuring it, as family and friends gathered, their faces pinched into mourning like it was a too-tight mask.

At the moment, Elijah was tired through with death.

"I goin' die some time. We all is," said Isaac. "I just saying I wants a good celebration like this one here. Can't you smell the gingerbread?"

Elijah couldn't. Death was stuffed up his nostrils.

A week later, Brother Joseph's son—also called Don Carlos—died, followed soon after by Hyrum's little boy and namesake. Elijah measured and coffined them both, and one by one, they visited his dreams. He was being haunted steady, like someone was trying to move or kill him.

Still, he played his part as undertaker, never mentioned the ghosts, and got to know Smith tears better than anyone's. He hadn't seen Sister Emma dry-eyed in a month.

There was no letting up of the trials, not even from God. The Saints kept saying, "Whom the Lord loveth, he chasteneth," but Elijah was feeling *enough is enough,* ain't it?

Which was the very thought in his head when he laid eyes on The Man once more.

Was it another dream, the man with the hate-eyes in Nauvoo? Maybe Elijah was taking in the swamp fever and it had perched on his brain, making him see things that weren't there, as the delirious dying did.

He looked again.

No, The Man was for real, and he was in Nauvoo. For whatever reason—and Elijah thought the reason was surely himself—The Man had come to Nauvoo, looking hungry and mad and still so full of hate it shone off his skin like skunk spray. He was probably carrying those old handbills, Elijah thought. Handbills and lies.

Maybe God had let Elijah get haunted as a sign for him to get out whilst he still could, before it was his own box getting cut and nailed, his own body getting measured.

As the last straw, Elijah Abel was called in to visit with Brother Alex Burke, a gangly, pious convert from New Hampshire who loved preaching loud and strong. You wouldn't imagine a voice could boom forth from such a frame as Burke's, but it did, though there was something practiced and empty in his sermons. He wondered once if Joseph Smith might have been referring to Alex Burke the time Brother Joseph said, "You don't have to bray like a jackass to be heard of the Lord." Seemed Alex Burke liked the sound of his voice maybe even better than the words he was speaking.

Elijah assumed he was being invited to visit with Brother Alex over some ecclesiastical matter. Perhaps he would be offered another mission call.

No. The subject was a white woman, the mother of a dead child

Elijah had boxed up. As undertaker, he had said a few polite things to the woman—Sister Carter, a widow in her forties—but couldn't remember much more than an exchange about the weather and the coffin wood. Brother Burke, seated behind a desk, suggested there maybe had been more, that Elijah had been far too friendly with Sister Carter, who was "white as a lily, and not to be defiled by the touch of any Negro finger." Alex Burke's face was upturned and reverent-looking like this was holy scripture, not a gut-kick insult.

Elijah thought, *Well, I didn't exactly mistake her for colored, sir.* He said only the last word of this thought, making it a question: "Sir?"

"Amalgamation is against the ways of God Almighty," Brother Burke stated, again like this was a verse found somewhere in the book of Luke or Matthew.

"Sir?" Elijah repeated, reminding himself that this was the very man who had sweated beside him in the Nauvoo quarry, gathering stone for the temple. Elijah had brought him water once when Brother Alex looked set to faint. If Alex Burke could say such things with the same voice he used to quote Bible, then who *was* Alex Burke? There were some white folk—like The Man who wore his hate like sheen—who you felt were hiding something monstrous under their faces, that if you peeled away the top layer of skin you'd find not a person but a wolf. And here before him was this Church leader. And dear Lord, who was this man? This wavy-haired, bushy-browed, flabby-cheeked Mormon man—who was he?

"Punishable by death in some cultures," Alex Burke said.

Elijah almost laughed. Punishable by death in you-name-the-city *white* cultures, he almost said. He had certainly seen it. Seen a man lynched over the accusation.

Elder Elijah Abel answered in his quiet, slave voice. It half-surprised him to find that voice so ready. (How long since he had used it?) "I never did intend no harm," he said. "Don't remember layin' a finger on so much as her glove . . . sir."

"Punishable by death," Alex Burke repeated.

"Yessir," said Elijah.

Burke dismissed him with a smile that looked harmless as a dove but which Elijah knew for sure was poison as a snake bite.

Thinking to complain over the false accusation and to demand some protection, Elijah went straightway to Brother Joseph at the Mansion House. Emma answered and directed him to the Prophet, who was seated in the parlor. But Elijah said none of what he had been practicing in his head. All he said was, "Time I get my mind out of the grave, ain't it?" His voice had filled out now; it wasn't the slave voice, which had returned to its hiding place somewhere down south.

Joseph smiled. "Hello, Brother Elijah."

"Time I find me a wife too, ain't it? Colored wife, of course." He wondered how the years had used Nancy. Their baby had died; he knew that and thought it was probably a mercy. Surely God knew where Nancy was and might guide Elijah there. It could well be Cincinnati, Ohio.

Joseph said nothing but motioned him inside and offered him a seat.

"There ain't no woman here for me, Brother Joseph." He sat, then stood, then paced a step. "And I'd never—." He knew what stories must've been spreading about him. Even if the Prophet didn't believe a word of the rumors, even if the Prophet gave a whole sermon at the Grove on the subject of Elijah's innocence, the stories would sit in Nauvoo's air like mildew. "Time I head back Ohio ways," he said. Then he waited.

No response.

"I'd do missionary work there too," he went on. "I believe I proved myself a pretty fine missionary."

The Prophet nodded.

"Besides, there's other members of the House of Carpenters." He was pacing steady now. "Of course I know, when we first come to

Nauvoo, you was in powerful need of my skills. There wasn't much of nobody else could work up woods the way I could." Elijah had to grin at this, because it was so true and it made him so proud.

The Prophet nodded again, still smiling.

"But times has changed. We got us a bunch of fine wood smiths now. Why, they can make coffins every bit as strong as mine . . . mostly."

Brother Joseph's smile widened. This was the look the Prophet wore when he challenged someone to a bout of wrestling or a stick pull. Elijah had been thrown more than once by the Mormon prophet. He didn't feel like eating dirt just now, so he quit pacing and stepped back. He stood behind a maple wood chair, facing Joseph Smith.

Joseph didn't move and didn't speak.

Elijah bowed his head. "I know why God wanted me undertaking, Brother Joseph. It was a good thing. I'm grateful." He lifted his eyes. "Only now's time for me to move on." He sighed long and felt his blood heat down his neck, pulse behind his ears. "And I ain't never laid no finger on no white woman, and I wouldn't."

At last the Prophet responded. "I understand that, Brother Elijah."

"I want your blessin'," Elijah said, "before I leave."

The answer was, "All right."

So Elijah knelt, and Joseph Smith laid his hands on the head of the best undertaker Nauvoo would ever know, releasing him to a new life in Cincinnati, Ohio.

Later that evening, Isaac asked Elijah to find two wives—one for Mr. Abel, and one for Mr. James.

The next morning, without even a farewell party, Elijah left Nauvoo, hauling his belongings in a single sack. He had enough money for passage on a steamboat but chose to go horseback anyway. Brother Joseph provided the horse.

Elijah would find a wife, but only one, and not for Isaac. Isaac

James would get himself a wife too, though not by hunting one down. The Lord would provide. His wife-to-be would come to Nauvoo herself. You might have guessed her name already: Jane Elizabeth Manning.

NOTES

The chapter title, "All Creatures of Our God and King," is from the title of hymn number 347 in *Hymns for the Family of God*.

As we have suggested in the text, a number of Saints from the South owned slaves, including Charles Rich, who owned at least six.

The statement by Joseph Smith "People from every land . . . and color," is from "Report of the President," *History of the Church*, 4:213.

The statement by Joseph Smith "Set them free—Educate them & give them equal Rights" is recorded by Willard Richards in his journal (quoted in Hill, *Joseph Smith*, 383). It is a response Joseph Smith gave Orson Hyde when asked what advice the Prophet would give a man coming into the Church with one hundred slaves.

The descriptions of Nauvoo in its burgeoning days are drawn from Hill, *Joseph Smith*, especially 372–73.

Elijah Abel, accompanied by Hosea Stout, Tarleton Lewis, William Hickman, John Higbee, Uriel Nickerson, and George Clyde, attempted to rescue Joseph Smith in early June after his arrest in Quincy. This attempt is recorded by Joseph Smith in *History of the Church*, 4:365.

The life of Don Carlos Smith is described in *History of the Church*, 4:398–99.

The statement by Joseph Smith "You don't have to bray like a jackass to be heard of the Lord" is quoted from Truman Madsen's lectures on audiocassette, *Joseph Smith the Prophet*.

We don't know exactly why Elijah Abel left Nauvoo for Cincinnati when he did; we have fictionalized a realistic motivation for his departure and made up the name Alex Burke. Certainly, the Mormon attitude towards "amalgamation" was typical of that of most Americans during this time. It seems significant that Elijah Abel was not in Nauvoo when the full temple endowment was given.

The Mannings

13

THE GOSPEL TRAIN

Take counsel together . . . for God is with us.
ISAIAH 8:10

Jane did enjoy preaching the gospel—especially to her family, which she did over a year's time after she was baptized. She kept her new religion a secret from the Fitches during this year, so she didn't get to the Mormon meetings often. But that was about to change.

The Manning family seemed to enjoy listening to Jane's gospel talk, especially Lew, though he kept breaking into giggles. Baby Sylvester, a fat little boy now who could outrun the chickens, was more interested in the ball of rag-cloth Jane had brought from the Fitches than anything she had to say. He called Phyllis Mama and called her Jane ("Zane," he pronounced it). Still, they had a relationship, though not exactly a mother-son one. But that would change.

Phyllis didn't usually comment while Jane preached, but eventually she concluded it felt like a good gospel and thought she'd join. The day Phyllis said that, Lew—lanky as a cornstalk and suddenly taller than Jane (she didn't get to see him all that often)—he just giggled. Then he announced he had been a Mormon two weeks now. Jane tried hitting him for keeping that secret. He dodged her, so she swung a pillow at his stomach and sent him sprawling to the floor, giggling still.

"Look at you," she scolded in a mock-mad voice. "You think you one big man to go change religion and not even tell nobody. Look at you! You easy to knock over as a dead dog!"

"I been goin' tell you," he said. "And how you know about knockin' over dead dogs anyhow? That your new scheme?"

"You just stop that gigglement. This be serious business here." She frowned. "And you the only dead dog I ever knock over." She stuck out her tongue and broke into her own giggle. "I'll be, Isaac Lewis Manning! You done that! Before I even give my ear to Elder Wandell, you done that!"

"I done it, Jane. Baptized by the hand of Elder Albert Merrill, that's me." He sat up proudly and spread his face into a grin.

"I'll be! I think you makes me happy."

Between satisfied chuckles, Lew asked her if she knew the Mormons were gathering in Illinois, a place the Prophet (and he named him right—Joseph Smith, sure enough) was calling Nauvoo. Himself, he planned on going there. He stood and puffed his chest out. He had figured on going alone, but they'd all just as well move together, as a family.

Jane sat on the rope-bed—the only real furniture in this one-room cabin—and breathed a long, loud sigh. She wiped her mouth, thinking hard. She wasn't sure she could move so far away. Wasn't sure she should, not without talking to Mrs. Fitch first. And she'd have to uproot Sylvester. This was no easy decision.

"Colored folks goin' too? You sure?" she asked her brother.

"Everyone goin', Jane. All the Saint folk: black, white, brown, purple, green, if they is some. This be one complete gatherin', ain't you been told?" His voice, well into its man-change but not established yet, squeaked.

She remembered something about Zion. Elder Wandell had described it. She had thought it was a state of mind or heart, not some city in Illinois. And since she hadn't gone to meeting much in the last while, she had never heard the name Nauvoo. At least she couldn't recall hearing it.

"How we get there?" she asked. "I ain't got no money to speak on."

"You got you some good legs last I looked," Lew said.

"Well, you'd best not look 'less you ready to die this instant."

"They's groups goin' all the time. They take the steamer, canal boats, coaches. They gets there."

Phyllis cleared her throat. She stood up straight, like she had a load of wash balanced on her head. This was her important posture. She was set to speak.

Phyllis mostly worked with her hands and fingers, not her mouth. She had been a slave, and talking had never bought her any favors. Phyllis had learned to save up words like some folks save up pennies. So when she stood to make a speech, the world stopped to listen. At least the world in that cabin did.

"Or we could walk," Phyllis said. "If this be the true gospel, and Nauvoo be a good place, it don't much matter how we gets there." She spoke the words like a hymn that ought to finish "amen."

"I think I better have me a long talk with Mizz Fitch," said Jane.

But the decision had been made. This family was moving.

So it was time for Jane to tell the Fitches she was a baptized Mormon. Maybe now she'd get her first lash of cowskin.

At first, the old widow just stared, eyes wide as raw eggs. Then her face puckered, and she sank into her deep-cushion chair, wailing, "Oh, Jane, now you've really done it. The devil has grabbed you good, and he's pulling you into that fiery place. And after all I've done for you!"

Jane had seen Mrs. Fitch weep many times before, so this was nothing new. Truth told, Jane had learned to ignore most of her miz-zus's tears, because they came so often and so fast.

She tried to excuse herself from the room, but the widow would have none of that. "You stay right here, girl. I haven't done with you!" Mrs. Fitch pushed herself from the chair and headed for the door, set to block Jane's exit. Certainly this was cowskin time. Which meant that the very moment had arrived for Jane Manning to leave her employment.

Nauvoo, Illinois. What a good name!

Mrs. Fitch stayed in the doorway with her back to Jane. Finally the widow turned, eyes wet. "You are not to leave us," she said.

Jane heard Melissa's steps coming downstairs, heard Melissa say, "Let her go, Ma."

Mrs. Fitch turned towards her daughter and then back to Jane. "You'll go anyway, won't you," she murmured.

"Yes, ma'am."

The widow stepped back.

"Good-bye, ma'am." Turning sideways to pass her mizzus, Jane gazed up at Melissa. This was likely the last time they would see each other. How Jane pitied that poor woman, trapped—sure as if she wore chains—in her mama's house! "Thank you," Jane breathed to Missy. Then she walked out the front door and started her last trip home.

At her mother's house, Jane announced that the Mannings should all leave Connecticut as soon as possible and head towards Zion. She had just up and burned her bridges, she said.

Phyllis had already put her house up for sale. Once Phyllis's mind was made up, it didn't get unmade.

So the whole Manning brood would go to Nauvoo—Mama Phyllis and every one of her children: Jane, Lew, Angeline, Lucinda, Sarah and her husband, Anthony Stebbins, and the baby of the family, Peter. A new life was opening for all of them. Elder Wandell was back in the vicinity. Surely he would help them.

It wasn't until hours later that Jane realized most of her dresses were still at the Fitches. She was picturing herself in rags, hitting her head for being stupid, when a knock sounded. There stood Widow Fitch, holding all of Jane's clothes and looking mad enough to do violence. The mistress had never in her life come out to this colored household. A rich white woman did not do such a thing.

Jane curtsied. She wondered if Mrs. Fitch was holding the dresses for ransom or if she might be hiding an arrest paper under the calico.

"I thought you'd want these," said the mistress. Her face, her voice, and her arms were stiff.

"Thank you, ma'am."

The widow stepped back and raised her brows. Jane wondered if she was expected to pay for her own clothes.

"Ma'am?"

"I thought you might at least have told Melissa good-bye." Mrs. Fitch began blinking. Yes, yes, the tears.

"I meant to," Jane said.

The mistress folded her fat arms and waited another moment. "I thought you might at least have thanked us for the opportunities we've afforded you by giving you a place in our household." She looked skyward. It struck Jane that such a pose took away Widow Fitch's double chin. If she could look up all the time, she'd hardly appear fat at all.

"Thank you, ma'am."

"I believe we have not been ungenerous."

"Not ungenerous at all."

"And perhaps you might have finished the ironing before your departure." This was the disappointed, why-do-I-tolerate-you scold.

"I'm sorry, but I been called away."

"Yes, I've heard tell that the converts to this new, this new— this so-called religion, or perhaps idolatry is the better term—that most of you will be leaving Connecticut." She lowered her eyes and made a tight smile. Her double chin found its place again.

"We are makin' ready to leave."

"Because I care deeply about your soul, as you know I do, I have come to invite you to stay. No one has sent me. I have come of my own accord to invite you to return to our household as though you were our own kin. No mention will be made of any of this silliness. All will be forgiven." The tight smile got bigger. The chins vibrated.

It was Jane who stepped back now. "You are very kind, Mizz Fitch. You know you are kind. Everyone knows that, and nobody will soon forget it, for you surely won't let them. But I've chose my path."

The widow gathered herself quickly. "Yes, and I am giving you an opportunity to choose again. Jane, don't go with this group of blasphemers. I have done my best. You know I have."

"All the whole world know that."

"I have forgiven your sins."

"Yes, ma'am. We all know that. We won't be forgettin' that any-time this century."

Widow Fitch knit her brow. "You're not—Jane, you're not mocking me, are you?"

"Me, ma'am? Oh, no!"

"Because you know I have tried to give you God's word—despite—. Heaven knows, I have taken you in rain and sun to the arms of Reverend Sylvester—"

"Actually, ma'am, he done that all hisself." She couldn't resist this and had to squeeze her lips to keep them from smirking.

"Pardon me?"

Jane backed up another step, reminding herself to invite no anger, to tempt no white man or white woman beyond what they were able to bear. "Yes indeed, you showed me Reverend Sylvester's church. Why, I named my boy after the good reverend! His example be that fine!"

"It's not too late."

"Thank you for my dresses. You can tell everyone how you brung me my dresses—my, my, visitin' us out here!—and all the world will know you for the good-hearted, brave woman you be. And thank you for all the care you give me, and please tell Melissa good-bye and I don't hate either one of you and I feel tender especially towards Missy, and please forgive me not finishin' up all that ironin', but they be all sorts of black girl—even some poor white girl—they iron good as me, and they surely appreciate such a right-hearted, forgivin', brave woman as yourself, Mizz Fitch."

The widow stood folding and unfolding her arms and blinking out tears. "So. You're determined as always. Perhaps I shouldn't be surprised."

"You have experience with me, ain't that true?" Jane smiled. The widow did not return her smile.

"I do indeed. So you're going with this group of—people?"

"Yes, ma'am."

"Jane Elizabeth Manning." In Mrs. Fitch's mouth, it had become the name of despair.

Jane looked at her mistress long and hard. "Yes, ma'am," she said in her own, strong, willful voice, no more restraints. She felt as peaceful and certain as just after her baptism. "I am goin' with the Latter-day Saint people."

"Don't you—"

"This here be free country. And Connecticut be a free state even to the black race, and my heart tell me—"

"Please don't finish that. Despite your decision, you must not back-talk me, girl. That is not your place."

Jane hugged her dresses so her hands wouldn't go where they wanted to—around the mizzus's neck. "My heart tells me go."

Widow Fitch looked skyward again. She wept for a full minute before speaking, her cries somewhere between hiccups and bird chirps. "Then, Jane," she managed, "though I love you nearly as well as if you was one of my own babies, I can only curse your steps." She sprawled her hand over her mouth and cried, "May God forgive you and put thorns in your way so you will feel the heat of his wrath and swing yourself full around." She turned and walked fast to her surrey, weeping like a mauled kitten.

"Thank you, ma'am," Jane called after her. "Very good of you! You give my best regards to Melissa! And you be careful ridin' home!"

And with that, Jane Elizabeth Manning closed the door.

NOTES

The chapter title, "The Gospel Train," is from Burleigh, *Spirituals*, 115.

Carter (*Negro Pioneer*, 13) reports Albert Merrill as the missionary who baptized Isaac Lewis Manning, though the year she gives for his baptism—1835—is clearly in error, "since Albert Merrill himself was not converted until December of 1841" (Wolfinger, "Test of Faith, in *Social Accommodation*, 158).

Henry Wolfinger explains the Mormon converts' devotion to "gathering to Zion" as follows: "In other religions, conversion might be the final stage of professing faith, but in nineteenth-century Mormonism, it was but an initial step followed by the convert's departure from 'Babylon' to 'Zion,' where he might join the faithful in the work of establishing the kingdom of God on earth" ("Test of Faith," in *Social Accommodation*, 128). Wolfinger quotes from a letter by Charles Wandell, written in Connecticut at the time of the Mannings' conversion: "The brethren here are very anxious to emigrate to Illinois; so you may expect to see all of us in Zion this Fall, that can possibly get there" (128).

That a year passed between Jane's baptism and the Mannings' trek to Nauvoo is stated in Jane's history, recorded in Wolfinger, "Test of Faith," in *Social Accommodation*, 151.

14

THE FAMILY OF GOD

*As God hath said, I will dwell in them . . . and
they shall be my people.*
2 CORINTHIANS 6:16

The Manning journey plan was simple: canal boat to Buffalo,
New York, where they'd meet up with the other Saints; river boat
to Columbus, Ohio, where Charles Wandell would help them pay
their fare; steamer to Nauvoo, Illinois.

The porter at the Buffalo dock was a sweaty-faced mulatto. He
was in his mid-teens like Lew, near the same height, but built like
a block. Everything about him was square: jawbone, shoulders, hips.
Even his words sounded like they kept corners. He spoke for the
captain: The Mannings' fare had to be paid right there in full if such
a fine steamboat were to take on so many Negroes.

"And who be you?" Lew demanded. "White man's lackey?"

The porter made slivers of his eyes. "Colored man pay here now,
not there later."

"But not the half-colored man?" Lew had always been feisty,
especially around fellows his own age. He knew they all were being

insulted by this teenager—not even a grown man, let alone a white one—keeping them off the boat.

Jane tried to hush her brother. He hushed her right back.

"Don't argue," she pleaded.

Of course Lew ignored her. "How far to Illinois?" he asked the mulatto, though it sounded more threat than question.

The porter set one foot onto the boat ladder and spread his mouth into a square snarl. "Eight hundred miles. Only that far. Your woman be right. You shouldn't argue too much. Things happen."

"Ain't my woman," Lew sneered. "She my sister!"

The boat whistle blew so loud and so long and so near that the Mannings had to clap their hands over their ears. After the horn's blast, Lew shouted to the porter: "You ought to stoke that thing better so it don't belch! Only thing makin' a badder noise is you flappin' your gums!"

The mulatto set his other foot on the ladder. He had delivered the message. This particular family would not be riding this particular boat.

Stepping forward, Jane called, "I put my trunk of clothes on board here. Paid for it. Will my trunk get to where I might retrieve it, sir?"

Lew hissed at her, "Don't call him sir. He ain't nothin' to be respected!"

Like something mechanical, the mulatto turned his head, sizing Lew up with slow eyes. He moved his gaze towards Jane, nodding once.

"I'll have my trunk in Nauvoo then, sir?"

The only answer was the whistle sounding again. The boat let out a geyser of steam and started shaking, coming to life. The water-wheel churned the river into froth.

And so it was on that chilly October morning that the Mannings started walking.

They slept wherever they could find shelter, often under bridges or pine boughs. It was a week later, after a fair snow, that Jane noticed the soles of her shoes had worn clear through. Her stockings were like spiderwebs. Sarah was in the same situation. Angeline's shoes were somewhat better, because her steps were so delicate. And Lucinda's shoes, the pair she had saved up six months' wages to buy, were just beginning to wear thin. Syl's were in the best shape, since he was getting carried most of the way, though they were getting raggedy. Peter, Anthony, and Lew were wearing boots which, being more sturdy, held up for a time. Before long, though, holes began showing in them too. Blisters answered the invitation, and took the place of leather, swelling, then bursting, leaving tender skin to get raked by the miles. Eventually, the Mannings could trace their steps by the blood on their path. Their footprints showed like rusty stencils in the snow.

It was Mama—Phyllis Manning Treadwell—who suggested out loud they ask for a healing, for every one of them knew they wouldn't make it on their own, not without God giving a miracle. They fell to their knees, and Jane started the prayer: "Father, we honor you, and we know you are with us and you brought us this far for a purpose. But Father, our feet are bloody, and we can't go on this way. We need your help. We need you to make a way as you made a way for Israel in the desert. We need you to deliver us same way you delivered Daniel. You always provide for your people, and we need you to provide for us. Bless our feet and heal them so's we can continue on our journey, Father. We know nothing is beyond your power. You have the means to provide all we need."

As Jane prayed, Sarah whispered, "Yes, Lord, we need your help, Lord." The other Mannings pleaded, "Make a way, Jesus" and "You know our needs."

Then they arose and began walking, feeling no need to wait. The Mannings knew their feet were being healed with every step. That had been confirmed in their hearts.

By the time they reached Illinois, they were a sight: tattered, dirty, bone tired. The women's head wraps were all dingy now. They had used these bandanas for washing themselves whenever they came across a horse trough or a stream. But their last washing had been a day ago, and the muddy trail they had crossed from Connecticut was etched like a map into every wrinkle on their faces: between their eyes, framing their mouths, crusting their brows like dirty snow. The men hadn't shaved since Buffalo, and their beards attracted every speck of grit in that cold air. Anthony complained that he couldn't even spit clean anymore. Baby Syl walked sometimes, but they all took turns toting him. The women either shawled him to their backs or balanced him on a hip. The men carried him on their shoulders, and Syl's chubby hands would burrow into the coarse, matted hair that had not known a razor in months. All of them looked to be runaway slaves, which a sheriff on horseback accused them of the moment they arrived at Peoria. He had a day-old beard and a long, gingery mustache that twitched when he said, "Who you belong to?"

Sylvester was riding Jane's hip. She undid his arms from her waist and set him down, looking straight at the white man's ruddy face. She would do the talking this time. "Sir, we don't belong to nobody. We Connecticut Negroes. I worked for Mr. and Mrs. Joseph Fitch."

The Sheriff gave her a look that said he had never heard the name Fitch and cared less. "Show me your free papers." He was fingering his rifle.

"We don't have free papers, sir. We Connecticut Negroes," she said more loudly, just in case he was deaf.

"You are in the state of Illinois, gal. Now you may have heard we gone abolitionist over a lot of business set forth by a Mr. Elijah Lovejoy? Just you know, it ain't so." Yellow tobacco juice dripped from his mouth.

"Who, sir?"

"A dead man. Troublemaker when he was living."

"Lovejoy?" She cocked her head and scrunched her face to show how deep she was thinking. "I don't recollect knowin' that name."

"Point being, this ain't no abolitionist state. I need to see your papers or set you in jail till we can find out who you are."

Jane straightened herself, her side sore from toting Syl. "Sir, we ain't never been slaves." That was mostly true. It was true of all the Manning children. It wasn't true of Anthony. He *was* a runaway. He still had a master down in Kentucky and one little sister there, ten years old, name of Sallie Mae. Anthony had been saving up his money since he first made it to Connecticut, hoping to buy Sallie Mae's freedom.

The sheriff spat tobacco juice, just missing Jane's feet.

"We Connecticut Negroes," she repeated.

He spat again, a little closer to her feet, and swept his sleeve over his mouth. His eyes rested where his gun had already gone: on Anthony Stebbins.

Mama Phyllis stepped forward. "I once been a slave." Mama's voice was deep, a strong, singing voice, made to praise the Lord. Though he was still looking down on her, sitting like a king on that horse, something in the sheriff's face changed once she started talking. "Up Connecticut, all us was freed some time back. It come gradual, but it come. My children, they never know the bond."

The sheriff eyed her. She was the tallest of the women, nearly as tall as Anthony. "We have us a list of runaways, with full descriptions." He moved his eyes towards young Peter and then to baby Sylvester, who was holding Jane's hand. "Pickaninnies too," he said.

At that, Sarah spoke. "Please, sir. We just be followin' God to the promise land."

Jane rummaged into her blouse and took out the Church certificates which identified them all as members in good standing. "These the only free papers we got."

Sarah commenced whispering the softest prayer she could, too soft for this white man to hear above his own proud voice: "Lord

Jesus, don't let there be any trouble. Don't let this man take any of us into jail, and please protect my Anthony. Just don't let there be no trouble, Lord."

Her whispers did not miss the sheriff's ears, though. He had appeared deaf when Jane kept telling him they were free Negroes, but he managed to hear Sarah fine. He said, "That's right, gal. Don't let there be no trouble." Lowering the rifle, he bit off a twist of chaw from the plug in his vest. "Mormonites. Lawless, thieving, cannibalizing Mormonites. That's about worse than being runaway slaves," he muttered.

"Sir?" said Jane.

He chewed like a cow, brown-yellow juice dripping down his beard. "Good luck, gal." Touching his hat—from habit, you understand, not from respect—he returned the certificates. "The last Negroes went to Nauvoo was never heard of again. Mormonites look for black flesh so's they can boil it in oil and clean it off the bones. You might want to know that. I could be the last soul you see who wants to do you some good."

"By puttin' us in jail?" Jane used her most innocent voice.

He grinned, showing teeth yellow as his tobacco juice. "You just might wish I'da done it. You just might wish you'da had that kind of protection, once they light a blaze under you." Again he spat, but this time shot it to the other side of the road.

Jane answered strongly, "No, sir. Ain't no cannibals amongst the Mormon folk."

"And those words will look fine on your gravestone, gal." He touched his hat again.

"Could you tell us, please, which way to Nauvoo?" Jane asked.

When he stared at her this time, she stared right back. "You don't believe a word I've said, do you," he chuckled.

She shook her head.

"Straight ahead, about a hundred mile." He wiped his mouth and then spurred his horse. The hooves raised dust enough to set the Mannings coughing. But at least they were coughing out in the open air, not behind steel bars.

"Awake and arise from the dust," said Jane as soon as the sheriff and his horse became a speck in the distance.

"What?" Sarah's rust-colored dress was torn at both sleeves and the waist, like it really had tarnished. Her apron was gray as ash. Jane's dress, a brighter orange, wasn't much better, its hem all frayed and ripped. She had discarded her apron miles back.

"'Awake and arise from the dust.' My best scripture Elder Wandell taught me. Means open your eyes. Get out from the dirt some white man's animal loose. Set your sights higher than horse-shoes."

Sarah offered God a quick thanks for sparing them again and asked Jane, "But what if that lawman be right?"

"Right how?"

"What if the Mormons do be cannibals? What if they wants us down Nauvoo so's they can eat us?"

Hands on her hips, Jane wagged her head. "And what if your eyeballs fall out this very minute because you believe such rabbit droppings as that?"

"My eyeballs ain't fallin' out."

"Don't be too sure. They lookin' mighty unstable to me. They lookin' unstable to you, Anthony?"

"A little wobbly," he said. The words described his voice too. It was still trembly from the sheriff's threat of jail. Anthony knew full well that his capture could've meant the Carolinas.

"Wobbly and bugly, I say," Jane declared without any shiver at all in her words. She was determined to fight the shake out of her voice with all her strength and all her faith—and a good dose of teasing. That was the Jane Elizabeth Manning way. "Oh, yes, ma'am, they goin' pop certain. We goin' be walkin' our path, and Sarah's eyes, they goin' pop clean out."

Sarah slapped her hands to her face. "My eyeballs is fine!" She pressed them, then turned on her husband, shook her finger at him. "Anthony, you support my sister in making a mock of me, I's liable to do something drastic to you!"

Anthony let himself laugh some, then grabbed his stomach and laughed big—bigger than what Sarah's words deserved. His laugh was overhappy, shaking with relief, shaking out all the fear which had been throbbing down his chest when the sheriff's eyes and rifle were on him.

"And what if the Good Lord should look down," Jane went on, "and the Good Lord see you fall for that white-man lie, Sarah, and he make it rain pitchforks on your head alone whilst the rest of us stays bone dry?"

"It ain't goin' rain." But Sarah was looking skyward.

"Don't be too sure," Jane said like a ghost.

"Jane, that a cloud I see there?" Anthony asked. There was still a quiver in his voice, but it was a glad quiver, the leftovers of his laugh. "A cloud just above Sweet Sarah's head?"

Jane nodded. "For sure look like a cloud to me."

Sarah stamped the ground. "Anthony! I's warnin' you!"

"You the funnest woman on this wide earth to tease at, Mrs. Stebbins," Anthony giggled. "And you so pretty when you mad. You get bright stars in your eyes."

"Well, you goin' get stars in yours once you tease at me again." When he put his arm around her shoulders, she sighed, "What do we know about the Mormons, really?"

Jane picked up baby Syl and swung him to her hips again. "You a cannibal, Sarah?"

"Oh, now. Stop it."

"Well, is you? 'Cause I know you be a Mormon. I seen you come out the water myself. You come out hankerin' after human flesh for lunch?"

Sarah hummed and pursed her lips. "Not at first. Only recent."

"When?"

"Why, just a minute ago. I's lookin' at you, Jane, and I's thinkin'—my, my, you'd make fine eatin'. A little cucumber and salt, and you taste just right. Don' you think so, Anthony?"

"Cucumber? Naw. Onion and garlic. Hot peppers maybe. Make the spice to match the flesh, I say."

"You right, honey. Cucumber way too cool for Miz Jane's flesh."

"Anthony," said Jane, "both of you had better learn to keep your tongues from flaggin' like daisies in the wind."

And with that, they started walking again.

By now, the Mannings had spent what little money they had, and they had stretched it far as it would go, foraging whenever they could. Sometimes they'd come upon a garden full of half-frozen tomatoes. No farmer would care about frost-split fruit, and often as not, worms and bugs had already claimed the cracks. There was always some droopy part of the harvest the Mannings could take and eat, gleaning the fields just like folks did in the Bible. Besides that, Anthony was a fisherman. He could grab catfish with his bare hands and nab crawdads before they'd even think to dart into moss. This was a cold time, but there were still occasions when he could use his gifts, whenever there was a pond or stream not wearing a skim of ice. So here were the Mannings, almost to their destination, and none had starved.

It was another two or three miles before they hit their next obstacle: a brackish river with foam currents stinking of sulphur, like the water flowed all the way from hell. This was the path of swill and sewage. *It'll probably kill us with the runs, if it don't freeze us first,* thought Jane. There was no bridge, not even a rope or vine to swing across the water. So Anthony put Syl on his shoulders, and without a word, they all stepped in.

Cold. The river was ice lightning. Their teeth chattered so much they couldn't even comment on the shock, just press forward. Anthony rode Syl on his back. Peter dog-paddled at first, then showed he could swim. Scrawny runt of a boy though he was, Peter could sure swim, even through such cold. It was a good thing he could, for halfway across, the smelly water was up to their necks. It covered most of Sarah's face, she being the shortest, and she screamed. Jane took Sarah's hand and pulled at her until the worst was over and their heads were above water. Still, Sarah seemed to be floating more than walking, and the currents were so strong. It wouldn't take much to sweep her downstream and underwater, so Jane clung hard, dug her fingernails into Sarah's wrist.

Sarah was sobbing when they made it out the other side, and Jane waited for the thank-you. It was a long time before Sarah said a thing, though, her teeth were chattering so bad, and she kept heaving and spitting and crying.

"It's all right," Jane whispered over and over. "We made it out fine."

Sarah burped loud. Then she lowered her head and put her face in her hands. Jane figured she was praying a weepy thanks to God, and let her be. But Sarah's eyes, when they looked up, were angry, not prayerful. She said, "Jane, you scratch me like a tiger!"

Jane stared at her hard before managing a comeback: "Maybe I shoulda just left you in there, then."

"You'd let me drown?" Jane knew that if Sarah had had the strength, those words would've come with a slap. The two of them had fought since they were babies. The day their daddy died, Sarah started a good slap-fight with Jane like if they hit each other, they'd forget to be sad. That was Sarah's way, and she still hadn't outgrown it, even as a married woman.

Jane's tears started when she let herself think on what they had just survived. She didn't feel like fighting. Her words came soft. "I thought you would drown. Thought I lost you, Sarah." She looked skyward and prayed, "Oh, Lord, thank you for bringing us across that water!" Then back to Sarah, "If you had drowned, I don't know what I'd do."

Sarah panted. Her head wrap had come off, and her hair was

wet cornrows. "I guess then you'd marry my Anthony," she breathed. The whole front of her was one big mud streak from pulling herself up the riverbank.

"You don't think I can do better than him?"

Sarah didn't strike out as Jane thought she would. She said only, "I coulda died in that water. You did save me, you know."

"Me and the Lord, sure enough. And the Lord saved me too, for I'da died if anything happened to you."

Sarah wiped her eyes and appeared to be setting up to gush something loving. Instead she said, "And you just tell me what so wrong about my Anthony!"

Jane let out a good laugh. "Girl, he's a southern Negro. He's a use-ta-be slave!"

"Not no more. He mine now." Sarah tried for a smile. It seemed frozen too.

"Your lips gone purple," Jane said.

"Yours too. And that water taste something awful, don't it?" She kissed her sister's cheek and said, "I'd follow you anywhere, Jane."

Jane said, "I know that. And thank you for not hittin' me, Mrs. Stebbins."

"Well," said Sarah, "the day ain't over yet."

But the day was nearly over. The sun was setting behind the gray sky. It didn't make any colors, just sank. The sky got dark, then darker, then so dark they couldn't see a hand in front of them. They knew they had to stop soon and build a fire and were making ready to do so when they spied a pin-prick of light in the distance. They marched towards it, tripping over stiff weeds. Their clothes stayed wet, starched with cold. Still, long as they kept moving, the cold wouldn't kill them.

The light was shining from a cabin, but no one was there. How could they have seen a light, Mama Phyllis asked, when no one was home nor any lanterns burning?

None of the Mannings answered. They didn't need to.

The next morning, they found deer jerky hanging on the porch, which they decided angels must've left. It would be breakfast, lunch, and maybe dinner.

"How far you reckon we come?" Anthony asked.

Sarah answered. "Since yesterday? Ten mile? Twenty?"

"Syl, you want to try reckonin' the distance?" Jane asked her boy, knowing full well he wouldn't have any idea. She just wanted him to say something, for he hadn't talked in days, only let himself be carried. "What would you say? A lot of walkin'? Too much walkin'? More walkin' than you ever hope you do in your whole life?"

His answer was a weak cry.

"You sick?" she said.

He cried some more.

"Mama sorry about the cold, Syl. Mama so sorry." Sylvester looked at Phyllis when Jane said mama.

"Not much further," Sarah said. "Sheriff say one hundred mile yesterday, and maybe we gone halfway."

"Maybe we gone halfway of halfway of halfway," said Anthony, sliding into an old slave song to make the walk more pleasant:

> *We raise the wheat*
> *They give us the corn*
> *We bake the bread*
> *They give us the crust*
> *We sift the meal*
> *They give us the husk*
> *We peel the meat*
> *They give us the skin*
> *And that's the way*
> *They takes us in.*
> *We skim the pot*
> *They give us the liquor,*
> *And say that's good enough*
> *for a nigger.*
> *Walk over. Walk over.*

There they were, walking over icy sticks and frosty weeds, making their own path, chewing the jerky the angels had left. By nightfall, they were in a forest, frost falling heavy as snow. The best shelter they could find was under some bare poplars and half-dead pines. By morning, their clothes were starred with frost ferns.

"What I'd give for a good pair of shoes or leggin's," Jane moaned when she opened her eyes. She had slept with Sylvester in her arms, had arranged her face so she'd breathe down his neck all night, keeping him warm that way.

"We got shoes," Anthony said. "Our feets done turn to leather."

"I'd rather walk on cow leather than Jane leather," she said.

The sun was rising, the sky had cleared, and it wasn't long before the frost took to melting.

"Would you look at that blue!" Sarah said.

"Oh my, what a mornin'!" sang Anthony, "I could die happy on a mornin' like this."

Sarah hit him. "Don't you sing me no death song, Ant'ny!"

"'Tain't no death song! That be a praise song! You just don't want me singin'!"

"I just tired. Ain't ready for another day of my legs walkin' and your mouth singin'."

"My singin' make you tired?"

"My sore feets make me tired. Just thinkin' how much better it woulda been ridin' on that steamship. I'm just wishin' Lew treated that porter better."

Lew scowled. They had gone down this argument before. "You think if I done different, we'd be steamin' down the Mississipp 'steada walkin' barefoot?" His tones were asking for a fight. Like all the Mannings, he had had his share of fights with Sarah.

"Who say?" Sarah answered. She'd blame him if she were pushed to it, that was clear.

Lew frowned deep. "You blamin' me?"

"Who say?" she repeated. (Wouldn't take much of a push either.)

"Ain't my fault," he muttered.

"'Course 'tain't!" cried Jane. She could see where this conversation was headed and jumped in before the blows began.

Lucinda helped in her own way, saying, "This whole journey was Jane's idea anyhow!"

"This whole journey was the Lord's idea," Jane said. "I just let you in on the information out of the goodness of my heart."

"Well, thank you so much," Lew answered. "I might've liked it more if the Lord had provided you a map and a boat along with his idea."

Jane stopped in her tracks, trying to decide whether to slap Lew for disrespecting the Lord or suggest they all sing a hymn. She chose the hymn, and Phyllis commenced it: "There is a holy city." Phyllis's voice was strong and steady as long, low bells:

> There is a holy city,
> A world of light above,
> Above the starry regions,
> Built by the God of love.

It was Jane who started the "Thank you, Lords!" between verses. "Thank you, Lord," she said, "for makin' our feet hard as mule's hooves!"

Anthony added his own: "Thank you, Lord, for givin' that sheriff such bad spit aim so's none of us got it in the eye!"

Phyllis started the second verse:

> An Everlasting temple,
> And saints arrayed in white
> There serve their great redeemer
> And dwell with him in light.

"Thank you, Lord," Lucinda shouted, "for wakin' us up with that good, icy water, lest we fall asleep on the path!"

"Thank you, Lord," Sarah chimed in, "for inspirin' Lew's rude tongue so's we could all enjoy this good family togetherness."

"Thank you, Lord," Lew said, "for givin' me such fine control over my emotions that I ain't killed Sarah to this day and will probably make it to nightfall with clean hands."

They all commenced the third verse with Phyllis:

> The meanest child of glory
> Outshines the radiant sun;
> But who can speak the splendor
> Of Jesus on his throne?

Now it was Phyllis giving thanks, but hers came serious and calm and peaceful: "Thank you, Lord, for keepin' us safe in your shadow, for bringin' us peace in every moment of our trial, for givin' us every tiny thing we needs to make it through the hard times, just like you always done, Lord, in all your tender mercy."

They had sung the song twice when they came to a sign: La Harpe.

Jane said, "I think La Harpe be real close to Nauvoo." Then she saw a cabin, a new one.

They knocked. A young mother, face pale as her hair, answered and said, "There's sickness here."

"Who sick?" Lew asked.

"My daughter. Might be catchin'."

"You hear of Latter-day Saint people?" Lew said. He was talking like this cabin was church.

The woman answered, "I am one."

"We close to Nauvoo for sure!" Jane whispered.

The woman nodded. "Thirty miles." It seemed a chore for her to lift up her head after that nod.

"All us be Latter-day Saints," Lew said.

"If you wants it," Jane added, "we administer to your child."

"Others have attempted to heal her. Twice the elders have come," the mother said. "But you're welcome to try."

Jane was surprised that this white woman let them in without any more words or questions. There was trust among the Mormon folk, whites opening their doors to blacks who identified themselves only by their religion. This must surely be Zion!

The Mannings surrounded the sick girl, who was lying on a cotton-tick mattress, her skin a dead gray, a curly-headed, blonde child, no more than three years old, dressed only in a shift. Even her curls seemed heavy with disease.

"Beautiful baby," said Jane.

"Yes," breathed the mother.

"How she called?"

"Angeline."

"Ah," said Jane. "My sister got that name too. That sister right there." Angeline curtsied. "Good name," Jane went on. "Your baby got a angel name. Sick as she be, she look like a angel too. But I know for true you don't want to lose her."

"Oh no, I don't," said the woman in a soft, soft voice. "But I will. I'm trying to ready myself. God's calling."

"Who say that?" Jane said. "Ain't no black border around your door."

The woman looked away.

It was Jane who laid hands on the child and whispered into her ear, "Angeline—you needs faith to be healed, darlin'. You needs to believe in Jesus Christ, that he can heal you. And oh, I know he can. There's a whole group of us here knows it, and if the good Lord take a mind to it, child, he will. Now, Lord, you got it in your power to heal this baby. You's the one who gave her life in the first place. If you don't have any particular need of her, her mama do. Heal this child. Touch her with your outstretched hand. Let your power be felt all through her little body. Let her be renewed. Overcome whatever sickness be in her. Lord, we praise your name. We know you can do anything you have a mind to, Lord, and we ask you to touch this baby. In Jesus' name, amen."

After a long moment, the mother said, "That was beautiful. Others didn't talk to her that way."

"My sister got faith lots of folks ain't," Sarah whispered. "I tried dyin' myself two times, but Jane prayed like that, and I'm still here."

"Hush," breathed Lew. "Somethin' be happenin'."

"Open them eyes, darlin'," said Jane. She had kept her focus on the child this whole time, stroking the little arms and cheeks. "Come on. Get them eyelids open."

The lids fluttered, then blinked.

"You thirsty, li'l one?" Jane asked.

No response.

"You want a sip of water? Jus' blink your eyes so I know," Jane said.

"Angie?" said the mother.

The girl's lips parted, and her lids fluttered again.

Jane turned to the mother. "Get her some water."

The girl blinked twice.

The mother stepped towards her child, pushing Jane aside.

"Talk to your baby," Jane said and ordered Anthony to fetch the drink.

The mother was embracing her child and weeping.

"She be comin' back to us now," said Jane. "You just gots to let God do his work."

Mama Phyllis, who had been steadily praying, lifted her head at that.

"Wasn't that child's time," Jane said. "I felt that straight off. Little Angeline just need a touch of the Lord's hand."

Anthony returned with the dipper shortly, and the child parted her lips.

"All in God's good plan," Jane said. "God keep his own clock."

Several hours later, the Mannings were eating all the food the woman could find to offer them, which wasn't much. Her husband was on a Church mission in England, and food was hard to come by.

That night, the Mannings slept in front of a fine fire. The woman herself didn't sleep for many hours but stayed up, rocking in a cane chair, watching her daughter on the mattress. Finally Jane roused herself and went to her.

The woman looked up, and Jane knelt to be on her level. "We been through a miracle today, and I still don't know who you people are—your family name," the woman said.

"We're the Mannings," said Jane. "From Connecticut. On our way to Nauvoo to be with the Saints. I'm Jane."

"I'm Ruth."

"Sister Ruth, you been missin' rest for a long time. You been stayin' up with this child night after night, not wantin' to be asleep in case the Angel come."

"That is true."

"But the Death Angel is on other errands now, sister. You got to let yourself sleep. Come on now. You rest." Jane put her arm around the woman's shoulders, and Sister Ruth let her head lie on Jane's arm. "Go lay down beside your baby. I'll watch her the rest of the night."

The woman obeyed and almost instantly fell asleep beside her daughter.

The next morning, Ruth gifted them her own dresses. She had only four, besides what she herself was wearing but said it was the least she could do. "You gave me my daughter back," she said.

"Oh, no, ma'am," said Jane. "That was God."

Ruth's were not rich-looking clothes but certainly better than what the Mannings had been wearing. There were not enough for all to have one, and Jane declared her own threadbare dress was just fine and the one she truly wanted to wear into Nauvoo.

"My dress feel more like a symbol than clothes just now," she said.

"Well, it sure look more like somethin' simple than it do a dress," Sarah answered.

"A *symbol*," Jane said. "Like the marks in Jesus' hands?"

"Oh, like them wounds of God's." Sarah rolled her eyes. "You plannin' on wearing it forever, then? Showin' off them rips like they was prizes?"

"Just wearin' it to Nauvoo." Jane pressed it with her hands. "After my other clothes arrive in my trunk, I start my new life."

When the Manning family left the cabin two days later, little Angeline was sitting up in bed and eating full meals.

After a rainy time of more walking, the Mannings approached Nauvoo at last. The first sight they beheld—way off—was the unfinished temple: the finest building any of them had seen or ever imagined. From a distance, it looked like a white ant hill surrounded by busy workers. As they got closer, the hill took on form and sparkle and had a presence that made them want to kneel. The workers were sweaty-faced men in muddy clothes, mortaring stones, carving wood, and loading wheelbarrows. It was dusk and November, but not one of the laborers was wearing a coat. Their work kept them warm. And likely, God's light was burning inside them too.

"All them is Mormons," Jane said. "Every one of them! We home now, among our own."

"Thank you, Jesus," Phyllis said. "You brought us all the way."

"And look at that building!" said Jane. "They makin' it into something God will visit for sure!"

They had heard about the Nauvoo Temple. Charles Wandell had mentioned it as the place where the Saints received new names. Jane had not known what he meant by that, but she liked the sound of it. And oh my, how she loved the sight of it!

But as they stared up at the temple, they all felt other eyes staring at them and not necessarily enjoying the view. They turned and met the glares of some middle-aged white folks, two women and three men. Lew looked behind him to see what might be attracting such ugly focus from these people. Sarah whispered, "We must be a sight."

But Jane knew it wasn't their wet clothes drawing these stares, and she didn't have to check for anything behind them. She knew that look, and it shrank her. She had not anticipated any rebuff from the Saints. She ached to return her eyes to the temple—it was calling her! But that look crowded out the Spirit of the Lord's house. She thought to say, "Elder Charles Wandell baptized and invited us here. Do you know him?" But such words wouldn't matter. These people would not view the Mannings as fellow Saints but as Negroes. Even showing their certificates of membership would do nothing. The realization chilled her. Every part of her that had been lit up with warmth and hope went weak and cold. She readied herself for whatever was coming.

Anthony stepped back. Both the white women were clutching their men's arms.

Finally, Jane spoke up. "Good evening. Ma'am. Sir." Her voice was flat. She had wanted to say, "Good evening, brothers and sisters," but her mouth would not form the words.

One of the men asked, "Who you after?"

"We Mormon folk," said Jane. "We after—"

"You belong to somebody? All of you?"

"No, sir, none of us," said Jane. "We come—"

"Joseph Smith," said Anthony behind her. Surely that name would get them somewhere or at least soften the stares.

Jane hadn't been able to locate Joseph Smith's name in her mind for the past minute. She was glad for the prompt.

"Can you direct us to Joseph Smith's home?" she asked.

No one answered. But it seemed one of the workers had heard the question from a distance, for he strode towards them. He was a tall man with dark features and a sunburned face. He wiped his brow and then offered his hand. "You were with the Charles Wandell company, weren't you," he said.

"Yes, sir," said Lew.

"I am Brother Orson Spencer."

Jane went teary and silently thanked God for the word *brother*. Phyllis murmured, "Thank you, Lord."

Orson Spencer shook Lew's hand first and then Jane's. "We didn't know if you'd get here," he said. The hard-eyed Mormons left as Brother Orson set himself to shaking everybody's hands. He then guided them to Joseph Smith's Mansion House. Last month, said Brother Spencer, the Prophet had turned his house into an inn, because new arrivals always stopped there and stayed on a while. Surely they would all be welcome.

They followed him, Jane wiping her eyes every now and again. Before she could get too comfortable in this new welcome, though, she sensed more wary eyes watching them. At one point, she heard someone ask, "What's that bunch of negras doing here?" She exchanged a glance with Sarah and kept walking.

Then there stood the Mansion House: white as could be, eight windows on either side of the front door and one more window just above it, two red-bricked chimneys, and a huge, brick stable attached. Brother Orson knocked on the door.

The women took off their head wraps, since they were soaked through. Their hair was still neatly cornrowed.

A doe-eyed woman in black silk answered, taking in the whole sight at once. Her hand flew to her mouth, and her face moved towards amazement. "Walk in!" she said.

Anthony stepped back. (Slave habits die hard.) "What?" fell from his mouth like a soft belch.

"Come in!" the woman said. Her voice was kind.

Brother Orson addressed her. "Sister Emma, this is the Manning family. They were with the Charles Wandell group. I know you'll take good care of them. And if you'll excuse me, I need to return to the site before darkness sets full in." He bowed and departed.

"All of you come in!" repeated Sister Emma.

"Oh, ma'am," Jane sighed, "we so wet and so dirty!" In her Connecticut dress, Jane was the dirtiest of the lot, but they were all equally wet.

"Come in!" Emma Smith repeated, and they complied.

Then a man's voice, deep and sweet, intoned, "The world looketh on the outward appearance, but God seeth the heart." There he was, coming down the stairs: Joseph Smith. Jane knew him from her dream, though in life he was taller than she had expected, and a bit more portly; his face brighter, his hair more gold than she had seen it. She certainly knew his happy, blue-green eyes. She hadn't expected his front teeth would be chipped and his lips somewhat scarred, but she didn't mind such details in the real man.

Beside Joseph Smith was another well-dressed fellow, whom he introduced as Doctor Bernhisel. The doctor's head was mostly bald, with tufts of gray hairs at the temples and darker hairs at the nape. His eyes were deep-set under thick brows, his skin fair, though his cheeks and nose were pink enough to make Jane wonder if he enjoyed wine too often. His nose was pointy, lips thin.

Sister Emma left at once and returned almost that fast with blankets, which she wrapped around each set of shoulders.

Jane could see a red carpet in the dining room, a chandelier of prisms hung above it. Why, this was like passing into heaven, where stars were hung not just for light but decoration!

"Let me feed them something," said Emma.

"My wife always thinks of the important things," chuckled Brother Joseph. "Yes, set on soup, Emma. But while it's warming, I want to hear about their journey." He peeked into the sitting room, told some girls there, "We've got company come," and then directed the Mannings into the parlor.

Dr. Bernhisel chose a red velvet chair, but none of the Mannings sat. They were afraid of staining or soaking the furniture.

"Please," said Joseph. He motioned to the chairs.

"We awful wet, sir," Jane repeated. She was still wondering at the surroundings.

"Call me Brother Joseph."

She folded her arms, holding her head scarf. "We soaked clear through, Brother Joseph, sir. Come thirty miles over two days in the rain."

"Thirty miles? I had thought it was perhaps a longer journey than that."

"Thirty miles from La Harpe," Jane said. "From beginnin' to end, I guess we come, oh—"

Anthony finished for her: "Eight hundred miles, sir."

The Prophet turned to him. "And you are?"

"Anthony Stebbins, sir."

"Eight hundred," Joseph repeated. He shook his head. "On foot?"

"Yes, sir," said Jane.

The Prophet motioned to the chandelier. "See the rainbows in those prisms?"

They all nodded.

"Those are your rainbows after the storm. God's sign. He still gives it, you know. Reminds us he's still at the ark's helm. Still watching over us. That wetness won't last. Please sit down."

They draped their blankets over the chairs before sitting.

Jane was naturally the spokesperson. Brother Joseph pulled up a ladderback chair and sat beside her, saying, "You've been the head of this little band, haven't you."

"I have."

He sighed, "God bless you," and clapped his hands once. His voice got excited. "Now I want you to tell me about some of your hard trials. I want to hear about those trials."

Jane did tell, blow by blow. The cold. The dark. The worn-off shoes. Sheriff. Freezing river. But, she said, they kept right on singing "Glory to God" and never bothering about any thorns or thistles in their path.

Brother Joseph slapped Dr. Bernhisel's knee. "What do you think of that, doctor? Is that faith?"

The doctor cleared his throat and nodded. He held a mahogany walking stick, which he tapped on the floor for emphasis. "I rather think it is. If it were me, I fear I should have backed out and returned to my home."

Brother Joseph's eyes misted. "You are among friends now," he told the Mannings. "You will be protected."

That was the moment Emma entered, inviting them into the dining room, where she had set out soup.

The tables were covered with white lace. The soup was chicken and pea. It was the most delicious meal any of them had ever tasted.

NOTES

The chapter title, "The Family of God," is from the title of hymn number 543 in *Hymns for the Family of God*.

The material about the Manning family journey is all extracted from Jane's own life history:

"One year after I was baptized I started for Nauvoo with my mother Eliza [Phyllis] Manning, my brothers Isaac, Lewis [that is, Isaac Lewis, which we know from other sources to have been her brother's name; Elizabeth Roundy, to whom the history was dictated, mistakenly inserted a comma between the two names] and Peter. my Sisters, Sarah Stebbings, and Angeline Manning. My brother in Law Anthony Stebbings, Lucinda Manning a sister in law and myself fall of 1840. We started from Wilton Conn, and traveled by Canal to Buffalo N.Y. We were to go to Columbus Ohio before our fares were to be collected, but they insisted on having the money at Buffalo and would not take us farther. So we left the boat, and started on foot to travel a distance of over eight hundred miles. We walked until our shoes were worn out, and our feet became sore and cracked open and bled until you could see the whole print of our feet with blood on the ground. We stopped and united in prayer to the Lord, we asked God the Eternal Father to heal our feet and our prayers were answered and our feet were healed forthwith. When we arrived at Peoria Illinois the authorities threatened to put us in jail to get our free papers we didn't know at first what he meant for we had never been slaves, but he concluded to let us go, so we travelled on until we came to a river and as there was no bridge we walked right into the stream, when we got to the middle the water was up to our necks but we got safely across, and then it became so dark we could hardly see our hands before us, but we could see a light in the distance, so we went toward it and found it was an old Log Cabin here we spent the night; next day we walked for a considerable distance, and staid that night in a forest, out in the open air. The frost fell on us so heavy that it was like a light fall of snow. We rose early and started on our way walking through that frost with our bare feet, until the sun rose and melted it away. But we went on our way rejoicing, singing hymns and thanking God for his infinite goodness and mercy to us, in blessing us as he had, protecting us from all harm, answering our prayers and healing our feet. In course of time we arrived at La harpe Ill., about thirty miles from Nauvoo. At La harpe we came to a place where there was a very sick child, we administered to it, and the child was healed. I found after the elders had before this given it up as they did not think it could live.

"We have now arrived to our destined haven of rest, the beautiful Nauvoo! here we went through all kinds of hardship, trial and rebuff, but we at last got to Brother Orson Spencer's, he directed us to the Prophet Joseph Smith's Mansion, when we found it, Sister Emma was standing in the door, and she kindly said come in, come in! Brother Joseph said to some White Sisters that was present, Sisters I want you to occupy this room this evening with some brothers and sisters that have just arrived, Brother Joseph placed the chairs around the room and then he went and brought Sister Emma and Dr. Bernhisel and introduced them to us, brother Joseph took a chair and sat down by me, and said, you have been the head of this little band haven't you? I answered yes sir! he then said God bless you! Now I would like you to relate your experience in your travels, I related to them all that I have above stated, and a great deal more minutely, as many incidents has passed from my memory since then. Brother Joseph slapped Dr. Bernhisel on the knee and said, What do you think of that Dr, isn't that faith, the Dr. said, Well I rather think it is, if it had have been me I fear I should have backed out and returned to my home! he then said God bless you, you are among friends, now and you will be protected. They sat and talked to us a while, gave us words of encouragement and good counsel."

In a reminiscence in *Young Woman's Journal* 16 (December 1905):

551–52, Jane says, "When I went there [Nauvoo] I had only two things on me, no shoes nor stockings, wore them all out on the road."

We can estimate the date of the arrival of the Manning family through at least one document, provided by Wolfinger in "Test of Faith," in *Social Accommodation*: "An ad in the December 6, 1843, edition of the *Nauvoo Neighbor* requests information on Jane's lost trunk, stating 'About six weeks ago a company of saints . . . escorted by Elder Wandell who had in his charge a trunk belonging to Jane Elizabeth Manning—Sister Manning was not here then but has since arrived and can obtain no intelligence of her trunk'" (171, n. 93). We know, then, that Jane and her family arrived after late October, when the Wandell group apparently reached Nauvoo, but before December 6. A mid- to late-November arrival for the Mannings seems a reasonable assumption.

Elijah Lovejoy was a printer in Illinois who was murdered after producing an abolitionist newspaper, the *Alton Observer*, and organizing the Illinois Anti-Slavery Society, all of which happened not long before the Manning family ventured there. There was surely still some strong sentiment—both for and against slavery—in Illinois at that time (see Filler, "Lovejoy").

The words to Anthony Stebbins's song, "We Raise the Wheat," are from Preston, *Young Frederick Douglass*, 61. It was a song Douglass reports having heard as a young slave. We have standardized the spelling.

The words to the hymn "There Is a Holy City" are taken from Harriet Beecher Stowe's account of a hymn sung by Sojourner Truth, quoted in Stowe, "Sojourner Truth," 108–9.

It should be noted that Sylvester Manning was not the only child on the trek. There was one more baby, probably the child of Sarah and Anthony Stebbins.

15

OH, PETER, GO RING THEM BELLS!

*But God hath chosen the foolish
things of the world.*
1 CORINTHIANS 1:27

Orson Spencer found Isaac outside the cooper's shop just after nightfall. Brother Orson said straight out, "I believe the Lord has heard your prayers, Isaac James."

Isaac, sitting on a bench, swiveled his head around to see who had addressed him. He half-expected an angel—which, in Nauvoo, was something many folks anticipated they might see some time. And he knew a good many religious people in the nation had been predicting the world would end right about now. Why, the Millerites up in Rochester, New York, had waited all day on October 22 for God to rapture them up to heaven! But God hadn't taken a mind to do so, and the Millerites had been disappointed. Now Isaac wasn't waiting on the Second Coming, but when strange voices called his name, he couldn't help but flash a quick thought on Jesus and the Rapture. The truth is, he didn't want to take on the clouds just yet, so he was relieved to see that the voice belonged to Orson Spencer. Brother Orson's face was handsome, but it wasn't no angel's face.

"Beg pardon?" Isaac said.

"I say, God has heard your prayers."

"Somebody die and leave me money?" Isaac had learned how to make white folks laugh.

Brother Orson chuckled just as Isaac knew he would. "Better than that."

"A woman too?"

"A whole group of women. Five of them. Black as you and looking lonely."

"Well, then!" Isaac spat on his palms and rubbed them together. "My life got good as a sweet potato pie, didn't it! Where do I go to collect my good fortune?"

Brother Spencer roared with such a laugh he could hardly pronounce "Mansion House."

Isaac squinted deep. "Brother Orson, you serious?"

"Oh, yes."

"They's colored women at the Mansion House?"

"I escorted them there myself. I counted five women, and I wasn't looking close."

"Five of 'em?"

"Not slaves either. Freeborn. From Connecticut."

Isaac stood up and grinned. "So I just strut myself up there," he said, "and I say—." He scratched his head and made himself look dumb for Orson Spencer's entertainment. "What do I say?"

"You say, 'Hello ladies! Anyone need a husband?'"

"'Hello ladies, anyone—.'" He stopped himself. "Aw, Brother Orson—you tryin' to make me appear the fool! I ain't sayin' no such thing."

Orson got out another belly laugh.

"It's been a while," Isaac said, "but I done some courtin' back in New Jersey. Come to think on it, I was somethin' of a legend."

"Well, Isaac James! I never suspected you had such a history!"

"Like I say, it has been a while. I'm afraid my tongue might twist itself up tryin' to recall what words I should say to a woman."

"How about you open the conversation this way: 'Hello, ladies—anyone care to see Nauvoo in the moonlight?'"

Isaac laughed at that. "Moonlight! They'd think I was disrespectin' them if I start out so fresh." But, he thought, he surely could teach a lady how to braid a palm hat, or he could start up conversation by telling how they had drained Nauvoo's swamp. It was true, he had been praying for a woman—and in Nauvoo, a person was not inclined to doubt that God had heard his prayer.

"The Lord will give you the words, Isaac," said Brother Orson and pointed him toward the Mansion House.

Isaac turned back only twice—once to see if Brother Orson was mocking him and once to smear a bit of tallow on his face. His skin was so ashy, it looked like he had run into a bag of flour. The tallow took out the dryness and all the marks of the day. He dabbed it on his hair too, and then walked himself to the Prophet's place and knocked on that big door.

The past week had brought clouds and a dust of snow, but this night was clear and chilly. Isaac wished he had something warmer than the two flannel shirts he was wearing.

When Joseph Smith himself answered, Isaac couldn't think what to say. He had almost expected one of the colored women would meet him at the door and tell him, yes indeed, God had sent her as a direct reward for the good job Isaac had done on that swamp clearing. (Remember, this was Nauvoo, and miracles were commonplace. You could anticipate angels or miracles wherever your path rounded a bend. In fact, it was recommended that you anticipate heavenly signs rather than the hellish ones—which were getting somewhat common too, mostly in the form of mobs or thieves or apostates. But if your mind was set on finding angels instead of devils around the corner, you walked happy.)

Brother Joseph grinned without saying a word, and Isaac peeked past him. Sure enough, there were a number of colored folk in the parlor. "Brother Joseph," he said, "I didn't know you had company."

"Isaac James," Joseph answered, "I didn't know you could lie so expertly."

"Now, Brother Joseph!"

"A good lie is like wearing a lightning rod on your head to test God's aim, you know."

Isaac wiped his forehead, feeling the tallow as he did. Cold as this night was, he was sweating. "All right," he said softly, "I heard you had company, but I didn't know they was such good-lookin' company."

Joseph ushered him into the parlor and introduced him all around. Isaac's eyes got their fill. Indeed, Orson Spencer had not exaggerated. These were fine, lively-lookin' women—and a few men with them. It was clear from their clothes and faces that they had come some distance, but they still looked fine! He heard all their names as Brother Joseph introduced them but couldn't remember a single one a second later. One of the women belonged to one of the men, he did recall that. And there was one holding a sleeping child and looking so gentle and kind he wouldn't have objected to trading that child places. The scene brought back a quick memory of his own mama, which he had to push out of his mind before any sadness set in.

He thought he'd do well to say something about the weather—about how cold it was or what November usually brought to Illinois. He meant to refer to the weather when he said, "Too bad you all can't see the moon from in here." As soon as the words were out, he knew they'd come wrong. Those were the words Orson Spencer had suggested—exactly what he had not wanted to say! Isaac tensed in every joint and muscle. Why, he did not know these women or their attachments, and besides, what would Brother Joseph think of him practically inviting a stranger to look at Nauvoo's moon? Seemed all the women in the parlor were staring at him like he was set to steal them away. His blood went rushing to his head. "What I mean," he said, "is it's a good moon night. Been cloudy, but it ain't cloudy tonight. And that moon paint the willows silver. We only get that on occasion this time of year."

Nobody made a move. Isaac wiped his forehead again.

One of the colored men spoke up. "Why, I would love to see that moon, Brother Isaac James. If you ladies will excuse me."

Not knowing what else to do, Isaac followed him outside and pointed skyward. "Well, there it is. Looks like a few of them clouds came back. The moon's there behind 'em."

"Yes, indeed. Nice moon."

"My name's Isaac James, in case you missed it."

"So's mine."

Now Isaac could see that this fellow was a playful rascal, and Isaac was not about to get mocked. "No, it ain't," he said.

"The Isaac part. I'm Isaac Lewis Manning. Folks call me Lew."

That seemed a fair response, and Isaac Lewis was grinning so big that Isaac James felt friendly at once. "So, Lew, which one of them women is your wife?" he asked. "Or is it all of them together?"

Lew made a face that could scare an owl. "All of them together? What sort of crime you think I done to get such a punishment? They all my sisters, except the one that's my mama. Why? You after a wife?"

"Me? No!"

"So you married already?" Lew asked.

"No."

"Then why ain't you after a wife?"

Isaac grinned. "Any you might recommend?"

Lew poked his tongue into his cheek and thought. "You'd be doin' me a favor takin' Lucinda. But you seem like a nice fellow; I couldn't do that to you. I'd recommend Jane. She got her a child already but no husband. She the best of the lot, providin' you treat her right."

"Don't I look like someone treat a woman right?"

"It's a little dark out here for me to say for sure."

"Don't my face look like a good man's face?"

"Seem fine, but the moonlight ain't all that showy."

Isaac whispered, "I feel like I'm sweatin' pebbles. Do I appear sweaty to you?"

"A little shiny."

"That's the tallow I put on my face. Make it gleam." He paced a step or two and then got brave. "So what if I was to come back here after you all settled down—tomorrow or next week, say—and you can introduce me to Jane. I can teach both of you how to braid hats sometime."

"That right? I never have learned how to braid cats."

"Hats! I said hats!"

"Either way," Lew said, "that sound fine. I go tell Jane you ain't lookin' for a wife, so she won't worry."

"That's right. I ain't lookin' for no wife."

"I tell her you ain't lookin' for a wife. Just a woman."

He stepped back. "You say that, and she'll never want to meet me! Now I'm a Mormon man, Mr. Manning. You tell her that. And I ain't after a wife." He let his sly smile appear. "But if one should be guided to me by the grace of God, I wouldn't go sour at the offer. Jane the one holdin' that child?"

"That's her."

"She got her a kind face."

"Kind and pretty."

"Don't say nothin' to hurt my chances, then."

"Truth is, Brother Isaac, I wouldn't mind havin' someone else take care of any of my sisters. I been doin' it long enough, and I growed tired with it. Whichever one you choose, I'll talk you up to her like you was honey on a comb."

When Isaac did see Jane close up, which was not for another three days, her face was kind indeed but wary. It was just outside the Mansion House, and Isaac was bringing a pumpkin to the Smiths. Jane was sweeping the porch. He asked how she enjoyed Nauvoo and if she would care to observe the arrival of the latest steamship. She answered that she enjoyed Nauvoo fine but would prefer to keep to herself for now, as she had caught a cold.

Isaac decided she was trying to preserve him from her sickness and respected her all the more. He would give her some time to recover. Meanwhile, he'd maybe explore possibilities with Lucinda or Angeline (he knew their names by now), though they were somewhat young. But if they were God's reward for all he had done in clearing Nauvoo's swamp, he figured age wouldn't make all that much difference.

NOTES

The chapter title, "Oh, Peter, Go Ring Them Bells!" is a traditional Negro spiritual from Burleigh, *Spirituals*, 198.

The Millerites, named for founder William Miller, a Baptist minister from New York who analyzed Old Testament scriptures and predicted the Second Coming would occur on October 22, 1843, were the precursors of the Seventh-Day Adventists (see Nichol, "Adventists").

The term "ashy skin" is commonly used in the black community to indicate dryness.

16

PLENTY OF ROOM IN THE FAMILY

*Once you were not a people . . . now you
are the people of God.*
1 PETER 2:10

The Mannings stayed in the Mansion House for a week. Brother Joseph would come in every morning to shake hands and check how they all were doing. Soon, they all found other places to live in Nauvoo—all except Jane, that is.

Jane was still waiting for her clothes to arrive on the steamship. She placed ads in local papers and waited at the dock, but before long she had to realize she had lost every one of her dresses—one of them silk, a hand-me-down from Missy. So there she sat, alone on her bed in the Mansion House, weeping. When Brother Joseph came in to wish her good morning, he looked around and said, "Why, where's all the folks?"

Jane stood, finger-combing her hair into place. It was done up in seven braids in the back, but the short hairs around her face were a mess. "They got themselves places, Brother Joseph, sir. But I ain't got any place." She burst out sobbing.

Joseph brought a handkerchief from his vest pocket and wiped her eyes. "Now, now," he said, "we won't have tears here."

She couldn't stop, though. The touch of his hand made matters that much worse. "And I just come from the landin', and all my clothes is stoled, and I ain't got no home!"

He patted her shoulder and wiped her eyes. She cried harder but calmed when he said, "You've got a home here—right here, if you want it. Now, you mustn't cry. We dry up tears here. Have you seen Sister Emma this morning?"

"No, sir." She wiped her nose and frowned against more weeping.

Brother Joseph left at once. When he returned, he had his arm around his wife's shoulders. "Emma," he said, "here's a girl who says she's got no home."

Jane's mouth wanted to pucker into a cry-kiss and work up another sob, so she deepened her frown against it.

"Don't you think," said Brother Joseph, "she's got a home here?"

Emma said simply, "If she wants to stay."

Leaning over Jane to wipe her eyes, Joseph asked, "Do you wish to stay here?"

She sniffed, waiting a long moment so her answer wouldn't come tear-choked. "Yes."

He straightened himself up. "Well, Sister Emma, why don't you talk to her and see how she is. And afterwards, why not go down to the store and clothe her up." He said good morning then and left.

Jane turned away for a moment, but Sister Emma put an arm around her and pulled her in to a mother's embrace. "Now, don't you worry," she said. "We don't turn souls away from this place. That's why we finally had to go make it an inn! That's why Brother Joseph built that brick stable."

"Couldn't miss that stable, ma'am."

"It houses upwards of sixty, seventy horses. We want room

available in this inn, just in case someone comes here to birth an important baby. Or if the Lord himself should appear in disguise. I don't suppose you're—"

"Oh, no, ma'am!" Jane interrupted. "I ain't the Lord. No! Nothin' holy, ma'am—not me! And I do promise on that!"

Emma smiled. "I was going to ask if you're hungry or feeling sick in any way."

"Oh, no, ma'am." In fact, she was getting stronger by the moment and more settled. Even happy.

Sister Emma asked the sort of questions then that Mrs. Fitch might've. But Emma's voice was different. It was tender. "So. What can you do?"

Jane stood straight and tall as she could, but she was still much shorter than Emma Smith. "Ma'am, I can iron. Very handy with the iron. Laundry. Extremely experienced. Housekeepin'—oh, dust run away the moment I enter a room. Cook—I can cook somethin' special. I been a household servant since I been six years old, ma'am. For some of the richest folk up Connecticut. Mr. and Mrs. Joseph Fitch. I don't suppose you heard of them way down here in Illinois."

"I'm afraid not."

"Never had no complaints about my ironin' or my housework, Sister Emma. "

"Only about joining the Mormons, hmm?"

Jane's mouth dropped. "How you know that?"

"This is Nauvoo. Hardly a soul here came without a fight." Emma glanced away and folded her hands. "And not every soul won it." She waited a moment and then said, "So, you are an expert with the iron."

"I must truthfully confess, that yes, ma'am, I do own long acquaintance with the iron."

Emma nodded. "That sounds very good. When you're rested, you may do the wash."

"Ain't tired. Not one bit."

"Why don't you commence your work in the morning? Meanwhile, let's have Eliza Partridge take you to buy a bolt of cloth and do you up some fine dresses, as Brother Joseph suggested. Eliza is always eager to please."

So there it was: Jane was a household servant for Brother Joseph and Sister Emma Smith!

Eliza Partridge was with Jane by the afternoon.

Nobody in Nauvoo was very wealthy, but Eliza carried herself like someone who once had been, and she was one of the prettiest women around. She resembled Emma Smith in many ways but was more delicate in bone and feature and much younger. Her hair was glossy brown, and her smile and voice were sweet. There was good-will all over Eliza Partridge's face, and Jane was pleased to let her choose the fabric: a good, sturdy calico for the dresses and cotton for a shift. Now Jane was ready to earn her keep and look right in style doing it!

And oh yes, Jane Manning knew ironing. She'd hold the iron on the woodburning stove—one of the few stoves in Nauvoo—until it was hot enough to steam. Then she'd flatten the pleats in Emma's dresses and iron the Prophet's trousers until the Smith clothes looked brand new. When the rim of Jane's head wrap got sweat-wet and her whole face was dripping, she thought of that icy, neck-high stream they had crossed not so long before, and she thanked God for such a good, hot job.

She was experienced with a washload too, an expert with bat-tlin' sticks and boards, and a fine soapmaker. Jane Manning could make lye soap nearly as fast as she could make corn pone. She'd dump the lye into the ash hopper and then check to see if it was strong enough by dipping in a turkey feather. If the feather got eaten up, the lye was all right, and she'd start a fire under the kettle, pouring in hog fat until the mix went ropey. With her soap ready, she'd boil the clothes in big vats behind the outback house, beating and twisting the sweat out of all the Smith threads.

In the first batch of laundry she did, she found some robes in the pile—robes unlike anything she'd ever seen. She looked at them close. White robes. "What this be?" she said out loud. And like an instant answer, something told her these robes had to do with the Nauvoo Temple. These robes had to do, that something whispered to her heart, with the new name she had been told about, given in that Nauvoo Temple.

Now how would it be, she wondered, to get you a new name? Not that you'd abandon the name you already had, for surely it was a fine name with some good heritage to it. But for a daughter of slaves to lay claim on a new name, a name having nothing at all to do with any white master in the past—for a slave's name was often the master's, just like a sheep brand told shepherds where their property belonged—oh, would that be glorious! Why, that would be a name only God knew, a name that claimed you his. She wanted that new name in that new temple!

But she kept such thoughts to herself. She asked no questions when she returned the laundry, all cleaned and pressed.

Lucy Mack Smith, the Prophet's mother, lived in the Mansion House too. Jane had to pass through Mother Smith's room to get to her own. By now, Mother Smith was a thin old woman with white hair like a mess of cobwebs. Her face was seamed, but her eyes were bright as a raven's. Often, she'd stop Jane and talk to her. She'd tell her all about Brother Joseph's troubles and how he had suffered for publishing the Book of Mormon.

One morning, Jane met Joseph coming out of his mother's room. After he said good morning and shook hands with her, she entered Sister Lucy's room on her way to her own.

"Good morning, Jane," said the old woman. Her voice had a nice warble, like a meadowlark.

"Good morning, Mother Smith," said Jane. She waited. It seemed the woman wanted something. And so it was. Lucy Mack Smith asked Jane to bring her a wrapped bundle from the bureau and then to sit beside her on the bed. Jane obeyed, and Mother Smith took the bundle, placed Jane's hands on it and said, "Handle this, then put it in the top drawer of my bureau and lock it up."

Jane did that too, feeling around the edges of the wrapping and then putting it away.

"Now," said Lucy. "You remember I mentioned the Urim and Thummim when I told you about the Book of Mormon?"

"Yes, ma'am."

"Well, Jane, you have just handled it. Sit down, girl. Now, you're not permitted to see it, but you have been permitted to handle it. Oh, Jane." Mother Smith moved her finger over Jane's jaw. "You will live long after I'm dead and gone, won't you?"

Jane could hardly speak but managed, "God willin'."

"I suspect God's willing in that. So you must do something. You must tell the Latter-day Saints that you were permitted to handle the Urim and Thummim."

"Yes, ma'am," Jane breathed, and then, "Oh, my!"

"Now, is that your brother who concocts the spicy cooking in the kitchen?"

It was, sure enough. After Jane got hired as a servant, Lew got hired as a cook.

"My brother Lew. And he do love the spices! Always generous with spices."

"Well, I love spices too. Or used to. When my stomach was younger. Could you tell him to be a little less generous with some of those peppers in my servings?"

Jane smiled big. "I be glad to do that."

"Otherwise, tell him he's a good boy. Fine cook. You go on ahead to your room now, Jane."

Lew's talents were being well used at the Mansion House inn, where most guests seemed to appreciate his generous spices. Lew was also teaching and showing dance at the Masonic Hall. He had always loved to dance. He could play songs with his feet. In

Connecticut days, and often on the trail from there to Nauvoo, Lew amused his family with the feet shuffle and the arm swing—doing it so fast, his arms and legs were sometimes a blur. He could make you smile in your worst hours. Lew could dance like a chicken and hoof it like a goat; he could do a slap dance, and a dance wherein his body got to spinning and gyrating like he was possessed of a spirit gone crazy with joy. His whole soul got expressed through his feet and arms and dancing body, and the Saints appreciated him almost as much as Jane did. Now, he didn't teach the white folk his more furious dances, but he did show them how to click their heels and smack their feet on the ground to make rhythm, and they enjoyed it.

Besides teaching dance, Lew, like most of the Nauvoo men, was digging rocks at the stone quarry for the temple. Oh, yes, this was a new life for them all. But not a life without tension. Some anti-Mormons were accusing Joseph Smith of conspiring to murder Missouri's former governor, Lilburn Boggs—that fellow who had issued the extermination order against the Saints. And talk of plural marriage and spiritual wives was everywhere.

Jane didn't think much about the plural marriage subject. But there came a day she was called on to think about it. It was a bright spring afternoon, and she was hanging laundry along with the other household servants: the Partridge sisters, Emily and Eliza, and the Lawrence sisters, Sarah and Maria. They were talking about Mormonism, when Sarah Lawrence glanced up and asked Jane, "What would you think if a man had more wives than one?"

Jane slapped a shirt on the line. Then she shrugged and said, "That's all right."

Maria started giggling, and before long all four white women were laughing like the laundry was a joke. Eliza's laugh was the sweetest.

"Well, what?" Jane asked, trying not to laugh herself. She sat down next to Eliza.

"We're all four Brother Joseph's wives," said Eliza and smiled bigger than her face seemed built to do.

Jane jumped right back up and clapped her hands. She said, "That's good!"

Eliza was laughing again, though Sarah wasn't. Sarah said simply, "Jane's all right. Just listen—she believes it all now." The four women gave her to know it was a secret, not even to be mentioned in the Mansion House.

Later that day when Emma dropped by her room, Jane wondered what she should say if Emma raised the subject. Should she let on that she knew, or should she play dumb? Emma had surely been unhappy about something lately, and Jane remembered how Emma had first introduced her to Eliza Partridge: "Eliza is always eager to please." There had been just a touch of bitterness in her tone.

"Sister Emma?" Jane tucked her hair into her head wrap.

Emma smiled. It was a good smile but a tired one. Couldn't hold a candle to Eliza's smile.

"Somethin' you needed, ma'am?"

"Yes."

"Ironin's satisfactory, ain't it?"

"You iron beautifully, Jane. And the laundry's fine."

The Prophet's wife entered and sat on the bed, waiting for Jane to close the door. Even then, Emma didn't speak for a long moment. Jane was sure she was likely to hear more about plural marriage now. She stayed at the door like a guard. It was one thing to hear about the subject from Eliza and the others, but she didn't think she wanted to hear it from Emma. It might be sad news coming from her.

"Jane," Emma said, "Brother Joseph wants me to ask you something."

"Yes?"

"It's not an easy question, and you should not give it a hurried answer."

Jane thought to speak but couldn't. Her heartbeat got so strong she could feel it in her ears and neck.

"My husband's question is, Would you like to join our family?"

Jane had been rubbing her hands together. Now they dropped to her sides. She had a testimony of Brother Joseph as God's prophet—why, she had seen him in a dream! And much as she admired him and thought him a good man—especially compared to Reverend Sylvester!—this offer to join the family came out of the blue. My my, what did it mean to be a servant in the Smith household?

"I don't understand," Jane said and truly hoped the details would not be explained just yet.

Emma answered, "Would you like to be adopted to us as our child?"

"Oh." Jane felt her knees would give way out of pure relief. "Your child?" She wiped her hands on her apron, thinking hard. "But I got me a mama," she said. "Phyllis Manning Treadwell is my mama."

Emma made that tired smile again. "I'm speaking of an eternal adoption, Jane. Would you like to be our daughter—Joseph's and mine—in the eternities?"

Jane went limp, still leaning on the door. "Oh, ma'am—I'm so green in this religion—I just don' know. I don't know what this 'eternal adoption' means exactly."

Emma stood. "You think it over, Jane. I told you there was no need to be hasty. Take your time. We'll talk again later."

Two weeks later, they did talk again about "eternal adoption." This time, Jane was ready with a response: "Both you and Brother Joseph—you so good and so kind to me, but—maybe I don't understand things like I ought to—but—no, ma'am. I don't think I should get adopted by you just yet. Can I wait till I understand it better?"

Emma nodded. "That's fine, Jane."

"Thank you, ma'am. I'll finish the wash then, if you'll excuse me."

NOTES

The chapter title, "Plenty of Room in the Family," is from the title of hymn number 552 in *Hymns for the Family of God*.

Besides the Wolfinger material, this chapter paraphrases quotations from an interview with Jane James from *Young Woman's Journal* 16 (1905): 551–52.

Jane's own history relates the events as follows: "We all stayed there [the Mansion House] one week, by that time all but myself had secured homes, Brother Joseph came in every morning to say good morning and ask how we were. During our trip I had lost all my clothes, they were all gone, my trunks were sent by Canal in the care of Charles Wesley Wandel, one large trunk full of clothes of all descriptions mostly new. On the morning that my folks all left to go to work, I looked at myself, clothed in the only two pieces I posessed, I sat down and wept, Brother Joseph came into the room as usual and said good morning, Why not crying, yes sir, the folks have all gone and got themselves homes, and I have got none. He said yes you have, you have a home right here if you want it, you mustn't cry, we dry up all tears here. I said I have lost my trunk and all my clothes, he asked how I had lost them? I told them I put them in care of Charles Wesley Wandle and paid him for them and he has lost them. Brother Joseph said don't cry you shall have your trunk and clothes again. Brother Joseph went out and brought Sister Emma in and said Sister Emma here is a girl that says she has no home, haven't you a home for her? Why yes if she wants one, he said she does and then he left us. Sister Emma said what can you do? I said I can Wash, Iron, Cook, and do housework! Well she said when you are rested you may do the washing, if you would just as soon do that, I said I am not tired, Well she said you may commence your work in the morning. The next morning she brought the clothes down in the basement to wash. Among the clothes I found brother Joseph's Robes. I looked at them and wondered, I had never seen any before, and I pondered over them and thought about them so earnestly that the spirit made manifest to me that they pertained to the new name that is given the saints that the world knows not off. I didn't know when I washed them or when I put them out to dry. Brother Joseph's four wives Emily Partridge, Eliza Partridge, Maria and Sarah Lawrence and myself, were sitting discussing Mormonism and Sarah said what would you think if a man had more wives than one? I said that is all right! Maria said well we are all four Brother Joseph's wives! I jumped up and clapped my hands and said that's good, Sarah said she is all right, just listen she believes it all now. I had to pass through Mother Smith's room to get to mine, she would often stop me and talk to me, she told me all Brother Joseph's troubles, and what he had suffered in publishing the Book of Mormon. One morning I met Brother Joseph coming out of his mother's room he said good morning and shook hands with me. I went to his mother's room she said good morning bring me that bundle from my bureau and sit down here. I did as she told me, she placed the bundle in my hands and said, handle this and then put in the top drawer of my bureau and lock it up, after I had done it she said sit down. Do you remember that I told you about the Urim and Thumim when I told you about the book of Mormon? I answered yes mam, she then told me I had just handled it, you are not permitted to see it, but you have been permitted to handle it. You will live long after I am dead and gone and you can tell the Latter-day Saints, that you was permitted to handle the Urim and Thumim.

"Sister Emma asked me one day if I would like to be adopted to them as their child? I did not answer her, she said I will wait a while and let you consider it; she waited two weeks before she asked me again, when she did I told her no mam! because I did not understand or know what it meant, they were always good and kind to me but I did not know my own mind I did not comprehend" (see also Wolfinger, "Test of Faith," in Social Origins, 151–57).

The time of Jane's being informed of plural marriage was likely the spring of 1844, a year after the Lawrence and Partridge sisters entered into plural marriage, taking Joseph Smith as their mutual husband. At the front of Eliza's handwritten journal are affidavits swearing that she was indeed sealed to Joseph Smith on May 11, 1843. Also at the beginning of the journal is a statement by Emily Partridge Smith Young (quoted in Woman's Exponent 14 [1 August 1885]: 38): "[Emma Smith] had always, up to this time, been very kind to me and my sister Eliza, who was also married to the Prophet Joseph with Emma's consent. Emma, about this time, gave her husband two other wives—Maria and Sarah Lawrence." These four women, all of whom Jane mentions, were sealed to Joseph by mid-May 1843.

Information on dances that Isaac Lewis Manning might have done are extracted from Blassingame, Slave Community, 45: "These dances were individual dances, consisting of shuffling of the feet, swinging of the arms and shoulders in a peculiar rhythm of time developed into what is known today as the Double Shuffle, Heel and Toe, Buck and Wing, Juba, etc."

The information on the Mansion House being used as a hotel as of September 1843 comes from History of the Church, 6:33.

The process of making lye soap is extracted from Remembering Slavery, edited by Berlin, Favbeau, and Miller, 97–98.

17

I'VE FOUND A FRIEND, O SUCH A FRIEND!

A friend loveth at all times.
PROVERBS 17:17

Lew took to Brother Joseph like a long-lost friend. The Prophet certainly enjoyed Lew's cooking. Oh, yes, Isaac Lewis Manning had found the most agreeable conditions of his life! No one had ever appreciated him this much before. And Brother Joseph was so kind—to colored as well as white. Why, when a slave named Chism got whipped by his master, the Prophet took the matter up himself as Nauvoo's mayor. Right there in the courtroom in the Mansion House, a Mr. J. Easton was brought up for whipping Black Chism. Lew was standing just outside the door when Joseph said in a voice like what God's must be: "Lynch law will not do in Nauvoo! Those who engage in it must expect to be visited by the wrath of an indignant people—not according to the rule of Judge Lynch, but according to law and equity!"

Lew didn't understand all the words, though he sure knew what "Judge Lynch" was about, but he appreciated the Prophet's passion for a right cause. Later, Lew prepared him the best sugar cake he could, took it straight to his office. Lew didn't want to say anything; he just wanted to offer a nice, sweet thank-you.

Brother Joseph smiled big when he saw the plate in Lew's hand. "What's this, Lew?"

"Not much. Just a morsel."

Joseph patted him on the back. "A sure answer to prayer and a rumbling stomach."

Lew started to back out the door and then looked up. Brother Joseph was already sampling the gift. "Delicious," said the Prophet. "Oh, you're a blessing, Brother Lew. I was feeling worn out and you're helping me get renewed."

"Glad I could do somethin'. We appreciate how fair you be to all of us. Only, Brother Joseph, sir, you oughta get yourself some sleep."

That suggestion brought a yawn from Joseph.

"If you like, I could fetch you some cool milk from the cellar to go with that cake. Might calm you some."

Joseph yawned again and said, "The cake is plenty. Thank you."

"I used good eggs in it. Two hours fresh. Brother Joseph, dinner won't be ready for another hour. Why don't you take a little nap? I'll be sure to wake you."

"Frankly, Brother Lew, you and my body think alike. I'm becoming persuaded. I haven't had much sleep, what with Mother being ill."

"And you been tendin' her yourself. Any mother appreciates a son carin' so much. Now, you go ahead and take that nap."

Joseph nodded. "I'll do that right now, and let this sugar cake send me sweet dreams."

Lew turned to leave and then stopped. "Sir? I jus' wants you to know, sir, I heard a little—not much—I been listenin' at the door, if you forgive me. Couldn't help myself." He straightened his back, because he was about to say words which should be said standing proud. "Brother Joseph, I thinks you one great law man. Or lawyer, whatever the name be."

The Prophet chuckled. "Do you know what my brother Hyrum says about lawyers?"

"No, sir."

Joseph twisted his mouth a little to make himself resemble his brother. "Hyrum says lawyers were created in gizzard-making time, when it was cheaper to get gizzards than souls. If a soul cost five dollars, a gizzard would cost nothing."

Lew laughed at the joke, though he wasn't sure he understood it. "Oh, no," he said, "now you ain't one of them sort." He stood tall again. "You one of the great ones, sir."

Joseph's eyes were half-open, looking heavy indeed. He took a last bite of cake. "Oh, yes," he said, "you write and tell the world I acknowledge myself a very great lawyer. I am going to study law. And this is the way I study it." He laid his head on his books, his hand still holding his fork. Then Joseph Smith fell asleep.

Lew tip-toed out.

It wasn't long, though, before the Mannings felt the hard side of Joseph's mayorship. It was Anthony, as Jane might have predicted, who broke the law, selling liquor on a Sunday. And it was Brother Joseph who caught him.

"Hello, Brother Stebbins," said the Prophet.

There was no escape. Anthony was caught in the act, red-handed. He gave a loud sigh and moaned, "Sorry." Now Anthony wasn't looking to give an excuse, but there was a reason for him doing this illegal thing. He explained: "Brother Joseph, down South, I got me a sister—Sallie Mae—still in slavery. To this day, that dear child be in bonds. I know I shouldn't be sellin' liquor on the Lord's day, but I wants so much—I gots to buy that child free, sir!"

Joseph stood quiet for a moment. "That does make me sorry,

Anthony," he said. "Sorry to the bone. But the law must be observed. I have to impose the fine. You know I do."

"Yes, sir."

"Which is ten dollars and twenty-five cents. And you must not continue with this work, regardless of any good intentions."

Anthony hung his head and promised to repent in full.

Come the next day, though, Brother Joseph showed up at Anthony's place with a fine, mottled mare.

"You come for the money?" Anthony said, eyes to the ground.

"You pay me the money; I'll make you a gift of this horse. How's that?" Joseph lowered his voice. "Now listen, Anthony, I want you to sell this good creature forthwith, and I want you to use the money to buy that child's freedom. You'll have no more need of vending liquor or anything else on the Sabbath. Is that a bargain between us?"

That moment was one of the few when Anthony Stebbins's eyes teared. He was not accustomed to such kindness. Not from a white man or a black one, either.

"Sir," he said, "if you buys my sister free, I will make a better deal than that: I will keep the Lord's day for the whole of my life, and I will do anything you ever asks me, Brother Joseph."

"And you'll be blessed." Joseph passed the reins into Anthony's hand.

Of course, by this time, tensions were rising all over Nauvoo—and they would get worse. There were outsiders claiming another extermination order against the Mormons was on its way. There were rumors that mobs were just waiting on the call to bring their torches and whips and ropes to bust up the Mormons and make of their temple one great blaze, like Hell itself. It was a dangerous thing to be a Mormon in those days.

NOTES

The chapter title, "I've Found a Friend, O Such a Friend!" is from the title of hymn number 220 in *Hymns for the Family of God.*

The case of Chism and "lynch law" are from *History of the Church*, 6:285.

An account of Joseph Smith nursing his mother as she suffered from "inflammation of the lungs" is found in *History of the Church*, 5:290.

The case of a black man named Anthony being fined for selling liquor (his purpose being to raise money to buy the freedom of "a dear child held as a slave in a Southern State") and then being presented with a horse by the Prophet to buy a slave child's freedom is recorded by Mary Frost Adams and quoted in Andrus, *Joseph Smith*, 33. The fine of $10.25 is recorded in *History of the Church*, 5:57.

Hyrum Smith's statement "[Lawyers] were made in gizzard-making time" is found in *History of the Church*, 6:240.

Joseph Smith's assessment of how to study law is found in *History of the Church*, 5:307.

Elijah in Ohio
1842

18

JESUS WALKED THIS LONESOME VALLEY

Did not our heart burn within us,
while he talked with us?

LUKE 24:32

Elijah Abel took a meandering way to Cincinnati through Indiana, where a number of Quakers asked him discreetly if he needed help. So he knew the Underground was still at work. "Wayne County," they told him was "safe territory," especially if he could find "Mr. Coffin."

Elijah had to laugh at that. Seemed he couldn't get away from "Mr. Coffin" however hard he tried.

But this "Mr. Coffin" was not of pitch pine but of flesh and bone and a fine heart. He was the president, so-called, of the Underground Railroad.

When Elijah met him, Levi Coffin was a lean and bearded forty-four-year-old. With his wife, he had been helping slaves escape for the past fifteen years. This, he had decided, was his mission in life.

Levi Coffin said only, "Company for supper, dear," when he answered Elijah's knock.

Supper was more than generous. Seemed the Coffins had killed the fatted calf for him and flavored it up with wild berries. Over such food, Elijah explained that he had free papers so had no need of the System.

Mr. Coffin said, just as Delilah had, that perhaps Elijah should use care. Free papers could be torn up and burned. It was not unheard of for a free black to be kidnapped, and Elijah would do well to follow the underground. Levi Coffin's voice was hoarse when he asked, "Where are thee going?"

"Cincinnati."

"Ah." Coffin nodded. "I've thought of making my way there sometime myself. Starting a free product store, perhaps." He cleared his throat.

"Sir?"

"Free product store—in which nothing is sold which comes from slave labor. There are such stores already in Baltimore and Philadelphia, you know."

"Baltimore," echoed Elijah. "I got born in Maryland. Never heard of such a store there."

"Times change," Mr. Coffin said.

Elijah told him about his adventure with the Underground Railroad years ago and offered to be of assistance in getting runaways north, if ever Mr. Coffin should need help in Cincinnati.

The Quaker nodded thanks and said that indeed, they might want to call upon him. Things were not looking any better for slaves. "New laws being considered all the time," Coffin said. "Fugitive slave laws."

"They got those already, don't they?"

"Not as harsh as the ones they're thinking on," Mr. Coffin muttered.

Elijah had heard nothing about more laws being thought on,

though he wasn't surprised. He set down his utensils and thanked Mrs. Coffin for the meal. She told him there was more to come—some ginger cake still in need of heat, which she'd have for him presently. Meanwhile, Levi Coffin let his guest inspect all the hidden doors and covered cellars in his home—hiding places for runaways. This whole house was a fortress with little caves to protect slaves in search of freedom. While Mrs. Coffin served his dessert after the tour, Elijah couldn't help but ask, "What is it make you Quakers risk so much for my people?"

Levi folded his arms on the table like he was set to pray. "Well," he said, "I read in the Bible it was a good thing to take in the stranger. Thee knows the Bible, Mr. Abel?"

"Yes, sir, quite well. Been a missionary."

"Ah. Then thee knows what the Good Book says. We are asked to administer to those in distress."

"We are asked that, sir. But not many folks do it."

"I thought it would be a safe thing for me to do right. The Bible tells us to feed the hungry and clothe the naked. I don't recall it mentioning skin color in those instructions."

Elijah nodded. "No, sir. Me either."

So once again, Quakers cared for Elijah Abel as he made his way.

Sprawling. That was the great city of Cincinnati. Like what Nauvoo could only dream of becoming. But Cincinnati was smoke fuming out of every chimney, blasts of steam, smells of fire and wood and melting ore and soot-blacked clouds. Cincinnati was dirty, noisy, and bustling, full of whole neighborhoods where every house was a mansion. Elijah had made it to the land of opportunity at last! It might smell like the devil's place, but it was bursting with money, jobs, and good-looking folks who wore fancier clothes than Elijah had beheld in all his days. No, it wouldn't be hard to find work in Cincinnati.

But not yet. There was something up north in this same state he wanted to see again. Kirtland. Elijah Abel wanted to pass his eyes over that temple—the best thing his hands had ever worked—to remind himself who he had become since lighting out from Maryland with free papers in his shirt. Like that temple, he was consecrated now; he had been burnished by the refiner's fire. The Lord had lit up Elijah's soul, just as He had lit up the temple when the Saints shouted, "Hosanna!" Elijah maybe didn't have the finished glitter of the Kirtland Temple yet but that would come in God's own time. So before even asking around for work, Elijah made that trip—careful of kidnappers, yes indeed—to Kirtland.

He arrived at dawn, February 6, 1842.

But the devil had visited this place!

Elijah's eyes took in the temple, but his heart couldn't. Part of the roof had been blown away—a too-close tornado, said a black boy whittling under a willow tree. Happened just two weeks earlier. Green sky, raging winds, and then one spiraling shaft of purple dirt and swirling rubbish.

"Why couldn't God have directed it elsewhere?" Elijah murmured. He didn't expect an answer.

There was dried mud and old mortar on the bricks. He picked up two bricks from the ground and struck them together, knocking the dirt off. His hands alone could do little to restore this temple, though. Nobody else was around save for that whittling boy. This temple had been abandoned—a ruin.

And the worst was inside. A door had been made in the downstairs wall and the basement strewn with grass and fodder for livestock. Cattle, sheep, and swine were grazing on this ground where angels once had walked. On the main floor, sheep had been herded into the few remaining pews in that sacred room where Elijah had heard his mama's voice. ("There's more to you," Delilah had said. Oh, he remembered!)

Sheep in that room—it was mockery, pure and simple! This was a desecration of Elijah's own handiwork, of his own consecrated skill—and even more, of the place God himself had accepted. Why, there was excrement on the floor! Half-chewed hay on the pews! Elijah could hear Old Testament Joseph whisper beside him, though he didn't see him now: "Defilers!"

"Apostates," Elijah muttered. He shook his head and returned to his horse. He didn't look back.

He was in Cincinnati the next day—sore in the seat and still angry.

That was his state of mind when he met Miss Mary Ann Adams. He didn't know her name as yet, or anything about her, but he could see she was returning from washing clothes in the river. Must be a cold job this time of year, he thought. The laundry basket was balanced on her head, just like Nancy used to carry hers. And she was wearing pink calico, like Nancy's. He remembered how that calico had stretched when Nancy was swollen with their baby. But this woman's shoulders were covered by a thick blue-green shawl, nicer than anything Elijah's woman could ever have dreamed of owning.

"Nancy," he breathed. The anger left like that name had blown it away.

The girl—and she was a girl, not quite a woman yet—glanced at him. No, it wasn't Nancy. This girl was not near so pretty. She was younger, yes, and her clothes newer. And she had the biggest set of eyes he had ever chanced on. But there was something in her not quite up to his woman. Maybe around the cheekbones. Nancy's had been high and shone like hot gold, especially in the summer. This girl had a round, flat face and some skin condition that reminded him of cauliflower. Still, there was a sweetness in her, even in the roundness of her face.

"Can I be of help?" He got down from his horse to ask this question. He hadn't changed clothes in a while and knew he looked road worn. His cape had caught a branch and torn down the side. And he was ripe—hadn't bathed in a good long time. He wished he had dipped himself in the river at least once before talking to this girl, but the river had been laced with ice, which froze that thought.

"Doin' just fine myself, thank you." Her voice was higher than Nancy's.

"Then maybe you could be of some little help to me?" He took off his hat—a good, gray wide-brim, which Brother Joseph had gifted him.

"How might I help you?" She didn't meet his eyes.

"New here, that's all. Lookin' for a place to stay. Place to work."

"What do you do?"

Elijah could give her a list of "what I do" long as his leg. "'Bout anything," he said. "Been a carpenter, ship worker, undertaker, stone mason some. Missionary."

"Missionary!" Now she looked. "You a preacher man?"

"Yes, ma'am." He switched his hat to the other hand. "I can preach you up a storm!" He grinned, looking her over. She was young, too young for him.

"Preach some to me, then, whilst I tote this basket home," she said.

He took that as a challenge. Leading his horse, he preached what he felt strongest about: The Joseph Smith story and the Book of Mormon. He finished up with a solid testimony of Jesus just as she approached a gray cabin, its old wood curling up. This place looked like a fine abode for cold termites.

"Well," he said, "I just proved I'm a preacher, and I don't even know your name."

"I don't know yours, either."

"Elijah Abel," he said. "Elder Elijah Abel."

"I'm Mary Ann Adams." She set the basket down to open the door as Elijah tied his horse to the hitching post. "You showed yourself a preacher all right. And if you lookin' for work, maybe my daddy can help. He's inside. Would you care to meet him?"

He hesitated, looking her over again. "How old are you?" He

whispered, for cabin walls weren't known for holding out wind or sound, and this girl's daddy would surely hear.

"How old you thinks?" she whispered back. Elijah knew she was trying to flirt but—bless her!—she didn't quite know how to do it. She was mimicking what she had seen others do.

He didn't answer.

Mary Ann opened the door, and an old man waved from the mattress. "That's my daddy, restin' his bones," she said. "Daddy, this is Reverend Abel. Reverend, this be Willie Adams."

Willie said in a weak voice, "Come on in and sit down. Warm yourself."

"Fire's low," Mary Ann said. "I'll stoke it some. Are you hungry, Reverend?" She was looking prettier every moment, and her mention of food brought out his first smile since Kirtland.

"I'm plenty hungry, thank you," he said.

"Ox tails been cookin' with potatoes all day, and I'll set some corn on to boil. We don't have much. Would you like some eggs and bread with your dinner?"

"That'd be fine," he answered, but he surely didn't expect such a runny egg as what she served. "My, my, you set a fine table," he said, staring at the slow-moving yolk, murmuring to himself: "You give this egg a good blessing, and you'd have yourself a chicken!" He spoke it so soft, Mary Ann thought he must be praying and closed her eyes in respect.

Even runny, the egg and all that came with it were tasty. Elijah hadn't taken a full meal since he was at the Coffins' place. And it was just the two of them at the table. The old man sipped soup in his bed.

"Your father sick?" Elijah asked.

"Dropsy," said Mary Ann.

That opened the door. Elijah explained all about priesthood, that he himself possessed it, and had the authority direct from God to lay hands on Mr. Adams and heal him straight out of bed, should that be the will of the Almighty.

"Oh, Reverend," she said, "would you do that?"

Elijah Abel stood at once, saying, "Of course," and walked to the mattress. He had a little tin flask in his pocket full of conse-crated oil. He dripped a few drops on Willie Adams's head and then set his hands there.

Elijah wanted to command that man to jump up and walk. In all sincerity, he wanted that because he knew how deeply it would impress Mary Ann Adams. But he did not feel such promises in his mind when he opened his mouth. After a long wait, he said, "I bless you with peace. God will hear the desires of your heart."

Mary Ann apologized that they had no bed to offer him. "No room in this here inn," she smiled. They were poor folk, but if he cared to, he could certainly stay the night, maybe sleep on the floor or in the corncrib outside. She did have some good wool blankets.

Elijah accepted the offer, choosing the corncrib, which seemed only proper.

Come morning, he awoke with Mary Ann leaning over him. He thought she was his mama at first, as though he had slept backwards through the years. Then he thought of Nancy—a quick, passionate thought. Then he remembered Mary Ann. Hers was not the face he most wanted to see leaning over him, but it was a pleasant face just the same.

"Good morning." Elijah licked his teeth.

"Mornin', Reverend." Her voice was teary. "I need your help. Papa died last night."

Elijah couldn't speak for a moment. He sat part way up and then managed, "Sorry."

"No, no," whispered Mary Ann. "He been tryin' to die for months. He so lonely since my mama fell dead three years back. All Papa complain about lately was how hard it been to die and why wouldn't God just take him?" She wiped her eyes. Elijah shook himself free of the cornhusk slivers and followed Mary Ann to the cabin. There, on the bed, lay Willie Adams. "Daddy asked me to pray for it once, but I straight-out refused," Mary Ann said. "Didn't want to be alone, and Daddy was all I had."

The old man looked bad: eyes half-open, mouth a frozen yawn. He would need some good laying out before visitors should call.

"He look peaceful," said Mary Ann. "Don't he look peaceful?"

Elijah agreed out loud, because he felt he should, but he didn't agree in his heart. He had seen all sorts of deaths. There were true peaceful ones, where the body seemed asleep and dreaming wonderful things—and this was not one of those. That was when he told her—the first time he had told this to anyone—how he had followed his own mama's wishes and prayed for her death and how she died right then.

"That so?" said Mary Ann.

"That so," said Elijah. "And I know how it is to be lonely, and I am sorry for your loss."

"You say you been a undertaker too, Reverend?"

"Yes, ma'am."

"Can you take care of my daddy?"

"I'd be pleased to do that," he said. "Why don't you spend some time with him right now?"

Mary Ann touched her father's hair. "I can't imagine not hearin' his voice again."

Elijah wanted to tell her she might hear it some time, coming through the veil. But this was not the moment to say so. This was her moment for grieving.

She ran her finger down her father's chin. Willie Adams's skin was already cooling. "Daddy," she said, "look like you got your desire at last. Now you and Mama's gone, and I don't know what I'm gonna do. Even when you was sick, you was still here to talk to, and I could hear your voice. Now don't you worry, though. I'll be all right. I'll be all right." She turned her eyes up to Elijah. "Some folks say the spirit tarries a while. Do you think he's still here? Or is he with my mama?"

"Maybe they both here," he said. "Both of them be concerned about leavin' you."

"I do feel left alone. You never heard my daddy laugh, Reverend. He didn't laugh at all in the last while. He had the best laugh you can imagine. Guess I won't be hearin' that again."

"Let me leave you with him for a bit," he said. "You say your good-byes. Where do you want your father buried?"

"Mama be buried out back. By that little grove on the south side. Daddy should be with her."

Elijah Abel left her and went about his work, purchasing wood and nails with his own money. He borrowed a saw from a down-the-road colored family and had the coffin built by afternoon. And this was how he made acquaintance with his soon-to-be friends just outside Cincinnati: they all started showing up at the cabin, bringing whatever they had for the funeral lunch. They were all free blacks, and all poor.

The colored community in this part of town already had a preacher: a tall, burly man who had bought his own freedom, then his children's, and then his wife's, and then turned his heart to God and memorized the Bible verses without ever learning letters. He preached a fine sermon for Brother Willie Adams, all about trumpets sounding on resurrection morning, and the dead rising up and praising God.

The mourners—around thirty—were gathered behind the cabin, where the grave had already been dug. They sang hymns and mourned the loss of one of their own. Many had known him their whole lives. Someone asked Elijah if he, being a minister, wouldn't care to speak a word.

Elijah complied, reciting scriptures they all understood in their own ways: "'He was despised and rejected of men, a man of sorrows and acquainted with grief; and we hid as it were our faces from him;

he was despised, and we esteemed him not.' Yet we here did esteem our brother Willie Adams, though, like many of us, he was stricken, smitten, and afflicted."

The other preacher said, "Amen."

The men lowered the casket Elijah had just built and pointed Mary Ann to the pile of dirt. She took a fistful and tossed it. The soil rattled as it hit wood. Then the women escorted her to the cabin, while the men commenced closing the grave.

Two weeks later, Elijah baptized two entire families into the Mormon church. He also baptized Miss Mary Ann Adams.

NOTES

The chapter title, "Jesus Walked This Lonesome Valley," is from the title of hymn number 217 in *Hymns for the Family of God*.

Levi Coffin, called sometimes the president of the Underground Railroad, worked in his chosen mission from the 1830s until after the Civil War. According to Anna Curtis, author of *Stories of the Underground Railroad*: "Readers of *Uncle Tom's Cabin* will remember the elderly Quaker, Simeon Halliday, and his kindness to fleeing slaves. Mrs. Stowe had Levi Coffin and his wife in mind when she wrote of Simeon and Rachel Halliday. Eliza, who crossed the Ohio River on blocks of floating ice, was also a real person who was sheltered in the Coffin home on her way to Canada" (37). Coffin opened a Free Produce Store in 1847 in Cincinnati, Ohio.

Though we have no evidence of any interaction between Elijah Abel and Mr. Coffin, it certainly doesn't seem beyond the realm of possibility that they were acquainted, given the likelihood that Abel used the Underground Railroad himself and the fact that Cincinnati became a major center for the Railroad, especially after passage of the 1850 Fugitive Slave Law (when Elijah was still residing in Cincinnati).

The information on the condition of the Kirtland Temple in 1842, when Elijah returned to Ohio, is extracted from Fields, "History of the Kirtland Temple," 81–83.

19

"ARE YE ABLE?"
SAID THE MASTER

*Are ye able to drink of the cup
that I shall drink of?*
MATTHEW 20:22

There was already a branch of the Church set up in Cincinnati—just in someone's log house, but it served fine. Joshua Grant presided. It was there that Elijah Abel and Mary Ann Adams took their vows as husband and wife. Neither of them was sure about their ages, though it was clear Elijah was considerably older than his bride. Still, she was old enough. He'd be a protector as well as a companion for her, and they both needed someone.

Elijah tore down the old Adams cabin and built a new one in its place. Mr. and Mrs. Abel were quite well accepted in the Cincinnati church of the Latter-day Saints, though all the members but those he had baptized were white. Elijah was, after all, a seventy in good standing, a friend of the Prophet himself, and now a married man with a fine job as a carpenter and a home that proved his woodworking skill. Considering his slave beginnings, he had found a good level of respect, certainly more than he ever dreamed of in Maryland.

But some of that respect turned a corner come July 1843, when Heber C. Kimball, Orson Pratt, and John E. Page visited the Cincinnati Mormons. Elijah had been invited to the church to meet these old friends of his, whom he hadn't seen in over a year. He shook their hands and then introduced his wife, who was showing signs of a nice, round pregnancy.

"You've done yourself proud. She's a pretty one," said Orson Pratt. Brother Pratt was a thin-faced, dark-eyed man. He looked and spoke refined.

"The Lord blessed me indeed," Elijah said.

These greetings spoken, the brethren called him into a back room. Elijah assumed this meeting would be to catch him up on the doings in Nauvoo—serious doings, no doubt. Maybe they'd invite him back to the carpenters' guild—an offer he would have to decline. He was set to say the words solemnly: "No, I chose Cincinnati, got Brother Joseph's permission, and this is where I be settled."

He never got a chance to make that speech. The brethren, all seated in a circle, invited Elijah to sit down as well. Brother Page began, "I respect a colored brother."

Elijah squinted. Something was coming, and it wasn't any invitation.

"Indeed, I respect the Negro members of this Church." John Page was looking beyond Elijah towards the other presiding officers. "Still, wisdom forbids we should introduce you, Brother Elijah, before the public."

Elijah let his neck and shoulders give in to the disappointment and go slack. He knew exactly what the agenda of this meeting was to be.

Orson Pratt had no problem looking him straight in the eye and saying, "I sustain the position of Brother Page."

Elijah sat stock-still for a moment. He used a quiet voice when he said, "I have no disposition to force myself upon an equality with white people." It was almost his slave voice. What amazed him was how suddenly his hope could be stripped away. Seeing these brethren had filled him with such joy and pride—introducing them to his wife and showing himself yet a faithful member of the Church. But all of that scattered the moment he was reduced to "a colored brother."

Heber Kimball accepted Elijah's humiliation with a brusque nod, no hint that he understood what it meant for Elijah Abel to abase himself in such a way. "Of course. We understand that, Brother Elijah. You've always been pliable in the hands of God, just like good clay. You've always been obedient to his commands."

Elijah recognized this as half-baked praise, coming from an experienced potter such as Heber Kimball. He tried to force a smile, which came out half-baked too.

"But, Brother Elijah," said Heber Kimball, "may I simply advise that you limit your activities here to the colored population?" To Elijah, the word *brother* suddenly seemed more condescension than true. He wasn't about to call this man—at whose side he had worked on two temples—"Brother Heber." He answered simply, "Yes, sir."

Elijah didn't talk to Mary Ann about the conversation in that back room. He was not about to be made less in his wife's eyes. They had grown close enough by now, however, that she sensed the change.

"Somethin' wrong?" she asked at supper.

"No."

"Somethin' I done?"

He said, "I knew the Prophet Joseph Smith" and then crumbled his cornbread into the greens Mary Ann had prepared.

"Those men make you remember him? Make you lonely for Nauvoo?"

"Prophet had the most powerful voice I ever heard, when God was in it," he said.

"Would it help you feel better to talk about him? I'd sure like to hear more."

He shook his head. "Not just this minute." He sipped his cup of cider and made himself smile. "Heber Kimball surely do approve of the wife I took," he said. "They all glad I'm helpin' out here. And it's plain we waitin' on a baby. Hope it don't embarrass you to get noticed that way. We startin' a whole generation of new Mormons. At least Brother Joseph might be happy about that."

"They'll probably brag on you to Brother Joseph. Probably talk like you was a king out here."

He didn't reply.

"Thou shalt be made equal to thy brethren," he quoted to himself as he tried to sleep that night. The words of his patriarchal blessing. From what the Brethren had said, Elijah was given to know new ceremonies were being performed in the Nauvoo Temple, which was now near completion. He wondered, would he have been included in them had he stayed in Nauvoo? Or would he have had to wait years, like Joseph of old, before he'd be allowed outside prison walls?

Old Testament Joseph came to him just as sleep approached, saying, "Funny thing is, they don't know you one bit. They don't even suspect what kind of power's waiting inside you. What a good messenger you are for the Lord. How very much the Almighty thinks of you. He got them glittering robes stored up for you."

"Well, I hope nobody steal them while I sits around waitin' on permission to get past the gates," Elijah murmured. He could imagine the glitter like all those bright stars showing through a little hole in his cabin roof. "Gotta fix that," he said and closed his eyes.

NOTES

The chapter title, "'Are Ye Able?' Said the Master," is from the title of hymn number 470 in *Hymns for the Family of God*.

Mary Ann Adams Abel is listed in the 1860 census as being twenty-eight years of age, and she was recorded as being forty-six years old at the time of her death in 1877, thus giving her a birth date of 1831 or 1832 (Bringhurst, "Elijah Abel," 137). If those records are correct, she would have been only eleven or twelve at the time of her marriage to Elijah. Vital records for people of color were notoriously badly kept, so it is possible that Mary Ann could have been born as early as 1827. If Elijah Abel's birth year of 1810 is accurate, Mary Ann Adams Abel was his junior by seventeen years or more.

That Joshua Grant presided over the Church members in Cincinnati is found in *History of the Church*, 5:337.

The incident of Church authorities restricting Elijah Abel to preaching only to blacks is detailed in Bringhurst, *Saints, Slaves, and Blacks*, 88. Elijah Abel's response, "I have no disposition to force myself upon an equality with white people," is an exact quotation.

Heber C. Kimball's statements on "good clay" are found in *History of the Church*, 4:478.

Nauvoo
1843–1844

20

I Am Not Skilled
to Understand

But where shall wisdom be found?
JOB 28:12

It was not far past midnight, Christmas Eve, when the Nauvoo angels started caroling. At least they sounded like angels to Jane Manning. They sang:

> *Mortals awake!*
> *With angels join*
> *and chant the solemn lay!*
> *Love, joy, and gratitude*
> *combine to hail*
> *th' auspicious day!*

Jane roused herself, set to behold a vision.

The half-moon was veiled by thin, blue-gray clouds, and every tree was frosted. The whole world shimmered with snow. There were no angels—not that Jane could see—but at the front door were Lettice Rushton, a blind widow, and six others, ushering in

Christmas Day. Jane joined the carol and heard Brother Joseph's voice just above hers. He had opened his window and was singing in a voice so lovely, it could melt that snow.

There was a party later that day, the likes of which Jane had never beheld even in the most festive times at the Fitches. Pine boughs, sweet cakes, songs, dancing, silk gowns, and lace headcaps—oh, this was a party! More than fifty couples! There was a moment when it appeared some long-haired drunken Missourian would dampen the fun, but the "drunken Missourian" turned out to be one of Joseph Smith's best friends, just escaped from a jail: Port Rockwell! When Joseph embraced him, the whole crowd shouted with joy, and Lew danced a jig.

Years later, when Jane thought back on that Christmas, she decided it was the best time she had had at Nauvoo. And it was the final best time too. That Christmas party signaled the end of all the celebrations in Zion.

Around February 1844—not long at all after Brother Joseph and Sister Emma had their seventeenth wedding anniversary—Joseph leased the Mansion House Inn to a fellow named Ebenezer Robinson. There were unspoken tensions that brought about this change, and Jane could venture a good guess about what caused the strain. She suspected Emma didn't care for Joseph's other wives dwelling under the same roof. Jane herself kept the secret she had been given and never mentioned a thing about plural marriage.

Several Smiths stayed on in the house, and Jane continued working there for a time. But that sense of family and home which had been the Mansion House was broke up.

Of course, Nauvoo itself was not broke up just because the Mansion House was. There was still hope for Zion in Nauvoo, and important announcements were getting made all the time—the most exciting being that Brother Joseph himself had decided to run for president of these United States.

Jane heard it not from Brother Joseph but from an outsider—a man with a pocked face, greasy hair, and pointy beard, who she imagined was probably a cattle rustler. There had been prolific thieving in Nauvoo—most of it blamed on the Mormons, though Joseph himself said that if anyone could prove Mormons were stealing other folks' property, he'd give his head for a football. There were bands of mean-minded men camped just the other side of the river who were the likely thieves, and Jane full suspected that sorry-looking fellow in front of her on the street was one of the band.

She was headed towards the cooper's to buy a small barrel, and the ugly man was talking with another fellow, this one younger and not quite so mean in the face. The ugly one was saying, "If Joe Smith gets himself elected president, he'll raise the devil with Missouri. And if Joe Smith ain't elected, he'll raise the devil anyhow."

"President!" Jane whispered to herself.

She asked Emma about it when she returned to the Mansion House, the barrel in her arms. "Brother Joseph, ma'am, he want to be elected president? Is that true?"

Sister Emma took the barrel and set it on the floor. "I suppose it is true, Jane."

"President! Of what?"

"Of these United States." At this, Emma's face took on the seriousness only she could produce: mouth down, all her face lines showing. "We can't support Van Buren, can we? He changes color like a tree toad. My husband visited him, you know."

"In the very White House?" She had never heard a word about this.

"The very whited sepulcher of a White House, yes, indeed. My husband told the head of our country, told him face to face, of the abuse we Mormons have suffered. Do you know what Mr. Van Buren's response was?"

"How would I know such a thing as that?"

"'Your cause is just,' he said, 'but I can do nothing for you.'"

Emma could do a fine mimic of how Van Buren might have sounded, doubling her chin and making her voice whiny. "Poor man," Emma said, "he was afraid he'd lose the election! And Henry Clay's not much better. He seems to think language isn't meant to express ideas but to conceal them. And Harrison—he's a Lamanite hater. Put Harrison in the White House and watch—the Lamanites will be annihilated."

In truth, Jane was unfamiliar with all of the names Emma had just mentioned, but she didn't let on. She simply shrugged when Emma said, "So, given the choices—and given my husband's boundless optimism—do you wonder he's offering himself?"

Brother Joseph entered then. "Offering myself?"

"As a lamb for the slaughter." Emma manufactured a smile like she was wringing the last drops of joy from her face. All of Emma's smiles of late were painful.

"It be true, then, Brother Joseph?" Jane asked.

"That I'm going to be slaughtered in this election year?" He smiled broadly, showing off his chipped teeth.

"I mean, you runnin' for president of these entire United States?"

He nodded but winked at her, so she still wasn't certain.

"Please say!" she persisted.

"Oh, yes, Sister Jane." But he shrugged, so it still seemed at least part joke. "That's been underway some time. Made some of the Eastern papers already. I'm surprised you haven't heard of it. My, when I get hold of one of those papers and see how popular I am, I'm afraid myself I'll actually be elected!" He chuckled and glanced at his wife. Emma's face had returned to its stony set.

"Then what would you do?" Emma said. There was an undertone to this question that sounded like a threat.

"God's will," Joseph answered.

"President!" Jane breathed.

"I guess I'd still prefer 'Brother Joseph,'" he said, "or 'Lieutenant General.' I have all the fine names I need in this life, thank you."

"But what if you do get it? What if you do be 'lected president? You mind my askin'—"

"Don't tell me. You want to be vice-president!" He gave her a quick hug.

She mustered a laugh, a weak one, and then said in a low voice, "About slavery, sir? If you do be president, what you do 'bout the slave?"

Joseph grew serious. "It's a large issue, isn't it."

Jane was thinking of the scar on her mother's right leg, just above the knee. Her mother's mizzus, in a sudden fit, had thrown a knife at Phyllis and then yelled at her for bloodying the carpet. That was the only incident of abuse Phyllis had ever spoken of from her slave years, but it was fixed in Jane's mind. Jane had often run her fingers over the scar, wondering what else might have happened to that black skin before freedom arrived in Connecticut. "It be the issue for my whole family. My mama been a slave."

Joseph nodded solemnly. "And your mama is a good woman."

"She the best woman I know." Jane's eyes teared when she said that. There were so many memories.

"Imagine someone considering her a thing to be enslaved!"

"And hurt. Cut up."

"It's a vile shame for this whole nation. I told Brother Orson Hyde—and I believe it completely—'You go into any city and find an educated Negro, and you will see a man who has risen by the powers of his own mind to his exalted state of respectability.' Do you know what Brother Orson replied?"

"Do I want to know?"

"He said, 'Put them on my level and they will rise above me.'"

Now, Jane knew Brother Joseph intended this as a sort of compliment to her race, but she saw Orson Hyde's meaning too—and his meaning surely came with fear and suspicion and probably memories of slave uprisings. She said only, "He say so?"

"And I answered, 'If I attempted to oppress you, would you not be indignant?'"

Jane whispered the only words she could think of, the words that filled her heart and soul: "I hate slavery."

"So do I, Jane," he said. "Well, would you like to listen to my platform? You would be my first Negro audience to hear it."

"Plat—?"

"My position on slavery."

Emma was looking anxious. Jane did not want to pursue a subject that would upset the lady of the house, but she did want to hear what Joseph would do about those in bondage.

"If you please," Jane said. "This is somethin' I want to know, down to the marrow of my bones."

Joseph set his hands on her shoulders and looked deep into her eyes. "I don't believe in shackles for any human soul. You should realize that by now."

"Oh, yes, Brother Joseph. From the beginnin' of my Mormon time, I realize that. From the day I step into the water of my baptism, I realize that."

"My platform calls on these United States to break off the shackles from the poor black man, to give liberty to the captive."

"Bless you, Brother Joseph."

"Freedom has always been God's will, hasn't it? I'm only after his will."

"Oh, yes, sir."

"God can show us a way out of slavery, our own or someone else's." His eyes looked suddenly distant. He was staring beyond her.

"I always know for certain," she said. "Heart down, I always know that is the will of the Lord God Almighty."

"Many will suffer if we don't do God's will in this." He was speaking more to himself than to her.

Emma left the room, either bored to tears or crying over some other matter.

"If we go counter to the Lord in this matter, I tell you—there will be war in this land."

She wondered if he might be having himself some prophetic vision and asked permission to go finish her ironing, lest she disturb any view of the future.

"Brother against brother, father against son," he said, nodding towards her but looking elsewhere.

NOTES

The chapter title, "I Am Not Skilled to Understand," is from the title of hymn number 94 in *Hymns for the Family of God*.

The words to "Mortals Awake" are taken from Smith, *Collection of Sacred Hymns*, 103. (Incidentally, Elijah Abel's missionary companion, Christopher Merkley, compiled another hymnbook.) The account of that Christmas carol being sung early Christmas morning 1843 by the blind widow and her family is recorded in *History of the Church*, 6:134, and is also given in Holzapfel and Holzapfel, *Women of Nauvoo*, 64.

The description of the Christmas party in 1843 is extracted from Telford, Black, and Everett, *Nauvoo*, 55.

Joseph Smith's statement "I pledge myself that if he finds the first farthing that we cannot show where it has been appropriated, I will give him my head for a football" is from *History of the Church*, 6:239.

The quotation from Martin Van Buren is from *History of the Church*, 6:243. The derogatory reference to Henry Clay is from *History of the Church*, 6:268. The observation that "if Joe Smith is elected president, he will raise the devil with Missouri" is from *History of the Church*, 6:248.

Joseph Smith's statement "When I get hold of the Eastern papers and see how popular I am, I am afraid myself that I shall be elected" is from *History of the Church*, 6:243.

Joseph Smith's comments to Orson Hyde about oppression of the blacks are from *Teachings of the Prophet Joseph Smith*, 259.

Joseph Smith's statement "Take off the shackles from the poor black man" is from his political pamphlet, quoted in *History of the Church*, 6:205.

That the Mansion House hotel was leased to Ebenezer Robinson in early 1844 is substantiated by Newell and Avery in *Mormon Enigma*, 171.

21

JUST AS I AM

*For he is our peace, who hath . . . broken
down the middle wall of partition between us.*
EPHESIANS 2:14

Even with Joseph Smith running for president and the anti-
Mormons making more noise all the time, there were pleasant
diversions in Nauvoo. Come spring, an actor named Thomas A.
Lyne got up a big theatrical exhibition in the lower room of the
Masonic Hall and performed a whole set of dramas. One of them,
Pizarro, Jane herself saw.

As for Lew, he still taught dancing in the Masonic Hall. He had
gained quite a reputation, becoming so popular with the Saints that
they'd stop him on the streets to comment on his talent.

The presidential speeches were something of a party, too. The
choir would sing songs like "O Stop and Tell Me, Red Man," and
Joseph Smith—dignified and tall and strong—would stand on his
stage and speak like the prophet he was and the president he was
surely meant to be. Jane knew she'd remember some of his speeches
for the rest of her life:

"If the tree of liberty," said Brother Joseph, "has been blasted in this nation—if it has been gnawed by worms, and already blight has overspread it, we will stand up in defense of our liberties and proclaim ourselves free in time and in eternity!"

She felt to shout hallelujah after that one. Lew did shout it—three times. Lew was anything but shy. And his admiration for Joseph Smith was enough to make his feet waggle and fly. "There ain't nothin' I wouldn't do for Prophet Joseph," Lew told his sister.

Of course, it wasn't just enthusiasm Isaac Lewis Manning felt for Joseph Smith. Lew loved the Mormon doctrine. His heart moved with it. It was April when a man named King Follett died, and Lew heard Joseph sermonize at the funeral. That day, Isaac Lewis Manning felt that angels were nodding their heads and clapping their wings. (He still imagined angels with wings, though angel Moroni, as Brother Joseph reported it, wore a white robe and had no wings, at least not any the Prophet could see.) Lew pictured happy angels all around the Saints, some three or four just above his own head—maybe watching for his feet to teach them rhythm.

The funeral sermon was all about eternity and said things Lew had felt but never dared utter, afraid they'd sound uppity, especially from a colored mouth. But when Joseph Smith said them, they sounded true, certain, and inevitable.

"All the spirits that God ever sent into the world," said Joseph Smith, "are susceptible to enlargement." The Prophet made no distinctions whatever. Lew felt as if Joseph had been looking directly at him as he spoke these words, like this was a personal message, like he could've been saying, "You, Isaac Lewis Manning, are capable of enlargement. Now, don't you be less than you can be. Don't you ever!"

"God found himself," Brother Joseph went on, "in the midst of spirits and glory, and because he was greater, he saw proper to institute laws whereby the rest could have the privilege of advancing like himself—that they might have one glory upon another." Again, these words entered Lew, filled him with fire. And again, it seemed the Prophet was looking directly at him. "I know that when I tell you these words of eternal life, you taste them," Joseph said.

Oh, Lew did taste them—such a sweet taste. The fruit of the good tree, he thought, that's what it was. He wasn't worshipping Joseph Smith, but he did love him, because when Joseph talked, Lew felt God all around.

Jane missed the King Follett sermon, though she heard Lew's account of it several times and felt Lew's faith. He wept every time he quoted the speech, though he did seem to embellish it sometimes. Lew could make a fine talk better, take it way beyond its words, but he was a good man anyhow. She didn't see him cry often, and it touched her to witness it. He repeated there wasn't a thing he wouldn't do for Brother Joseph.

Jane herself was doing very specific things for Brother Joseph and Sister Emma too—the ironing. Since the Mansion House had broken up, Jane had gone to live with her mother in nearby Burlington, accompanied by her sister Angeline. But she still ironed the Smith clothes, and they told her there wasn't a better iron-mistress in all of Illinois.

She was halfway through a good batch of clothes (it was June now) when Isaac James knocked on the window. Jane wiped her apron across her sweaty forehead.

"Can I come in?" Isaac mouthed.

She pointed to the back door and said, "Ain't locked."

Isaac's face was mostly teeth when he entered—the biggest grin he could offer. In his hand was a stained handkerchief, holding a bunch of blackberries, juice dripping on the floor.

"Oh, Mr. James," she sighed, trying not to sound disappointed at the new work he was making for her. She grabbed a clean rag to mop the juice.

Apparently, he heard no disappointment. His face was still all teeth. "Guess what I got in here?" He held the bag high and four more drops of juice fell. One splashed on Jane's just-washed apron. She wiped the drops without looking up.

"Don't tell me." She met his eyes and gave a tiny smile. "You been to Lima."

"Blackberry capital of the wide world!" Three more drops. Jane wiped them up and suggested he might do well to set the bag in a dish. "Sweetest blackberries you ever taste in all your days, Miz Jane."

She got him the dish. "A bit early in the season, ain't it? These here berries look more pinkish than blackish, Mr. James."

"You think so? A little on the pinkish side, maybe, but go ahead and taste one." He undid the handkerchief and held the berry to her mouth. She took it with her fingers instead.

"I been able to feed myself many a year, Mr. James," she said. "I don't need your foolishment."

"Sometimes, Sister Jane, you ought to let a man do for you." He stepped back to watch her eat. "Wouldn't kill you to let a man do for you."

She puckered. "Sour. Wouldn't set right even in a pie. Not without three, four cups of sugar."

"Which I would love." He was all teeth again.

"Well, you just might at that," she laughed.

He grinned bigger, shifted his weight, and then looked around the room as though some good words might appear on the wall to help him start off a conversation. What he finally said was, "You one lucky lady being here in Burlington 'stead of Nauvoo just now."

"Oh, I miss Nauvoo somethin' fierce. I'd go back tomorrow if I could." She set the iron next to the fireplace.

Isaac shook his head. "Gettin' right scary in Nauvoo, Miz Jane. Death threats 'most every day against Brother Joseph. He declared martial law, you know that?"

She had heard rumors but didn't believe everything. Gossip could churn up all sorts of dust and make you think it was a tornado when it was just a swirl of garbage. She lifted the iron and began pressing another shirt. "What that mean, 'marsh law'?"

Isaac considered it, squinching his face, blinking. He hadn't figured on that question. "It refer to that marsh around Nauvoo. That marsh be our new border and any stranger come across that marsh is like to get hisself shot. That's it."

Jane raised her brows and smiled. "And I think you been sipping blackberry wine, not just eating berries."

He laughed like a horse and hedged again, still looking for words on the wall, or inspiration. "You so pretty when you smile, Miz Jane," he managed.

She uprighted the iron and turned away. "You tryin' to spark with me, Mr. James? Sour blackberries and sweet words?"

"Now you look at me, girl!" He took her shoulders, made her face him. "My, my, you pretty! And you know what I love best of all? I never see you dirty. Of course, when you first come to Nauvoo, you look like somethin' the dog drag in off the street."

She tried not to laugh. It was plain this man hadn't gone a-courtin' in a long while. Maybe this was his first attempt, and he was awkward as a newborn goat. "Thank you kindly," she said.

"I don't mean no disrespect. Wasn't your fault. You come all that distance! Why, you couldn't look bright and new after such a journey! But since that day, you keep yourself so clean. Somethin' like that sure do impress a man."

"Is that so?"

"Except for that bit of berry juice on your apron—"

"Your fault—"

"Except for that—and I full accept the blame—you the cleanest woman I ever seed."

"I just set this apron two hours in the bluing tub. I guess I be settin' it there again."

"And I beg pardon for my berry stainin' it. Still, you the cleanest woman I know."

"Is that the only thing you like about me, Mr. James? That I'm clean?" She had some motherly instinct to help him along in his efforts—and some womanly instinct to resist them.

"You clean as a new shaved lamb."

She looked at him straight. "Now is that really the best you can do?"

"No." His face took on a bold and ready cast, like he was aiming a gun at a squirrel and set to fire. He breathed in deep. "How's this? Marry me, Jane."

Her head fell back, and she stared at him. Yes, that was one serious face he was wearing: round as a cabbage and black as hers and fixed somewhere between proud and scared. She took the iron and put it to work, stroked the shirt sleeve twice. "Well, right at the moment," she said, "I'm a little bit busy an' a little bit sweaty to be a bride."

"Aw, Miz Jane, you know I don't mean right this moment."

"I know," she sighed.

"So. That be a yes or a no or a let's-wait-and-see?"

"One of 'em, sure 'nough."

Again, he showed off his teeth. "Then I keep bringin' you blackberries until they full ripe, Miz Jane, and you makes your answer solid." He touched her shoulder.

She stepped back, shook out the just-pressed shirt, and laid it atop the ones she had already finished.

"Jane," he said. "Jane?" Seemed he wanted her to say his name. She didn't, only set another shirt across the table. "I make you one good husband, Jane. I ain't very much, but I's all I got to offer. Never had me a wife before. Kept the Mormon faith many years now. Even paid tithing, poor as I be. Now, I may not seem to you all that grand a fellow to look on, but maybe—I say maybe—you might want to think things over good."

She glanced at him. He was watching his feet.

"Miz Jane, I jus' don't know how you goin' do better'n me," he murmured.

The iron was ready. She went to work again, pressing another collar before answering, "You mean because I got me a son without a proper daddy?"

Isaac cleared his throat, spoke softly. "His daddy white, ain't he?"

"Good and white. A minister."

"Oh. Best kind o' white." He sucked in his lips and bit down. "If that's what you want," he said after considerable silence.

She let her breath out slow. "His daddy wasn't my doin'. I got took."

He hummed a sad "I already knew" sound and said, "Them white men pretty good at sirin' babies. Ain't good at marryin' the baby's mama if she dark, though."

"Like I say, I got took. But Sylvester Manning is surely my boy, and I won't have you bad-mouth him."

"Now, Miz Jane, I didn't mean nothin' by it. What you gettin' your jaws so tight about?"

She pointed the iron at him. "When it come to my baby, I get my jaws and everythin' else tight. I don't want nobody takin' a bad view of my son."

Isaac stepped back. "Miz Jane, I know Sylvester be a good boy. Ain't you seed me with him? Oh, we's friends!"

Jane took in a simmer-down breath and changed the subject. "So. This law of the marshes—"

"I seed it myself, Miz Jane," he answered fast. "Brother Joseph, he all dressed up in his finest, you know? Lieutenant General of the Nauvoo Legion! And he lift his sword high as he could, like a king's—what? What you call that thing a king hold?"

"Scepter."

He sighed, "You smart too, woman. You know all the right words."

"I recognize a few."

"Joseph, he hold up that sword like one bright scepter. I seed it with my own eyes. He take it out of that carryin' thing, and he say, 'I calls God and angels to witness'—other words like them, I ain't rememberin' everything. Most powerful words I ever hear from his mouth, though. He say we goin' keep free."

"We colored folk?"

"We Latter-day Saint folk, Jane. Brother Joseph, he hold his sword up to heaven like he summonin' all the host of God and them flamin' chariots too."

"Was all the Nauvoo Legion alongside him when he done that?"

"Yes indeed!"

She wished she had seen it. She always did love it when the Nauvoo Legion got out uniforms and put itself in lines. She loved the sound of that bugle and the choir singing and the perfect march steps of the soldiers who did look like God's own elect troop. Someday, she hoped Syl might join them.

"'Course, you must know things is bad—oh, very bad—for Brother Joseph now," Isaac went on. "He was in hidin'. Last I hear, he give himself up to the ones goin' after him. They was takin' him to Carthage Jail. I don't know as he goin' be wearin' them shirts you pressin' so fine. Leastwise, not anytime soon," he said so soft she could barely hear. "Some folk say he won't be comin' back to us. Not alive, anyways. Next time he be wearin' one of those shirts, might be in the coffin."

Jane wanted to slap Isaac for saying that. "He be God's prophet! Lord ain't goin' let nothin' happen to that man!"

Isaac popped a berry in his mouth. "People is turnin' against him fast, Jane. Even Brother William Law from the First Presidency. You hear 'bout that?"

"Brother Law?" She could hardly imagine. Brother William was one of Joseph's truest friends. She had seen William and his brother Wilson at the Mansion House for supper—joking, chatting, enjoying the good company and Lew's cooking. How could William Law become an enemy?

"Both them Law brothers be against him. William and Wilson."

"No!" She felt all her blood sink to her feet.

"Turnin' on him like they was wolves. Sayin' spiteful things." He nodded, taking himself very seriously and eating another berry. "Printed up a paper claimin' all manner of hurtful business, from what I been told." The berry juice dribbled down his chin. "'Course the paper never seed the light of day. The Saints decided it might be better to bust up the press than to let the press bust up Zion. But them apostates was set—the Laws and ol' Higbee too—set to tell the world Joseph Smith was a fell-down prophet. Callin' for his blood. Thirstin' after it, sure 'nough."

"Brother Joseph's blood?" She stared at the black juice on her apron and then at the little drop falling down Isaac's mouth.

Isaac nodded, paused a long time, and then begged, "Aw, marry me, Jane!"

She cut her eyes away. "I'll give you my answer later. You just now give me a lot to think on. I need some time, Brother Isaac. Some good time."

"Well, I need me some good times too!" he said. "When I come by later on, the berries be black as night and sweet as you."

"That so? I might get out a pie yet."

"And I hope your answer be sweet as that pie."

"Whatever the answer, it be the right answer, Mr. James."

"Oh, I like that word. *Right*. I like that word much as I like that other one—that—what a king has?"

"A scepter?"

"That's it. A scepter. You make me feel like a king, Miz Jane, teaching me a word like that one there. Wish you could've seed Brother Joseph. They's somethin' about a man with a scepter."

She met his eyes. "Careful now."

He was all teeth again. "Yes, ma'am, Miz Jane," he said.

NOTES

The chapter title, "Just As I Am," is from the title of hymn number 417 in *Hymns for the Family of God*.

Jane records her departure from the Mansion House in her history as follows: "Soon after they broke up the Mansion and I went to my mother, there was not much work because of the persecutions, and I saw Brother Joseph and asked him if I should go to Burlington and take my sister Angeline with me? He said yes go and be good girls, and remember your profession of faith in the Everlasting Gospel, and the Lord will bless you. We went and stayed three weeks then returned to Nauvoo."

1844

22

OUT OF MY BONDAGE

The Lord . . . hath sent me to bind
up the brokenhearted.
ISAIAH 61:1

Now all this time, while the Manning family and Isaac James were living in Nauvoo and Elijah Abel was in Ohio, a number of other Mormons of color were down Cotton Country—in this case, Mississippi.

Samuel Chambers, a thirteen-year-old slave, was baptized in a pond. It was a secret baptism; his master knew nothing about it. A new convert named Preston Thomas preached the gospel to this boy, despite any policy set against converting slaves without their masters' consent. Preston Thomas, you see, was burning with gospel. He knew God was no respecter of persons and that the Church of Christ could use some color. Now maybe he couldn't find anyone else to listen to him besides this slave boy, and maybe he was tired of being cast out of folks' homes when they found out it was the Mormon gospel he was preaching, but the truth is, Preston Thomas was so fired up that he told the good news to anyone who'd listen. He found ready ears on Samuel's black head.

Of course, Samuel Chambers had heard something about Jesus already, for the Good Book was preached every week where Sam lived. Massa himself read the words to his slaves. Massa's sermon usually said things like, "Blessed are the patient; blessed are the faithful; blessed are the cheerful; blessed are the submissive; blessed are the hardworking; blessed are the obedient." And the scripture that for sure got overworked was: "He that knoweth his master's will and doeth it not shall be beaten with many stripes." Another of Massa's favorites was "Servants, obey your masters." Oh, they all knew that verse!

So Samuel was ready to hear new words about Jesus, who came to the world to save sinners. Preston Thomas told this slave boy that the Good Lord had a fountain of pure water where all were invited to drink and the Lord had a feast of good food where all could eat whether or not they had money to pay for it. This good food and this pure water was the gospel itself. You could close your eyes and feel it moving down your throat and warming your insides, he said. And Samuel Chambers, skinny child though he was, his voice not yet sunk to its man-tones—he felt it. Warm indeed.

After dark, when sometimes the slaves buried their dead, Samuel went to be buried in the water and brought back out again, just like the resurrected Lord from the tomb. Then, dripping wet, Sam returned to the slave quarters behind his master's mansion. No one but him and Elder Thomas knew his life had just turned a corner.

He'd lose contact with the Church before long but not for good. Eventually, he'd join the Saints out west—after he grew up and got made free, though at this time, freedom was a ways and a war away.

Three other Mississippi slaves would have a big hand in the Mormon future: Hark Lay, Oscar Crosby, and Green Flake. They were good friends already, and Hark and Oscar had the same mama, though different owners. Their masters, Billy Lay, William Crosby, and James Madison Flake knew each other well. James Flake was from North Carolina, where Green had been born, but he sold hounds in Mississippi, so he, Billy Lay, and William Crosby got acquainted over a passel of dogs. William Crosby got baptized first, after two missionaries (James Brown and Peter Haws) preached to him. Then Brother Crosby converted Billy Lay's wife. James Flake got converted by Benjamin Clapp. All of these men would be together in the Mormon migration later on, headed by the very man who baptized Green Flake on April 7, 1844: John Brown. It may strike you as funny that a Brown baptized a black named Green, but that's how it was—colorful.

Green Flake was a tall, muscular young man, sixteen when he went into the waters of Mormonism. And he could sing—oh, he had a voice could fill a canyon! Even so, his singing was not quite as good as Hark Lay's. Green's voice was powerful; Hark's was not only big but sweet. He had the right name, that's for sure. His mama had given him that name after hearing the words "Hark, hark, a lark!" and liking the sound.

Now Hark was a large, brown lark with a very deep song, but his name and his voice seemed like they had wings indeed and came straight out of heaven. Hark Lay had a voice that knew the depths of the soul and could go there easy, just like sinking under water. He could baptize a song and confirm it with the Holy Ghost. Together, Hark and Green, close in age and size, would blend their deep tones many a night in later years on the trek west.

Oscar Crosby, already approaching thirty, wasn't the singer these two teens were; he was a silent and steady man. But he enjoyed listening to song. Song was part of everyday life. Oh, yes, most of us sang back then as we worked the fields. We sang about Jesus, how he endured his load even when he got whipped, slapped, and finally killed on a cross. We sang how even after dying at Calvary, our Lord came back, full resurrected. Jesus had that spirit in him that never could be killed, at least not in a permanent way. We sang with the rhythm our ancestors had brought out of Africa, rhythm that set the plow's speed when we furrowed the ground, that matched the picking of the cotton and the weeding of those fields. We sang words that made it seem the Lord was working right alongside us:

> Well, you seen how they done my Lord—
> But He never said a mumbling word.
> Well, they cut and hewed him out a cross.
> But He never said a mumbling word.
> Well, they pierced him in his side,
> But He never said a mumbling word,
> Not a word,
> Not a word,
> Not a word.

And there was Jesus, dropping the seeds into the earth, never saying a mumblin' word, just being there because we were singing him there.

We sang how the Lord punished those who disrespected him or disrespected his creations. We sang about our ancestor, Noah, for example, and about God's anger when the children of men became so wicked, God decided enough was enough; it was time to flood the earth. And only Noah had an ark. One of those songs went like this:

> Well, God got angry on his throne
> Angels in the Heavens begin to moan,
> And God says, 'Go down, angels—stir up a flood!
> Block out the sun; change the moon into blood!'
> They tell me, Great God, when it started to rain,
> The women and the children, they begin to
>   scream,
> They knock on the windahs, knock on the door,
> Cryin', "O Brother Noah, won'cha take on more?"
> Noah says, "I am sorry, my friend,
> But God's got the key and you can't come in."
> Rain, children! God's gonna send the water from
>   Zion!

And He's gonna raise the Heavens up higher,
And it's gonna rain! It's gonna rain!

At the time, it seemed like a song to help us plant seed faster, but it was prophecy as much as melody. For before long, it was going to rain once more in this nation because of man's wickedness. Only this time, it'd be blood drenching the land.

But that flood was some years away yet. There were more immediate troubles—and high waters too—for the Mormons.

For a brief while, the Flakes were in Nauvoo. James Madison Flake used Green's labor as tithing now and again, and Green built his master a brick house and once took the Flakes' young son, William, to the top of the Nauvoo Temple so they could survey the city which they thought would be their fixed dwelling place.

Little did they know how soon everything would change.

Nobody knew.

Elijah Abel, in Cincinnati, was settled. He certainly was not ready for bad news from Nauvoo. The news he was getting now was that Joseph Smith was running to be president of these United States.

Brigham Young, that broad-faced, auburn-haired president of the Quorum of the Twelve Apostles, and apostle Heber C. Kimball, who wore whiskers down his jaws, had reached Cincinnati on May 26, 1844, at 6:00 P.M. They were carrying that grand news about Brother Joseph's candidacy. Elijah saw them at church the next day, greeting them with a good handshake but no embrace. He reported that there were a number of white sisters—named three specifically—in the Cincinnati ward who were far too accustomed to speaking evil of the Lord's anointed. Elder Abel expected at least some acknowledgment or praise for this report but was pretty much ignored. These men were attending to other business.

At 8:00 A.M., May 27, all the elders were summoned to a conference. Elijah attended too but mostly held the door for the others. At the meeting, Brother Brigham discussed the need of government reform. Then two thousand copies of Joseph Smith's platform, "Powers and Policy of the Government," were distributed.

Elijah, a good reader now, was pleased but not surprised by Brother Joseph's words on slavery: "Petition, ye goodly inhabitants of the slave states, your legislators to abolish slavery by the year 1850, or now. Pray Congress to pay every man a reasonable price for his slaves out of the surplus revenue arising from the sale of public lands and from the deduction of pay from the members of Congress. Break off the shackles from the poor black man and hire him to labor like other human beings; for an hour of virtuous liberty on earth is worth a whole eternity of bondage."

Yes, sir, Elijah knew he could count on Brother Joseph to take a stand against slavery!

"America," said the tract, "is not an asylum for the oppressed as long as the degraded black slave is compelled to hold up his manacled hands and cry, 'O liberty, where are thy charms that sages have told me were so sweet?'"

Good words, thought Elijah. Brother Joseph said such good words!

It was with this tract in hand that Elder Abel set out to the Cincinnati streets and there noticed an announcement: an abolitionist oration to be delivered by a former slave named Frederick Douglass. The rough sketch of the orator showed a familiar lion-face, with hair like a combed mane. Why, this was that old caulker, Fred Bailey! Elijah was sure of it. Fred Bailey had not only escaped slavery, he had gone and got himself a new name! A nice one too: Frederick Douglass. That name had some music to it!

Elijah was in the audience when the abolitionist rally began. A large, fair-haired woman named Elizabeth Cady Stanton spoke first, followed by the famous newspaperman, William Lloyd Garrison, who stood stiff as a fence post to introduce Mr. Frederick Douglass.

Elijah, on the back row, squinted to be sure he knew this face. Oh, yes, it was Bailey. But this wasn't Bailey's voice. This voice matched the lion's head: sure of itself, able to rise in fierce waves or to whisper in a way that could pierce any real Christian's heart. Why, it wasn't a far cry from Elijah's own preacher voice!

Douglass began with a pretend dialogue between a master and a slave, dramatizing each role:

"What can you do for me that will compensate for the liberty you've taken away?"

"Providence," says the master, "decreed that one man should be subservient to the other."

"The robber," said the slave (and Douglass made each word a lesson on theatrical possibility), "who puts a pistol to your breast may make the same plea. Providence gives him a power over your life and property. But it has also given me legs to escape with, and what should prevent me from using them?"

The audience laughed, though Elijah heard a pair of finely dressed men say, "I don't believe that man ever was a slave. I never heard a slave talk like that. I'd bet my father's watch this fellow's a trained pretender. Maybe even a painted white man."

Elijah wanted to bear his own witness: "Now, you listen to me, sir! I knew Fred Bailey—Frederick Douglass—when he been a slave!" But Elijah understood how powerless his own words would be when Douglass himself was being disregarded.

"I was broken in body," Douglass continued—and these are his real words—"in soul and in spirit. My natural elasticity was crushed, my intellect languished, the disposition to read departed, the cheerful spark that lingered about my eye died; the dark night of slavery closed in upon me—and behold a man transformed into a brute!" At this, Douglas stripped off his shirt and showed the whip marks on his back. The women in the audience gasped. One of them fainted.

Oh, Elijah knew this life Douglass was showing! But again the white men ridiculed the former slave. One asked, "When was the last time you heard a nigger use a word like *languished?*" The other laughed and shook his head. Elijah wanted to slug them both, so he pocketed his fists and tried repeating scriptures in his mind about the blessed state of peacemakers. Soon he was clenching his fists so tight his knuckles felt brittle. If he were to hit one of these know-all white men, his hands would certainly shatter, a riot would start up, and he might get to meet Judge Lynch face to face. He dug his fingernails into his palms and told himself again, "Blessed are the peacemakers. And may those making a mock of freedom go straight to hell and burn like dry tinder."

"I had now penetrated to the secret of all slavery and oppression," Douglass finished. He turned to his audience and clothed himself again. "Slaveholders are only a band of successful robbers, who left their homes and went into Africa for the purpose of stealing and reducing my people to slavery!"

"Yes, yes," breathed Elijah.

"And I deny that the black man's degradation," Douglass said in a louder voice than before—a voice of conclusion—"is essential to the white man's elevation. I deny that the black man should be tied, lest he outstrip you in the race of improvement. I deny the existence of any such necessity, and affirm that those who allege the existence of any such, pay a sorry compliment to the white race!" Douglass pounded the podium at the end of every sentence. "The more men you make free, the more freedom is strengthened, and the more men you give an interest in the welfare of the state, the greater is the security of the state!" Now he pounded the podium twice and lifted his arms. Oh, Elijah knew what Frederick Douglass was feeling—that lightning which said your words had gone straight to the listeners' hearts and were throbbing there. Elijah stretched his fingers, lifted his hands from his pockets, and began the applause, which applause soon sounded like a roar all around him. It lasted a long time but did not include the two white "gentlemen" who refused to believe a slave could know the meaning of such a word as *languished*.

Elijah wanted to make his way to the stand, to ask if perchance Mr. Douglass had any remembrance of him. But Frederick Douglass, with Miss Elizabeth Cady Stanton, was thronged. And Elijah, turning to leave, found himself face to face with Levi Coffin.

"Mr. Elijah Abel," said Coffin.

"Yes, sir. You remember my name, sir."

"And thee remembers mine?"

"I do, Mr. Levi Coffin."

"There could be times when it would be best if thee did not remember it," he whispered.

"Understood."

"So thee are here now. In Cincinnati."

"Some years. Married."

"Good. Marriage is an honorable state. There are many honorable states, of course. Most of them to the north."

Elijah laughed.

"We may have need of thee," said Coffin quietly.

"I'm ready to help you however and whenever I might." He gave Levi Coffin his address.

Over the next weeks, Elijah Abel gave Brother Joseph's platform to all the colored folks he knew, though most of them couldn't read—and even if they could, the platform words were very big and complicated. So Elijah would explain what "shackles" were, and what it meant to have "manacled hands." Now of course, colored people couldn't vote during this time, but many had acquaintances who could, including some abolitionists who would take comfort from Joseph's bold stand. Elijah told his colored friends to get these papers into the hands of any sympathetic whites they could find, and he worked to get the platform into good hands too. Maybe the Brethren didn't want him preaching to the white population, but they surely couldn't object to his giving Joseph Smith's presidential words to a man who could vote!

It was a July day, after Elijah had taken copies of the platform to yet another abolitionist meeting, that he returned home to find Mary Ann weeping.

"What?" he said, his mind raking up possibilities.

She couldn't speak for a moment. Then, "Oh, 'Lijah!" she sobbed, "they killed your prophet. Joseph Smith. His brother too. Killed 'em both. A mob done it. Shot 'em stone dead!"

NOTES

The chapter title, "Out of My Bondage," is from the first line of hymn number 401 in *Hymns for the Family of God*.

Samuel Chambers was born May 21, 1831, in Pickens County, Alabama, but grew up in Mississippi and was secretly baptized there. Details about his life are mostly from "Saints without Priesthood," 18.

The "Slaves' Beatitudes" ("Blessed are the patient," etc.) are recorded in Blassingame, *Slave Community*, 63.

Green Flake was born in Anson, North Carolina, January 6, 1828, a slave of James Madison and Agnes Flake. When he was sixteen, Green was baptized in the Mississippi River on April 7, 1844. James Madison Flake offered freedom to his slaves when he prepared to go to Nauvoo, but Green and his fellow slaves Liz and Edie elected to remain slaves and to accompany the Flake family, though Edie eventually returned to Mississippi (see Joel Flake, "Green Flake," citing Carol Read Flake's *Of Pioneers and Prophets*, 60). The Flakes were in Nauvoo shortly before Joseph Smith was killed, where Green built them a brick house.

Green Flake's baptism date is recorded in Brown, *Pioneer John Brown*, 46. Church records show the date as August 8, 1847, but that is the date Green was rebaptized by Tarleton Lewis and reconfirmed by Wilford Woodruff (Flake, "Green Flake," 7). Though at least one source (Bullock, *Pioneer Camp of the Saints*, 112) reports that James Madison Flake gave Green to Brigham Young, the data strongly support the view that until James and Agnes Flake departed for San Bernardino, Green was their slave, his labor used and accepted as tithing. It is true that upon their departure to California, Green was "given" to Brigham Young, but again, this was considered tithing. One oral report from Green's last living grandchild, Bertha Marie Udell, says Green was traded for a yoke of oxen (quoted in Flake, "Green Flake," 16). If that is the case, it may have been the same yoke the Flake family used on their journey to San Bernardino.

Hark Lay, according to Kohler, "had been born on the Crosby plantation in Monroe County, Mississippi in 1825." His mother, Vilate, called her son Hark "after overhearing a visiting actress dramatize a lovely poem about 'our feathered creatures.' The words 'Hark! a lark!' were oft repeated in the performance and stuck in her mind." Kohler notes also that Hark Lay "loved music and could usually be located by following the sound of his clear and mellow voice as he sang while he worked." She further states that a fiddler in Hark's pioneer company, named Hans Christian Hansen, often played his violin at night during the trek west and could get Hark to dance a mean jig (*Southern Grace*, 58–59).

Oscar Crosby, Hark Lay's brother, was born around 1815, making him the oldest of the three slaves in the lead pioneer company (Kohler, *Southern Grace*, 17). His master, William Crosby, had been converted by two missionaries, James Brown and Peter Haws, "who had travelled through Monroe County on their return to Nauvoo" (Kohler, *Southern Grace*, 42).

The song lyrics quoted in this chapter, typical of early spirituals, were part of the music collection (records) of Elsie Gray, Darius Gray's mother. We do not know the lyricists' names.

That Brigham Young, Heber C. Kimball, and William Smith were in Cincinnati in late May 1844, campaigning for Joseph Smith and meeting with the elders of the Church to do the same is documented in *History of the Church*, 7:136.

That "Elijah Abel 'preferred a charge' against three women for their failure to attend church meetings and for 'speaking disrespectfully of the heads of the church'" in Cincinnati is supported by Bringhurst, *Saints, Slaves, and Blacks*, 88.

The statements by Frederick Douglass are authentic, all found in Preston, *Young Frederick Douglass*, or in any compilation of Douglass's orations.

23

IN THE HOUR OF TRIAL

Blessed are the dead which die in the Lord.
REVELATION 14:13

Willard Richards's handwritten message was sent from Carthage to Nauvoo on June 27, 1844, at 8:00 P.M.: "Joseph and Hyrum are dead. Taylor wounded. I am well. The job was done in an instant."

By the time the letter arrived, the Saints had already heard of the murder. It had been a rainy day. Come nightfall, dogs were howling as though the news was sitting like crows on branches, and the dogs could sense it. The people of Nauvoo beat drums, striking out rhythms of grief and warning, beat them till dawn.

Lew, still the Mansion House cook, was awakened by Emma's wail before the drums even started. Emma was pregnant; he thought at first she might be having her pains. Then he knew it wasn't that. A cold certainty filled him. He understood exactly what had happened and went into the hall. When Samuel Smith approached, his steps so slow, like he was carrying the very body of Joseph, Lew knew for sure.

"Brother Joseph dead, ain't he," Lew said.

Samuel, looking much like the Prophet, nodded once.

"Hyrum too?"

Another nod. Samuel tried to speak several times before the words came, and they came weak: "We're heading to Carthage to get their bodies." Samuel's eyes focused somewhere above Lew's head. "We could use some help," he said.

Lew whispered, "I'da laid down my own life for him, sir. If I coulda."

"We all would have."

No one spoke as they set out, late at night, horses pulling the two wagons, Dimick Huntington leading the way. Each wagon carried a rough pine box, ready to hold the burdens waiting at Carthage. By the time they arrived, it was the morning of June 28.

Willard Richards met them a short distance from the jail, told them the whole story: how Joseph had known he would be slaughtered, how on the way to Carthage, the Prophet had stopped at the Nauvoo Temple, looking it over, and then run his eyes across all of Nauvoo, saying with sad satisfaction: "This is the loveliest place and the best people under the heavens. Little do they know the trials that await them."

The mob had their faces painted "to look like a gang of Negroes," Brother Willard said. Lew didn't voice his thought that a "gang of Negroes" would never have been so brutal as a white mob.

Hyrum had fallen first, taking two balls to the head, crying, "I am a dead man!" He had stared at Joseph for a moment while the Prophet moaned, "Oh, my dear brother Hyrum." Then Hyrum's stare went glassy, and Joseph Smith had no time for any more goodbye than that. Shots were coming fast. Joseph rushed to the window and was murdered as he stood, his last words being, "O Lord my God." He fell through the window. Dead.

John Taylor had been wounded. Richards hadn't been able to find help for him until past midnight, as everyone seemed to have fled Carthage, sure the Mormons would seek revenge.

Brother Willard didn't weep as he told the story. His voice shivered sometimes but more from fury than grief. Or maybe it was shock. His mouth was moving fine, the words understandable, but he was so stiff and tight, he looked like he had been cemented from sinew to bone. Or sometimes he would stand perfectly still and move just his eyes down. Such as when he said the word *dead*.

Willard Richards was a big man, husky, round-faced with a shiny pate, a set-back hairline, and brown eyes now hard and fixed as a doll's. To no one in particular Richards commented, "Joseph knew he'd be killed. He had a good deal of anxiety after leaving Nauvoo, anxiety he had never before had when he was under arrest. He seemed depressed."

"He knew," Lew murmured. "For sure he knew."

Brother Richards looked on him briefly but seemed blind. "They promised us safety," he said. "Joseph asked me, 'If we go into the cell, will you go in with us?' And I answered, 'Brother Joseph, you did not ask me to cross the river with you. You did not ask me to come to Carthage. You did not ask me to come to jail with you. Do you think I would forsake you now?'"

Dimick Huntington observed, "You were with him to the end, Doctor Richards."

Brother Willard went on. "I said to him, I said, 'Brother Joseph, I will tell you what I will do: if you are condemned to be hung for treason, I will be hung in your stead, and you shall go free.'" Briefly, Brother Willard's eyes watered. He pressed them with his fingers, which still had lines of dried blood in all the creases. "Joseph said, 'You cannot.' And I replied, 'I will.' But I could not." Now, the doctor bowed his head. His shoulders shook like a great sob was coming, but it never arrived. He resumed his stiffness. "When we heard the mob shout, I glanced an eye by the window curtain. I saw a hundred armed men 'round the door. There was no escape."

Lew found his own eyes tearing for Brother Richards. But these were little tears compared to those he soon shed on first seeing the Smith brothers' bodies, both of them laid in the parlor of a place called Hamilton House. Joseph. Hyrum. Lew turned away and put his hands over his mouth to keep from sobbing out loud. Then he wiped his eyes and returned to the others. They were lifting Hyrum into one of the boxes. Lew helped them and then looked at Joseph, the bloody clothes, the bloodless face. The Prophet had been shot in the heart. Lew took Joseph's shoulders and on the call, hoisted the body into the second box. They covered both boxes with branches to shade them from the sun, which had decided to show itself at last.

They returned to Nauvoo in silence, until just before the city limits a brass band came together, sounding dirges. An honor guard of twelve men surrounded each wagon, and thousands of Nauvoo citizens lined the streets. Brother Richards spoke again, his words loud but hollow. The doctor felt drained. "Brothers and sisters, keep the peace. I have pledged my honor and my life for your good conduct."

Both pine boxes were set in the Mansion House parlor. Then the doors were shut. Lew stayed outside but could see through the window as Dimick Huntington and William Marks laid the bodies on tables, washed the brothers' wounds, and put camphor in all the places the gun balls had entered. When Emma came in, she knelt and put her hands around Joseph's face. She was wearing mourning clothes, black wool buttoned to the throat. Lew could see her quaking shoulders, could even hear her words: "Oh, Joseph! Joseph! Have they taken you from me at last?" Then Brother Dimick noticed Lew was watching and closed the curtain.

When Lewis Manning saw the bodies again the next morning, they had been placed in good coffins, not those rough-hewn pine vaults. Each coffin was lined in black velvet and fastened with brass nails. Each lid held a square of glass to protect the martyrs' faces.

Ten thousand Saints passed before their dead prophet and his brother before day's end.

Again, it was Samuel Smith who found Lew that night in the Mansion House garden and repeated the words: "We could use some help." Lew wasn't sure what kind of help was called for this time but followed Samuel inside. There, the coffins were placed in a small bedroom. The pine boxes would be used again now, as decoys. For fear that bloodthirsty men might unbury and mutilate the bodies, bags of sand were placed in these roughshod, outer caskets. It was these "coffins" that Dimick Huntington would drive to the funeral the next day.

At midnight, a group of men, led by Brother James Emmett as musketed guard, carried the real coffins to the basement of the yet unfinished Nauvoo House. That was where Isaac Lewis Manning, under Brother Huntington's direction, had already dug two graves.

NOTES

The chapter title, "In the Hour of Trial," is from the title of hymn number 122 in *Hymns for the Family of God*.

The statement by Joseph Smith "This is the loveliest place and the best people under the heavens" is from *History of the Church*, 6:554.

The record of Joseph Smith's anxiety for his safety, as reported by Willard Richards, is found in *History of the Church*, 6:592.

Willard Richards's promise to die in Joseph's place is in *History of the Church*, 6:616.

Isaac Lewis Manning's claim that he would have laid down his own life for the Prophet had he been allowed to is quoted from his obituary (in Carter, *Negro Pioneer*, 13). His obituary in the *Deseret News* also records that he was among those who went to Carthage to collect the bodies of the Smith brothers and helped dig their graves (in Carter, *Negro Pioneer*, 13).

The report of rainy weather, dogs howling, and the Nauvoo citizens beating drums on the day of Joseph's martyrdom is taken from Madsen, *I Walked to Zion*, 118.

The fact that Joseph and Hyrum's bodies were laid out in the Hamilton House after their martyrdom is from Allen and Leonard, *Story of the Latter-day Saints*, 211.

24

I Know Who Holds Tomorrow

*Fear ye not . . . ye are of more value
than many sparrows.*
MATTHEW 10:31

Jane Manning had been in the crowd when Willard Richards addressed them. Isaac James was beside her. She allowed him to take her hand. "I like to die myself," Jane whispered. "I could just lay me down and die, Isaac." This marked the first time she had called him by his name without attaching "Brother" or "Mister."

"Now, Jane," he answered in a voice reverent as hers, "you can't want to die just because he did. We should all want to live now and do much good as possible." He wiped her cheeks.

That was not the time or place for him to bring up the subject he wanted to, but he did bring it up three days later, while Jane was sweeping the floor. He entered after two knocks and started talking before she could even say good morning.

"Jane," he said, "the truth is, Brother Joseph would agree what I'm about to say."

"Hello, Isaac."

"We need to get on with livin'."

"Pleasant to see you this fine mornin'."

"We need to go ahead and get married and move forward, even with the Prophet gone."

She had the impulse to hit him with the broom, let him catch it hard for approaching this idea so soon after the Prophet's death. She resisted, though, and waited for the rest of his speech.

"Truth is, you and me is the best we got, and it's time," he said without any pause. He had practiced. That was clear.

Jane looked at him long.

"Jane Manning," he said, "I love you." Now he waited for her answer. She turned her attention to the broom instead and let him stammer around for his next words. He finally came with up a few: "We was meant to raise families, and you looks like a woman who could bring forth a good many children, and God say we was meant to multiply and punish this earth."

"How you plan on punishin' this earth?"

"Ain't you heard about me? I be one of the best farmers in Nauvoo! Got me a whole vineyard of grapes. I punish this earth like it never been punished before."

"Them the best courtin' words you can find?" She swept dust from a corner.

"Truth told, I ain't used to courtin' much. I court the fruit of the vine, and it don't usually answer back."

"Maybe because you punish it too much."

"But that's what God say to do, ain't it? That be His will."

"Mr. James, the word is *replenish*. 'Multiply and replenish.'"

He sighed. "See how you be? You so good with words! Now, I know I ain't good with words like you. Ain't much for courtin' either. But I ain't lyin' when I say I loves you."

Jane let herself look at him and stopped the broom. "Isaac, you doin' fine with this courtin' business. Problem is, I'm still mournin'

Brother Joseph, and I ain't ready to think on gettin' punished and multiplied."

"All right." He touched her cheek with one finger, gentle as could be. "Will you let me know when you is ready?"

"You be the very first to know. I promise on that."

In Nauvoo, the Saints would continue to build the temple. But with Brother Joseph gone, who would lead them? There were several claiming that right, and things got unruly fast—some following Sidney Rigdon, some Brigham Young, and some following their own selves.

Though Sister Emma opposed it, Jane chose to go with Brigham Young, even moved into his place as a servant. The other Mannings decided not to continue on in Nauvoo, nor maybe even with Mormonism. It wasn't just confusion that kept them on the fringes; it was a subtle change in attitude—or the subtle revelation of an attitude that had always been lurking. The temple was nearly done, but no Negro was let inside to be endowed. It was the curse of Cain and Canaan, some said, that meant the black man had to stay outside.

In their patriarchal blessings, Hyrum Smith had told the Mannings they were descended from "Cainaan." That was all right, but none of the Mannings had heard mention how that lineage meant some sort of permanent position on the rough side of the holy gates—leastways, not amongst the Mormons. Of course, most religions talked about lineage some, and "the curse of Cain" was no fresh news. But the Mannings had hoped for better turns of conversation in Zion.

Isaac James commented on the lineage only in passing. Nauvoo was still a better place for a colored man than anywhere south of Mason-Dixon, he said, and his life was better—more opportunities available—than it had ever got in New England. He was a "whittling deacon," a member of the Nauvoo Legion who'd follow the Gentile marshals everywhere they went, whittling innocently but sending the sure message with every bowie-knife notch that he'd just as soon whittle a Gentile's finger as wood, should that finger set itself to harm the Mormon folk. It was a proud position to hold. Indeed, Isaac was contented and didn't look for any more than came on his plate—except a wife.

Two months after the martyrdom, Jane went to him while he was harvesting grapes, taking him cornbread and well water. He showed off his pearly whites at this silent announcement that she was ready to pursue their previous conversation.

"Well, will you lookee here!" he bellowed.

Now Jane was not quite ready to give this man all control of the matter. She offered the water but spoke at him like she was mad, and fingered her ears: "You one noisy man! Ow! Maybe you best watch your mouth and quiet it down some."

He set down his basket of grapes and took the cup, rolling his eyes as he drank, like he'd die of happiness. "Tasty, tasty!" he said. "And I tell you straight, there's another mouth I would prefer to watch. That be your mouth. I prefer to watch it all day and all night long."

"What you'd better watch is your whole self, Mr. James," she said. "Just because I be bringin' you cornbread and drink don't mean—."

"Mr. James?" He made his face mock-hurt and bit into the bread.

"You prefer 'Brother Isaac'?"

"What I prefers is 'honey doll' and 'sweetheart.'" There were cornbread crumbs all around his lips.

"Then you'd best check out a sweets market."

"Wherever you be, Jane Manning, there's enough sweets for me, honey."

"I warn you, Brother Isaac—you best watch yourself."

"I's watchin' myself in your eyes, Miz Jane." He laughed, catching the sound before it got too loud, cutting it off sharp. "And I think," he whispered, "your eyes is gettin' 'customed to me. Maybe to like me a little? Huh? Jus' a little?"

"You likely get the same impression from a lookin' glass, Isaac."

He sighed. "Aw, say me that again."

"I say you likely—"

"My name. Say me my name. I want to watch your mouth say me my name." He finished the cornbread, wiped his mouth with his sleeve, and then took her elbows in his hands. She squirmed, but he held tighter. "Say it, Jane. Come on now, honey."

She looked away, frowning as big as she could—because if she didn't keep the frown, she knew she'd bust out laughing.

"My name. Say it, woman."

"Isaac."

"That's fine." He took her full into his arms then. "I be good for you, Jane," he said. "I promise you that. Life with me will be sweet as sweet can be." He knuckle-kissed her hand.

"Isaac," she said, practicing the name of the man who would be her husband. "Isaac Ja—."

He kissed her full on the lips before she finished the last sounds.

Jane Elizabeth Manning and Isaac James were married in Brigham Young's house, Jane looking grand in blue silk; Isaac in his Sunday-best grays, his pant hems only slightly frayed. They entered the parlor, sitting in the chairs set up for them at the center of the room. The guests—not many, mostly family—surrounded them. Lew handed the marriage license to Brigham Young, who read it aloud. Jane and Isaac stood and said the words that made them husband and wife—though for time only, not (as Jane had heard was done in the temple) for "time and eternity." Brother Huntington gave a prayer, and then they all sang, "Praise God from Whom All Blessings Flow." Afterwards, wedding cake, berry pie, clusters of grapes from Isaac's garden, and good cold water were passed around.

"Mrs. James" liked her new husband fine. She didn't feel she loved him all that much, but love would surely arrive. Besides, some of the Nauvoo women said love wasn't the most important part of marriage, anyway. Respect was. And she could respect her husband. Certainly she enjoyed the sound of "Mrs. James," and she enjoyed giving Syl a daddy. All in all, it was a good wedding and a good day. And Nauvoo days of late were not particularly good. Fact was, Nauvoo days were getting worse and worse, so a good day was more than welcome.

The mobs weren't too troublesome just after the Martyrdom. For a time, Nauvoo seemed to be prospering again. Yet even then, the Saints knew they'd be heading west. Every fine thing they were doing in Nauvoo, every task they were finishing, was to leave a legacy when they set out for another Zion: some valley nestled in the Rocky Mountains. So it wasn't much of a surprise when the persecutions started up once more, though slow at first. These little scourges were just the early hints that the Saints had best get ready for their exodus. When the violence hit full—mobs raging and shrieking like devils at a party—it was simply God's way of moving his people. Just like the Egyptian plagues.

It was no surprise that the closer the Saints came to finishing the temple, the worse the mobs got. Jane herself saw an old white man—his name was McBride, a former soldier of the Revolutionary War—getting half-lynched by a mobber. She had never seen a white man lynched, not even halfway. Never imagined it. It was a ways past dusk. The mobber, one ugly man with greasy hair, stood in the road like he owned it, holding a torch of bundled pitchpine. The torchlight made a yellow circle around him. Then of a sudden, there were three other mobbers with him, also carrying torches. Some words passed between McBride and the men who were set to pester him, though Jane couldn't hear. She could see, though, as these white rascals grabbed the old man and hoisted him up by his roped neck. She clapped both hands over her mouth to hold her scream in, for she certainly knew what these men would do should they discover her. Helpless, she watched them half-hang McBride. They let him down before he finished dying. The moment the mobbers took to their horses, Jane ran for help, which arrived shortly in the form of two good-sized Mormon boys. But McBride ended up passing to his glory anyway, right there beside the tree he had been hanged on.

Such mean men, Jane thought after the mobbers. She was weeping. Meanest men God ever wattled a gut into. *Enjoy hell!* she thought at them. *Seein' you sizzle won't make me drop no tears!*

Soon there were fires—sudden ones started by horse-riding men with ash-blacked faces. These flames could take whole neighborhoods. Then came whippings—white men whipping white men and whatever black men they could find. Why, the whole world had gone mad. Jane knew mankind must be all right at the core, or why would God bother with them? But from what she could see now, mankind's goodness had got wrecked or knotted up somewhere down the line. Leastways, in Illinois it had.

So yes indeed, God was declaring it time to move. Brother Brigham himself made the announcement, and the work of preparation went forward day and night: Men cut up wagon oak, and blacksmiths kept their fires blazing all the time to forge chains and wheel spokes.

When Mrs. Jane Manning James asked her brother, Lew, if he'd be going west, he shook his head no.

She hadn't expected this. All along the trail from Wilton to Nauvoo, he had followed her lead, as he had done his whole life.

She looked at him long, but held her tongue from trying to persuade him of what he didn't want. They had changed. Lew was no longer a little boy or a teenager; he was a man.

"Your mind set on stayin'?" she asked.

"Janey, everything got took out of me when Brother Joseph

died." He sucked in a deep breath. "I just can't see me headin' cross country with these people. Not now."

His words took everything out of her too. "Well, as for me," she said, "you know, I be headed west."

"I do know that."

"God's callin' me to Zion."

"I thought Nauvoo was goin' be Zion," Lew murmured.

"Wherever it goin' be, that's where God's callin' me, and I will answer the call."

Their eyes met, and Lew took her into his arms, the first time he had ever done that. They both were weeping. "You got you a good man, Janey. I trust him look after you same as I would my own self if I was with you. And if he don't, you find you some way to get me word and I come all the way over the prairie jus' so's I can beat the tar outa him." She could feel his tears on her neck.

"Oh now, Lew," she said, "you know he treat me good. Besides which, you couldn't beat the tar out of nothin' but a blackbird— 'less you dance a fellow to death."

"That much trust!" He kissed her lips lightly. "I hope it is God what be leadin' you."

"I full believe it is."

"We meet again. I feel that in my soul."

"I take that as a promise. And I want one more promise from you before I go: Look after Mama."

"I will. You know I will. You look after yourself. You be careful."

She gazed up at him, then turned away, and hurried back to Isaac.

Lucinda announced the next day that she would not be heading west, for she had a good life singing for steamship passengers. She had even found a beau, a young colored fellow who worked the ship's horn like God making thunder. To which Jane teased, "Sound like about the right man for you. Someone who can drown out your saucy words by just pullin' a rope." Lucinda laughed a little and presented Jane with a long-billed, indigo bonnet as a going-away gift. "To keep the sun from your eyes," Lucinda said, then squeezed her own eyes shut and let a few tears drop.

It was no surprise Lucinda was staying behind, but Jane wondered out loud why Anthony and Sarah wouldn't join the trek. Anthony said he had had enough walking to suit his whole life, thank you, and looked to settle down now right there in Lima and raise him up a family—keeping the Sabbath every seven days, just as he had promised Brother Joseph. Sarah was in that way, near ready to bust with new life. And Anthony's sister was due to join them any time, her freedom having been purchased by Joseph Smith's gift.

Jane told her sister, "Sarah, I think I already miss fightin' with you."

Sarah started for her, and Jane thought she'd get one more slap to remember her sister by. But it was not a slap Sarah gave. She threw her arms around Jane's neck and took to sobbing, "I goin' miss you so much! I've never knowed life without you near."

"And I've never knowed life without you. But however far apart we are, we still sisters. We always be sisters. Never forget how much I love you," said Jane.

"Go with God, Janey," Sarah whispered.

Jane let go the embrace and begged, "Come with us."

Anthony stepped forward, shaking his head. No, the Stebbins family wouldn't be walking west.

Neither would Angeline or Peter, who had found steady work selling palm hats.

And neither would Mama Phyllis, who was just too old for another trip. Jane would be the only one of the Mannings who would make this journey across the prairie and the plains.

Leaving her mama ached the most, for Jane knew for true they would not meet again in this world. Mama's husband, Cato Treadwell, had finally got to Nauvoo by steamship, not on foot. He promised he'd be "watchin'" over Phyllis, but he was a poor, weak man. His "watchin'" wouldn't amount to much. Phyllis's friend, Eliza Mead, another former slave who had found the Mormons, was more help than Cato.

In their last moments together, in the Manning cabin at Burlington, Phyllis called Jane to her side. It was just the two of them now. The others had all said their good-byes. "I wanna pray with you, daughter. I wanna ask God to bless you," said Mama. They knelt next to the bed, and Phyllis took Jane's hand. "God, I'm losin' one of my babies," she said, "and she has been so much more than a baby to me and to my family. You raised her up and strengthened her and gave her the wisdom to know what to do, which way to turn. But with all that, she still my baby. Father, I ask you to continue blessin' her. Stay with her and guide her own steps as she journeys away from this family. Bless her the same ways you always bless us: with your love and your abiding care. I ask that you stretch forth your hand of mercy and protection and cover my baby girl with your Spirit. Father, I love her so much, and I feel so full of thanksgivin' that you gave her to me as a daughter." Phyllis looked at her then and put her hands on Jane's head. "My daughter, here in the presence of God, remember to lean on Him and let Him direct you in all things. Bless her, Lord, with every good thing. I call down your angels to watch over her, and I acknowledge your goodness forever. In Jesus' name, amen."

Strong, unwavering love filled Jane Manning James and made her certain of God's call, as though Jesus Christ himself had come down from the skies to issue it.

NOTES

The chapter title, "I Know Who Holds Tomorrow," is from the title of hymn number 96 in *Hymns for the Family of God*.

Jane's reaction to Joseph's death is taken from a reminiscence in *Young*

Woman's Journal 16 (December 1905): 553. The response "You don't want to die because he did" that we have attributed to Isaac James was actually given by Jane's "teachers" (home teachers). Her life history records the following: "I shall never forget that time of agony and sorrow, I went to live in the family of Brother Brigham Young, I stayed there until he was ready to emigrate to this valley. While I was at Bro. Brigham's I married Isaac James, when Brother Brigham left Nauvoo I went to live at Bro. Calhoons. In the spring of 1846 I left Nauvoo to come to this Great and Glorious Valley."

The assignment to the lineage of "Cainaan" in their patriarchal blessings, given by Hyrum Smith, is authentic (Bringhurst, "Elijah Abel," 144, n. 33).

The story of McBride's death is extracted from an account by Eliza Dana Gibbs, quoted in Holzapfel and Holzapfel, *Women of Nauvoo*, 162.

The description of Jane's and Isaac's wedding is based on the description of a typical wedding found in Holzapfel and Holzapfel, *Women of Nauvoo*, 80.

The "whittling deacons" are described in Stegner, *Gathering of Zion*, 39.

That Cato Treadwell, Jane's stepfather, was in Nauvoo at some point is suggested by Wolfinger's research ("Test of Faith," in *Social Accommodation*, 261). Treadwell apparently married Eliza Mead after Phyllis Manning Treadwell's death. One source—Van Hoosear—claims Cato came in the initial trek from Connecticut to Nauvoo (Wolfinger, "Test of Faith," in *Social Accommodation*, 261), but given that in her own history Jane does not mention him as a member of the trek, and given Treadwell's age (he had fought in the Revolutionary war), we think it possible he found an easier path to Nauvoo than the eight-hundred-mile trek on foot.

25

'TIL THE STORM PASSES BY

A man shall be . . . as the shadow of
a great rock in a weary land.
ISAIAH 32:2

On February 4, 1846, Charles Shumway crossed the Mississippi, setting off the Mormon migration. About three thousand Saints, maybe a fifth of Nauvoo's population, loaded all their possessions onto flatboats and skiffs and moved themselves from Nauvoo to the Iowa side of the Mississippi River. They were the vanguard company, led by Brigham Young, and they faced a wilderness as broad and fearsome as the one the Israelites took on centuries past, when God led them to Jericho. Surely God would repeat himself now and show the Saints their land of promise.

On February 15, Brother Brigham ferried across the river to the growing camp beside Sugar Creek. A number of Saints were waiting there in tents and dugouts and quick-made cabins, suffering the cold like it was refinement. Alongside Brother Brigham were two hundred armed men, the Mormon Security Guard.

Jane and Isaac, with Sylvester and a coming baby making its presence known in the swelling of Jane's womb, went with the George Dykes family, not Brigham's or Reynolds Cahoon's, though Jane had lived with the Cahoons after leaving the Youngs. Jane would do the Dykeses' laundry, soaping it in the icy sludge of the Mississippi. Isaac would break and train the oxen which would guide their wagon west, for the oxen knew nothing of the job before them. An unbalanced yoke could tip the whole thing.

From Sugar Creek, the caravan of wagons—called "the Camp of Israel"—snaked west to the Missouri River, slogging through mud sometimes, and muscling wagon wheels out of marshy ruts. And these wagons were something else! Pots and churns and barrels hung onto the sides, banging and clattering with every bump on the trail. Oh, they traveled noisy and resembled a troop of peddlers setting off to sell their wares to the Indians. You wouldn't be surprised to see a whole chicken pen latched on to a wagon's rear! The Saints would not be coming back to this place, so they were taking everything they could, sitting on travel chests, using kettles or soap boxes as foot stools.

By May, they reached Garden Grove—the "magic city of the Woods," some hundred and fifty miles west of the Mississippi. It was a grove indeed, tall, shell bark hickory trees, and short flowers of all description everywhere. It was a brief stay in that beauty, though it did afford Syl an opportunity to play with the herd boys, who were making stick fences for crickets and pretending the ugly bugs were cows trapped inside a corral. They'd stack pebbles on the crickets' backs and make bets over how long it'd take before the pebbles would fall. Syl even won a bet: a promise of hardtack once they got to Zion. What the herd boys did not mention, though, was that they meant the heavenly Zion, not the earthly one. But Syl dreamed of hardtack until he could taste it.

Any food would have been fine, actually. There was grass aplenty for the animals in this place, but hardly a bite for humans except an occasional squirrel or a bird shot down by a good hunter, and then the meat would be so full of buckshot you could break a tooth satisfying your need. Once, Syl ate grass alongside a flock of sheep. He never did confess to his mama, for she would have found it undignified. As though starvation were the proper thing for a Mormon to do!

The next real stop was Mount Pisgah, smack in the middle of Potawatomi Indian lands and Potawatomi plum trees. Parley P. Pratt had named this place, for it reminded him of where Moses viewed the Promised Land. And no wonder—it brimmed with glades and groves and plenty of timber. It was here Brigham Young celebrated his forty-fifth birthday, fiddlers and a brass band making him a proper party.

Sylvester didn't have a for-sure birthday, though he was near seven years old, give or take. He sure did act like a seven-year old, and was far too busy to get sick. Jane worried her hands through his head anyway, checking for death-carting lice and fever—neither of which ever hit him. He endured her exams, but how he hated them!

What Sylvester James loved was watching the older boys, like twelve-year-old George Smith Rust, do their duties—driving loose animals on foot. Sheep, cattle, oxen. The herd boys had a dirty job. Sylvester knew for sure that grubbing in dirt was part of the fun and wanted to be a "herd boy" himself. He hung back from them only after they yelled at him to leave off. But even hiding in a tree or behind a patch of scrub oak, he could see the herd boys hazing unwilling cows from the river—cows that seemed to be constantly turning their heads to find their own mothers or maybe to spy on Syl. He loved the way the boys looked: tanned almost dark as him, hair uncombed, skin chapped, clothes ragged. There was something about the herd boys more animal than human, and Sylvester admired it. He figured a herd boy could howl like a beast, and nobody would even take notice.

What Jane took notice of more than once was Syl's absence.

She herself couldn't move much, her belly had gotten so baby-big, but she could call Sylvester's name like she had learned to yell from the most cantankerous owl in the woods. Jane Manning James could shout the name of her son louder than the Nauvoo Bell itself, which had once been part of the temple and was now the token of everything left behind, toted in one of the lead wagons.

Travel started up again on June 1. Part of the way, they followed an Indian trail to the Nishnabotna River, passing right through a Potawatomi village. They camped near the Nishnabotna for two days—long enough for Jane to feel her going-down pains and get set to deliver her baby. It was June 10, 1846, that Sister Patty Sessions came to "put Black Jane to bed" after administering to her and anointing her with consecrated oil.

Baby time indeed. Jane lay beside the Dykes wagon behind some makeshift tents. Isaac set some blankets under her head.

Syl had a few hours to himself that day where he could have trailed after the herd boys, but he didn't go far. He could hear his mama's cries, sometimes more like a cat than his mama. He didn't want to venture out too distant.

Isaac took him to the river, hunting for lazy catfish—so he said. Syl understood it was really so he wouldn't hear his mama hurting. A baby's birth was no place for a man anyhow.

"You figurin' on a brother or a sister?" Isaac asked him.

Syl shrugged. "Don't matter. What you want, Brother Isaac?"

Isaac shook his head like Syl had disappointed him mightily. "Now, you tell me, Sylvester, I give you my good name, and you still calls me 'Brother Isaac' like I be nothin' more to you than Brother Brigham or Brother William. Boy, I's your daddy now. Whyn't you call me somethin' like 'Papa' or 'Father'?" He squinted hard. "'Brother Isaac?'" he mimicked. "I's your mama's husband, boy! Legal and lawful."

"Ain't 'ccustomed to it, that's all," Syl said. He wiggled his remaining front tooth. The other tooth had fallen out last week—

not from black canker (though Jane had feared that awful, child-snatching disease), but because time had come for it to fall out.

"So 'customate youself." Isaac folded his arms hard.

"You want you a son, Brother Isaac?"

"Now see? There you go! 'Brother Isaac'!"

The words seemed more observation than anything begging answer, so Syl ignored them. "I mean when Mama done with that there. You wants it a boy?"

Isaac sighed and pointed to a muddy-looking catfish swimming circles in the creek. "You fry up catfish with good butter, and you ain't never tasted a better thing this side of heaven, son." It was a warm day. Isaac's sweat curled around his forehead wrinkles as he spoke.

"That so?" Syl pocketed his hands in his overalls.

"And I got me a boy. A big boy. Boy so big his baby teeth fallin' out right and left. A big boy son named Sylvester James." Isaac took a handkerchief from down his shirt and wiped his brow.

"Son?" repeated Sylvester.

Isaac knelt to be on eye-level with him. "Come on, now. I want you say 'Papa.'"

"I don' think we got no butter."

"What?"

Syl squinched his lips up. "To fry catfish. Should we catch one."

Isaac shrugged. "No matter. We ain't goin' catch nothin' this good mornin'. Only Sister Sessions goin' catch somethin' this good mornin'. Somethin' with a good cry, I hope."

"Yes, sir."

He took Syl by the shoulders and stared at him hard. "Say 'Papa.' Just once. For me. Say it."

The boy looked away. "They's no butter even if we did grab us that fish. Papa."

Isaac embraced him fast, before Syl could resist it. "That's right. That's what I want you call me. Now, when your mama done in there, you and me gots to be good friends. You got to quit runnin' after them herd boys and scarin' my Janey half out of her wits. You promise me that, son? She ain't goin' be able to chase you for some while now. And I expect what with all this yellin' she be doin' now, she ain't goin' have much voice to call you home."

"That's good news!" Syl said.

Isaac shook his head. "Now, listen. You gots to stay put. Repeat after me: 'Papa, I stays put now.'"

Sylvester wiggled his tooth.

"Well?" Isaac said.

He wiggled it again. "If you decide to beat me some? Say, hit me in the mouth? This tooth'd come clean out."

"What?"

"One hit in the mouth, I bet this tooth go straight down my gullet."

Isaac asked softly, "You got beat up before?"

Syl looked skyward, still wiggling his tooth. "No, sir."

"Whupped?"

"No sir."

"Excuse me?"

"No sir, papa."

"Then why you think I goin' beat you, boy? I look like the beatin' sort to you?"

"No, sir, papa."

"Then just give me the words I ask you."

"They slip outa my head."

"Repeat after me: 'Papa—'"

"Papa?"

"'I stays put now!'"

"I stays put now."

"And all together one breath: 'Papa, I stays put now.'"

"Papa, I stays put now!" He grinned.

"That's my good boy!" He rubbed Syl's hair. "And who knows?

Maybe some butter might just appear if that catfish decide to jump out of the water and let itself get catched."

Jane was screaming and hissing now. Isaac and Sylvester were a long ways off, but they could hear her without straining.

"Baby comin'," Isaac said. He stared straight ahead and bit down hard. His jaws looked like long stones. He seemed more angry than excited. Maybe even guilty. "Some of the sisters be pickin' strawberries nearby. Maybe we should get some for your mama, for afterwards."

"Sister Hobbs die when her baby come las' week. Baby die too," Syl commented. Then he yanked his tooth out.

Isaac squinted at him. "Who told you such lies as that?"

"I seen the grave myself. Both of 'em got put under together."

"Sometimes death do stalk a new mother," Isaac admitted. "Not this time, though. Your mama fight too hard to let death snatch her up. And Sister Sessions—"

"I know."

He fixed his eyes on Syl. "Boy! You all bloody, son!"

"My tooth." He showed it.

"Well, stop up the bleeding with some cotton, then. You scarin' me! An' you know what your mama might think."

"What?"

"Aw, put your brains on it!"

"Black canker?" He bit down on his plaid sleeve. The blood spread into the design.

"I guess so. Now, I don't want you scarin' your mama. You got you a fever?" Isaac touched Syl's forehead.

"No, sir, papa." He bit down again. He liked the way he whistled now when he said "sir" and started hunting out "s" words in his head. "Certainly not, sir. Hey. Hey, sir. Listen. I can whistle without tryin', Isaac—papa—listen. Listen."

And that was the moment of Silas James's first cry, which set them running towards the Dykes wagon and the birthing tent.

Some minutes later, the newborn was presented to them, wide mouth bawling. Jane was sitting up, smiling proud.

The Jameses paid Sister Sessions with twenty-four pounds of flour and that night were serenaded by a brass band. It was a fine welcome for this child.

The very next day Jane had her first visitors: Zina Huntington Smith Young (once Joseph Smith's plural wife and now Brigham Young's—and out in the open too, for plural marriage was getting addressed above whispers), accompanied by a new convert, a lively-looking woman named Annie Thomas.

Zina was tall, dark-haired, and had stark features. She already had some fame among the Mormons as one of the powerful women at camp. She, Patty Sessions, and Eliza R. Snow were often speaking in tongues and giving blessings. It was no wonder Zina had learned of Silas's birth. God Himself might have let her in on the news. But Jane hardly felt ready for company. She spit-combed her hair, but it was an unruly fleece at the moment. "Please excuse my appearance," she said.

Zina assured her they had not come to check on appearances, only to see the new baby.

This seemed Sister Thomas's cue, and she started jabbering, "You must be Black Jane. I'da guessed it. You mind I look at the pickaninny?"

Jane said, "My baby's name is Silas," and pulled back the shawl where he was cradled. Sister Thomas took to jawing then: "Oh, Zina—look! Cutest little nigger baby I ever did see! I owned me a pickaninny once," she whispered like it was a secret only for the white women to share. "I inherited it for my sixteenth birthday. Four years old and black as a crow. I gave it up once we joined the Saints. My husband asked me to, and I obeyed—but it was hard." Now she turned to Jane and spoke up. "So when I heard you'd had you one, I told Sister Zina to take me to you right this minute! Oh, just looking makes me miss my own. I left so much behind—my good clock, all my china, my pickaninny, and a fine silk dress."

Zina Young interrupted to ask if Jane was recovering all right.

"A little tired yet," Jane admitted. "The birth wasn't easy."

Annie was off making more words: "Childbirth—that's a pleasure I'm still waiting on. I've only took my husband eight months ago. Why, I hardly know how to—"

Zina cut her off. "Thank you, sister. We'll let Jane take her ease now."

"I am a bit tired," Jane said.

"There are many sick these days. The Lord has blessed us." What Zina Young meant was that there were many women set to deliver babies. That was how they said it in those days: "sick." She went on, "Eliza Lyman is almost ready herself."

"Is that a fact?" Jane said.

This Eliza Lyman was formerly Eliza Partridge, daughter of Bishop Edward Partridge, who Elijah Abel had attended as an undertaker. She was that same glossy-haired woman who had bought Jane her first lengths of cloth in Nauvoo and later told her about plural marriage. Since the Martyrdom, Eliza had married one of the Church's Twelve Apostles, Amasa Lyman. The way Jane understood things, Eliza was sealed to Brother Joseph for eternity, but Amasa would be her earthly husband. Zina Young was also sealed to Joseph for afterwards and married to Brigham Young for now. Besides being sister-wives for the eternities, Zina and Eliza were also step-sisters in this world, so it made sense Zina would know all about Eliza's condition.

"You take your ease," said Zina, "and when you're ready, you might call upon Sister Lyman."

"Yes, ma'am," said Jane.

But ease was not meant to be a part of this journey. They were on their way to Keg Creek the very next day, traveling through high, rolling prairies. Workmen up ahead were building a bridge for the caravan. Sometimes the pioneers built bridges over the waters they had to cross, sometimes they were ferried, and sometimes they just forded the currents, hoping the bottom rocks were not so big they'd tip the wagons.

On June 13, 1846, they were at a place rightly named Mosquito Creek Camp. Mosquitoes had claimed this area for sure, and frogs hopped out of wild grass in whole families. It was here that Captain James Allen of the United States Army found Brigham Young, and asked if the Mormons might lend the government five hundred men to fight in the war with Mexico. Well, President Young didn't resist. This seemed an opportunity to get on the government's good side, so Brother Brigham asked any willing men to accept the army's invitation and serve as the Mormon Battalion in the Mexican War.

"Like the U.S. government deserves such as that!" Isaac James muttered when he heard the news. He and Jane were sitting beside the Dykes wagon.

Jane, nursing baby Silas, said that what the U.S. government deserved was some of the same lashing it meted out to Mormons and Negroes. It might be a fine thing, she concluded, for some Saints to witness a cavalry or two getting rousted by Mexicans.

"You soundin' somewhat unpatriotic," Isaac whispered.

"U.S. government ain't provided me nothin' to brag on lately," she said, and Isaac kissed her full on the mouth.

Others of the Saints were more suspicious than vengeful, certain that calling their men into service was a cover for one terrible scheme: mass extermination. Captain Allen promised that no such thing would happen, that he himself would lay down his life if any Mormon man got killed without good cause. The U.S. government, he swore, was nothing if not honorable.

Jane's response to that was, "Then I guess the U.S. government is nothin'." And Isaac kissed her again. She figured the more she said against the government, the more kisses she'd earn—which could result in another baby, so maybe she'd best keep her quiet.

Many Mormon women, including some in the Jameses' company, gave up their men to the government for a time. On the evening of the Mormon Battalion's departure, right there at the camp, a great farewell ball was held in a just-made bowery. Sylvester James thought the ball was the most magnificent thing he had ever seen. All the men were out in their Sunday best, and the women wore white socks, silk dresses, and bright petticoats. Nearby sat Indians in scarlet blankets and leggings made of bright feathers. Syl was perched high in a hickory tree to watch. The music was something else: violins, horns, sleigh bells, and tambourines. And what dancing took place that night: Copenhagen jigs, Virginia reels, French fours. Everyone had happy feet that night. What Syl wished was that his Uncle Lew were there. No one could dance like Uncle Lewis Manning. But when some rich-voiced lady sang "By the Waters of Babylon We Sat Down and Wept," the dancing stopped and the crying began. Then someone prayed out loud for God to bless all of them with pure hearts and brotherhood. Syl found himself crying as bad as the women.

There wasn't time for too many tears, though. The Saints were moving again. On June 29, four thousand of them were ferried across the Missouri River. At Cold Spring Camp, just after the crossing, Eliza Partridge Lyman gave birth to her first son.

Jane did make a visit to her friend, though she gave Eliza a bit more recovery time than Sisters Young and Thomas had given her. With Silas in her arms, Jane walked to the Lyman wagon and then fast wished she had not gone at all. Eliza was sick, Brother Amasa told her with some sharpness in his voice. She had the childbed fever, and nobody knew if she would survive or not. She had received blessings, but the matter was in God's hands, he said.

Jane found a grove of birches right after getting that news. She was remembering the white child Angeline, who had regained her strength directly after Jane and her family had blessed her. And she was thinking of how Brother Joseph had prayed in the Sacred

Grove. So, clutching Silas to her chest, she opened her mouth to ask God out loud to please let Eliza stay on the living side. She felt great affection for this particular woman, and it didn't seem right that God should take her. Now, Jane James would surely not judge the Almighty. She might nudge Him a little, though. That wagon was an awful place to deliver a baby anyway, what with the summer sun beating on it every day and the night air almost frosty. After a woman suffered in such conditions to bring forth a child, she surely should have a chance to raise him! That's what Jane told God.

And God listened. Or seemed to. At least, Eliza did not die from the fever. A few weeks later, when Jane returned to see how Eliza's health was doing, a living woman answered her call. But Jane could hardly believe this was her friend from Nauvoo. "Lord, Lord," Jane prayed silently, "you took her pretty hair!" Eliza was wearing a loose-fitting cap, but her hair was gone, her skin was pale, and she was so thin Jane could hardly believe she could still be breathing.

"Sister Eliza?"

Eliza's mouth shaped into something like a smile. Her voice was familiar and sweet but so quiet Jane had to listen hard. "Jane?"

"I heard you was poorly," Jane said. "I come to see if you improved any."

"I'm better," Eliza said. She was sitting in the wagon, which Jane figured was about all that spent body could manage.

"Well, then, praise the Lord."

"I'm glad you know me," Eliza said.

"Ma'am?"

"I'm so much a skeleton, those who used to know me do not— until I tell them."

"Oh, Sister Eliza! Why, I'd know you anywhere! 'Course I would! That smile alone would tell me this was you. And how's the baby?"

"His name is Don Carlos—after dear Joseph's brother. I was so sick, I could hardly care for him. I thought we might lose him too.

But God has blessed us." At this, she brought the child from his cradle. He was plump at the cheeks and looking healthy—and fast asleep.

"I know your hair will grow back."

"Oh yes. It will. I do believe there is a power that watches over us and does all things right," Eliza said. "And I was not meant to be bald."

"So you and me, we both got us sons!"

"And you still have your hair."

"For what it's worth, ma'am. Now, I don't want to stay too long. I think you should rest as much as your body wants. Can I get you anything?"

"Oh, Jane—would you? A cup of cold spring water would set so fine just now."

"And I'll be back with that directly," Jane said. She did as she promised, watching this shadow of Eliza Lyman sip the water like it was life itself.

The next long-stay camp was Cutler's Park, which they reached in September. This was where Syl saw a sight he hoped would never meet his eyes again: Three young men were taken out to a grove and given eighteen whip lashes each. They had done some "immoral" thing, and nobody would tell Syl what it was. That was the first time he saw someone whipped. He was not supposed to have seen it, of course, but he knew how to hide himself in a tree like a squirrel. He paid attention to these grown boys crying and the sound of the whip slicing air and then skin. Sylvester James decided then and there that he would not be "immoral"—whatever that meant.

In October, the James family forded the Missouri again with a good many other Saints to set up what they'd call "Winter Quarters." This would be a long camp, a place where some would build comfortable dwellings, though many would manage in half-made houses where only one side was chinked and mudded, and the rest was a tent. Jane, Isaac, and Syl lived in a dugout, just beside the Dykeses' sod hut.

The settlement was built in fort style, on a second bluff up from the river, some sixty feet above the water. At first, it seemed like paradise—wild grapes, plums, and nuts growing on the river bottoms, and water close at hand—easy to haul in barrels from the brooks at either end of the place. It was a refuge for near four thousand Mormons.

But all of them soon endured the dead of winter. And this winter meant "dead" to a good many, too—especially the children, or those who took the black canker, which stripped their gums of teeth before it snatched the breath from their lungs. On December sixth, Isaac Haight and his wife lost their eighteen-day-old son, who had been named for his father. On December 12, Don Carlos Lyman, that baby son of Eliza and Amasa who looked so healthy when Jane viewed him the past summer, passed on. Jane heard about it alongside a whole group of weeping women, just outside the cabin Amasa had built his family. She heard someone say that when little Don Carlos was washed for burial, the water formed ice on his body.

Eliza appeared at the cabin door. Her hair had grown back in tufts, almost like she had pulled some of it out. She was pitiful, still pale and thin, using all her strength to keep tears from gushing as she told her tale: "My sister Caroline and I sat up with him every night. We tried to save him—we could not bear to part with him. But we were powerless. The Lord took him." Finally, Eliza broke down and wept, "I will try to be reconciled."

Sister Zina Young was present. She took Eliza into her arms, urging her to remember that God was over all. There were many mothers in this crowd who had lost their babies to this winter.

Jane felt to stand back and listen. She had not lost a child, and she did not fully fit into this world of white grief.

"Oh, Zina!" Eliza was sobbing, "he was my greatest comfort—he was always in my arms!"

Sister Zina did not answer but stroked the sprouts of Eliza's hair. Another Eliza—Eliza R. Snow—recited a poem of comfort, as she often did at a pioneer death:

> *Beloved Eliza, do not weep*
> *Your baby sleeps in quiet sleep.*
> *Although in dust its body lies*
> *His spirit soars above the skies.*
> *No more upon your throbbing breast*
> *It lays its little head to rest.*
> *From all the pains of nature freed,*
> *Your fond caress he does not need.*
> *Sweet was its visit, but its stay*
> *On earth was short; 'twas called away*
> *By kindred spirits to fulfill*
> *Its calling and Jehovah's will.*
> *Then soothe your feelings, do not mourn*
> *Your noble offspring will return*
> *And with its friends on earth remain.*

They were pretty words but did little to console Sister Lyman at this moment. Here was the time for crying, and Jane shed a number of tears herself. When she returned to the dugout, wrapped tight in a wool shawl, she held both her boys to her long and hard.

January found Hosea Stout hard pressed to locate enough healthy men to guard the city. Then came a frozen February and a mean March. Roaring winds yanked up tent poles and cracked them. Seemed the poles were nothing more than Lucifer matches. The rain shined in the firelight like silver pine needles—or the devil's own darts set to flatten flames into coals.

And so it was night after night. Jane began to think of Noah and to wonder if boats might be called for instead of wagons. Maybe, she considered, the Saints ought to be gathering their livestock two by two and just leave this land to the curse.

Among those who lost their lives to cold or canker were some slaves from Mississippi belonging to Brother John Brown and

Brother John Bankhead. "Winter fever" was what the white folk called it. Jane herself watched Brother John's slave, Henry, struggle to find his last breath, heave for it, his mouth chomping air, none of which could make it down his swollen throat. Then he fell backwards, eyes rolled up, and gave up his ghost—which he seemed relieved to do. Brother John said, "The cold is extremely hard on the Negroes." He had not known she was listening, had not noticed her. Jane thought the Southern Saints were maybe in the habit of not noticing blacks. Maybe to them, blacks were their own shadows.

She felt to make her presence known and to suggest that could be an extra blanket or two might have helped this particular Negro, who had slept outside on the cold ground while the white family occupied the wagon and the shelter directly under it. But she didn't introduce either herself or her thoughts, didn't choose to invite disharmony. She was feeling bad, though, with the dead man's eyes staring at her. She was wondering if she could've done something for him while he lived and told Isaac as much. He responded that it didn't bring much good to harp on the past. Besides which, that poor slave would no doubt be treated better by angels and the Good Lord Jesus than ever he had been by Brother Brown, even if Brother Brown was a kindly one.

The Browns seemed truly sad at their slave's death. As many other pioneers did with their loved ones, the Browns buried Henry in a tarp and marked his grave with a stick.

All those deaths would define Winter Quarters for Jane James the rest of her life.

For Sylvester, though, death was distant, and Winter Quarters had some fun times. One snow-covered night under a clear sky and a full moon, George Rust and a dozen of his friends found a hickory drag and a steep hill. They decided the best use they could make of this wood and that hill would be to go coasting.

Now Sylvester was not invited to participate in this fun, but they couldn't keep him from watching. Up a fine-sized hill the boys went, hauling the drag. Then they all climbed in it, and down it slid, faster, faster—and Syl could see the boys weren't doing much steering. They were riding this sled down until it stopped—which it did by ramming into a sod house.

The boys were bruised but not hurt bad. Sylvester never told a soul what he'd seen.

Now you should know that the James family and those slaves who died in the worst of the cold were not the only colored folks at Winter Quarters. There were several others, including those three slaves you've already heard about: Green Flake, Oscar Crosby, Hark Lay.

Green Flake was a teenaged trickster, packed to the skin with energy and fun. He was simply too lively for sickness to stalk or even consider baiting. James Madison Flake had no hesitation in using every muscle his slave could offer, come rain or sun. As Green told it, he had been working this way from the time his body found its size—breaking soil, chopping cotton plants, picking those prickly bolls, separating the seeds, and packing the fiber into bales. He never had balked at his work and didn't balk now, not once. Green was exactly the sort of fellow Syl would turn out to be, Jane decided—except Syl would be free. It was a pretty good future, though it had its risks. If Syl could be as loyal to God as Green was to his master, everything would turn out fine.

Many nights the pioneers asked Hark and Green to sing. Their songs were so happy that a good dream might bounce around before settling into a body's mind. So often, the last moments before sleep took her, Jane was hearing deep music about Jesus. Not the traditional Mormon songs, but the ones her own mother had sung years ago:

> Some days are dark and dreary;
> Some days our hearts grow weary;
> Some paths may not seem cheery—
> These things will cease someday.

The slaves' voices made a pleasant path to sleep. Even the rain seemed to calm, and one night stopped entirely when they sang:

> It was early in the mornin',
> It was early in the mornin',
> Jus' at the break of day,
> When he rose, when he rose
> And went to heaven on a cloud.

The congregation of clouds seemed shamed by those words. Maybe the clouds were reminded of better purposes they had once served than pouring water on God's people and stealing the most helpless for Mr. Death. With a weak flash of light and a soft groan, the thunderheads dispersed. Hark and Green kept on singing until a sprinkle of stars appeared like a sign of redemption. But it rained again the next day, though it was a gentle rain by nightfall, and no hymns could persuade these nervous new clouds to quit fidgeting and let the moon show through.

Oscar Crosby was a quiet one, a hard worker, not a talker. Jane knew there was pain in this man and maybe whip stripes on his back. She didn't want to know about them, though. She didn't want to think one of her own faith, even though he was a Southerner, might whip his slave.

It was those three—Oscar, Hark, and Green—who left in the first company to Zion, April 1847. They would clear the path for everyone else to follow. They'd hack down pine branches and willows, roll boulders away, kick aside pebbles, scuff and cut out a trail, set mile markers, and sometimes construct bridges over fast-current rivers. Once in the Salt Lake Valley, these slaves would build cabins for their masters, and all would be ready for Zion to set up.

I should mention one other colored man who made an appearance at Winter Quarters: Pete McCary. Now, Jane had heard of Black Pete before—the half-Negro, half-Indian who had once tried to fly by making himself some sort of featherless wings, jumping from a lake bank, and landing on a treetop. Pete was not the sort of man she figured she'd put any trust in, but he was so tall and he claimed so certainly to be a prophet and to have personal knowledge of plural marriage that several of the more desperate women took it into their heads to sleep with him. It was Parley P. Pratt who hounded him off and then lambasted the ones who followed or believed him: "Will you follow a man who has no right to the priesthood?" Jane wasn't sure what the apostle meant by "no right to the priesthood," but she thought Pete was crazy and didn't mind seeing the back of him. Seemed to her that straightway after Pete left, the weather improved permanent.

Emily Partridge, now another of Brother Brigham's plural wives and an acquaintance of Jane's from Nauvoo days—Eliza Lyman's sister—asked straight out: "Jane, are you offended by what Brother Parley said?" They were gathering Jerusalem artichoke during this conversation—a bit of green which would heal black canker in short order.

Jane answered that Brother Parley had said a good many things, and she hadn't stopped to consider which ones offended her.

"What he said about Black Pete," said Emily.

"He say somethin' about that man?"

"Brother Brigham says it's nothing to do with blood, Jane. God made all flesh of one blood."

"I know." But she also observed that Emily called her "Jane," never "Sister."

"Brother Brigham says we have one of the best elders in the Church, who's as black as you are. Africa-black. Walker Lewis is his name, and he's preaching somewhere in Massachusetts."

Jane repeated the name and assured "Sister Emily" that she was more offended by Black Pete's shenanigans than by anything Elder Parley P. Pratt might say.

That finished their conversation. The women filled their baskets with artichokes and pig weeds, then headed to their separate dwellings to feed their separate families.

NOTES

The chapter title, "'Til the Storm Passes By," is from the title of hymn number 501 in *Hymns for the Family of God*.

The description of "pots and churns" and other items hung on the wagons is based on Patty Sessions's diary as recorded in Godfrey, Godfrey, and Derr, 147.

That the Nauvoo Bell was carried in one of the lead pioneer wagons is documented by Stegner, *Gathering of Zion*, 54.

As suggested, food was indeed sometimes scarce for the pioneers, and "in spite of the time and admonitions the Saints had been given to prepare, many had left Nauvoo inadequately supplied" (Godfrey, Godfrey, and Derr, *Women's Voices*, 148).

That Jane and Isaac James lived with the George Parker Dykes family and paid for Silas's delivery with twenty-four pounds of flour is documented in Patty Sessions's journal (Smart, *Mormon Midwife*, 54). Sessions refers to Jane as "Black Jane." Since George Dykes joined the Mormon Battalion, he is not listed in the Jameses' immediate pioneer company. We are conjecturing that with George in Mexico, the James family might have inherited the Dykes wagon.

Jane's history lists Silas's birthplace as Hog Creek, which is almost certainly a misrendering of Keg Creek. Even so, the birthplace is not accurate, although it's close. According to William Hartley (personal interview), Silas James's birth is listed in Brigham Young's journal as occurring at the Nishnabotna River. The date of his birth corresponds to the brief pioneer camp at the Nishnabotna (Kimball, "Iowa Trek," 43) rather than Keg Creek, which was the next stop.

Brigham Young's journal is also the source of two other details in this chapter: the brass band that played the night of June 10, 1846, and the presence of wild strawberries in the area (Hartley, personal interview).

We can identify the birthplace of Don Carlos Lyman as the Cold Spring camp (Omaha Nation) from pioneer journals (Kimball, "Iowa Trek," 45).

We have used many of Eliza Lyman's own words as recorded in her journal, describing the conditions of childbirth, the heat of the wagon, and the grief of losing her firstborn son, Don Carlos Lyman. The Eliza R. Snow poem is taken from the holographic journal of Eliza Maria Partridge Lyman, 42. As Stegner shows in *Gathering of Zion*, 48, this poem is typical of the poems Eliza R. Snow wrote for grieving parents.

That Eliza Partridge Lyman lost her hair as a consequence of "childbed fever" is also mentioned in Eliza's journal and is documented in Albert Lyman's biography of his grandfather, *Amasa Mason Lyman*, 156.

The close relationship between Zina Diantha Huntington Smith Young, Eliza R. Snow, and Patty Sessions is documented in various sources, including Jenson, *Latter-day Saint Biographical Encyclopedia*, 2:697–99. Zina's relationship to Eliza Partridge was not only as a sister-wife (both having been sealed to Joseph Smith) but also as a stepsister. As Eliza Lyman says in her journal, Zina's father had married Eliza's mother after the deaths of their original spouses (transcribed in Carter, *Treasures*, 2:219). Patty Sessions also records a number of times she and the other women of the camp (often including Eliza Snow and Zina Young) "blessed and got blessed." Sister Sessions reports giving a pioneer woman a blessing "by laying my hands upon her head, and the Lord spoke through me to her great and marvelous things" (in Godfrey, Godfrey, and Derr, *Women's Voices*, 197).

"Lucifer match" is an early term for a match.

Amasa Mason Lyman was married to Maria Louisa Tanner in 1835. He took as plural wives Caroline Partridge, Eliza Partridge Smith, and Cornelia Eliza Lott (1844); Dionitia Walker (1845); Paulina Eliza Phelps (1846); and Lydia Partridge (1853) (Van Wagoner and Walker, *Book of Mormons*, 163).

Details of the great farewell ball for the departing Mormon Battalion are extracted from Jensen, "Beneath the Casing Rock," 26.

The whipping of three young men at Cutler's Park for "immoral conduct" is reported by Hosea Stout, quoted in Jensen, "Beneath the Casing Rock," 29. Reportedly, the crime they committed was "punishable by death."

The depiction of at least some of the houses at the beginning of the settlement of Winter Quarters is extracted from Eliza R. Snow's journal of October 28, 1846: "The house into which we mov'd was partly chink'd & only mudded on one side & only covered on one side, the other having the tent thrown over it" (in Godfrey, Godfrey, and Derr, *Women's Voices*, 148).

The death of Isaac Haight's namesake son is documented in Jensen, "Beneath the Casing Rock," 31.

The death of Don Carlos Lyman on December 12 is recorded in Eliza Lyman's journal, transcribed in Carter, *Treasures*, 2:230.

The deaths at Winter Quarters of Henry Brown and the unnamed slave of John Bankhead are documented in Carter, *Negro Pioneer*, 8. We have extracted details of the conditions that likely contributed to the deaths of these men from Lorenzo Young's journal, as quoted by Stegner, *Gathering of Zion*, 58–59. The information about Green Flake, Hark Lay, and Oscar Crosby is also in Carter, *Negro Pioneer*, 7–8. The names of Flake, Lay, and Crosby are engraved on the statue of Brigham Young near the intersection of Main and South Temple Streets in Salt Lake City. All three are described as "colored servants" (as good a euphemism as any for slaves). All three were, in fact, well acquainted long before the Mormon exodus, the white Lay and Crosby families having intermarried and having had much interaction with James Madison Flake, who before the trek west would "come down from North Carolina" with his hunting hounds, a number of which he had sold to the Crosby and Lay families (Kohler, *Southern Grace*, 44).

The account of several young men "coasting" down a hill on a hickory drag and running into a sod hut is from Jensen, "Beneath the Casing Rock," 31.

There are conflicting stories about whether Green Flake traveled back to Winter Quarters for the Flakes or remained in the Salt Lake Valley to build them a cabin. We do know that when the Flakes reached the valley in October 1848, the log house Green had built was awaiting them in Cottonwood. Whether or not Green was actually the driver of Brigham Young's coach is subject to speculation, but Van Wagoner and Walker (*Book of Mormons*, 86–88) report several sources as so claiming, as do Joel Flake, "Green Flake," 15, and Coleman, "History of Blacks in Utah," 33.

We have extracted the idea that Green Flake had experience in cotton fields from the statement in Kohler, *Southern Grace*, 44, that many Flake "family members and friends had . . . moved to [Mississippi] and developed it into fine cotton-producing country."

The hymn "Some Days Are Dark and Dreary" was written down, though not composed, by Elsie Gray, Darius Gray's mother. In her Pentecostal church, there were very few hymnbooks, so she and others wrote down the words to the hymns. We do not know who the author of these verses was.

The hymn "It Was Early in the Mornin'" is taken from Painter, *Sojourner Truth*, 105.

Information on the controversial Black Pete is taken from a variety of sources, including Bringhurst, *Saints, Slaves, and Blacks*, 36–37. Parley P. Pratt's words mark the first recorded use we have of the Pearl of Great Price sanction against blacks holding the priesthood (so interpreted from Abraham 1:27). Esplin quotes Parley P. Pratt ("Minutes for 15 April, 1847," Brigham Young Papers, LDS Church Archives) as saying, "[Some] want to follow this Black man [McCary] who has got the blood of Ham in him which lineage was cursed as regards the Priesthood." Though the origin of the priesthood policy is ambiguous at best, referred to vaguely in 1845 by Orson Hyde discussing "the curse upon Blacks" as "among the mysteries of the kingdom" that Joseph

Smith had privately taught during 1843–44, it was not until 1852 that Brigham Young publicly pronounced the policy (Esplin, "Brigham Young," 395, 398).

The quotation from Brigham Young (March 1847) that Black Pete McCary's expulsion from Winter Quarters had "nothing to do with blood for of one blood has God made all flesh, we have to repent (and) regain what we av lost—we av one of the best Elders an African in Lowell—[i.e., Walker Lewis]" is found in minutes for 26 March 1847, Brigham Young Papers, LDS Church Archives, cited in Bush's "Whence the Negro Doctrine?" 215, n. 11.

Lythgoe cites a letter from William I. Appleby (June 2, 1847) referring to Walker Lewis: "At this place I found a colored brother by the name of Lewis, a barber and an Elder in the Church, ordained by William Smith" ("Negro Slavery and Mormon Doctrine," 334).

That Jane was usually referred to by her first name rather than "Sister Jane" or "Sister James" is implied by several sources. The one mention of Jane in Eliza Lyman's journals refers to "Jane James, a colored woman" (April 25, 1849, transcribed in Carter, *Treasures*, 2:235), whereas all other Mormon women but Eliza's immediate family are referred to as "Sister" in the journal. Likewise, as previously cited, Patty Sessions refers to her as "Black Jane" rather than "Sister." Similarly, Wilford Woodruff's journal of October 16, 1894, calls her "Black Jane" (quoted in Wolfinger, "Test of Faith," in *Social Accommodation*, 150), and President John Taylor addresses his response to her (which she signed "Your sister in the gospel") "Mrs. Jane James" (cited in Wolfinger, "Test of Faith," in *Social Accommodation*, 148). We do know, however, that Jane was sometimes called "Sister," for the George Albert Smith papers (quoted in Wolfinger, "Test of Faith," in *Social Accommodation*, 150) report: "President Woodruff informed the Council that Sister Jane James, a negress of long standing in the Church, had asked him for permission to receive her endowments." The implication that she was usually referred to by her first name is not surprising given the customs of the time—which customs have extended even into the present day. Darius Gray reports that his mother, for example, a domestic servant, was also addressed by her first name by whites, even when it was a child addressing her.

"Black canker" was a form of scurvy. The Jerusalem artichoke, which became plentiful in springtime, did much to alleviate the sickness (Jensen, "Beneath the Casing Rock," 32).

26

I'll Go Where You Want Me to Go

*I know that it shall be well with
them that fear God.*
ECCLESIASTES 8:12

The James family's time at Winter Quarters ended on June 18, 1847. They were called to move on to their destiny: the Rocky Mountains.

Brother Horton Haight, in a skiff, pushed his heifer into the water, and a number of men urged the cattle forward. The wagon oxen came last, and most of what Sylvester James saw was splashing—foamy, sparkly splashes like the animals were kicking up crystal. Then the herd boys dived in and commenced to swim the cattle across the river. There were six boys, buck naked, their shirts stuffed into the legs of their pants, which were balled up and held overhead. The boys were whooping and hollering for the herd to press on to that other side or go to hell. (Sylvester liked the way the herd boys talked too, though when he quoted a phrase to his mama, she slapped him one and said to watch his tongue or she'd pull it clean out.) The animals pressed on, looking bothered.

The James family had their own wagon now, and Syl was assigned to count the wheel notches, checking on how many miles they went each day. Papa Isaac would drive the oxen, walking along the left side of the lead team, using a willow to provoke them to righteousness and the true path God had set out and the trailblazers had marked. Isaac would yell gee and haw, and the team would obey. Jane would often sit up front, looking useful and pretty, wearing her long-billed indigo bonnet and a plaid dress.

The James family was assigned to the Ira Eldredge company, with Isaac Haight their immediate captain. Silas was one year old now. Jane often kept him strapped either to her own back or to Syl's.

So they were bound for the land of milk and honey. Wagons rolled onto the flatboat that would ferry them across the Elk Horn river. The trail up the Platte River was set. They followed it when they could, covering near fifteen miles daily, through dew-soaked prairie grass, past a large Pawnee village—its lodges made of skins—and across the Loup River with frothing rapids, ugly sandbars, and hungry quicksand. There were many surprises over the prairie: occasional fires in the distance, small lakes full of sunfish, and wild flowers of every shade Syl had ever in his life imagined—deep blues and pinks and purples; bell-flowers that never seemed full open, and others that were simply conceited, flagging their petals like they were for sale. There were prairie dogs ducking unto their burrows, owls scared up from their nests, and occasional rattlesnakes showing off the rhythm of their fancy tails.

And there were Indians.

The Potawatomis had not been too exotic. They were mostly poor, like the Mormons. Vagabonds. The Pawnee were a sight, though, with their plucked eyebrows and face paint, their heads all shaved except for a hair-stripe from forehead to midway down the scalp—a hairstyle that might put the word *skunk* in your mind.

There were other tribes too. The scariest appeared as though they had slunk up from the grave, their hair strung with white clay and stiff as shaggy bark.

Sylvester James enjoyed seeing Indians and especially liked the word *Potawatomi*, sometimes reciting it for hours on end as his rhythm maker. "Potawatomi right. Potawatomi left. You wanna potawatomi? Thank you, no, no potawatomi for me, jus' a good pota potatoes'll do. Or a pota what-a-you wanna call it."

On occasion, they'd see other pioneers—of the Gentile sort—headed west in the gold rush. There were good opportunities to trade for supplies, for the Mormons were equipped to ferry the Gentiles' possessions across any river and enjoyed being paid for their services. Mostly, though, the Mormons kept to themselves. They had been driven out of enough places that trust was not their first instinct when they saw a stranger.

Before long (though it certainly felt long), they were out of the prairie and on the Great Plains—buffalo country.

Those lumbering, bearded critters were a rare sight at first, but it didn't take long before the Mormons were a line of white-topped wagons in a sea of brown buffalo. For long stretches, the animals were everywhere—and when they weren't plodding along lively, their bleached bones showed where they'd dropped dead.

Periodically, the members of the Haight company went hunting. There were good marksmen among the men, so they rarely lacked for meat in this terrain. On one of the more exciting days, Isaac Haight got thrown by his horse while giving chase to a buffalo. Brother Haight recovered nicely—and so did the buffalo. Next day, bruised but proud, Isaac Haight went after buffalo again. He killed two. The company ate hearty that night.

There were buffalo stampedes sometimes, and sometimes stampedes of cattle. Once, when a herd of cattle was setting to act up, Syl himself called the warning. The almost-stampede had been caused by a Sioux Indian trick. Those sly Sioux would spook the cattle herd and then steal what they could; they had done it to other companies. But Syl saw the hoof dust, wailed a warning, and some skilled men leaped onto their horses and set them loping, circling the cattle so only a few were lost.

Sylvester James was the day's hero. He would remember that fondly, especially as the day-after-day travel set in.

Which it most certainly did.

There were no trees now to give firewood, but the Saints had new fuel for their cooking: buffalo chips. Syl would hunt them out, and then his mama would dig a hole in the ground and set the food in a good kettle, slow cooking on what the buffalo had left behind. If they were lucky, they'd get Potawatomi plums or wild strawberries too.

At night, he'd sometimes dance all alone while a fiddler played and the white Saints did their fancy steps—many of which they had learned from Uncle Lew. Jane and Isaac danced too, but apart from the whites. More than once, Syl fell asleep while the fiddle was still going strong. He never had problems sleeping, curled under the wagon and wrapped up in a buffalo hide. Dawn light always seemed an intrusion, and his heavy eyes closed so easy during morning prayers.

Soft sand soon made hard pulling for the ox teams, and it took more than a willow switch to urge them forward. The pioneers had to help each other. At the Loup River, they had put ten men to a wagon to haul each one across. Now they put a number of men with the ox teams to move them on. And that wasn't the worst part. There were dust storms here which turned the air grainy for hours. Once they had to stop the wagons to wait on the dust settling, for they could hardly see a hand before them. The grit stuck in their hair and teeth and on their eyelashes and brows. It stung their eyes so bad, most of the company went face down inside or under their wagons. The whole world seemed a mess of bad weather.

"Arise from the dust," said Jane when the way cleared and the dust mostly settled. They washed their faces in the Platte, but bits of dirt kept irritating Syl's eyes and making him cry—a true embarrassment—long after the storm had moved along.

"Why'd Jesus send us that one?" he asked out loud, though he didn't direct the question to anyone in particular.

Jane heard it, though. Jane had a mother's ears, and they didn't miss much. "Don't you go questioning the Lord," she said.

Syl hardly wanted to see what else the Lord had in store. But the sights were pretty interesting, and he was willing to look as long as dust didn't come at his eyes. The terrain changed from sand bars, to bluffs, to ridges of rock, to buffalo grass and weeping willows. The Platte changed too, got sluggish. In this part of the country, their life-giving river looked black and cold. Its smell hovered in the air, like rocks and dead fish all mixed up.

Syl pretended Mormon-hating Gentiles were waiting just the other side of the Platte and that by using a deer bone like Moses's rod, Brother Isaac or George Rust or Syl himself could part that river and go smack the Gentiles on their noses or send them straightway to the devil for being so inhospitable to Latter-day Saints. Syl thought he'd enjoy such a miracle as that.

Now one of the things the Lord had in store for the James family—and for all the pioneers—was a view of the most interesting rock forms in this world. There was one rock that looked exactly like a huge frog head. Syl concluded that a mischievous angel had dreamed it up and thought he'd like to meet that being and get some instruction on how to design a rock of his own. Syl's creation would be a gold-brown mountain wearing his mama's face—all dark rock, with deep caves for eyes and nostrils and the deepest cave for his mama's tired smile. He'd call that mountain Potawato-me-mama.

Chimney Rock, which (according to Isaac Haight) resembled a big, tarnished chimney on a British mill, wasn't a bad sight either, its main cliff sticking up straight as a pipe. It seemed everyone's favorite, though Syl preferred the frog head.

Days later, way off in the distance, they could see the Laramie Peaks, which would introduce a whole range of rocks and cliffs and hazy valleys. There was snow on those faraway mountaintops.

They set up camp at a place called Scott's Bluffs—high, steep, broken rocks, which some said could pass for ancient ruins. It was Scott's Bluffs where a number of the Mormon Battalion joined them, reporting that the Mexican War was nothing at all and they'd all been dismissed to come home. They'd already been to the Salt Lake Valley and were headed back to Winter Quarters to get their families.

George Rust, who Syl considered maybe his best friend (though George never gave him more attention than a head nod), learned that his gone-soldier papa had been kicked by a mule and hurt bad in the leg and so had been sent to Pueblo, Colorado, with other sick army men. George, dressed in buckskin and worn boots, his hat more holes than felt, took the news without showing a lick of emotion. Syl wanted to offer some comfort but knew he was either too young or too black.

They were on the road again soon, headed to Fort Laramie, the ox teams' feet and necks sore and the grass inadequate to keep any of the animals satisfied. When the wagons had to head down a gully, Isaac James urged the hungry critters forward with an occasional switch and steady comfort: "Ain't much more. You doin' fine. You was made for this very purpose. You doin' fine."

Fort Laramie was a fur trading place—or had been. It was in poor shape now, but still a good resting spot, a place where a body (human or animal) might catch its breath, get new shoes, and contemplate the journey. They ate quite hearty there—meal, bacon, beans, and short cake, though flour at the fort was sold for the outrageous price of twenty-five cents a pound. Jane and some of the other women gathered pig weeds, so they could have greens for supper too.

Five hundred and forty-three miles they had traveled. Syl could hardly remember a day he had spent doing his own pleasures instead of following the hardly-there path or sneering at the wake-up bugle or coughing against a dust storm or helping to guide the wagon into its place in the nighttime circle and then saying prayers and singing hymns.

Back in Nauvoo, he had had a real-looking wood gun. With his cousin, he had pretended to be a soldier of the Nauvoo Legion. Somehow, that toy got left behind with that cousin, though at times, when the day's travel was done and no one was paying him mind, Syl'd snatch up a deer bone for his weapon and pretend Brother Joseph had just invited him to be the youngest colonel in the Legion. He found a good-sized goose feather once, and used it as a sword. He called heaven's wrath down on the Gentiles exactly as he had been told the Prophet had done before getting killed. Silas was too little to be a good playmate, and the white boys wouldn't play much, so what games Syl invented, he did on his own.

Silas was big enough to run now, though his legs hadn't had much chance to do it. So here at Laramie Fort was Syl's opportunity to teach his brother how to sprint as if the Gentiles were on the chase, set to shoot a ball straight into your ribs. The brothers raced, Silas's bow-legged steps wobbly and full of falls, Syl's so long and graceful he thought he should be a mountain cat.

But what truly he was, was a tired pioneer boy making ready for more walking.

After leaving Fort Laramie, there were some other things that took Syl's mind off the step-after-step—like the ant hills with their red guards protecting tiny Indian beads. Syl loved collecting those beads. Jane didn't mind him doing it, though Isaac thought it a pretty stupid pastime, given the certainty of ant bites. Besides which, Isaac considered the worst white folk he knew were the collectors. Slave owners were the biggest collectors of any, he commented to Jane as Syl claimed more beads. White masters were always gathering porcelain china to show off, wasn't that so? Silverware, glass figurines, lacy tablecloths. And Africans.

He laughed but took on a bitter face when he said this, and Jane wondered what parts of his past he hadn't told her yet. He was a free black, he had said. From New Jersey. Had he always been free? He avoided that subject but lashed out with these resentments—which set her to wondering.

Even if they got stung or bit, Isaac went on, white masters kept on collecting, claiming, toying with Africans and then stinging those Africans harder than those Africans could ever sting back, putting the bit on them—shutting up their mouths with that metal mask that ripped the sunburned flesh clean off their faces. No, for whatever reasons Isaac wouldn't talk about, collecting was not a hobby he admired. But he didn't raise a ruckus over Syl's new game. Isaac wasn't one to raise a ruckus over much of anything.

They were ferried over the river a few days after leaving Fort Laramie and then climbed hills spiked with pine timber. At the summit of one hill, they got a full view of snow-capped Laramie Peak. They had to lock the wagon wheels to descend that hill, but the vision of the peak had been worth the climb. Besides which, they had had to make the climb anyway, so they found reasons to be as grateful as they were tired. One reason for gratitude was the gladed creek, which awaited them not too far distant. Isaac Haight and John Potter set off after antelope and deer directly after they made camp there. The two returned within the hour, toting a buck with antlers almost as wide as Brother Isaac was tall. They all had good meat that night.

It was here Syl saw his first bear: a brown one and her cub. He felt he could paw a good fish from the river just as well as any bear and decided he'd fight a bear for a fish, should the opportunity arise. In fact, he'd enjoy the fight more than he'd enjoy the fish. He'd relish living like a Potawatomi and wrestling bears for food, and even dreamed about it that night.

The dream ended too soon, of course. The next day they made twelve miles up and down hills, camping on a stream Isaac Haight named Dry Creek. Next day, they walked and walked again, and come evening, camped in their usual circle. Sylvester heard a number of wolves howling this particular night—closer than usual.

Now Sylvester didn't mind distant wolves, as long as they kept distant. He didn't care for the up-close view of that sleek silver-black hide, those hungry, colorless eyes, those pink-white noses. He had seen a wolf up close once, though the wolf had been dead. Sometimes in his bad dreams (which he did suffer on occasion) he saw wolf packs sniffing around the camp like they were identifying who'd die next so they could decide if the corpse would make enough meat. No, Syl did not care for the direct company of wolves, prowling around with their one-mind purpose and ready teeth, and he certainly did not care for their nighttime howls, especially as he knew they sometimes dug up the Saints' graves. He thought, though, that he would indeed enjoy a wolf puppy, which he would name Potawatowolfey.

That name made Papa Isaac laugh when Syl mentioned it the next morning, but it made Jane angry. "I ain't raisin' no wolf in my house!" she said.

"Well, now," Isaac said back, "you can't, can you? You ain't got you no house. Not yet, anyhows."

"Well, when I do, I ain't raisin' no wolf 'less it be for eatin'."

"Eatin' what?" Syl said. "Eatin' Silas? Sometimes he cry enough I wouldn't mind a wolf eat him." He backed up just in time to miss Jane's slap, but his ears caught her scold, which came in the full yell only Jane Manning James could execute.

"You say one more word like that, you be punished greater than you can bear." She hollered like he was a mile off, though he was right beside her.

"Sorry." Syl's repentance was always quick with his mama.

"You jus' watch that tongue," Jane said. She joined her husband in front of the wagon, while Syl dropped to the rear. He could hear Isaac defend him.

"He only jokin', Janey Liz."

"I don' know where from he get a tongue to say such things."

"You don't?" Isaac sounded shocked.

"I just pray God he don't have no tongue like one I remember. Nor soul like that one either."

"Like—? Oh, his white daddy, you mean."

This was the first time Syl had ever heard mention of his "white daddy."

"Naw, he don't," Isaac was saying. Syl strained to hear. "He got a better soul than that one, I can promise that with no fear o' retribution whatever."

"Pray God he don't have the kind of soul that use up a body just because it be available," Jane went on. They were hitching the wagon. "Pray God he don't have the kind of soul that feed a body straight to the wolf's teeth just because that soul ain't learned love."

Isaac paused before answering. "Now, honey, truth is, Sylvester James get his tongue straight from his mama. Honey, he teasin' you, that's all. Just like you tease me, like you used to tease your brother and Sarah. Oh my, you sure did tease Sarah! Honey, that be your own tongue you hear flappin' in his mouth."

Jane gasped as if that thought stole her breath. "Isaac James, I would never joke 'bout feedin' a baby to a wolf!" She was near tears.

"And that boy love baby Silas. That boy love him crazy. You jus' tired, Janey. You jus' so weary of all this bounce ridin', day after day. That's all."

"Weary of all the travel." She climbed inside the wagon. "And in a family way, I expects."

Syl knew he was not intended to hear this, so of course he listened harder.

Isaac groaned. "Aw, no! How'd that happen?"

She gave him a look. "You ain't figured that out yet?"

"Aw, Janey. I don't want you sick in such conditions."

"Well, it wasn't my plan either. You know when this happen."

"So you just' barely in that way, then."

"Isaac James," she said like accusation, "you either there or you ain't there. Ain't no in between, no barely, no mostly. You is or you ain't, and I most certainly is, and I ain't in no mood to argue."

He sucked in his cheeks and then blew out. Syl could see him in profile. "Well, look like I's payin' for my passion now." Again, Syl knew this was not intended for his ears. "And from on your lack of humor, look like Syl payin' too," Isaac finished, loud enough to reach the back of the wagon and any other Saints who were having difficulty hearing the whole fight.

Jane stretched her head around the tarp. Sylvester was standing still, head down, pretending to examine the spokes. "Hey, Syl!" she called.

He lifted his head just enough to make eye contact.

"Hey, Syl! How 'bout 'stead of a wolf pup you raises you some rabbits and we eat rabbit stew every week and we make you a whole coat outa rabbit cottontails so's you look just like the lamb you be!" Jane called.

He knew this was her way of apologizing. His almost-smile was his way of accepting it.

The next camp was Deer Creek, which came supplied with more tasty fish. Again, after a good meal and a fine sleep, they followed the life-giving Platte. They followed it every day, until time came for the Last Crossing. That was August 19, 1847.

By now, the sun was beating down hot enough to make you resist temptation if there was a chance the devil's place was any hotter. These were days could cook your brains.

And after that Last Crossing came forty high and dry miles. Three days' worth.

The first morning dawned to bright haze. The sun itself was hardly visible, though its light was everywhere. That sun seemed to stretch itself full out to cover the sky, and these pioneers were thirsty as newcomers to hell.

Silas was starting to make a few words by now. The one he made on this day was "Water."

"Swallow your spit," Syl told him.

Silas gave him a blank look.

"I'd give you some of mine if I had any," Syl said.

They had put some water in a jug at the Last Crossing, but it hardly lasted a day. Jane was surprised to see so little of it—just drops—when she tipped the jug for Silas's mouth on the second day of desert. She wanted to accuse all the men around her of stealing their liquid life. Isaac told her nobody had drunk the water. That mean ol' sun had pulled it out of the jug and into the sky.

When Jane looked skywards with her angry eyes, Syl said, "Don't you go questionin' the Lord, Mama." He didn't want to smile. His lips would bleed if he did.

"If I had the strength, Sylvester James, I'd slap you hard for gettin' saucy with me." Jane's speech was as slow as his.

"Ain't got enough water in me to get saucy, Mama. I jus' be repeatin' good words."

She sighed. "Good words at that. Wish we could drink 'em 'stead of jus' sayin' 'em." Then she quit talking. Every word made her tongue stick. Her teeth and eyeballs were so dry.

The third day, they didn't even have drops of water. They could hardly speak, for their tongues had swelled up and their lips were scabbed and bleeding. They all learned that blood doesn't quench thirst one bit.

Independence Rock waited at the end of that long, dry pass, looking for all the world like a huge, bumpy wart half a mile wide, complete with a fine cavern where the whole company could hide in case Indians or gentiles got feisty. Here, hundreds of travelers had etched their names for history, in red or black or yellow paint. And Independence Rock came with a reward: the Sweetwater River.

A few of the Saints tried a restrained swallow of the clear water, but most of them jumped full into it, including every member of the James family. There was never sweeter water anywhere on that trek.

It was August 22.

A canyon called Devil's Gate came next—and they could hear the Sweetwater rushing like blessed thunder all through it. The South Pass followed—the gateway to the Rocky Mountains. But this gate was not something you went through, it was something you went over. It was like going up and down a huge saddle.

Here, Jane and other sister Saints gathered a mineral called saleratus from a lake bed. Syl thought it was maybe to be held in reserve as poison should any enemies venture after them, but Jane promised it was merely for bread leaven.

This was sage bush country now, and there were jagged mountain ranges in the distance. No more plains, no more prairie. The Lord's peaks were up ahead.

The date was September 1, 1847. They camped at a meadow called Muddy Springs. Here they met a group of pioneers heading back down the trail to find their families or to encourage other Saints by giving them testimonies of how glorious their Zion would be. Among them was Green Flake, who had built a cabin for his master's family down the Salt Lake Valley, all the logs split open and pegged together. In fact, Green had driven James Flake's white-topped carriage with Brigham Young himself inside it! But Brother Brigham got too sick to abide the last bends and curves forking off what they'd soon call Echo Canyon and decided to stay behind, either to rest or to die. What Brigham had was the Rocky Mountain fever—a nasty sickness dug into the blood by a mean and measly tick. But tiny bugs can do mischief to powerful folk, given the chance—and that's a fact of life.

Brigham told Orson Pratt to go down to the valley with a bunch of strong men and build up bridges and roads.

Now, Green Flake was one of the strongest—near two hundred pounds already—so naturally, Brother Orson chose him to help dig out the last of the trail. They all used axes and shovels and poles and whatever else was handy—most especially elbow grease and muscle. So Green Flake, a slave, was one of the very first to enter the valley—or better put, to cut and dig his way there. In fact, he was in the first wagon through Emigration Canyon! And now he was headed back to his Massa and Mizzus, set to guide them and their babies to their new home. Green's "sister"—his fellow slave, Liz— was a pioneering Flake family member too, eager as anyone else to settle her bones down.

Among these returning pioneers was Brigham Young himself. And also among them was William Walker Rust, George's father.

It was Syl who gave George that news.

George Smith Rust, a big buck of a boy now, was walking behind a lazy group of sheep and hardly paid attention when Syl called, "Georgie?"

George glanced at him. Truth told, Sylvester James had tried his patience more than once. But this time, every bad thing Syl had ever done would be forgiven. Syl had the news of a lifetime.

"There's a comp'ny of men ahead." Syl looked up into George's sun-squinty eyes. Syl was the age for baptism now—eight years, give or take—and realized suddenly that he wasn't much shorter than young Rust. Syl didn't know how tall his white daddy had been, but he knew he had height coming on him, and he'd probably be taller than George, given a year or two more growth.

"So?" George's voice had gone deep since the journey began.

"Our men." Syl wished his had gone deep too, but he still sounded like a girl.

George shrugged. "Negroes?"

"Well, one at least. Green Flake. 'Member him?"

"No," said George.

"But a group of white folk too." He grinned. "Including your papa."

George stopped in his tracks and took off his old hat. The sun had bleached his hair just like it bleached the deer bones and antlers. "You tease me, Syl, and I kill you flat before you can say—"

"Potawatomi?"

"Before you even say *pot*, that's how fast."

Sylvester giggled. "Ain't teasin'. I seen him, Georgie! With my own eyes! Your papa!"

And at that moment, George saw his papa too, running towards him. George flung his hat into Sylvester's hands, yelling, "Keep it!" and was dashing, leaping into his father's arms.

That night, lit by flickers of campfire, President Brigham Young and other apostles spoke. Brigham had recovered from his fever and had surveyed the whole of Salt Lake Valley. It was exactly the place he had seen in vision, he declared. Why, Zion was so near the Saints could breathe it in, should they just fill their nostrils. All would be well.

What he didn't mention was that before "all would be well," they'd have to get through the next stretch—between the Big Sandy Creek and Green River. That would mean another thirty-five miles with only a little water.

Brigham Young, Green Flake, and the others continued their return trek, while the Ira Eldredge company pressed on towards the valley, trying to stay close to the Big Sandy. But there sure were some dry spells! Jane tried to breathe the air of Zion into her nostrils as Brigham had suggested, but all she got was a hot nose.

When the Saints did find water, they learned mosquitoes had already claimed it. Why, you couldn't swallow without hearing a mosquito whine past your ear, and you had to wonder if you might ingest a few just by breathing.

Baby Silas was getting ornery, over a year old and still walking like there was a big apple stuck between his legs. The trek had not been good for baby Silas's muscles, and Syl planned on working him well once they reached Zion—teaching him to wrestle just like the Prophet Joseph and to pull sticks and play ball.

By now, they could see Indians' wickiups. These Indians were said to be friendly, though Jane had heard one returning pioneer claim that Jim Bridger labeled the Snake Indians "bad people" and told the Mormons not to kill them but to make them into slaves.

She had winced when she heard it.

They would be at Fort Bridger soon—the famous trapper's way-lay trading station staffed by Frenchmen and Indians. It consisted of two double log cabins about forty feet long, and a ten-foot-high pen for horses. Bridger had chosen a fine place for his fort, sur-rounded by knee-deep grass, with cold, clear water nearby. When the Saints arrived, even Isaac tried his luck at fishing for the speck-led trout, said to be plentiful in this place. He used grasshoppers for bait but didn't get a bite except from a swarm of mosquitoes.

Other pioneers wanted to do a little shopping at the post. You could trade two rifles for nineteen buckskins, three elk skins, and a mess of other materials for making moccasins or coats. Of course, things weren't cheap. You wouldn't expect them to be. A pair of pants, for example, cost six dollars.

Fort Bridger was a good rest but a brief one. The bugler woke the pioneers after only one day's stay. The cattle were rounded up, teams hitched to their wagons, and the trek continued. They crossed a valley dotted with cedar trees and tasted the coppery water from a red-sand spring. The wet sand looked like rust, or blood.

The path was lined now by stinky swamps—surging, bubbling, yellow foam with lazy balls of scum. Any cattle that indulged in the smelly water would sure bloat up and keel over dead. Syl held his nose for a few minutes, until he grew accustomed, but he knew better than to drink that poison.

They were entering real mountain country now, following the

same trail the Donner-Reed party took towards California—and you know how that party finished up: with people eating each other. Well, it was no wonder the Donner-Reed folks met disaster on these narrow ridges. This was not a path you'd want to take without an angel as your guide and prayer as your protection.

The Mormons had both—Angel Moroni and daily prayer. And the Mormons made it through without even considering turning cannibal. At least nobody said they were considering it.

At Bear River were berries—ripe and sweet. Isaac James took special delight in feeding berry after berry to Jane, like each one was a secret they shared. They camped there, hearing the swishing willow boughs dance to the stars as night came around them. In the morning, Isaac and Sylvester James rounded up overeager cows who had managed a midnight escape. There were yet many rivers to cross, waist-high grass to wade through, and narrow passes with sheer drops ahead. But they took each difficulty as it came. That's the only way to get where you want to go: one step at a time.

At last, they passed through Echo Canyon where the wagon wheels sounded like carpenters banging boards. A single pistol shot would repeat itself like volleys of thunder, and the animals would low and bray, talking to themselves and getting many answers. Sylvester shouted his name and heard it return four times.

It was a grand introduction to what followed: thirty-six miles of mountain.

When they had first seen the mountains, the pioneers were awestruck. This had to be God's country for sure, with such giant guardians as these! Oh yes, the towering Wasatch Mountains were a glory to behold. But the Saints got past their awe pretty quick, once they started climbing with wagons and ox teams. You might've cursed the cliffs yourself, if you'd been there—that is, after you'd prayed and reminded yourself you could come across a Burning Bush at any moment.

Crooked trails, rugged rocks, tangled bushes, sudden streams, and blunt-cut willows tore up the wagons' tarps and wheels, and made Jane feel as if she was swimming in a horse's belly and that horse was galloping—not to God, but taking the other direction, because it sure was getting hot. It didn't help that she was expecting. More than once, Jane James had to visit a ridge or a bank to vomit.

Finally, they rounded a road near the mouth of Emigration Canyon. There were still some big climbs ahead, but at last, at last, from the Big Mountain summit, they could glimpse the valley: Zion. Or Deseret, as some were already naming it. Which seemed to Syl a long, weary way to pronounce *desert*—like the word was warm tar in the mouth and you had to say it slow. The most noticeable thing in Zion was the span of silver light stretching to the west. The Great Salt Lake.

Well, it would be Zion someday, proclaimed Jane Manning James, even though she was feeling sick as a dog at the moment. The Saints could make anything flourish and bear fruit. "You just watch us, Syl," she said to him. "I seen it done already down Nauvoo. You watch."

"Yes, ma'am," he answered.

"You watch," she repeated, then stepped aside and let herself throw up.

On September 22, 1847, after a steep descent down the Big Mountain, and six miles through Emigration Canyon, they arrived at their last camp. The company fixed their wagons in a circle at Temple Block.

A group of Saints had already dammed a pool in the creek flowing by the temple site. This would serve for the pioneers' rebaptism. Everyone participated, including Sylvester James, this being his first time under the waters. Isaac Haight took his hand, made the baptism prayer "in the name of the Father and of the Son and of the Holy Ghost," then dropped him down and brought him back up, born again.

On May 8, 1848, Jane and Isaac James became parents of Mary Ann, the first colored child born in Utah. Once again, Patty Sessions "put Black Jane to bed."

NOTES

The chapter title, "I'll Go Where You Want Me to Go," is from the title of hymn number 502 in *Hymns for the Family of God*.

Jane's history describes the trek as follows: "In the spring of 1846, I left Nauvoo to come to this Great and Glorious Valley. We travelled as far as winter quarters there we stayed until spring, at Hog Creek [Keg Creek] my son Silas was born. In the spring of 1847 we started again on our way to this Valley. We arrived here on the 22nd day of September 1847 without any serious mishaps, the Lords blessing was with us and protected us all the way, the only thing that did occur worth relating was when our cattle stampeded, some of them we never did find. May 1848 my daughter Mary Ann was born, all of my children but two were born here in this valley, their names are Silas, Silvester, Mary Ann, Miriam, Ellen Madora, Jessie, Jerry, Boln, Isaac, Vilate, all of them are with their heavenly father except two Sylvester and Ellen Madora."

The Ethel R. Jensen history of the George Smith Rust trek (the Rust family being in the same company as the James family) lists the company's departure date from Winter Quarters as June 18, 1847 (34).

The names of those in Jane's immediate company, led by Isaac Haight, are Joseph G. Baxter, Eveline Mattin Boggs, Mary Boggs, Esther Jones Brown, Catherine Adelia Hatwick Curtis, Alanson Eldredge, Alma Eldredge, Edmond Eldredge, Esther Ann Eldredge, Hiram Eldredge, Ira Eldredge, Nancy Black Eldredge, Martin Luther Ensign, Caleb Haight, Caroline Eliza Haight, Eliza Ann Snyder Haight, Isaac Chauncy Haight, Sarah Aldridge Haight, Temperance Keturah Haight, Isaac James, Jane E. James, Silas James, Sylvester James, Ruth Martin, Hannah Potter, John H. Potter, William Potter, Ann Elizabeth Roper, George Smith Rust, Amanda Spencer, Anna, Twin Spencer, Charles Henry Spencer, Claudius Victor Spencer, Daniel Spencer, Edwin E. Spencer, Emily Spencer, Frances C. Spencer, Gilbert H. Spencer, Hirum Theron Spencer, Mariah Antoinette Spencer, Mary Leone Spencer, Elizabeth Howard Standage, Ephraim R. Whitney, and Harriet Whitney (Crockett, *Thursday June 17, 1847*, "Elkhorn River," Nebraska, par. 3).

The men who joined the Mormon Battalion—including William Walker

Rust and George P. Dykes—are not listed in the company. Dykes's service in the Battalion is documented in Jenson, *Latter-day Saint Biographical Encyclopedia*, 2:762.

The cattle stampede is mentioned in Jane's life history and also in the unpublished history of the George Smith Rust Family, "Beneath the Casing Rock," by Ethel R. Jensen, which we have relied on heavily for details of the Jameses' trek west.

Though a number of the Mormon pioneer groups suffered terribly, especially some of the later-arriving handcart companies, apparently the James group did not suffer much, at least by comparison. As Stegner puts it, "Perhaps because of their sanitary precautions, perhaps because they were a little ahead of the sickly season, they were in good health as they prepared under the tutelage of Ira Eldredge, Isaac Haight, and Cyrus Wheelock to make their way over the old Nauvoo-Council Bluffs road to the Missouri" (*Gathering of Zion*, 215).

Details of pioneer children finding beads in ant hills and corralling crickets are taken from Madsen, *I Walked to Zion*, 112.

We have relied on several sources in re-creating the trek west from Winter Quarters. For this chapter, the most important were Nibley, *Exodus to Greatness*; Bullock, *Pioneer Camp of the Saints*; and Knight and Kimball, *111 Days to Zion*. Even more indispensable than these sources was information gathered in interviews with William Hartley (May 8, 2000).

The quotation from Jim Bridger that the native peoples (the Snake or Shoshone Indians) near Wyoming were "bad" and should be enslaved rather than killed is from Knight and Kimball, *111 Days to Zion*, 195.

Saleratus is like baking soda. Sometimes, the lakes were only saleratus, and pioneers would chip off pieces. That the saleratus polluted some rivers and killed cattle who drank from them is mentioned in Jensen, "Beneath the Casing Rock," 39.

"Muddy Springs" is now known as "Pacific Springs" (Nibley, *Exodus to Greatness*, 409).

That Brigham Young and other apostles addressed the Haight (Ira Eldredge) Company at Pacific Springs in early September 1847 is documented by Jensen, "Beneath the Casing Rock," 40.

Knight and Kimball, *111 Days to Zion*, quotes Wilford Woodruff's memory of Brigham Young's earlier impression of the valley. "Brigham had seen the valley in an earlier vision. Looking over the expanse below, the president saw the future glory of the valley and said: 'It is enough. This is the right place, drive on'" (252).

We have paraphrased William Clayton's description of Echo Canyon, as quoted in Knight and Kimball, *111 Days to Zion*, 235.

The Saints' ritual rebaptisms upon entering the valley and at other times are described in various sources, including Eliza Lyman's holographic journal, 85.

Elijah Abel Returns to Nauvoo October 1847

27

IT WILL BE WORTH
IT ALL

*Let us run with patience
the race that is set before us.*
HEBREWS 12:1

Elijah Abel had wanted to visit Nauvoo since he first learned of
the Martyrdom. He wished he himself could've built the coffins for
Joseph and Hyrum—oh, they would've been the best death-boxes
this side of England! He would've carved sunstones and cloudstones
and moonstones into the wood, as though each case were a temple.
It concerned him to know someone else had built the boxes, for he
was certain he could've done better than whatever carpenter got
that job. More than likely, the whole carpenters' guild had participated. All of them excepting Elder Elijah Abel. He was sure they
had done the best they knew how, but he was also sure he could've
added a suggestion or two. How he wished he could've loaned his
own wrist-strength to the sanding, agitating away the rough wood,
just like God had smoothed off Brother Joseph's roughness, and then
making that wood to shine.

He would've gone Nauvoo-wards that very June 1844, but Mary Ann stopped him. "Them people out there?" She waved her hand towards where she figured Illinois must be. "They don't make nothin' of fillin' a white Mormon full of lead balls. How much you think they make of lynchin' a colored Mormon first sight?"

He had to agree: a trip there would be inviting the noose.

Besides, Mary Ann had been in a family way. That baby girl had lived about an hour beyond what their first daughter had. (The first one managed only about five minutes of breath before giving up on it.) More than likely, Mary Ann was still too young to bring a living child into the world. But there was time. Mary Ann herself was becoming more woman, and they'd get themselves a for-keeping baby sometime soon—perhaps very soon, for she was rounding up again, and this baby kicked so hard Elijah could feel the thumps himself.

Brother Joseph had been dead three years. Most of the Saints had left Nauvoo, and Elijah figured it was safe enough to make a visit. It was a need he had. He wanted to see the Smith graves—all of them. He wanted to see the completed temple. He had a sense that if he didn't see that temple soon, he never would. Same thing would happen to Nauvoo's temple as happened to Kirtland's. He wanted to see the temple his hands had worked on before any animals took shelter inside and before God set his winds upon it.

He traveled by coach and steamboat and then was ferried into the familiar place: the City Beautiful, Brother Joseph's dream, gone quiet while Brother Joseph slept. And there was the temple: a huge rectangle of nearly white limestone. There were sunstones and moonstones and starstones carved into the thirty pilasters and the frieze. The tower—which had not been finished when Elijah headed off to Cincinnati—stretched nearly one hundred feet above the eaves, complete and strong, topped with a weathervane angel. That angel was in the likeness of the Angel Moroni, the very messenger who had shown Brother Joseph the gold plates engraved with scriptures: the Book of Mormon. That name, Moroni, was one good name, one beautiful name. That would be his son's name, Elijah decided right there, should God give him a son. And as that thought entered his mind, the weathervane angel made a full circle, like an answer and a promise.

The carvings had turned out grand. Elijah liked the sunstone in particular. He had heard Brother Joseph refer to the "highest degree of heavenly glory" as a place bright as the sun. That was where Elijah knew he'd find his glittering robes. And Joseph of the Rainbow Coat was already there, no doubt, with those twins of his. Bringing some color into the place. Which Elijah would do too.

Elijah still held an occasional conversation with Old Joseph, more out of habit now than need. And sometimes he felt Old Joe was really there beside him, doing his part to make the dialogue interesting.

"So how you gets to that bright place after you dies?" Elijah thought at his imaginary companion. His thoughts came in the language of his childhood. "You climb up a ladder? Like Jacob's ladder?" He was still gazing at the sunstone.

"You figure that's how it is?" Joseph of the Rainbow Coat answered. "Step by step, and then you arrives?"

"Ain't it?"

"Not hardly."

"How then?"

"'Lijah, you listen. That sunny state ain't somewhere you gets to; it's somethin' you become."

"Hmm? I figured they must be steps—each one a commandment. You takes one, and some angel body stand in your way and he ask you, 'Does you steal?' When you says, 'No, sir!' why, that angel stand hisself aside. You takes you another step, and one more angel body put itself in your way and ask you, 'Does you lie?' And when you says, 'No, sir!' that angel body stand hisself aside, and up you goes like that, the lights gettin' brighter all the time till they bright as the sun."

Old Joseph of the Rainbow Coat wiped his forehead with his head wrap. It was October but sunny still. Nauvoo's leaves shimmered like pennies—new coppers and old ones—all down the valley. "Too many folks thinks that way," Old Joseph sighed. "It ain't steps makes us bright. It's strippin' away anything that keeps us from being all God made us to be. You already bright, Mr. Abel. You just need to open up more to let it shine."

"My patriarchal say to me my soul be white in the next world."

"We talk this one over already, ain't we?"

"Maybe so. We talk over a whole mess o' things. What do you think it mean—my soul be white in eternity?"

"Not that you necessarily goin' change color, sir! Jus' goin' shine is all. Shine so bright."

"And what make a soul to shine, Joe?"

"Now don' you know that?"

"Maybe I do and maybe I don't."

"Love. That's all. Jus' pure love, with nothin' gettin' in its way."

Elijah grunted. "Well. I figured as much."

Much of Nauvoo had been abandoned. It had become a typical river town—except for the temple, which still had holiness around it. The city itself had gotten wild—and not just in overgrown bushes and rambunctious weeds. It had the feel of danger to it, a sense of lurking robbers. This was the opposite of that stripping away Joseph of the Rainbow Coat referred to. Here was a tangle of neglect, unpruned canes, happy weeds, and the return of that swampy stench suggesting sickness was waiting around the next bend in the week. Nauvoo was dirty and bitter. Strange that a place could feel bitter, but it did—as if spiders had been instructed to build cobwebs in every corner and remake Nauvoo into a refuge for poisonous bugs.

The Mansion House was still there, but it was an inn now, with a huge brick stable attached. He could hear the horses shift in their stalls.

Elijah knocked on the familiar door. After a moment, Emma Smith answered. Yes, this sad-looking woman was undoubtedly Emma, though the years had not been kind to her face. She couldn't have climbed far into her forties, but she looked much older, one eye droopy, her shoulders bent, threads of gray shimmering in her dark hair. She was dressed all in black.

"Sister Emma," he whispered.

Her eyes brightened. "Elijah Abel?"

He removed his top hat. "Come to pay my respects, ma'am. To you. To the Prophet. Wanted to lay some flowers by his grave. Hyrum's too."

Emma smiled, and her face got younger. "The graves are secret, Elijah. Protected." Her voice was quiet, but it had aged just as her face had. There was a hoarseness to it, like it was worn out with wailing, though he could not imagine Emma Smith giving in to loud cries.

"Their coffins made good?" he asked.

"Oh, yes. Beautiful coffins." She seemed reluctant to let him in to the house.

"Wish I'da been here to add my touch."

Emma nodded. "I'm sure you would've carved something fitting."

"Ma'am, I can promise that much."

"Please come in." She opened the door wide.

In the sitting room, Emma introduced Doctor John Bernhisel, a boarder at the house.

Bernhisel seemed a fine enough man to Elijah, just closed up some. His face resembled likenesses of Martin Van Buren Elijah had seen in the newspapers—which likeness was maybe not coincidence. There was something presidential about Bernhisel. It was in the way he dressed so perfect with that pressed black suit, a fat gold watch peeking out of his vest pocket, gold chain running to his waist. Most impressive was his stand-up collar and silk cravat, woven in all the colors oil made on wet tar. Or maybe the doctor made his impression in the way he moved—ever on the awares of what might offend. The doctor's fingers seemed primed to play a pianoforte or drink a cup of tea, should the occasion arise. Here was a true gentleman, middle-aged, trained in every detail of refinement, and then dressed to show it.

Dr. Bernhisel carried on a polite conversation with him, reporting that most the Saints were heading towards the Rocky Mountains and reviewing the persecutions which had come before that exodus. Elijah said he had already heard about most of it. News made it to Cincinnati, he said.

The conversation lagged, spurting into comments about the weather or Washington politics and then jerking to a halt when Elijah couldn't think of anything to answer. For a moment, the two men just sat there, Sister Emma rocking on the chair between them, rubbing her hands.

"I don't believe we've met before now, have we?" said Dr. Bernhisel.

"I left Nauvoo 'round 1842, sir."

"That's right," Emma said distantly.

"And that's when I arrived," Dr. Bernhisel said. "We must've barely missed each other."

"By the skin of a goat, I'd guess. I used to be head undertaker here. Founding member of the carpenter's guild." Elijah felt he should stand, that Bernhisel was uncomfortable talking to a seated Negro. Stand—or maybe kneel and offer to shine the gentleman's shoes?

"Fine undertaker," Emma added, her voice and face still unfocused.

"Ah. And I'm the man who hopes to keep you undertakers free from too much work." Bernhisel pointed at him with his cane. "I'm a doctor. Specializing in apoplexy."

"Good for you, sir. Glad to know that."

"Fine doctor," Emma added. Then she asked "Brother John" to tell "Brother Elijah" about the Mannings.

Dr. Bernhisel nodded vigorously. There was hope for this conversation yet! He proceeded to describe another black family: the Mannings. They had arrived in Nauvoo not long after Elijah had left. Several free women, he said, and Elijah caught the meaning.

"I got me a wife up Cincinnati," he announced.

Emma clapped her hands at this—something spontaneous, which relieved Elijah. The Emma Smith of his memory had always been spontaneous, not this restrained, nervous, sad shadow. "Oh, good!" she said. Her smile was real.

"A wife! You found a wife!" Dr. Bernhisel chimed in.

"Oh, yes. My wife," Elijah said, "she named Mary Ann."

Emma clapped again. Seemed she was applauding the name.

"Ah." Dr. Bernhisel nodded. "Fine name. A fine, fine name indeed."

"Thank you."

"Congratulations," the doctor said. For a moment, Elijah thought he was being congratulated for finding him a wife with such an acceptable name. Or maybe the congratulations was for Elijah's keeping his place well enough to say the right thing. Then he realized it was for getting married. He was four years wed, so didn't expect the good wishes to still be flowing.

"Thank you much," he said anyway.

"I have recently become a married man myself," Bernhisel stated. This was a speechifying man, no doubt of that. Elijah could imagine Dr. John Bernhisel saying with exactly the same clarity: "I have recently become a candidate for the United States Senate." The doctor tapped his cane. "Julia Ann Haight Van Orden."

Elijah's head fell back. He knew Sister Van Orden, and she was already married! "Sister—"

"Brother Van Orden died," Emma explained. "Dear Julia was a

poor widow. It was a most charitable thing for the doctor . . ." Her voice trailed off. She took distance again. Some memory had called her away. Elijah had no idea what it was, though he guessed it surely had to do with Brother Joseph.

"That's correct," said Doctor Bernhisel. "Widow Van Orden. Now Sister Bernhisel. I inherited six children when I took her on." He shook his head, seemed suddenly worn out by his burden, and glanced at Emma. She was staring out the window. Two of her sons were playing outside, including Joseph Smith III. Elijah hadn't seen Junior in near five years. The boy was nigh his teen years now and near as good looking as his daddy, the Prophet.

"Six children! Bless you, sir," Elijah said. "Sorry to hear about Brother Van Orden. But bless you, sir!"

"Thank you." The doctor stood and excused himself to take a walk and prepare his bowels for supper. Sister Emma likewise excused herself "to catch up on some sewing."

Elijah couldn't think of anywhere else he wanted to go at the moment, so he stayed alone in the room. He could almost hear Brother Joseph's voice in this place, saying, "Why Brother Elijah! You've come back at last!" He let his eyes close, hoping for a good dream.

When it came supper time, he was awakened and invited to the table, across from Dr. Bernhisel. Sister Emma was still sewing upstairs, so it was just these men and a pair of strangers who witnessed the arrival of Major Lewis Bidamon, who, Bernhisel announced confidentially, was courting Sister Emma.

Elijah raised his brows but asked no questions. Sister Emma's life was her own, he figured, though he couldn't imagine how she could think of replacing Brother Joseph. Standing in the courtyard, Bidamon, wearing a tall hat, made a deep bow to Sister Emma, who he could apparently see in an upstairs window. He put his hat back on and marched towards the door, not noticing a clothesline, which grabbed off not only his hat but his fine toupee, scalping him clean.

Bidamon was saying, "Damn that wig!" when Brother Joseph's namesake son answered the door.

So this was the fellow seeking the Prophet's widow! He was as tall as Brother Joseph and well dressed but otherwise just a man-sized monkey. And only a major at that! Why, Brother Joseph had been lieutenant general of the whole Nauvoo Legion!

Elijah departed soon after the major's interesting entrance and a bite of supper. Visiting the outback shed, he let himself laugh hearty. Later, though, when he thought on his visit to Nauvoo, there wasn't much to laugh at. Poor Sister Emma had grieved herself into early old age, and the brightness in her eyes seemed more angry than glad. She was holding on to anger like it was something precious. She wasn't shining, not the way Old Joseph of the Rainbow Coat described a body could shine.

Emma's anger was aimed mostly at Brigham Young, he gathered, for he heard her speak to Dr. Bernhisel of it, heard her say, "It is possible for those people to make me poor, but they could never make me poor enough to induce me to follow Brigham Young!"

Elijah had wanted to tell her then, "Let go the anger!" but it would have seemed an uppity thing for a colored man to say to a white woman. And it would've been hypocritical besides. There was plenty of anger inside his own self, still itching under his skin.

He did lay yellow mums beside the tombstones that memorialized Joseph and Hyrum, though he was given to understand their bodies were not under these stones but hidden away.

Still, he got what he came for: a last look at Nauvoo and the temple. He returned silently to Cincinnati, where his son was born three months later, just as the new year—1848—was beginning.

Elijah and Mary Ann named him Moroni, after that holy harbinger of the restoration of all things. And somewhere nearby, just after baby Moroni let out his first mortal howl, Elijah could hear Ancient Joseph saying, "I loves my boys—my dark little boys—like you can't count it, Elijah."

Elijah answered, "That's how I loves my boy, Joe. Exactly how."

Later, as the midwife was working Mary Ann over, Elijah took his baby into his arms and traced the tiny nose and chin, same way Delilah Abel had done all those years ago when Elijah himself got pushed into this world. "He's everything to me," Elijah whispered to Ancient Joe. "And I will raise him right. I will keep him out of the pit."

"Well, you try. Wasn't my father cast me into the pit, you know," Old Joe was saying. "It was my brothers."

"Imagine that!" said Elijah. "Imagine a child's brothers doin' such a thing to him! Sellin' him into slavery!"

"I don't have to imagine, 'Lijah. I just close my eyes and I remember."

"Oh, yes," Elijah said to that and kissed his baby's forehead. "I remember too, Joseph. Oh, yes, I do remember!"

NOTES

The chapter title, "It Will Be Worth It All," is from the title of hymn number 135 in *Hymns for the Family of God.*

The interior of the Nauvoo Temple was burned by an arsonist on October 9, 1848. Three of its exterior walls were destroyed by a tornado on May 27, 1850, and the remaining wall was leveled in 1856 for safety.

The details and dates of Dr. Bernhisel's life are extracted from Van Wagoner and Walker, *Book of Mormons,* 15–18.

The incident of Lewis Bidamon's "scalping" by the clothesline is reported in Newell and Avery, *Mormon Enigma,* 246. That Doctor Bernhisel was residing in the Mansion House at the time is reported in the same source (245). Emma's bitterness towards Brigham Young is well documented. Her statement "it may be possible for [them] to make me poor, but [they] could never make me poor enough to induce me to follow Brigham Young" is from Newell and Avery, *Mormon Enigma,* 246.

The children of Elijah and Mary Ann Abel are listed in the 1860 Salt Lake Census (13th Ward) as Moroni (sometimes spelled "Maroni"), age twelve; Enoch, age eight; Anna, seven; Delilah, four; and Elijah, one.

POSTSCRIPT

This book's long enough now. You've met just a few of the pioneers of color in these pages. Of course, they all knew each other before long: Jane, Isaac, Elijah, Green, Hark, Oscar, Samuel. Eventually, they all became well acquainted.

But that's for the next book to tell.

BIBLIOGRAPHY

Allen, James B., and Glen M. Leonard. *The Story of the Latter-day Saints*. 2d ed. Salt Lake City: Deseret Book, 1992.

Andrus, Hyrum L. *Joseph Smith: The Man and the Seer*. Salt Lake City: Deseret Book, 1960.

Berlin, Ira, Marc Favbeau, and Steven F. Miller, eds. *Remembering Slavery*. New York: New Press, 1998.

Blassingame, John W. *The Slave Community: Plantation Life in the Antebellum South*. New York: Oxford University Press, 1972. Reprint, 1975.

Botkin, B. A., ed. *Lay My Burden Down* [a compilation of slave narratives]. Chicago: University of Chicago Press, 1945.

Bringhurst, Newell G. "Elijah Abel and the Changing Status of Blacks within Mormonism." In *Neither White Nor Black*. Edited by Lester E. Bush Jr. and Armand L. Mauss. Midvale, Utah: Signature, 1984, 130–48.

———. *Saints, Slaves, and Blacks: The Changing Place of Black People within Mormonism*. Westport, Conn.: Greenwood Press, 1981.

Brown, John Zimmerman, ed. *Pioneer John Brown*. Salt Lake City: Daughters of Utah Pioneers, 1941.

Bullock, Thomas. *The Pioneer Camp of the Saints: The 1846 and 1847 Mormon Trail Journals of Thomas Bullock*. Edited by Will Bagley. Vol. 1 of *Kingdom in the West*. Spokane, Wash.: Arthur H. Clark, 1997.

Burleigh, Harry T. *The Spirituals of Harry T. Burleigh*. Miami: Belwin Mills Publishing Corp., 1984.

Bush, Lester. "A Commentary on Stephen G. Taggart's *Mormonism's Negro Policy: Social and Historical Origins*." In Bush and Mauss, *Neither White Nor Black*. 31–52.

———. "Mormonism's Negro Doctrine: An Historical Overview." In Bush and Mauss, *Neither White Nor Black*, 53–129.

————. "Whence the Negro Doctrine? A Review of Ten Years of Answers." In Bush and Mauss, *Neither White Nor Black,* 193–220.

Carter, Kate B. *Negro Pioneer.* Salt Lake City: Daughters of Utah Pioneers, 1964.

————. *Treasures of Pioneer History.* 6 vols. Salt Lake City: Daughters of Utah Pioneers, 1952–57.

Cleary, Calista. "Little Egypt." Unpublished paper, Barton L. Weller Scholarship Competition, 2 May 1989. Available through the LDS Family History Library, 35 N. West Temple Street, Salt Lake City, Utah 84150.

Cockrum, Col. William. *History of the Underground Railroad.* 1915. Reprint, New York: Negro Universities Press, 1969.

Coleman, Ronald. "A History of Blacks in Utah." Ph.D. dissertation, University of Utah, 1980.

Crockett, David R. *Thursday, June 17, 1847.* Retrieved June 8, 2000 <http://www.goodnet.com/indirect/www/crockett/150/jun1747.html>

Curtis, Anna L. *Stories of the Underground Railroad.* New York: Island Workshop Press Co-op, 1941.

Esplin, Ronald K. "Brigham Young and Priesthood Denial to the Blacks: An Alternate View." *Brigham Young University Studies* 19 (spring 1979): 394–402.

Fields, Clarence. "History of the Kirtland Temple." Master's thesis, Brigham Young University, 1968 .

Filler, Louis. "Lovejoy." *The World Book Encyclopedia.* Chicago: World Book 1988.

Flake, Carol Read. *Of Pioneers and Prophets.* Boise, Idaho, 1974. (Privately published.)

Flake, Joel. "Green Flake: His Life and Legacy." Unpublished paper for History 490, Brigham Young University, August 11, 1999.

Flanders, Robert Bruce. *Nauvoo: Kingdom on the Mississippi.* Urbana: University of Illinois Press, 1965.

Godfrey, Kenneth W., Audrey M. Godfrey, and Jill Mulvay Derr. *Women's Voices: An Untold History of the Latter-day Saints, 1830–1900.* Salt Lake City: Deseret Book, 1982. Paperbound ed., 1991.

Habenstein, Robert Wesley, and William M. Lamers. *The History of American Funeral Directing.* Milwaukee: Bulfin, 1955.

Hartley, William G. "'Almost Too Intolerable a Burthen': The Winter Exodus from Missouri, 1838–39." *Journal of Mormon History* 18 (fall 1992): 6–40.

———. Personal interview with Margaret Young. May 8, 2000.

Hill, Donna. *Joseph Smith: The First Mormon*. Midvale, Utah: Signature, 1977.

Holzapfel, Richard N., and Jeni B. Holzapfel. *Women of Nauvoo*. Salt Lake City: Bookcraft, 1992.

Huggins, Nathan Irvin. *Slave and Citizen: The Life of Frederick Douglass*. Boston: Little, Brown and Co., 1980.

Hymns for the Family of God. Nashville: Paragon Associates, 1976.

Jensen, Ethel R. "Beneath the Casing Rock." Unpublished history of the George Smith Rust family, 1981.

Jenson, Andrew. *Latter-day Saint Biographical Encyclopedia*. 4 vols. Salt Lake City: A. Jenson History Co., 1901–36.

Johnson, Charles, Patricia Smith, and WGBH Research Team. *Africans in America: America's Journey through Slavery*. New York: Harvest–Harcourt Brace & Company, 1998.

Jones, Barbara. *Design for Death*. Indianapolis: Bobbs-Merrill, 1967.

Kimball, Stanley B. "The Iowa Trek of 1846: The Brigham Young Route from Nauvoo to Winter Quarters." *Ensign*, June 1974, 36–45.

Knight, Hal, and Stanley B. Kimball. *111 Days to Zion*. Salt Lake City: Deseret News, 1978.

Kohler, Charmain Lay. *Southern Grace: A Story of the Mississippi Saints*. Boise, Idaho: Beagle Creek Press, 1995.

Lyman, Albert R. *Amasa Mason Lyman: Trailblazer and Pioneer from the Atlantic to the Pacific*. Delta, Utah: Melvin A. Lyman, 1957.

Lyman, Eliza Maria. Holographic journal. In Special Collections, Harold B. Lee Library, Brigham Young University. Reprinted in Carter, *Treasures of Pioneer History*, 2:213–85. Salt Lake City: Daughters of Utah Pioneers, 1953.

Lythgoe, Dennis L. "Negro Slavery and Mormon Doctrine." *Western Humanities Review* 21 (1967): 327–38.

Madsen, Susan Arrington. *I Walked to Zion: True Stories of Young Pioneers on the Mormon Trail*. Salt Lake City: Deseret Book, 1994.

Madsen, Truman G. "Joseph's Personality and Character." *Joseph Smith the Prophet*. Audiocassettes. Salt Lake City: Bookcraft Recordings, 1978.

McConkie, Bruce R. "All Are Alike unto God." Address delivered to religious educators, Brigham Young University, Provo, Utah, 18 August 1978. Also in *A Symposium on the Book of Mormon*. Salt Lake City: The Church of Jesus Christ of Latter-day Saints, 1979.

Merkley, Christopher. *Biography of Christopher Merkley Written by Himself*. Salt Lake City: J. H. Parry, 1887.

Newell, Linda King, and Valerie Tippetts Avery. *Mormon Enigma: Emma Hale Smith*. Garden City, N.Y.: Doubleday, 1984.

Nibley, Preston. *Exodus to Greatness: The Story of the Mormon Migration*. Salt Lake City: Deseret News Press, 1947.

Nichol, John Thomas. "Adventists." *World Book Encyclopedia*. Chicago: World Book, 1988.

Packer, Boyd K. *The Holy Temple*. Salt Lake City: Bookcraft, 1980.

Painter, Nell Irvin. *Sojourner Truth: A Life, a Symbol*. New York: Norton, 1996.

Preston, Dickson J. *Young Frederick Douglass: The Maryland Years*. Baltimore: Johns Hopkins University Press, 1980.

"Saint without Priesthood: The Collected Testimonies of Ex-slave Samuel D. Chambers." *Dialogue* 12 (summer 1979): 13–21.

Seabury, Samuel. *American Slavery Distinguished from the Slavery of English Theorists and Justified by the Law of Nature*. New York: Mason Brothers, 1861.

Smart, Donna Toland, ed. *Mormon Midwife: The 1846–1848 Journals of Patty Sessions*. Logan, Utah: Utah State University Press, 1997.

Smith, Emma. *A Collection of Sacred Hymns for the Church of Jesus Christ of the Latter Day Saints*. Kirtland, Ohio, and New York: F. & G. Williams Co., 1835.

Smith, Joseph. *History of The Church of Jesus Christ of Latter-day Saints*. Edited by B. H. Roberts. 2d ed. rev. 7 vols. Salt Lake City: The Church of Jesus Christ of Latter-day Saints, 1932–51.

———. *Teachings of the Prophet Joseph Smith*. Selected by Joseph Fielding Smith. Salt Lake City: Deseret Book, 1977.

Smith, Lucy Mack. *History of Joseph Smith, by His Mother, Lucy Mack Smith*. Edited by Preston Nibley. Salt Lake City: Bookcraft, 1958.

Stegner, Wallace. *The Gathering of Zion: The Story of the Mormon Trail*. Lincoln: University of Nebraska Press, 1964.

Stowe, Harriet Beecher. "Sojourner Truth: The Libyan Sibyl." In *Narrative of Sojourner Truth*. Edited by Nell Irvin Painter. New York City: Penguin Books, 1998. 102–17. (*The Narrative of Sojourner Truth* was originally published in 1850.)

Taylor, Margery. Personal interview with Margaret Young. February 10, 2000. LDS Family History Library, 35 N. West Temple Street, Salt Lake City, Utah 84150.

Telford, John, Susan E. Black, and Kim C. Averett. *Nauvoo*. Salt Lake City: Deseret Book, 1997.

Van Wagoner, Richard S., and Steven C. Walker. *A Book of Mormons*. Salt Lake City: Signature, 1982.

Wangeman, William C. *The Black Man: A Son of God*. Bountiful, Utah: Horizon Publishers, 1979.

Wolfinger, Henry J. "Jane Manning James: A Test of Faith." In *Worth Their Salt: Notable but Often Unnoted Women of Utah*. Edited by Colleen Whitley. Logan, Utah: Utah State University Press, 1996. 14–30.

———. "A Test of Faith: Jane Elizabeth James and the Origins of the Utah Black Community." In *Social Accommodation in Utah*. Edited by Clark S. Knowlton. American West Occasional Papers. Salt Lake City, 1975. 126–72.

Woodruff, Wilford. Papers. Historical Department, The Church of Jesus Christ of Latter-day Saints. Salt Lake City, Utah.

Young Woman's Journal 16 (December 1905): 551–53. Also in *LDS Collectors Library*. Salt Lake City: Infobases, 1997.

Young, Robert. *Young's Analytical Concordance to the Bible*. Nashville, Tenn.: Thomas Nelson Publishers, 1982.